Bobbie Faye's
Very
(very, very, very)
Bad Day

TONI McGEE CAUSEY

St. Martin'

NEW Y

This is a work of fiction. All of the characters, organizations, and events portrayed in this novel are either products of the author's imagination or are used fictitiously.

BOBBIE FAYE'S VERY (VERY, VERY, VERY) BAD DAY. Copyright © 2007 by Toni McGee Causey. All rights reserved. Printed in the United States of America. No part of this book may be used or reproduced in any manner whatsoever without written permission except in the case of brief quotations embodied in critical articles or reviews. For information, address St. Martin's Press, 175 Fifth Avenue, New York, N.Y. 10010.

www.stmartins.com

Book design by Gretchen Achilles

LIBRARY OF CONGRESS CATALOGING-IN-PUBLICATION DATA

Causey, Toni McGee.
    Bobbie Faye's very (very, very, very) bad day / by Toni McGee Causey.—1st St. Martin's Griffin ed.
        p. cm.
    ISBN-13: 978-0-312-35448-0
    ISBN-10: 0-312-35448-7
    1. Cajuns—Fiction.   2. Beauty contestants—Fiction.   3. Trailer camps—Fiction.   4. Kidnapping—Fiction.   5. Brothers—Fiction.   6. Nieces—Fiction.   7. Lake Charles   (La.)—Fiction.   I. Title.

PS3603.A8988B62 2007
813'.6—dc22

                                                            2007003241

First Edition: May 2007

10   9   8   7   6   5   4   3   2   1

For
Carl
and
Luke and Jake

Those who say a thing cannot be done need to get the hell out of the way of those who are doing it.

—*bumper sticker seen in Lake Charles, Louisiana*

Chapter One

You know how some people are born to Greatness? Well, Bobbie Faye Sumrall woke up one morning, kicked Greatness in the teeth, kneed it in the balls, took it hostage, and it's been begging for mercy ever since.

—a former Louisiana mayor after Bobbie Faye accidentally ran her car into his office, knocking pages of fraud evidence into the street, which helped land him in Federal prison

Something wet and spongy plunked against Bobbie Faye's face and she sprang awake, arms pinwheeling. "Damn it, Roy, you hit me with a catfish again and I'm gonna—" *Whoa.* Everything was dark in her cramped trailer. There was no catfish, no little brother Roy pretending innocence. Of course she'd been dreaming, because Roy was twenty-six now, not ten. Still a complete pain in the ass, though.

She swiped at the cold rivulets of wetness running down her face. "What was that?" she muttered to no one in particular. "And why the hell am I wet?"

"You gots a s'imming pool inside."

Bobbie Faye squinted in the half-dark and focused on Stacey, her five-year-old niece, whose blond pigtails were haloed in the blue bug light emanating from just outside the trailer window. Then she peered at the wet Nerf bat Stacey dropped to the floor.

1

Check that. A Nerf bat *floating* a good two inches above the lime green shag carpet.

"Shit!" Bobbie Faye stood, flinching as the icy water covered her ankles. "Fuck. Damn fuck fuckity shit."

"Mamma says you shouldn't cuss so much."

"Yeah? Well your mamma should quit drinking, too, kid, but that ain't likely to happen either."

Shit. That was evil. She checked Stacey's reaction, but her niece was preoccupied with the soggy Nerf bat again and hadn't seemed to hear. Thank God. She didn't mean to harm the little rug rat. And how was she supposed to remember to be nice at four-freaking A.M.? Who the hell would expect her to be nice anyway? Lori-freaking-Ann, that's who. Her pill-popping, wine-swigging lush of a little sister whose plastered-on Grace Kelly smile made her look efficient and serene, even when she wobbled into a wall and fell on her ass.

Bobbie Faye never got to look serene.

Sonofabitch. And today was the day the Social Services lady was scheduled to come by. At four-thirty that afternoon. To judge whether Bobbie Faye was providing Stacey with a safe and stable home. Bobbie Faye shuddered as the icy water lapped at her ankles. Somehow, she was supposed to fix . . . whatever the hell *this* mess was . . . in time to preside at the opening ceremony of the Contraband Days Festival and get back before four-thirty to prove she could be a good foster parent while Lori Ann was pulling her court-ordered four-month drying-out stint at the Troy House.

Oh, flipping yippee.

Water splashed against her knees, and she looked down at Lori-Ann's little ankle biter stomping on the carpet as they squish-squished their way down the hall.

"Your hippos are s'imming." Stacey laughed, pointing at the glow-in-the-dark hippos dancing across Bobbie Faye's thin white cotton PJs. Then the monster child jumped again, hard, splashing water up to Bobbie Faye's elbows.

"For Christ's sake, Stacey, if you hop around one more time, I'm gonna turn you into a frog."

Stacey giggled, but at least she stopped jumping.

Bobbie Faye stood in front of the cramped utility closet of her tiny, dark trailer and glared at the culprit: her washing machine, run amok. Water geysered from somewhere behind the vibrating piece-of-crap appliance. If she'd had a gun, she'd have shot it. Several times. Happily. She twisted knobs, pressing buttons broken so long ago, there was no telling what they had originally been meant to do.

She wanted to stomp or snarl that this was so not happening to her, but she was awake enough now to be mature in front of Stacey. She could do mature. She was twenty-eight years old, the oldest sibling and the one the other two constantly turned to when they screwed up; of course she could do mature. And solve problems. She was a paragon of problem-solving, and she slammed her fist down on the machine, hoping to dislodge whatever it was that was causing the crisis. The machine shuddered, the water gushed higher, and in that moment, seriously mature went straight to hell. Bobbie Faye hauled off and kicked the machine, then yelped and squirmed in pain because frozen toes do not take too well to sudden impact with metal.

Bobbie Faye squeezed her eyes shut, hopping on the other foot and biting her lip to keep from spouting a new stream of expletives. *Way to use a brain cell, genius.* Stacey took one gander at the hopping and went straight back to jumping with the enthusiasm of a five-year-old on a post-Easter-morning sugar high, soaking everything in her path.

And this is the kid who throws a tantrum if I even look like it's time for her bath.

There were two things Bobbie Faye knew for certain. One, a day without disaster would be a day in someone else's life. And two, she was going to kill her brother Roy for not showing up to fix the washing machine like he'd promised.

She sloshed through the kitchen to the back door and opened it, hoping the water would rush out; it barely trickled. The trailer floor had already sagged below the threshold, turning her ancient trailer into a bowl.

Wonderful. The bathtub leaks, the trailer doesn't.

Bobbie Faye slumped a moment, barely resisting the urge to pound her head against the door frame. This was her one day off. She'd worked extra hours all week just to be able to relax this morning and take her time to get ready for the festival's opening ceremonies. She hadn't thought anything could top the thunderstorm that blew through on last year's opening day and knocked a tree onto her first truly pretty car, a slightly banged-up purple Nissan 300ZX. Sure, it was used, high mileage, and pulled heavily to the left, but it was shiny, with only two rust spots. The tree could have fallen in any other direction and nothing would have been damaged. Of course, that would mean this was someone else's life. It didn't help when she learned she had, just that day, received a cancellation notice from her car insurance. (Not a single person, not even her friends, ever believed she really hadn't seen that fire truck barreling through the intersection with all of its lights on and sirens blazing. She thought the fireman was clearly at fault, though she did feel pretty awful when, to avoid hitting her, he slid into a light pole, knocking it through the roof of the grocery store on the corner.) Her insurance company paid all of the claims. And canceled her.

The bastards.

But this year? It was going to be different; she was going to have a pleasant, peaceful day if she had to maim and kill to get it. There were no storms, the insurance was paid up on the rickety cracker-box-on-wheels Honda Civic she'd bought to replace her cool little sports car, she had planned to have plenty of time to get ready and avoid the traffic jams, she had washed her clothes last night and all she'd had to do was toss them into the dryer. . . .

So, of course, she was standing in two inches of water *inside* her trailer.

There was no way in hell she was bailing all of this by herself. Roy was going to get his sorry ass over here and help. She went to the phone to call him, flipped on the living room light and gasped. Waves rippled across the floor. Water slapped at the bottom of the more-shabby-than-chic sofa and chair and filled the video bay of her ancient VCR set on the low shelf below the TV. And on the carpet near the sofa where she'd left it was her mom's Contraband Days scrapbook. Drowned.

Bobbie Faye's face hurt with the strain of holding back tears. Her mother had kept that scrapbook for more than twenty years. When Bobbie Faye was seven, her mom had let her glue a pirate eye patch on the cover, denoting the history of the festival. Well, her mom had been drinking and hadn't really seemed to notice the eye patch and sequins until a few days later, but she let Bobbie Faye keep them on there and showed them proudly to her friends, so that was almost as good, especially when her mom made her an eye patch to wear to that year's pirate costume contest.

Pirates, Bobbie Faye had learned the way other kids learned catechism, had found the multitude of bayous and marshlands in south Louisiana perfect for transporting loot and contraband into the growing territory. The pirates had hidden in south Louisiana for the same reasons the Cajuns had fled there from Nova Scotia: sanctuary. It was a place to be whoever the hell you wanted to be. A close-knit, family sort of place, where watching your neighbor's back was as standard as having a nodding awareness that they just might be crazy as loons, and that was okay, too.

After years of digging up half of Calcasieu Parish in a vain attempt to find the buried treasure, the locals eventually, reluctantly, gave up. Well, not entirely. Bobbie Faye remembered when she was a kid and learned there was a place named *Contraband Bayou* which was said to have been the home of a few pirates who supposedly hid jewels and gold somewhere back where the bayou ended. She tagged along when Roy and Lori Ann's dad took them fishing because he was going to go right by the famous bayou and Bobbie Faye was sure if he'd just let her out, she'd find that treasure. All she got for her trouble was a bad case of poison sumac and a good view of a bunch of deeply dug holes. So much for history.

As it was, history settled lazily into myth, which eased along into celebration, and the Contraband Days Festival was born. It was a crazy, lively festival where everyone dressed up as pirates for twelve days in May for parties, music, dancing, and all sorts of events. Tractor pulls! Races! Parades! Buccaneers! There were "official" pageants every year, but Bobbie Faye's mom (and her mom before her, and so on) were the unofficial "Queens"—a title started so far back in time, no one really remembered how it was handed down generation to generation. Bobbie Faye's mom had kept a scrapbook of all her Contraband memories . . . and gave it to Bobbie Faye just before she died, when she had also passed her the duty of being Queen.

Bobbie Faye pulled the scrapbook out of the water, her heart sinking as she slowly turned the first sodden page. Spidery scrawl ran in an inky river, washing most of the words to nothingness; the water had faded the old photos to murky shadows and all of the mementos were a soggy mess. The once-dried petals of a rose her mother had worn on her last parade fell apart under Bobbie Faye's touch.

Fury slammed her adrenaline up another notch; at any moment, the back of her head was going to pop clean off, especially as the cold water wicked farther up her PJs. The scrapbook was Bobbie Faye's hold on a tenuous place, the "before" as she liked to think about it. Before her mom started wearing the big floppy hats when her hair was getting inexplicably thinner and thinner, before she started wearing the weird combination of clothes and her morning eggs smelled just a shade more like rum than eggs ought to smell, before Bobbie Faye recognized her mom was a little *too* dancey-happy most days, jitterbugging on the coffee table (before it broke), before Bobbie Faye knew what the word *cancer* meant. She looked back at the destroyed scrapbook she held. If Roy had shown up like he promised and fixed the damned washing machine, this wouldn't have happened. Bobbie Faye stared out her front window, past the gravel road, and fantasized briefly that she could zero in on wherever Roy was with a laser intensity that would fry his ass on the spot.

There was just no telling where he was, and getting him on the cell phone would take an act of God. Check that. It would take an act of some willing life-sized Barbie type. He could be anywhere: his fishing camp south of her trailer park, where there were hundreds of little bayous and marshy wetlands (or as Roy put it, plenty of escape routes); or, just north of her trailer park, hiding in a hole-in-the-wall bar somewhere in the muddy industrial city of Lake Charles, a place Bobbie Faye thought of as the kind of cranky, independent southern town that had never really given a rip what its image might be, although if someone had labeled it "home of the hard drinkers who make Mardi Gras revelers look like big fluffy candy-asses," it might have staggered to attention and saluted. Knowing Roy the way she did, she figured he wasn't anywhere near his own apartment in the heart of the city. Probably in some stupid poker game or, God help him, at one of his many girlfriends' places. *He can run,* she thought, *but he can't hide.*

H iding was exactly what Roy was trying to do right at that moment. He slammed on his jeans and then squirmed his six-foot frame into a large, dusty compartment under the window seat situated in the bay window of his married girlfriend Dora's house. He wriggled silently to try to ease the contortion, but his toes were already starting to cramp. The layers of dust inside the seat tickled his nose and he pinched it to keep from sneezing. He squinted through the decorative tin grill on the facing of the window seat and saw two sets of Muscles of the steroid persuasion barge into the room. Dora, his very tanned, very bosomy (bless Jimmy and his penchant for giving his wife all the plastic surgery she wanted), very blond girlfriend who was sitting above him on the window seat, shifted her legs to block the view into the grating, to better hide him.

"Where's Roy?" the smaller of the two sets of Muscles asked Dora.

"I ain't seen Roy since he left the bar. Besides, I'm married. What would Roy be doing here?"

"Same thing he's been doing ever since your Jimmy's been out on the oil rig," the shorter man said. He peered around the room and allowed himself a small shudder. "You get attacked by lace or something? This is a fucking nightmare. No wonder Jimmy's always gone out on the rig."

Roy knew without being able to see her that Dora had poufed out her collagen-enhanced bottom lip, pouting.

"Nice doorknobs, though," the larger man said, and Roy grimaced. If he was in a bar, and really really drunk, he'd fight a guy that size for mentioning Dora's boobs. Even if you're boinking another guy's wife, there was a certain etiquette to maintain.

"I don't know nothin' 'bout Roy," Dora insisted.

"You know where he is," the smaller of the Muscles said. "Roy's got something we want, and we know he came here."

"Yeah," the other mountain of muscles chimed in. "He always *comes* here. Don't he, Eddie?" He broke into a giggle, and although the Mountain was almost double the smaller guy's size, Roy pegged him as younger and a little simple, maybe; despite the fact he lost at poker every other Friday, Roy considered himself a pretty good judge of character. Whoever they were, they couldn't be here for his bookie debts because he was kinda sorta caught up, and the three he still owed usually didn't send knee breakers until you were more than a couple of months past due (he still had eight days). And he was pretty sure the guy who bought that boat hadn't figured out that Roy hadn't owned it in the first place. No, these guys had to be here about something personal. Nothing he couldn't talk his way out of. God knows he'd done it a hundred times before.

Roy saw Dora's calf contract as she inhaled quickly. Past her very fine calf, Roy could see that the smaller set of Muscles, apparently named Eddie, had a gun aimed at her.

The seat creaked as Dora shifted above him, and dust fell into his twitchy nose just as Roy's cell phone, adjusted to maximum volume so he could hear it in the bar, vibrated against his jean pocket and trumpeted the LSU fight song. His heart ramped up three billion beats in .02 seconds as he frantically tried to slap the phone off.

And managed to turn it *on* so everyone in the room could hear Bobbie Faye's shout, muffled, but not nearly enough, by his jeans.

"Roy! You sonofabitch! You promised you would fix this washing machine for me and I even *paid* you already! Now get your *ass*—" He slapped it off and stayed very still, pretending to himself it hadn't really happened and no one heard it.

Bedroom light flooded into the window seat as the lid snapped open and Eddie bent over, grinning, his horribly disfigured face inches away. Roy flinched at the grotesque features where his nose zigzagged from having been broken too many times and the right side of his face looked slightly caved in and sagged lower than the left.

"H'lo, Roy. I know somebody who wants to see you."

"Uh, well, um, thanks. But see, that was my big sister on the phone and I gotta get over there and fix that thing, or she's gonna kick my ass." Roy eased out of the window seat, trying for nonchalant, until Eddie pointed the gun at his chest.

"Seriously, guys. She'll kill me."

"If there's anything left of you when we're done," Eddie said, "we'll pay to watch." He jammed the gun into Roy's side and Roy turned to Dora with a pleading gleam.

"Babe? Can you call Bobbie Faye and tell her I might be running late?"

"No calls," Eddie told her. "You stay quiet, we don't need to come back. Got that?"

Dora nodded, clutching her robe around her as they hustled Roy out of the room.

"Man, I hafta call her," Roy said, turning his charm smile onto full wattage. "You have no idea how crazy Bobbie Faye is."

"That's the least of your worries," Eddie said.

"Hmph," Dora said, following them down the hall. "Y'all don't know Bobbie Faye."

B y five in the morning, as she banged a wrench against the shut-off valve of the washing machine, Bobbie Faye was beginning to feel like the poster girl for the "Pissed Off and Deadly" crowd. She had pulled the machine away from the wall and partially into the hallway in order to get to the pipe; the water had not only *not* shut off, it spewed at a rate that would make a firefighter putting out a five alarm fire proud. It also happened to be a rate matched only by the speed of new swear words she'd been muttering under her breath.

There was an odd, rubbery scrunching sound behind her and then the watery echo of waves rippling against the walls. Bobbie Faye turned around to find Stacey hell-bent on "rafting" on her plastic Big Bird floatie, her butt dragging on the floor as she scooted it down the hall.

"Stace. For. The. Last. Time. This is not a swimming pool. Go find your sand bucket like I told you to and bail the water out the front door."

"What's 'bail'? Mamma says you bail Uncle Roy outta jail a lot."

Aaaaaannnnd it was official: they had screwed her up by age five, a record even for the Sumrall family.

"Well, kiddo, it's kinda the same thing as scooping up water and throwing it out the door. It's getting somebody outta trouble and Aunt Bobbie Faye ends up broke before it's done."

After settling Stacey to scoop out water at the front door, Bobbie Faye had the distinct impression that everything around the perimeter of the room sloped toward the center. She walked to the middle of the room, and sure enough, the water was deeper there—nearly four inches versus just two near the door. This little funhouse event definitely fell into the *oh fuck* category.

Bobbie Faye decided she wasn't going to panic. Not at all. There would be no panicking in the Sumrall household. Which was just when she noticed the trailer starting to make creaking and groaning noises. So not helping with the whole not-panicking decision.

As the daylight ripened into actual morning, Bobbie Faye ventured outside to see if there was any other way to cut off the water. It struck her that the trailer looked swollen, and with the floor sagging on sad little piers supporting the structure, it looked like a bloated PMS-ing woman forced to wear stilettos.

No word from Roy. No clue how to shut off the stupid valve. No choice.

She was going to have to call the emergency line at the water company. Which meant talking to Susannah. Who still blamed Bobbie Faye for the entire Louisiana State University hearing Susannah lose her virginity to the Assistant Dean of Accounting when Bobbie Faye inadvertently left the intercom system turned on in the Dean's office during an extremely brief stint as a student-worker. (And really . . . who knew accountant types could be so loud?)

It didn't help that Susannah's parents were faculty and heard everything firsthand.

But this was a certified emergency, and Susannah was just going to have to dispatch someone.

T he larger of the two sets of Muscles, which Roy had silently nicknamed The Mountain, zip-tied Roy's hands behind his back and then shoved him into the rear seat of an all-black Town Car. By the time they had hit the interstate heading east, Roy's arms ached, his nose itched, and he was starting to think these guys might be worse news than pissing off Bobbie Faye.

He leaned forward a little, scanning from Eddie, who was driving, to The Mountain, whose stomach was growling in the passenger seat.

"Is this about Dora?"

Neither of the men answered.

It was unlikely; Jimmy was a roughneck, but he was also pretty straightforward, and if he had suspected Roy of boinking Dora, Jimmy wouldn't have wasted good money on goons. He'd have just beat the hell out of him.

"Ellen?" No answer. "Or . . . Vickie? Thelma?"

Still nothing.

Maybe it was the thousand bucks Roy owed Alex after dodging out of the last poker game. But . . . as much as Alex might want to kill him, Roy knew Alex didn't want to have to deal with Bobbie Faye again. Ever. And hurting Roy would mean lots of Bobbie Faye in Alex's face. The other guys at the poker table had made Roy promise not to mention Bobbie Faye any more because every time he did, Alex twitched, and nobody wanted a gunrunner twitchy.

As Eddie and The Mountain drove Roy toward Baton Rouge, Roy pondered his ever-growing list of ex-girlfriends and their husbands who might want him hurt (or a little bit dead) if they'd been able to find him, but he couldn't see any of them going to this much trouble and expense when a good rifle and a bateau were enough to drop him to the bottom of some little-known bayou.

B obbie Faye grabbed her cordless phone and dialed the water company's emergency number.

When Susannah heard Bobbie Faye's voice, she hung up.

Fifteen minutes later, Bobbie Faye managed to force her to stay on the line and listen to the problem.

Susannah laughed.

And called the local radio station.

When she finally got back on the line, the DJ could be heard on the three-way conversation as he broadcast her latest disaster, and Bobbie Faye knew Susannah was enjoying her revenge. To make it even more fun, Susannah's big helpful advice to Bobbie Faye was to shut off the water at the valve.

"Well, duh. I did everything but sacrifice chickens to get it to budge. If God Himself tried to turn it, He'd get an inferiority complex."

"Fine," Susannah said, a bit too happily. "I'll send someone out. They'll be there sometime between noon and three."

"I can't *wait* until three for someone to show up. You ever see *Titanic*? Nothing. *Nothing* compared to this, Susannah. And I can't turn off the main valve—there's a lock on it and the lot manager is gone for the wee—"

Click.

She looked at the dead phone and then at the base unit perched on the arm of her more-shabby-than-chic sofa when it struck her that the lamp was off. And the hall light. She growled her way past Stacey, who had not only ceased to scoop out water, but had somehow found not one, but two, frogs, and was letting them swim around the living room.

Something clinked and rattled outside on the side of her trailer.

She sloshed her way through the sagging living room to her front door, pulling the wet and now clingy PJs away from her body, knowing she ranked skankier than a nutria straight out of a mud pit, but if it was who she suspected, she didn't have time to waste changing into clothes. Sure enough, there on the gravel drive, facing out, its engine running for a fast getaway, was a Gulf South Electric Utilities truck.

She hurtled down the stairs and around to the electric meter. The utilities worker saw her just as he clipped the red tag-wire onto the metal box, preventing her from rigging her meter back on when he left. He cringed as she marched toward him, using his clipboard to shield his face, then his groin (then his face, then his groin; he finally chose his groin).

"Good choice. Which is not going to help you one little bit to keep that"—she gestured—"area. Safe. If you don't turn my electricity back on."

Before she could launch an actual attack, he looked at her and then blushed, thoroughly, from his oversized collarbone to the tips of his rather large and now crimson ears. Then, pointedly gazing away from her, he thrust a letter into her hands.

"I'm sorry, Miss Bobbie Faye. But your check bounced."

She snatched it, read, and fumed.

"How in the hell am I supposed to come up with a deposit of two hundred and fifty bucks when I obviously couldn't come up with one-freakin'-eighty-seven for the bill in the first place?"

He had inched a step back with every word she spoke, still not meeting her eyes. "I'm really sorry. I wouldn't do this to you for anything in the world, you being the Contraband Days Queen an' all, but, you know, it's my job. They would fire me."

"You work for dickheads, you know that? I can't get this money until later, but I've got to have the electricity on so I can borrow Nina's wet-vac to suck up the whole freaking lake in there." She gestured at the trailer and he gaped a moment at the small trickle of water leaking from one of the bottom seams. "See that? You gotta cut me some slack here. I'm supposed to be at the festival's starting ceremony in just a couple of hours!"

"I . . . I just can't. I'm really sorry!" He turned and fled, climbing into his truck before Bobbie Faye could catch up.

"Coward!" she yelled as he peeled out. "Come back here and fight like a *man*!"

She examined the bill he'd handed her and made a mental list of items she might be able to pawn to cover it, then remembered she'd already pawned them to help pay for her sister's stay for her "sobriety mummification" (Lori Ann was ever the positive thinker) in a decent detox addiction center.

Bobbie Faye stood in front of her trailer, water dribbling from the front door. The good news was, as bad as things were, at least they couldn't get any worse.

Roy's stomach dropped a little when the Town Car veered into the industrial heart of Baton Rouge, where the black-water Intercoastal Canal intersected the roiling Mississippi River. They parked behind a plain brown stucco building which squatted with all the glamour of a working-class hooker, bland and scarred and ignored by most of the city passing by. Cast-off broken-down desks and chairs, many from the sixties, were piled in haphazard stacks, filling the lobby, and it looked more like a government-surplus auction center than an office space. The acrid scent of stale body odor mixed with tobacco clung to the stained veneered walls of the ancient elevator.

They stepped out into the tenth floor, where a utilitarian sitting area was lined with rickety metal chairs listing in rows. Eddie didn't bother to press the call button beside a door whose green paint was chipped and mottled and looked as though it had leprosy; instead, he reached below the last broken chair to a lever. A hidden panel beside a dusty plastic ficus swung open. Roy thought that might be a big bloodstain under the ficus, but he wasn't about to ask. His balls retracted a little (*only* a little) when they stepped into the room beyond the leprosy door. His adrenaline jumped and his sense of balance wobbled as though he'd stepped through some sort of portal. A line of sweat beaded just above his collar and the air frozen in his chest acted like it hadn't a clue how to escape back out again.

This might be something I can't talk my way out of.

The foyer sported an impressive imported rug, rich in honeys, golds, and russets. Sculptures perched on granite pedestals and were specially lit from above. There were fancy paintings on the wall, and Roy started wondering just who in the world he had screwed whose dad might have been in the Mafia. This place reeked of money, and not the kind the IRS knew anything about.

They walked through the foyer and into an even more sumptuous office. A thick blue tarp covered yet another expensive rug. Roy looked from the tarp to Eddie.

"Please tell me that's 'cuz y'all have a roof leak."

The Mountain clocked him on the side of his head and Roy crashed down on the tarp, jamming his shoulders when they caught the brunt of his weight, sending waves of pain through to his toes and back again. Nausea spun through his stomach and swam upwards, and then The Mountain yanked him up, planted a fist into his face, and this time when Roy hit the tarp—well, once the black dots cleared from his eyes—he saw the toe of an expensive wingtip inches from his face.

"Tie him in the chair, boys," a baritone voice purred from somewhere above the wingtips. "We have a phone call to make." He leaned over Roy, his face looming in Roy's clouding vision. "You'd better hope your sister's home, dear boy."

. . .

R oy didn't remember blacking out, but coming to was far more painful than anything he'd experienced after a drinking binge, and pretty much everything on his right side was fuzzy and dim.

He was tied to a chair and positioned in the middle of that blue tarp. The ropes cut into his arms.

Something . . . someone asked him something. Slowly, noise seeped in. They wanted something Bobbie Faye had.

"I . . . uh. Why'n't you ask Bobbie Faye for it?" he slurred, squinting through hazy vision in one eye (the other swollen shut) until the angular face of a well-dressed man came into focus. Roy guessed him to be mid-forties, maybe, and oddly happy. He wore a flawless silk suit, perfectly tailored, which almost managed to give him an appearance of sanity and stability.

He introduced himself as Vincent.

"You see, dear boy," Vincent said, "we don't want to kidnap a Contraband Days Queen. There would be far far too many questions, especially with her associations with the police. And your niece? Cute little blond-haired five-year-olds get the Amber Alert, and the country would pay attention. As a last resort? *Yes.* However, *you?*" Vincent leaned down, filling Roy's blurry vision. "You are expendable. You're always disappearing, hiding out from one girlfriend or another. No one will even believe you're missing until days later, when it no longer matters to us."

Roy noted the playful tone, the warm smile, and pondered how he was going to charm Vincent. Everything about the man struck Roy as pointy: a chin sharpened to a razor edge, angular eyes, pinched nose, a slash of a mouth, and thin, clothes-hanger elbows. Realizing it was unlikely Vincent would know his way around a John Deere backhoe didn't cheer Roy up like it usually did. Vincent might be a challenge.

B obbie Faye approached the steps leading to her front door at the same moment Stacey was dragging something not quite above water level toward the trailer door.

"Your purse was ringing."

"Stacey! For crying out loud."

Bobbie Faye jogged up the steps, dug into the damp purse for a cell phone, and scanned the last caller's ID through the condensation forming on the cell's small screen. Roy's name and number flashed, and Bobbie Faye resisted the urge to project her frustration with him onto the phone by squeezing the phone to death. She glanced back at her soaking wet niece splashing and laughing just inside the door.

"Stacey, honey, go find something dry you can wear to school and bring it here." As Stacey scampered back to her room, Bobbie Faye hit the dial-back feature and got Roy's voice mail.

"Damnit, Roy, it looks like the Mississippi River just decided to detour through my trailer. You better call me back or I'm going to rip your head clean from your shoulders. You got that?"

She snapped the phone off and steamed. It wasn't humanly possible to be any more frustrated until she glanced down and made a startling discovery: the silly glow-in-the-dark PJs she'd bought just to make herself laugh were transparent when wet. She thought back to the electricity guy's blush and realized she'd flashed him. Completely. She wasn't entirely sure which was worse—to have exposed herself, or to have done it with yellow and pink see-through hippos over her boobs. She would have prayed for a lightning bolt to put her out of her misery, but with the way her luck was running, it wouldn't kill her, just maim her and give her bad hair for the rest of her life.

Her cell phone rang again and she snatched it open. "Roy. You *asshat*. I don't care what bottle blonde or redhead you're with, if you're not over here in five minutes—"

"I'm sorta tied up right now," Roy said, his voice husky and muffled.

Bobbie Faye pulled the phone from her ear, stared at it a second, then slapped it off for fear of what she might say to him. After all the times she'd bailed him out of trouble, hidden him from girlfriends, hidden him from armed and ticked-off girlfriends' husbands . . . she wanted to kill him. No. Wait. She'd just take out an ad in the paper with a list of all his girlfriends and watch him run. Carmen might go after him with a meat cleaver again, but the idiot almost deserved it. In fact, she might just plan a surprise party for Roy and give all the girlfriends their choice of weapons at the door. As she tallied the list of his exes she could call, the phone rang again and Roy blurted, "Emergency! Don't hang up!"

"You have got to be kidding me," she said, gazing back at her trailer, which was now making grating, rumbling noises.

"I'm serious, Bobbie Faye, they're gonna kill me."

"Hmph. Like I'm buying that again."

"I swear, it's true."

"Right. Ask 'them' if they need any help."

W ith his left eye swelling, Roy could barely make out Eddie and The Mountain in the shadows of the room where they relaxed in deep leather chairs. The Mountain snored. There was a niggly part of Roy's brain—the part that usually warned him to get his pants on and get the hell out of the window just in time—sending out bursts of alarms. Two knee breakers this casual might just be used to way more violence than Roy had first suspected. This could be a world of bad. Best not to think about that. He tried, instead, to stay focused on Vincent, now holding Roy's own cell phone to Roy's bleeding ear and leaning in close enough to listen to Bobbie Faye's ranting.

"You," Bobbie Faye was venting over the cell, "are the lowest human scum, Roy Ellington Sumrall, so don't even try to con me."

Vincent eyed him and Roy shrugged, saying, "I've sort of used the old 'life or death' thing a couple of times before."

"A couple of times!" Bobbie Faye shouted, mistaking the point as being directed to her. "Try a *couple of dozen*. Just get over here and help me. *Now!*"

The cell clicked off again, and Vincent drew it away from Roy's ear, tut-tutting him the way he might a child who'd plunged his hand too often into a cookie jar.

"So much for sisterly love, dear boy," Vincent said, and Roy shuddered at the finality in Vincent's mock-sympathetic tone. "Maybe I should dispose of you and find someone she cares about."

"No, really, she cares. I swear. She's a good sister. You know, when she's not all batshit crazy. Let me call her back. I'll convince her. Really."

Vincent considered Roy for a moment. Roy tuned up his most earnest expression, hoping the swollen lips and bruised eyes didn't subtract from his attempt at charming Vincent. Vincent laughed and shook his head. At that, Eddie stood up and withdrew the largest blade from the largest sheath Roy had ever seen.

"I believe, dear boy, that you're trying to stall. Truly, I admire your chutzpah, Roy. A few more years, and you might have managed to elevate it to the level of artistry."

Vincent nodded to Eddie, who moved closer to Roy, turning the blade so that the light glinted off of it and into Roy's eyes.

"In fact," Vincent continued, "I like to think of myself as an artist, too. It takes a true ability to con the conmen when you deal in black market artifacts and expensive stolen art. And while I admire your attempt, dear Roy—and in another situation I might have even taken you under my wing and trained you—right now, I simply have too much money invested in this venture to waste any more time."

Eddie moved forward and Roy strained to hop his chair away from the men, but the deep plush pile of the rug beneath the tarp kept him from being able to actually hop.

Eddie chuckled. "You havin' a hernia or something?"

"I promise," Roy told Vincent, "she really loves me. She'll give it to you. Easy. I have always been able to count on Bobbie Faye, even if she is certifiable."

Roy gritted his teeth, trying to hold his "charming" smile. Vincent studied him, then surveyed the desk, the painting on the wall, and the nearby statue on a black granite pedestal, until his gaze rested on a yellowed, water-stained handwritten journal lying open in a glass box in the center of the desk. Then finally, slowly, he turned back to Roy.

"Last chance." Vincent hit redial on the cell phone and held it to Roy's ear. "No excuses."

As soon as Bobbie Faye answered, Roy asked, "Have you got a newspaper somewhere around you?"

"Jesus H. Christ on a pogo stick, Roy, you promised you wouldn't drink before noon."

"On Mom's grave, Bobbie Faye, I swear, I have not been drinking. I need your help. Please . . . do you have a paper?"

O n Mom's grave? *He had better not be lying and then swearing on Mom's grave.* Bobbie Faye, who had shrugged into a robe in between calls, peered out the door and saw a newspaper on Old Man Collier's front steps next door, still rolled in a rubber band. She stomped over toward it.

"Yeah, I've got one," she said, picking up the paper.

"Look on page A-five. Top right photo."

Bobbie Faye wedged the cell phone between her ear and shoulder as she walked back toward her trailer, keeping an eye out for Stacey. The trailer made more worrisome groaning sounds, and as she opened to the right page, she pulled the phone away from her ear and shouted, "Stacey? Honey? Come out here where I can see you, okay?"

On the page in question, there was a photo which showed a blue tarp over a body, and judging from where the hands and feet stuck out from under it, the body had obviously been dismembered.

Bobby Faye recoiled and dropped the paper. "What *is* that? And what the hell are you showing me that for? Are you nuts?"

"Not 'what,' Bobbie Faye. Who."

She recognized something in his voice she hadn't noticed before: fear. Real fear; trying to be brave, but not doing so well.

"Remember cousin Alfonse?" he asked.

"The one who used to dress like a chicken mascot down at the Pluck & Fry or the one who used to grow moss for a living?"

"No, not them. The one in jail."

"Roy, they're all in jail."

"Right. I mean Letta's son. That's him."

"No way."

"Way. He got out early."

"Oh, bullshit, Roy. This could be anyone. I don't have time for whatever game you're playing—"

"I'm serious! Remember when he tried to set the alligators free at the zoo?"

"Oohh. He was missing half of . . ." She peeked down at the photo on the ground, at the arms and legs sticking out from under the tarp, with one foot definitely a stub. Bobbie Faye's knees wobbled, a bit watery, and she leaned hard on the railing to her stairs.

"Roy. He's dead! Oh, geez!" Her stomach flipped and seemed to want to do toe-touches. "What's this got to do with you?"

"He got out a month ago. These . . . um . . . people here . . . Bobbie Faye, they wanted something and he said he could get it, but when he didn't, well. You see?"

Bobbie Faye stood outside her creaking trailer, trying to breathe evenly, struggling to comprehend the reality of bright morning sun, water turning her living room into a lake, and now, murder. Nothing seemed to fit, as if someone had tossed hundreds of random jigsaw puzzles together, thrown five pieces at her, and expected her to make some sort of finished picture.

"God, Roy, I really don't have any money," she said.

"It's not money, Bobbie Faye. They want . . ." She heard the pause, and her stomach knotted. "They want Mom's tiara."

Bobbie Faye stood dead still, her head echoing with his words, the normal sounds of the morning—the birds, alarm clocks from nearby trailers, a pick-up crunching up the gravel drive—all assaulted her senses, rendering her displaced, disoriented. Anger battled fear, and she wondered if she was being had again.

"You," she said evenly, "had better be kidding. Mom gave that to me. It's the only thing I have left of hers."

"I swear to you, Bobbie Faye. I swear. I don't know why, but they want it. Real bad."

"Roy, the last time you conned me out of the tiara, it was so you could wear it to some stupid Mardi Gras parade and you damned near forgot it at a bar in the French Quarter!"

"It's not like that!" His voice had risen, like he was in pain, and Bobbie Faye could hear him breathing faster. She could also hear the trailer now making bizarre moaning sounds. As she talked, she hurried to the doorway to scoop up Stacey, who was sitting on the threshold tying her wet shoelaces.

"Do they know that tiara's not worth any actual money?"

"I don't know. They just want it."

"But it's only an old silly thing of Mom's. She used it for fun, for the Contraband Days parade. *I* use it for the parade. Anybody could've taken it during the parade, easy. Why do this now?

"Besides, it's not even worth the cost of the safe-deposit box. Hell," she said, moving away from the trailer with Stacey on her hip, "if Lori Ann hadn't been drinking again and stealing everything Contraband Days-related to sell on eBay, I would have just kept it here."

Stacey's face screwed into in a concentrated frown, absorbing the insult to her mom.

"Sorry, kid." She hugged her niece.

There was a scraping metal-on-metal sound behind her, and Bobbie Faye whipped around in time to see the front half of her trailer's floor sag from the enormity of the water weight. The trailer burst open and the piers pierced through the floor until the front half rested on the ground. It knelt there like a dying behemoth, the sloshing water forcing it off-balance. Then it slowly leaned away from Bobbie Faye, moaning until it collapsed to the ground with a great metallic ripping and grinding. Water sloshed out everywhere as it died.

Bobbie Faye dropped the cell phone to her side in shock, forgetting the call for a moment. All her brain could process was, "Ohmygod. My trailer. My trailer. Shit. Holy shit."

"Bobbie Faye?" Roy shouted, his voice dim and tinny from far far away.

"My trailer. Geez, Roy. It's . . . it's . . ."

"Bobbie Faye? I need you to focus, sis!"

"Focus?" She held the cell phone away from her like it was an alien device and then slowly, remembering, put it to her ear.

"Bobbie Faye? Are you there?"

"Yeah."

"You sound weird."

"Don't mind me. I'm just having an aneurysm."

"Oh. Okay. Good. So you'll bring the tiara?"

The tiara. She snapped back to the problem. "Yeah, Roy, I'll go get it."

"You can't contact the police or tell anybody."

"Like someone would believe me."

"They said they're watching you. They'll know if you call anyone. And they want you to be subtle about it, Bobbie Faye."

Bobbie Faye frowned at her flattened trailer. "I'm all about subtle right now, Roy."

"As soon as you get it," Roy continued, rushed, relief in his voice, "you gotta call my cell. Okay? And then they'll tell you where you've got to take it."

"Get the tiara, be subtle, call you after. Check."

The call clicked off and Bobbie Faye glanced from her cell phone to her flattened trailer to Stacey on her hip.

"Is Uncle Roy okay?" Stacey asked.

Bobbie Faye hugged her. Roy was the closest thing to a father figure the kid had ever had. "I'm sure he is, kiddo."

"Mamma says you can fix anything."

Hmph. Bobbie Faye could imagine the sarcasm dripping off Lori Ann when she said it, but the hope in Stacey's expression squeezed her heart; Bobbie Faye wondered how in the hell she was supposed to live up to that hope. There were people holding her brother hostage, threatening to kill him, and she had no idea where he was.

That's when she felt it: that fire in the pit of her stomach, that knot of big-sister determination in her chest that had nearly gotten her killed more times than she could count. There were people. Threatening to kill her brother.

Which just fucking pissed her off.

"You gonna fix Uncle Roy?"

She hugged her niece. "I'm gonna give it a helluva shot."

Chapter Two

Bobbie Faye *is* the "chaos theory."

*—former karate teacher whose reconstructive nose surgery after
telling Bobbie Faye to "go for it" is coming along nicely*

Bobbie Faye shanghaied a few neighbors to help her get as much as she could rescue out of the trailer. The rest of the neighbors, who loved a good trauma when they saw one, were already setting up grills and cracking open ice chests overflowing with beer. A couple of rowdy drunks debated the merits of betting on whether or not she would kill someone by the end of the day.

"That's like bettin' a duck's gonna fly," one drunk protested. "Throw somet'in' else in." She moved out of earshot while they set up a disaster betting pool, similar to a football pool, where a board was constructed with a grid and disasters were listed in columns across the top, while time of day was denoted in rows down the side. Bobbie Faye had heard that since disasters were so common around her, to win, a person had to place a bet on the time of day the disaster would occur.

It was barely 7 A.M.

The bank didn't open until nine. She didn't know how she was going to not kill and maim before nine. The drunks just might make a fortune.

Bobbie Faye struggled out of the trailer with the last of her treasured possessions—her family photos. Stacey hovered and watched as she wiped the condensation from the interior glass and then reassembled each, trying to salvage the cheap wooden frames. These were simple color candids: one from when she lost her first tooth; one from graduation; one from the time she had her arm in a cast; another of herself at ten, with Roy, eight, and their baby sister Lori Ann, four, all sitting on an old-fashioned playground merry-go-round beneath an iron canopy of stars and half-moons. It was one of the few happy memories she had of their childhood.

She was just finishing with the photos when her best friend, Nina, arrived, fashion-plate runway-model perfect in her rosy stilettos and a gauzy translucent blouse so blush pink and skin-toned, Bobbie Faye had to double take to make sure there was a shirt there at all. Her male neighbors seemed to be having the same problem, and two men fell off Old Man Collier's front stoop as they rubbernecked Nina gliding past.

Bobbie Faye grimaced at the only semidry clothes she'd been able to salvage from her waterlogged closet: a pair of low-rider jeans a shade too tight and a skimpy white baby-doll T-shirt that read, SHUCK ME, SUCK ME, EAT ME RAW (subtitled LOUISIANA OYSTERS), which her sister had given her as a gag gift one Christmas. Her old, beaten-up cowboy boots completed the ensemble.

She sighed; she was, of course, used to Nina's regal beauty. Half of the time, she could barely run a comb through her own tangled mess, whereas Nina could have taken over a small third world country without even slightly disheveling her cool blond bob. They'd been best friends since kindergarten, nicknamed "Fire and Ice" their senior year, and Nina was one of the few people Bobbie Faye would trust to watch over all her worldly possessions. She glanced at the chartreuse plastic peacocks in the barren flowerbeds that she'd meant to turn into a garden one day, and thought maybe she should delete "worldly" from that description.

Nina cast a merciless grin at Bobbie Faye as she peered over her Ray-Bans. "B, you are the first person I know who's managed to drown a trailer."

"Bite me."

Stacey's eyes opened wide as she swiveled from Bobbie Faye to Nina, who picked up Stacey and gave her a hug.

"Don't worry, Stace. You'd be a big wad of grumpy, too, if you'd just killed your home." She turned to Bobbie Faye. "I got your message to bring the wet-vac, but something tells me we're way past that." She waited for the glare, and grinned again. "What can I do? You want me to take Stace to school?"

"Um, no, not exactly." Bobbie Faye had never, ever not told Nina a secret. She'd maybe held off a couple of hours, but never a full day, and she expected Nina to see right through her now. "I'll do that. I've got to go run an errand."

"I'll go. Whaddya need?"

"No, thanks. It's something I've got to sign for."

As expected, Nina peered over her sunglasses with a who-do-you-think-you're-kidding expression.

"I need you to stay here and guard my stuff." She and Nina glanced at all of the barbecue grills and the two dozen or so neighbors sitting in lawn chairs. The sound of pull-tabs popping on beer cans hammered the morning quiet. "I've seen some of these people pick a garage sale table clean in five seconds flat, and it wasn't even anything they wanted."

"And just how am I supposed to stop the looting?"

Bobbie Faye grabbed a pair of ice tongs and thrust them into Nina's hands. "Show no mercy."

Nina regarded the naked greed on the neighbors' faces, then scrutinized the plastic tongs. "Please, God, tell me this is secretly a Taser."

Bobbie Faye snatched up her purse, transferring Stacey from Nina's hip to her own. A few moments later, she and Stacey pulled out of the trailer park lot, her rusty yellow Bondo-and-duct-taped Honda Civic chugging hard and billowing black smoke.

R oy watched as Vincent leaned back in a leather chair behind a gleaming burled walnut desk. Vincent flipped through the photos in Roy's wallet, thumbing past glamour shots of various ex-girlfriends. He stopped, a wicked grin spreading across his face.

"Nice family photo," Vincent said, his voice dropping to a purr, and the hair on the back of Roy's neck stood at attention. Vincent examined the shot of Roy, Bobbie Faye, and their younger sister Lori Ann, who was holding a then-three-year-old Stacey. "Quite . . . enticing. Particularly Bobbie Faye."

"How do you know which one's Bobbie Faye?"

"My dear boy, *every*body knows the Contraband Days Queen. Besides, she has what I want. I made it my business to know." His lips twitched at the photo. "I bet she'd be much more delightful tied up than you, dear boy. I think I'm looking forward to meeting Bobbie Faye."

Protectiveness surged through Roy, which was quickly replaced by futility as he strained against the ropes tying him to the chair. Even though he suspected Bobbie Faye could take care of herself, Roy didn't ever want her to have to deal with the lascivious expression on Vincent's face.

"Oh, you'd probably hate her. The last guy she dated wanted to kill her." Roy grasped suddenly that Vincent might take that as a suggestion, and added, "Not that you would. You know. Want to kill her. The one before that became a priest." This wasn't getting any better. "She's kinda a handful."

"Feisty? I like feisty, as long as it doesn't interfere with my plans."

"Oh, she wouldn't. I swear. She'll get the tiara and go straight to wherever you tell her."

"You'd better hope so, Roy. It'd be a real shame to have to torture you *and* kill you."

Vincent smiled and Eddie and The Mountain chuckled, as if it was a great joke. They were jovial, having a little fun, right? Roy ground his teeth, though he tried not to show his concern. This was just perfect. Bobbie Faye rarely did what anyone told her to do, nor did she seem to care about other people's opinions of her . . . which made her so unlike all the women Roy had been able to con, he sometimes wondered if she was really Southern. Or even American. In the words of the lovely singer, Jo Dee Messina, Bobbie Faye's give-a-damn was busted. Now his life depended on Bobbie Faye following directions.

He was doomed.

Roy's stomach lurched and dropped, and sweat popped out in places he didn't even know had sweat glands.

Bobbie Faye's sad little car coughed its way up the drive of Goutreaux Elementary School, which was not much more than a series of small brick buildings slung low in a line and hunkered down as if they were on permanent hurricane watch. The sidewalk teemed with little kids lining up before the first bell of the day. Her car was billowing so much black smoke, the kids backed up as a unit and held their breath as soon as they heard her car approach. Stacey climbed out and bounced her way to a small circle of girls who hugged her and immediately enveloped her in the group. The rest of the kids moved back in unison and held their breath again when Bobbie Faye pulled out of the drive, her car belching its protest at being accelerated again so soon.

Every instinct screamed at her to zoom to the bank as soon as possible, breaking every traffic law in the process. But Roy's kidnappers wanted *subtle* and that meant she needed an excuse to go to the bank since she wasn't due to take the tiara out of the safe-deposit box until the final day's parade. Not to mention *zoom* wasn't in her car's vocabulary, though *humiliation* apparently was. A teenaged boy on a John Deere tractor actually passed her, shaking his head at her pathetic excuse for a ride.

Bobbie Faye's car hiccupped to a stop in front of her place of employment, Ce Ce's Cajun Outfitter and Feng Shui Emporium. The hand-lettered sign on the old Acadian-styled house, converted years earlier, had seen better days, and previous manifestations of Ce Ce's businesses were showing through the paint. The faint outline of print indicated it had once been the Outfitter and Pet Rock Emporium, proving there was no fad Ce Ce was afraid to embrace full throttle.

Bobbie Faye was pretty sure Ce Ce wouldn't know Feng Shui if it jumped up and bit her in the ass. As Bobbie Faye opened the front door, she chuckled. Ce Ce had apparently received another shipment of crystals, and if one crystal would help someone achieve balance and enlightenment, she obviously had concluded a hundred would be Nirvana. Ce Ce was apparently ready just in case every living soul in Louisiana wanted a few thousand. Crystals were stacked in every nook and dangling from the ceiling. Bobbie Faye could see fourteen billion reflections of herself as soon as she walked in the door.

As strange as that was, it fit with the jumbled sense of the place that Bobbie Faye had loved from the first moment she'd walked in at age sixteen. The old Acadian house had been added onto several times over the decades; rooms opened onto random porches and sometimes a person would have to travel through a closet to get to another room. The former owner had started the business selling crickets and bait to fishermen headed for the lakes or the Atchafalaya swamps and, over the years, had added rods and tackle, hunting gear and everything cammo, camping equipment and portable Coleman stoves, lanterns, fish scent, deer scent, biscuits in the morning, the best gravy in the world, and any sort of odds and ends that someone might want in a camp on the river or back in the swamp. When Ce Ce took over, the odds and ends quotient had jumped exponentially and she became the place for that weird thing you had heard about that might help with fishing, hunting, or your love life, but couldn't find anywhere else. It didn't hurt a bit that Ce Ce was also the go-to Voodoo priestess if you wanted a love spell thrown, or a revenge spell, or even just a plain old good luck charm. She had every angle covered.

Bobbie Faye passed through the over-stacked aisles, the warm glow from the antique overhead lights giving the place a cozy, homey feel (and hiding layers of dust). The smell of freshly baked biscuits made her stomach growl. She hurried past her own section (guns and knives) of the store and waved to Alicia and Allison, the twins no one had ever been able to tell apart, who were manning the live bait register. Then she pasted on a perfectly calm "nothing-is-wrong-here, move along" expression and zipped into Ce Ce's office.

Ce Ce was on the phone. Ce Ce was almost always on the phone, solving someone's problems all while weaving something or other into her dreads the way other people doodle. Today it was colorful beads. She could barely wedge her barrel-shaped body between the desk and the wall and Bobbie Faye chuckled when she saw Ce Ce using her large breasts as a shelf for the bags of beads. She hadn't known how much she needed to see Ce Ce's warm smile until it spread across the woman's face to her eyes.

"That's right, sugar," she was saying. "Better sex. How many crystals should I put you down for?" Ce Ce listened as Bobbie Faye looked askance at her, then said, "A whole gross? Honey, are you sure? You want your man to live through it, don't you?" Then she laughed, marked down a gross next to a client's name, and hung up.

"Tell me you're not actually selling those crystals as an aphrodisiac for better sex," Bobbie Faye said, weaving around stacks of oddball items and mountains of office clutter. She dropped into a chair opposite Ce Ce.

"Of course I am, honey. Confidence breeds confidence, don't you know that?"

Bobbie Faye just shook her head and laughed.

"Now what you want, honey?" Ce Ce asked, her chubby cheek propped on a fist. "'Cuz you got that look."

Bobbie Faye had barely had the words "I need an advance" out of her mouth when Ce Ce was already writing out a check.

"I don't get it," Ce Ce said. "Why're you paying for electricity when it's dead on its side? Seems to me you should just shoot it, bury it, and get yourself a man."

"Only if they let me shoot and bury him when he's useless, too."

"No wonder you're still single." Ce Ce handed the check to Bobbie Faye. "It ain't like you to throw good money after a bad cause, unless it's your . . . dammit. It's Roy, ain't it?" Ce Ce asked, her all-too-knowing gaze making Bobbie Faye uncomfortable. "What're you up against?"

"I told you. Gotta get the electricity turned on to wet-vac out the place." Bobbie Faye swallowed, wondering if Ce Ce had heard that wobble in her voice. "You know, once I get it standing back upright."

The only way she had been able to think to be subtle when going to the bank was to have something normal to do, like cashing a paycheck. Ce Ce didn't owe her one for another week, but Bobbie Faye could rationalize asking for an advance instead of telling Ce Ce the truth. Thing was, Ce Ce was the smartest person Bobbie Faye knew, and one of the kindest, and if there was anybody who might be able to figure out a way to help Roy, it might be her. Then Bobbie Faye remembered the picture of their dismembered cousin and shuddered, knowing she could never put Ce Ce at risk.

"It's nothing, Ceece. I gotta run."

Ce Ce gave Bobbie Faye a big hug, and said, "You call me if you need anything, *chere*. You got that?"

Bobbie Faye nodded and hurried out of Ce Ce's office, grabbing a biscuit from Alicia (or maybe Allison) before going back out to her car. She checked the time on her cell phone; a quarter 'til nine and the bank was just one block over. She would get the tiara, she'd give it to the creeps who had Roy, and he'd be safe.

The car hiccupped. And wouldn't start. After the starter throbbed a bit to no effect, Bobbie Faye put her head on the steering wheel and tried not to scream. She then calmly opened up her glove box, got out a small ball-peen hammer, went around to the front, lifted the hood, and smacked a few engine parts indiscriminately.

"You," she said, seething through gritted teeth as the ball-peen hammer made contact, "stupid," smack, "car." smack. "You're going to be," smack, "tin cans," smack, "if you don't freaking *start*." *Wham*. She got back behind the steering wheel, turned the key. The car chugged a bit, but the starter wasn't quite catching.

"I swear. You'll be a freaking toaster!"

She stomped her foot and the engine roared to life.

Bobbie Faye backed out of the lot, edging onto the main street through town as the car's engine surged and paused, surged and paused, surged and paused, all while billowing more black, acrid, eye-watering smoke than normal. The engine's surging worsened as she sputtered through the red light and turned toward the bank, and all Bobbie Faye could think about was how on earth she was going to get the tiara to whoever the hell was holding Roy if she didn't have a way to drive there? Lake Charles wasn't exactly big on cabs, especially ones who'd drive her around for free.

She couldn't pull Nina off guard duty or else she wouldn't have a single thing left to come home to, Lori Ann's car had been repossessed last month given that she'd drunk up all the car payments, Ce Ce's car was in the shop, and the last guy Bobbie Faye had dated had decided that life would be much calmer in war-torn Iraq and so had sold all his worldly goods, including a perfectly usable go-cart. Which, at this point, would have been a step up for Bobbie Faye, but noooooooo, he had a sudden desire to help people in a combat zone. He'd said he now understood their need, after having dated Bobbie Faye. His leaving the country couldn't possibly have been because she'd come home early from work and found him at her own trailer, comatose next to a prepubescent hussy he'd picked up and, in a drunken stupor, brought to Bobbie Faye's trailer instead of his own. She wondered if his hair had grown back in yet from where she'd shaved him bald in his sleep, or if he'd ever been able to remove the dye she'd used to paint "Little Dick" on his forehead.

The car lurched toward the bank, clanging into the parking lot of the re-purposed former Texaco station. Bobbie Faye gripped the steering wheel, swearing every curse word she knew under her breath and making up a few new ones as something loud popped under the hood and black smoke poured out in earnest, as if all the previous smoke had been amateur tryouts and this was now the pros.

Then the car died. Deader'n hell.

Four feet away from an actual parking spot, with not even the grace to coast the rest of the way in, and she was blocking the bank entrance. She put the car in neutral, got out, and pushed with every single cell she had to get the car into the spot, then saw too late that it was in crooked and blocked another spot. At that point, she kicked the door. Which fell off.

"You goddamned *fucking* pile of crap!"

There was an audible gasp behind her from the three nuns and four other customers clustered in front of the bank. Bobbie Faye straightened up, tugged at her tight SHUCK ME, SUCK ME T-shirt, which was riding up her ample boobs, grabbed her soggy purse, and joined the line forming at the bank entrance as if everything was perfectly normal. She pretended not to notice when everyone edged slightly away from her.

Besides the three nuns, the other four customers were comprised of two geeky twenty-something boys spastically air drumming to music beating through their headphones, a weathered older man in a welder's cap, and a skinny man hunched into a permanent question mark. She bit her lip to keep from trying to push her way past them to be the first in line; several more customers arrived and lined up loosely around her, everyone having that casual competitive air of wanting to be the first in line but not wanting to appear to be the kind of person who'd push a nun out of the way.

Chapter Three

Warning: Bobbie Faye crossing

—homemade sign placed by Bobbie Faye's neighbors

When the bank opened, the nuns were first inside; this being a heavily Catholic town, Bobbie Faye suspected the likelihood of lightning bolt revenge made everyone walk slowly behind them. This didn't stop everyone from cutting in front of each other, putting Bobbie Faye farther back in line than she'd begun. On any normal day, she'd have drop-kicked anyone who was being an ass, but Roy had stressed *subtle* and so by God, she was going to be subtle if it killed her.

She examined the check Ce Ce had given her, hoping that the activity made her seem normal. Whatever the hell *normal* was. She wasn't entirely sure she'd ever met up with *normal*. With the line not even moving, Bobbie Faye craned to see who the teller was, and sighed as soon as she saw it was little Avantee Miller, who was barely nineteen and already thoroughly bored with the world.

The skinny, bespectacled man stood in line directly behind Bobbie Faye. As she bounced on her toes, fidgeting, watching Avantee ever so slowly help the very first nun, the man behind her twitched and flinched and gawked at her as if she was something from another planet. She thought she'd reassure him with a little friendly banter, because that's what normal people who are being subtle do, right?

"We'd have to drive a stake in the ground to see if Avantee moved," she joked, expecting to get at least a hint of a grin from him. Nothing but a blank stare. "You know, create a fixed mark? Something to measure from?" He sort of shuddered, barely grimaced acknowledgment, and tried to avoid meeting Bobbie Faye's gaze, which made her wonder if she'd even remembered to brush her hair.

She was now officially scaring the locals.

Then she noticed a small puddle of water, thanks to drips from her purse. She tried to look completely innocent and gladly took a step forward when the first nun was finally finished.

Fifteen minutes later, Avantee had just progressed to helping the third nun and Bobbie Faye decided it was a good thing she'd had to wear old clothes, because when she spontaneously combusted, at least Lori Ann could take some of her better clothes and sell them. Bobbie Faye caught herself bouncing again in rhythm to the snores wheezing from old Harold, the eighty-year-old bank guard, and her impatience was definitely not improving the twitchy nerves of the poor nerdy guy behind her.

She noticed Melba, the insect-thin bank manager, darting over to a desk, and Bobbie Faye, filled to the brim with all the patience she could manage for an entire week, much less one morning, said, "I hope you have a good retirement plan, Melba. I've been here long enough to apply for one."

Melba sighed the very long, drawn-out sigh of one who carries the entire weight of the world, which did not faze Bobbie Faye one whit. Melba had been sighing like that since first grade. She sighed again, more resigned this time, and said, "What can I do for you, Bobbie Faye?" in a tone that implied she had met her quota of helping people back in the womb.

Bobbie Faye rushed to Melba's desk and handed over the check that Ce Ce had given her.

"I need to cash this," she said, trying to sound entirely normal, like her brother's life didn't depend on it. Before the words *you have to wait in line* could form in Melba's plodding thoughts, she added,

"And I need to, um . . ." She slid a glance around, then dropped her voice. "Check on my safe-deposit box."

Melba arched a painted eyebrow so high, it stabbed her hairline. Bobbie Faye tried not to flinch.

Melba asked, "You have your key, of course?"

Shit. Key.

Bobbie Faye rummaged in her soggy purse, knowing it had to be in there, that was the last place she put it, and please God don't make her have to go home and try to find a *key* in the middle of a trailer lying on its side, with most of her belongings strewn in the middle of her lawn. She tossed all the debris from her purse out of her way. Finally, from the bottom, she pulled up a box full of hairpins and various important things and lo, there was the key. Melba cleared her throat and Bobbie Faye looked up. She'd covered Melba's entire desk with the wreckage from her purse; most of it was wet and already leaving water marks on Melba's prized leather blotter.

"Oh. Sorry, Melba." She raked the contents back into her purse and ignored Melba's sour expression.

The safe-deposit boxes were stored in the former oil change pit, which still smelled like mud and oil decades after it had been converted. Bobbie Faye sat at the little student's desk the bank used for a table and stared at the box, her hands shaking. Melba turned her key and waited for Bobbie Faye to put her own key in.

When the box was unlocked, Melba said, "I'll go cash this for you while you visit your box." She turned to hurry out, then paused a moment at the door. "Your mamma would have been tickled pink to see you takin' such good care of her tiara. I always figured you'da lost it."

Bobbie Faye frowned at Melba as she left. She turned to the box and, holding her breath, opened it, moved the tissue aside, and lifted out the tiara. It was made from iron, molten and beaten into shape with four odd half-moon curves at the top, two on each side facing each other, and a star in the center, taller than the half-moons. Nary a gem, diamond or otherwise, not a single ounce of precious metal, just iron. Slightly rusted, scratched and plain. Bobbie Faye stared at it, flabbergasted that someone could put so much value on something her great-great-grandfather made as a toy for his daughter; save that it was old, it had no more value than an antique horseshoe.

She held it tight to her chest a moment, getting a few rust marks on her white T-shirt. She closed her eyes, her thumb absently running across the first half of the inscription, the only part still visible: TON TRÉSOR EST TROUVÉ. The rest of the lettering was so worn, only faint marks remained. Her mother had made a little ceremony out of "passing the flame" when she first crowned Bobbie Faye with the tiara. There were flowers for their hair and beads and silly costumes. Her mom read the inscription, saying, "My little treasure," and Bobbie Faye had imagined that's what her great-great-grandfather would have said to his daughter when he first crowned her.

It was the only thing her family had passed down besides the gene that made them all screwups, and the tiara was worth more to her than gold. She remembered her very first parade as the Contraband Days Queen, stepping into her mother's place, feeling wrong, out of sync. It was the first time she'd been forced to acknowledge that the cancer was going to win and her mother wasn't always going to be there. Then she remembered her mother's delight when she had first worn the tiara, and she blinked away the tears.

I'm sorry, Mamma. She lifted her face to the ceiling. *Roy's in trouble, and I need this.* "And then I'm going to beat the crap out of him," she said, aloud. Catching herself, she looked back up at the ceiling and amended, "I mean . . . help rehabilitate him."

By the time Bobbie Faye made it back to the lobby, Melba stood motionless at her desk, one hand holding out Bobbie Faye's cash from her check, the other hand hovering midair, holding a telephone receiver halfway to her ear.

" 'Bye, Melba." Bobbie Faye grabbed the cash and shoved it into a plastic bag with the tiara. She tied the bag closed as she hurried across the lobby floor, eyes down on her task, until she bumped into the twitchy guy, who was now standing in front of the line, twittering with nerves.

Bobbie Faye glanced over to Avantee, who held a wad of cash intended for the twitchy guy. She had paused there with her arm stretched halfway out, as if all of the synapses regulating efficient motion had finally short-circuited. Bobbie Faye rolled her eyes, snatched the cash from Avantee's hand, said, "For God's sake, how hard can it be to hand it over?" and turned to hand the cash to the twitchy guy.

Who was holding a gun. On Avantee.

"Thank you," the twitchy man said. Then he yanked away her plastic bag and, waving his gun at her, added, "I'm very sorry. I'm going to be needing this as well."

"Oh, you have so got to be kidding."

He indicated his chest, beneath a lightweight windbreaker, where sticks of TNT were strapped.

"This is your first time," she said, and he blushed.

"I didn't know whether to use a gun or dynamite."

"Well, next time you paint your paper towel rolls, try to make sure 'Bounty' isn't showing through."

When he looked down to see if she was right, she grabbed for her tiara bag, and what she'd assumed was a fake gun went off—shooting the ceiling—all while Harold the guard slept soundly.

Plaster fell and smacked Bobbie Faye in the head, coating her hair with white dust. She gaped at the bank robber.

"That's not my fault," he said, pointing at the ceiling dust.

"Fine. Give me back my ti . . . uh. *Lunch.* Now."

"Hey, Professor Fred," one of the two geeky boys said from the front door. "I think I hear sirens. We need to go!"

Fred turned to run just as Bobbie Faye lunged again for the tiara, and it seemed like the next moment took a billion years.

The welder guy edged closer as—

Professor Fred slipped in the puddle from Bobbie Faye's purse—

And as the Professor fell, he threw the bag-o'-tiara-and-cash to the two geeky boys freaking out at the bank door, next to a still-sleeping Harold. The tiara arced high, way beyond Bobbie Faye's reach, and she leapt up—

Tripping over the Professor just as the welder guy pounced on him, knocking the gun from the robber's hand.

The gun slid one direction on the concrete floor and Bobbie Faye rolled in the other.

She scrambled across the welder and Fred, grabbed the gun, and ran out just in time to see the geeky boys climbing into a white Saab. They sped out so fast, she didn't have time to even get a plate number, and she spun around in the parking lot, desperate, her brain chanting *no no no no no no no*.

Sirens screamed a few blocks away, heading toward the bank, and there was her car, dead to the world and no hope of reviving it, much less managing a high-speed chase. There were several other cars in the parking lot—an old station wagon with a harried dad and four kids; a Volkswagen Beetle piloted by the librarian; a silver Ford Taurus helmed by a nattily dressed blond guy; a couple of work trucks, one obviously belonging to the welder inside; a red tricked-out Ford step-side that gleamed in the morning sun, whose driver hunched down at the wheel; and, beside it, a blue Porsche, whose owner was nowhere in sight.

Bobbie Faye picked the logical and obvious choice. For Bobbie Faye. She ran to the passenger side of the tricked-out step-side, knowing that it was going to be occupied by some sort of testosterone-fueled gangly, pimply teenage boy who measured manhood in just how many inches the truck could be jacked up on supersized tires. This kid apparently had a deeply insecure ego because the Monster Mudders were at least three times any normal tire size. A kid like that was usually persuaded easily enough by breasts, but on the off chance that hers might not do the trick, she held Fred's gun on him.

Except he was so not a teenage boy. Instead, the guy was about mid-thirties, weathered hard, tall, muscled. His hottie factor jump-started her hormones with a vengeance, especially the really nice biceps, which unfortunately led to a hand holding a gun on *her*. One glance at his expression soured every single surging hormone, because Bobbie Faye knew instantly he was the type of guy with the mean pit-bull attitude of someone who was ex-military, ex-cop, ex-husband, and seriously lacking in the patience department.

Shit. Why couldn't he have been a wimp?

"I need your truck," she said, keeping her gun on him. "I need to follow that Saab."

"You need a psych exam." Then he saw the Jolt Cola he'd knocked over fizzing all over his jeans. "Sonofabitch! Look what you made me do."

"You drink that? That stuff will kill you."

He nodded pointedly at both guns, facing off.

"I don't have time to argue." She moved the barrel of her own gun slightly and shot the truck over his head, putting a crisp hole just inches above him, and then just as quickly had the gun aimed at his face again.

"You shot my truck! I can't believe you just shot my truck."

"You need a grown-up truck, anyway. What is the deal with you?"

"You're nuts!"

"Yeah, like that's a news flash. I need you to follow that Saab." She climbed in, keeping her gun trained on him.

The sirens were closer now.

He gazed past her to something in the parking lot, and his expression darkened, though she wouldn't have thought it possible. "Lady," her hostage said, seething and obviously straining not to fire his Glock, "unless you want a bullet hole in that cute shirt, you'd better get out. I've got my own emergencies."

"You think calling my shirt *cute* is going to make me go all wilty and fluttery and step out of this truck? You have seriously been dealing with the wrong kind of woman." She aimed Fred's gun at the fancy GPS/DVD/CD player. "Either you follow that car, or the DVD bites it."

"What's so all-fired important about that Saab anyway?"

"They stole . . . something." She followed his glance to the Saab a couple of blocks away and disappearing fast. "I'll make it worth your while if you help me get it back."

He holstered his own gun. "Fine. *Just don't shoot the truck.* It took me three years to get this thing in shape."

"Start sharing life stories, and I may have to shoot *you*."

"Promises, promises."

He raced after the Saab, cutting off the silver Taurus which was pulling out of the bank's exit.

Wow, that was easy. Really easy. Too easy. What was wrong with this picture?

"What kind of reward?"

So much for freaking *easy*. She had no money for a reward. Nothing to hock. And the Saab was so far away, if this guy didn't keep going . . . She glanced his direction and caught him reading the text on her shirt. And grinning. What had he paid Satan to have a grin like that?

"I am not even a part of the reward," she said, waving the gun in his face. "It'll be a real reward. Of some sort."

"If I'm going to risk jail time, lady, it better be worthwhile."

Holy freaking geez, what on earth could she give a guy who was such a guy's guy that he obviously liked stupid big-wheeled trucks and guns and . . . oh. Yeah.

"I know where there's a 1929 Indian Scout you could have."

He eyed her. She didn't blame him for being suspicious.

"Almost completely restored. It was my brother's."

"Was?"

"You help me get back that thing they took, he'll sign it over to you."

"Why in the hell would he sign over an expensive collector's motorcycle?"

"Do I strike you as the kind of big sister that takes 'no' for an answer?"

"You strike me as a total loon, but I suspect that works in your favor."

Chapter Four

If I have to take on Bobbie Faye as a client, I quit.

—*Diane Patterson, former high school guidance counselor*

Bobbie Faye crowded the truck's driver as they passed the intersection where Eva's Grocery sprawled, all four hundred square feet of it, with two whole gas pumps and three locals in the gravel parking lot selling everything from shrimp to watermelon out of the back of their camper-trucks. She spied the car running along a parallel street, and as she craned to get a better perspective, she blocked the driver's view of the road. He whipped the truck into a sharp left turn and the momentum smacked Bobbie Faye against the passenger door.

"You did that on purpose!"

"Yeah, it's called 'driving' and I thought that was the point."

Her cell phone rang; it was Nina. She snapped it on while watching the Saab ahead of them make a sharp right turn. "Not a good time right now," she answered.

"Sure, B. I just thought you might want to have a say in whether or not your trailer got winched up."

"Winched? . . . What the hell? I thought you were going to protect my stuff?"

Bobbie Faye heard the crack of a whip and she sunk her face into her free hand. "Oh, God, please tell me that wasn't the whip."

"The whip?" the hard-assed pit-bull driver asked, but she ignored him.

"Okay. That wasn't the whip."

"Jesus, Nina, it isn't even ten a.m. Don't you think it's a little early?"

"There's an appropriate time for a whip?" her hostage asked.

Bobbie Faye scowled. "It's not *my* whip, so quit looking hopeful."

"Oooooh. You have a man there interested in my whip?"

"No. He is not a *man*."

"He definitely sounds like a man to me. And he sounds sexy."

"Don't even go there. He's not a 'date' kind of man. He's my *hostage*."

"Oh, Bobbie Faye. Not again."

"Lady, I am *not* your hostage. Aside from the minor detail that you said there'd be a reward, I only *let* you in the truck since you seemed so distraught."

Nina laughed. "You know how to look 'distraught?' Is that anything like 'homicidal'?"

"Quite a lot like 'homicidal,'" Bobbie Faye said pointedly to the driver, who obviously could hear Nina. "I shot his truck."

"Is it nice?"

"No, it's a big candy-ass monstrosity."

"Figures. But at least he was interested in the whip. He shows potential."

"No. He is most emphatically not interested. In the whip or any of the other, um, things, you might be carting around in the trunk of your car." Bobbie Faye cast a questioning look toward the driver, whose wicked grin made her want to throttle him. And then she mentally slapped herself, because she definitely did not care what he was interested in, no matter how nice those biceps were.

"What a shame," Nina said, and Bobbie Faye heard her crack the whip again and a male voice yelped. "You planning to tell me what the hell's going on?"

"Maybe later. I have to go get something first."

"Like your mind?"

"Why are you my best friend again?"

"I'm the stable one."

"Yeah, you and your whip."

"Well," Nina drawled and Bobbie Faye could sense the catlike satisfaction of her toying with the men around her, "this whip is way more efficient protection than the ice tongs. Right now, however, you have a decision to make. I can either protect your trailer or your stuff."

"What do you mean, 'protect the trailer'?"

"The LeBlanc brothers are here and they've both got winches on their trucks. They're pretty convinced they can pull your trailer back upright, but I thought you should know your neighbors have them at two-to-one odds of failing badly."

"Oh, holy shit."

"If it's any consolation, the disaster betting pool has completely filled up, though there was a huge fight over who got the spot where you definitely killed someone."

"If Claude winches up my trailer, someone's gonna win, quick. Put Claude on the phone."

The Saab made another left turn, and they followed, gaining.

Bobbie Faye could hear Nina calling nineteen-year-old Claude over, and when he sounded reluctant, she heard the whip crack and she cringed. The pit-bull truck owner was still following the car through the industrial backside of Lake Charles when Claude came on the line.

"We're just tryin' t' help," Claude said, and Bobbie Faye could picture his scrunched-up earnest expression, the one she always associated with a chubby overgrown puppy who really, really didn't mean to pee on the rug. Again.

"Claude, I swear to God, if you and Jemy try to winch up my trailer, I will tell everyone I know that you were kissing your cousin and that's why Mother Superior fainted dead away when she saw y'all."

"When the hell was this, seventh grade?" her driver asked.

She mouthed, "Last year."

"I was just practicing!" he claimed. "I had a big date and how am I s'posed to learn? You won't teach me."

"Claude, we had this discussion already."

"But how am I supposed to get out of the T-ball league if I don't have a coach?"

"League rules, Claude. Sorry 'bout that."

Bobbie Faye heard the phone being handed back to Nina.

"Oh, B, he's pouting now. He's too precious for words."

"Do not, under any circumstances, get any ideas."

"You are so not fun."

"And sit on the damned trailer if you have to. Can't you pile the stuff close enough for that whip to reach both?"

"I'll see what I can do," Nina said, and hung up.

Bobbie Faye frowned at her driver and squelched an irrational urge to punch him in the middle of his amused grin.

"Just shut up."

"I didn't say anything."

"You didn't have to."

"Have you always been *this* cracked?"

"Buddy, this is normal. You don't want to see *cracked*."

"It's Trevor. You know, for when I'm dead and they ask you who you kidnapped."

"You are a real positive thinker there, Trevor."

"It's a little something I've picked up as a result of the female nutcases like you in my life."

"I am *not* a nutcase."

"So far, you've kidnapped me at gunpoint, you have what sounds like a homicidal friend with a questionable whip fetish doing things to people I am afraid to ask about, and you're threatening a Tennessee Williams play on one poor soul who sounds like he's just trying to help. You're not driving in the 'normal' lane today, that's for sure."

"Oh, bite me. Where are the geek boys?"

"I kinda want to hear about this whip thing, though."

"I kinda want to shoot your truck again. The geek boys?"

"Just up ahead."

"Thank you. Was that so hard?"

"Lady, you have no idea."

"It's Bobbie Faye."

She strained to see the white Saab, leaning into his line of sight. He pushed her back to her side of the truck just as her cell phone rang. Bobbie Faye noted the caller ID, paled, and answered.

"I swear, Roy. I'm trying to get it. Really."

"Where are you—wait a minute. What do you mean, 'trying'?"

"Well, there was a robbery at the bank." She smacked Trevor on the arm, motioning him to hurry. "They got the thing, and I'm trying to get it back. It's got to be on the news by now."

She glanced out toward the Saab, which was gaining distance on them, and waved the gun toward the dash, saying to Trevor, "Do you even *know* where the gas pedal is?"

Trevor grumbled something about how he just should have shot her, pleaded self-defense, and he'd have been home for breakfast already. She ought to just shoot his dash on principle, except she'd probably shoot the engine, too, and fry them both to crispy critterdom. Then she heard Roy babbling something about the TV footage and she snapped back to attention.

Roy watched Vincent hit a remote control, and ebony wood panels on one wall folded aside revealing a state-of-the-art TV and satellite system. News footage on one TV interrupted the local programming to show an aerial view of the bank parking lot swarming with police and reporters.

The picture cut to a young and overly enthusiastic reporter who flailed her arms toward the bank behind her as if she thought she was still competing for cheerleader tryouts; Roy half-expected her to whip out pom-poms at the end of the telecast.

"We're speaking to eyewitnesses here," the reporter said, waving her microphone toward the bank teller, Avantee Miller, knocking her in the nose. "How many people were in this gang?" she asked, oblivious to Avantee's pain.

"At least six," Avantee squeaked. "Lots of big guns, too."

"Did you fear for your life?"

"Oh, totally. They were shooting up the whole place, threatening our lives. And that Bobbie Faye, man, she's really scary when she's in a bad mood."

"You've heard it here, folks," the reporter shouted, flailing again as Avantee ducked to dodge the mic. "This brutal, vicious gang, *allegedly* led by local clerk, Bobbie Faye Sumrall, gone mad."

Roy leaned forward as the station cut to the bank surveillance footage.

"Hey, your sister looks pissed," Eddie said, now a little less bored. He even set down his interior design magazine.

And sure enough, there it was, in grainy black and white, Bobbie Faye walking over, grabbing the money from Avantee and then handing it to a nervous little guy with a gun; they spoke (there was no sound) and then, suddenly, both ran—and fell—and Bobbie Faye grabbed the gun as it skittered across the floor, and then out the door she went.

Roy shouted, "Holy *shit*, Bobbie Faye, you robbed the bank!"

Chapter Five

Bad luck: 10,381
Bobbie Faye: 0

—Graffiti seen on overpass

I did *not* rob the bank," she shouted back, still leaning forward as if that would urge Trevor's truck to speed up. "I may have *accidentally* robbed the bank, which is not at all the same thing."

"You robbed the bank?" Trevor said, slamming a palm against the steering wheel. "What the hell was I thinking? Of course you robbed it, you had the gun. And I fell for your sob story."

"I didn't *tell* you a sob story, you jerk, I shot your truck. And you," she said to Roy over the phone, "should know better. The other people robbed it. If I *had* robbed it, I'd have the money, and the, uh . . . thing." She glanced at Trevor, aware he was listening. "And we're going after it."

"We?" Roy asked.

"Not important."

"What the hell is this thing they took?" Trevor asked, and she waved him off just as another man's silky baritone voice eased over the line.

"Bobbie Faye," the man said, a seething level of impatience cutting through the silken tones. "I want that tiara. Now."

"I'm working on it!"

"Work faster," he said, "or I'll start sending you pieces of your brother." He hung up.

"Wait!" But there was no "wait" and she sank back against the seat, thoroughly frustrated.

"What's going on?" Trevor asked. Not an unreasonable question, she knew, but she couldn't risk explaining anything to him. He was in it for the reward. The last thing she needed right now was for him to have second thoughts and bail on her.

"Nothing but my life disintegrating rather spectacularly," she said, watching the car ahead of them.

"So these guys took something important?" he asked, and she rolled her eyes. Maybe he wasn't as sharp as he'd seemed at first.

"And you're sure it wasn't someone else, right? We're chasing the right guys?"

"You think I don't know who the hell stole the thing I need?"

He swerved to the curb, parked, reached across her, ignoring the gun, opened her door, and pointed. "First floor, chocolate to your left, electroshock to your right, watch your step and next time, call a cab."

"But . . . but . . . what about the reward?"

"Accessories to armed robbery don't usually have free time to ride a motorcycle. Out."

He kept looking behind him, and Bobbie Faye followed his glance, wondering if the police were sneaking up on her.

"I don't have any money for a cab," she said.

"Lady, you *robbed* the bank."

"I did *not* rob the bank, will you please quit saying that? I mean, for crying out loud, do I *look* like the kind of person who . . ." She stopped when she saw his glance and she followed it down to her SHUCK ME, SUCK ME T-shirt and the gun in her hand. "Never mind, don't answer that. Here's the deal: I've got to get something back. If I don't—"

"Yeah, sure, it's life or death, right?" he asked, interrupting her before she could turn on the patented Sumrall charm. He tapped the

GPS box on his truck as if it was far more interesting than she was and Bobbie Faye gritted her teeth behind her best "charming" smile, fighting the urge to shoot the damned GPS box just for kicks.

"Not buying it, lady," he continued. "You're a magnet for disaster and you're costing me every single minute you stay in this truck. While you're cute and all—"

"I'll pay you," she said. "To help," she added when he smiled. She did not like that smile. That was a very dangerous smile; he could convince someone it was okay to jump off a cliff when he smiled like that. She also did not like that brown curly hair or the scar next to his eye, or how blue his eyes were against his tan. Brown eyes were way the hell more trustworthy. Somehow she had to get the upper hand here, and obviously the gun wasn't really going to do the trick unless she actually wanted to shoot him, and while that wasn't totally out of the question, she was already in enough trouble.

Bobbie Faye eyed the Saab, which had stayed on the same street, getting caught by heavy cross traffic at each red light, clearly afraid to risk running the lights. She tried batting her eyelashes at Trevor, hoping to God she had maybe possibly at some point brushed her hair, and hopefully there was nothing in her teeth when she tried the patented "you-want-to-help-me" smile.

He shook his head. "How are you going to pay me? You can't afford a cab, remember? I don't need this. Get out. Tell the cops you were having a nervous breakdown in the bank because of your . . . was it your brother you mentioned? And they'll go easy on you."

"I am *not* having a nervous breakdown, and if you shove me out, I'm going to tell them the robbery was all your idea. And no one— not you, God, or anyone else in between—is going to stand in my way of helping my brother. Now *drive*."

The expression on his face shifted from "no" to "hell, no." Never try to con a man who was so well-practiced in the art of "no" he had a repertoire of expressions. She had to do something, find some way to crack that armor, because she didn't know if there was a way to catch up with the boys once they turned off this street into the busy grid of the city proper.

She gave up the pretense, itching to just shoot him and get it over with. "Do you have any brothers or sisters?"

"Are you planning on kidnapping them, too?"

"If it would help, yes. Do you?"

"Three bratty sisters from hell."

"No wonder, with a brother like you."

"Please tell me there's a jar somewhere with your picture on it, collecting for therapy."

He glanced back in his rearview mirror and frowned.

"I've got to get that thing they took from me, or the people who want it are going to hurt my brother."

"This is why random murder was invented," he muttered as he watched something in his rearview mirror.

"Don't give me ideas. C'mon. We're losing the car."

She leveled her gun at him, watching him stare at that rearview mirror, frowning way more than he had when she'd first held the gun on him. She stole a fast glance out the back window and saw a silver Taurus parked at the curb a few car lengths behind them. A yuppie guy whose suit fit nicely across his broad shoulders climbed out of the driver's seat and went to stand in front of a storefront. He seemed familiar, but she couldn't place why. She squinted and realized that the storefront was empty, and the guy seemed to be staring a little too intently, his body half-turned away from where she and Trevor were parked at the curb.

"Hey," she asked, "is that guy . . . watching us? Through the reflection in the glass?"

"Did that guy have anything to do with the other guys who stole your stuff?"

"No . . . well, not that I know of, why?"

A helicopter roared into view above them all, and Bobbie Faye met Trevor's grim expression.

"Goddammit, lady, you owe me. Big."

He floored the truck, and Bobbie Faye bounced against the dash, slamming her wrist into it, and accidentally fired the gun, blowing a hole in the floorboard. Instantly, before she had fully righted herself, bullets ripped into the tailgate, coming from somewhere behind them.

"Not the *truck*! Sonofabitch. This is getting personal."

And then he did the thing that made her realize barging into his truck might not have been such a clever idea after all: he started shooting back at the yuppie guy running after them.

"Stop doing that! You could hurt someone!"

"*You* shot at *me*," he reminded her.

"Did not. I shot your *truck*."

She ignored his glare. He probably would have followed through on the threat to throw her out, except he was flying down side streets in the same general direction the Saab had taken. Contraband Days Festival banners were strung across the street from lamppost to lamppost. People had already turned out by the dozens, dressed up in pirate costumes with fake swords, beers and soft drinks in hand. Bobbie Faye yelped as Trevor wheeled around a curve and almost plowed into a batch of schoolkids crossing the street.

Trevor spun the truck in a sharp right turn and she slammed up against him. (And damn, guys aren't supposed to smell good in the middle of running for your life, are they?) Before she could sit up to see just where they were, his bicep tensed against her cheek. He nearly elbowed her to death as he spun the wheel, avoiding something she couldn't see as he punched the gas. She gawked at the view out of the windshield as the truck suddenly angled up, going airborne, Trevor laying on the horn to scatter pedestrians.

The truck landed. Hard. Inside something red. It was one of the parked parade floats waiting in the prep area.

"We just landed in a crawfish," she said helpfully.

"Thank you. I noticed that." He didn't sound particularly appreciative.

Two cop cars sped past, and she considered the red pincers around them and appreciated that they were camouflaged. But only briefly, because a helluva lot of pissed off Cajuns started emerging from various floats in the prep area, including the float they were straddling, searching around for someone's ass to kick. Bobbie Faye scanned past the chaos, the cops, and the crazed pirate wannabes running around, past the roadblock created by the logjam of the first floats which had already begun traveling down the parade route.

And then she saw it: the Saab, trying to extricate itself from the same unholy mess, just a few blocks away.

"Hot *damn*, there they are. We've gotta hurry."

Trevor gaped at her as if she couldn't be serious, and when he made no move to hurry, she hit the low-wheel-drive gear and stomped on Trevor's accelerator.

The truck dug down into the bed of the float, grabbing traction, and Trevor had to manhandle the steering wheel to keep control, all while blowing the horn to warn bystanders on the sidewalk to get the hell out of the way. The truck climbed off the float fast, dragging a good portion of the rest of the crawfish with them for a couple of blocks, causing everyone to stampede.

Everyone except the cops, who tried to U-turn and get back to them, but who were slowed by the floats lumbering out of the giant crawfish-truck's way. Bobbie Faye grabbed for the steering wheel when Trevor started turning away from the Saab. He wrestled it back, pointing to the passenger side.

"You," he seethed. "Stay over there."

"You don't know what you're doing!"

From the fury radiating from him, she decided maybe sitting in the passenger seat wasn't so bad an idea after all.

He glared at her, muttering, "One quick shot to the head, no one would have been the wiser."

She pretended not to hear him, peered out the back window, and almost seizured when she saw just how many cops were trying to cut through the jammed streets to follow them.

Chapter Six

Not only *no*, but *hell no*! We already had the Alamo. We sure as hell are not taking Bobbie Faye.

—*the governor of Texas to the governor of Louisiana*

In the lead cop car, State Police Detective Cameron Moreau blared his sirens at the idiots in the red truck, relying on his quarterback reflexes to outmaneuver the other cars in his way and watch downfield in case the red truck made a break for an opening. For one second, he had a clear view of the truck and a woman in the passenger seat. When she glanced back, his heart sunk to his size eleven shoes.

He grabbed his microphone and keyed for dispatch.

"Jason," he said, "get me backup. Bobbie Faye's in that damned truck ripping through the parade."

"Our Bobbie Faye?"

"I sure as hell ain't claimin' her."

"Shoot, Cam," Jason said, barely hiding the laughter. "You just been pissed at her since fifth grade, when she sold lemonade she made out of holy water and told the priest it was your idea."

Sonofabitch. Why'd he have to live here where everybody knew every damned fart anyone had ever taken in their life? And why in the hell did it have to be Bobbie Faye in that damned truck? He could feel Jason laughing without even being in the same room.

He keyed his mic again. "Just shut the hell up," he said. "I need me some backup."

"You're gonna need the army, is what you're gonna need." This time, Jason didn't even bother to hide the laughter, and Cam slammed his mic down, breaking the hook. He accelerated, trying to keep the truck in sight without mowing down curious onlookers in the process.

His radio crackled again; this time Jason sounded more worried than amused.

"Cam? You still following Bobbie Faye?"

"No, I thought I'd have a tea party out here. What the hell do you think I'm doing?"

"Well, she robbed the bank."

"You're kidding me."

"No, they got her on surveillance tape. It looks like she's robbed Moss Point First National, her and some college kids or something."

"I didn't even know Moss Point had graduated to surveillance tape."

"I guess they figured Harold was going to sleep through the end of the world, so they might as well. And what makes them think they ought to call the bank 'First National,' huh? Doesn't that seem a little—"

Cam interrupted him. "Jason. Philosophize later. Just tell me who-all is after her and where they're coming from."

"I'll get back to you on that." The radio went silent again.

Great. Just great. It had to be Bobbie Faye. Sonofabitch.

Cam shoved all thoughts aside, particularly the ones where he understood he wasn't even surprised that there was something as bad as a bank robbery involved with Bobbie Faye, or that he knew he'd be happy if she was in cuffs. Instead, he focused on not running down anyone while he zigzagged through the crowd, staying hot behind the truck. He peered up and saw the news helicopter and realized they were tracking the truck as well. He grabbed his microphone again.

"Jason? Contact Channel Two news and patch me through to their helicopter."

"Copy that," Jason answered, abrupt and official, which told Cam all he needed to know: the Captain and God-knew-who-else were listening in to see exactly what happened next. *Just great.* Given that it was Bobbie Faye they were dealing with, he could kiss his promotion good-bye.

B obbie Faye saw the car hang a left ahead. When Trevor didn't seem to be about to turn, she snapped and pounded her fist on the dash, shouting, "Left! Left! Is it against your religion to turn left or *what*?"

"Do you want out? Because if you keep hitting my dash, you're getting out."

"What is the deal with you? It's just a truck."

He screeched to a stop, turning to face her full-on.

"It. Is. Never," he said, his words measured, "*just* a truck." He turned back to the steering wheel, took a breath, then floored it, his truck practically leaping forward with the sudden acceleration, and momentum pushed her hard against the back rest.

"All righty, then," she said, shaking. "That's more like it."

She gaped behind them at a metric buttload of cops with blaring sirens and lights. Shit. Was that Cam driving that lead car? Noooooo, no no no no no. Please, God, anyone but her ex.

Trevor whipped the wheel, slamming her against him again, knocking the breath from her for a moment. Maybe he was doing it on purpose. Sadistic bastard was enjoying it. Though he had an arm across her to hold her steady. And damn, that arm was like a band of steel. Impressive. As he steadied her, she forgot about Cam behind her. Or, more like, chose denial, because no way could her luck really be that bad.

W hen Bobbie Faye crashed against the passenger side of the truck, Cam fought the urge to identify with the driver.

The scanner crackled with static as Jason radioed him.

"I've got the pilot patched in to you."

Cam grabbed his mic and asked, "Who's up there?"

"Allen," the pilot answered.

"You've got a good sight on the truck?"

"Yep," he said. One word answer. Obviously not a Southerner.

"Could you elaborate a little for me here?" Cam said, spinning his steering wheel to avoid a little grandma in a Volvo who was determined to cross the intersection in the middle of the chase. "I don't exactly have a periscope in this thing."

"Gotcha," Allen answered. "Looks like the red truck's winding its way toward . . . wait a minute. There's a white . . . maybe a Saab? I'm not sure, but it's maneuvering like mad. I think it's trying to get out of the jam."

"Describe the Saab's driver."

"Early twenties. Glasses. He keeps looking toward the red truck, from what I can see."

Just then, the red truck swerved hard again and Cam saw Bobbie Faye slam against the dash. It would be just like Bobbie Faye to not put on her seat belt. How many times had he reminded her? Damn freaking woman.

The driver seemed to be shouting at Bobbie Faye, and he was pointing emphatically to the passenger side. Cam watched in awe as Bobbie Faye slid over to the passenger side and actually put her seat belt on.

Damn. He was starting to really like this guy.

Or maybe hate him.

He'd decide later.

"Hey," the helicopter pilot cut in, "the Saab's broken loose of the crowd. And the truck's jumping through the opening—looks like the truck's chasing the Saab."

Cam focused on the chaos of the crowd as he followed the truck through its opening, zigzagging to avoid angry people piling out of cars. Wrecked floats spilled flowers and tissue paper in a riot of colors all over the road. A couple of the cops behind him would handle the rowdy crowd. Still, he would almost trade places with them to have someone else handling the impending disaster that was Bobbie Faye.

On days like this, he wished he'd taken the job in Austin. A very nice city, very nice people, and no Bobbie Faye. Instead, he'd come home from a successful college football career, a local hero, happy to be back in his hometown, loving the spicy food, his good-natured people with their own unique customs.

Except that he woke up some mornings with a heavy sense of dread on his chest, and he couldn't quite pinpoint why. It didn't help that most of those mornings coincided with a Bobbie Faye disaster, which had already cost him two promotions.

He didn't *want* the sixth sense of knowing when to predict a Bobbie Faye crisis. He didn't want a single fucking thing to do with the woman, specifically since their dating had ended so spectacularly badly. Not that he thought about it. He didn't (much). Plain and simple, she was a catastrophe that he had to prepare for, just like any other. He would remain professional. Detached.

"They're turning," the helicopter pilot said, breaking into his reverie. "McCaffery Road. I'm going to lose them under those trees."

Cam understood: McCaffrey was a curvy road that wound beneath dozens of hundred-year-old live oak trees whose branches intermingled above the road to form a complete canopy. The trees followed the undulating bank of Lake Prien, and the road sometimes double-backed on itself in sharp turns. He'd worked more accidents on this one road than he cared to remember. And the helicopter would never be able to track them there.

The good news, though, was that the trees ended just before the road crossed the bridge and entered the marina. There was nowhere for Bobbie Faye to go.

"I'm flying ahead to the bridge," the pilot said and Cam heard the helicopter veer away. "We'll watch for them to come out on the other end."

Cam kept behind the truck, worrying about the way the driver kept accelerating into the curves—impressed when the truck didn't flip over in the sharp turns. Just what in the hell had Bobbie Faye gotten herself into *this* time?

The Saab sped up in one longish curve, at least a half-mile ahead, racing into the turns far less expertly, cutting across the lane in order to handle the turn at such a high speed. Cam winced, panic burning his gut. The kid driving wasn't considering the fact that there just might be oncoming traffic in that lane in the curve. Cam had backed as far off as he could so he wouldn't intimidate them into rushing and losing control. Even the driver of the truck had slowed a bit, though from the little Cam could see of Bobbie Faye, she was leaning forward, pushing against the dash as if that would make the truck speed up.

B obbie Faye heard the noise from up ahead well before they were out of the curve, and she knew all the way to her bones that this was not going to be good. The air stuttered with the staccato drumming of an eighteen-wheeler employing its Jake Brake, a most definite non-reassuring sound.

As they ramped out of the curve, the awfulness of what was happening seared into Bobbie Faye, and the animal part of her brain saturated her body with a shot of *get the hell out of here* adrenaline. The eighteen-wheeler, hauling one enormous metal oil-rig pipe, had careened off the road to their left in order to miss colliding with the Saab, which was in his lane . . . and now to avoid hitting the oak trees, the trucker had yanked the truck back toward the road . . . over-compensating, crossing the double-yellow line, only to see them in his path in that singular moment.

She could see the trucker's face, the absolute terror and anger of it all as he dodged away from them and Trevor cut to their right. But there was only so far each of them could go without ramming the oak trees, and that's when Bobbie Faye's world crawled into agonizingly slow motion:

The Saab passing the back end of the eighteen-wheeler's flatbed trailer . . .

The eighteen-wheeler starting to jackknife, with the trailer end closing in on them . . .

Just as the metal pipe as large as Trevor's truck broke free of the bindings on the back of the eighteen-wheeler's trailer and rolled off.

It seemed like it hung forever in that second just before it hit the road. Her gut knew that if Trevor kept going forward, they would be crushed under the pipe, if he didn't keep going forward, they would be crushed by the eighteen-wheeler's cab, and if he tried to go to the right, the pipe would sandwich them against the oak trees.

Bobbie Faye knew they were dead.

She wouldn't be able to get to the tiara. Or Roy.

And then she grasped that she had hijacked a psychotic, because he was aiming the truck *at* the rolling pipe. At the opening.

There may have been screaming.

Bobbie Faye thought it might be coming from her, but she was powerless to stop it as they shot into the pipe, speeding forward for a few feet until there was metal screeching against metal, whiplash as their sudden forward momentum snapped to a complete stop and then *whoosh,* the whole world spun crazily out of control as the truck continued rolling with the pipe. They dangled upside down, hanging by seat belts, then upright, then over, then upright, then over, and *wham.* They slammed into something.

And kept rolling.

Oh, it must be the trees, we've mowed down the beautiful oak trees, Bobbie Faye thought, realizing she was having a quiet, analytical thought right before dying, how very very strange.

The pipe kept spinning, picking up speed, and then for a brief second, the truck and pipe felt weightless. Airborne.

And then *kaplunsh.* There was a deafening sucking sound as water from the lake rushed into both ends of the pipe. She grabbed her gun from the floorboard as water gurgled into the truck from the bullet hole she'd put there and now water was covering her boots and *whose stupid idea was it to shoot the truck anyway?* She jerked back up to see the level of water rising fast on the outside of the truck, over the hood and then against the windshield, water pouring in through the firewall in the dash. The doors couldn't open, wedged as the truck was against the interior of the metal pipe.

Trevor shook her and he was saying something . . . she could see his lips moving, but there was all that damned *shrieking* and if that didn't stop, she was going to have to *kill someone soon,* and he shook her harder and kept mouthing something and why didn't he just *speak up* for crying out loud and then he slapped her and she focused every atom in her body into rage aimed at him.

Then she realized the shrieking had stopped.

He grinned, way too smug for a split second there, and she decided she might as well have the satisfaction of shooting him since she was probably going to drown anyway.

Chapter Seven

We separate our male clients into four categories: single, divorced, widowed, and those who survived Bobbie Faye. That last group is usually so shell-shocked, we don't let them date through our service until they've had counseling and can form complete sentences again.

—*Christina Donatelli, owner of Bayou Dating Service, Lake Charles, Louisiana*

Bobbie Faye had barely turned toward him when Trevor took her gun—so quickly, she hadn't even known he'd done it until he waved it at her.

"You can decide to shoot me later."

"Oh, sure, make promises you won't have to keep after I've drowned already," she said, hugging herself, trying to sustain the snark in order to fake the calm while the water rushed into the truck and crept up her calves. She *was* calm, damnit. Of course she was calm. She was so one-with-the-freaking-calm that after she had drowned, they were going to call her St. Bobbie Faye, Patron Saint of the Calm People. There was a big drawback to that, because calm people don't really need any help and only the crazies would be haranguing her in the afterlife. Fuck.

Trevor snapped his fingers in front of her face and she lasered a glare at him.

"Am I interrupting something?" he asked, leaning past her, grabbing the flashlight from his glove box.

"I'm a little busy working out my afterlife schedule, thank you very much."

"Sorry to interrupt." He motioned toward the back window. "Now, I'm going to shoot it on 'three.'"

"But the front window's bigger. Why not go that way?"

"I just *told* you. It's shatterproof glass. Can you hold your breath long enough to swim to the surface?"

His doubtful expression annoyed the crap out of her. She threw her shoulders back, defiant. "Of course I can. I took P.E. I can be athletic."

"Yeah, somehow I think the Olympics are safe from you." He ignored her glare. "On two, take a deep breath. The water will rush in fast."

He counted, one finger up, then two (they took deep breaths), then three and *bam bam bam bam*. Four shots across the back window. The explosion of sound in the confined space startled Bobbie Faye, and she nearly forgot to hold her breath as water poured in.

While she looped her purse over her head, Trevor used the flashlight to break out the rest of the window and rake shards of broken glass out of the empty window casement. He swam through first. Panic jolted her and the metallic taste of adrenaline saturated her mouth as she watched his feet disappear out of the window into the inky blackness cast by the pipe and muddy lake. She hated to admit she felt relief when she saw him crouch in the truck bed and reach back to help her through the truck window. They kicked away from the pipe and swam toward what Bobbie Faye hoped was the lake bank opposite from where the police were no doubt gathered.

It was a long freaking way to the surface, she thought as she swam through the cold, dark, primordial soup that was Lake Prien, and wondered if Trevor was taking the long way just for spite. She brushed past scary giant catfish near the bottom of the lake, and then a little higher the bream and sacalait and bass darted away from her. The water above her head seemed marginally lighter with daylight trying (and nearly failing) to shimmer into this murky world. Bobbie Faye gritted her teeth, fighting to hold her breath.

How the hell did she *get* into these things, anyway? When she woke up that morning, she was expecting a normal day. Well, a fun day of cutting the ribbon for the opening ceremony to the Contraband Days Festival and waving and taking pictures with a billion babies and sticky-fingered pirate-costumed kids who were always so excited to be at the coolest festival on the planet.

Her lungs hurt. There was this odd constriction across her chest and she had to keep reminding herself to fight that sensation by not breathing. Water, bad. She couldn't really see Trevor in the murkiness and what if they were going the wrong direction?

She needed oxygen. She needed to breathe. The water pressed in around her, a heavy blanket of cold and dark. Bobbie Faye followed behind Trevor, losing momentum. Dizzy. And fuzzy. How did the world get fuzzy? And what was it she was supposed to be doing with her arms again?

Water rippled against her as Trevor slowed down, grabbed her hand, tugging hard to hurry her through the last few feet of watery prison. They surfaced behind one of the many fallen rotting trees which sufficiently hid them from the opposite bank.

Bobbie Faye wheezed for air, sucking it in and sputtering. Trevor helped hold her afloat until she could breathe normally again, which surprised her and annoyed her all at once, because he really *shouldn't* be being nice right now, given the fact that his truck was at the bottom of this very lake. It worried her, when someone was unexpectedly kind. She eyed him, wondering if he was being helpful just to have the pleasure of turning her in to the police.

When she peeked through the branches of the deadfall, sure enough, there were cops and onlookers and media on the opposite shore. She saw Cam; his lanky frame, shock of dark, straight hair shorn too short for her tastes, and easy rolling gait of an athlete were unmistakable. Her heart sank. He was too damned good at his job, the bastard. Add in the nice little bonus that they pretty much hated each other and how he would thoroughly enjoy arresting her, and really, this day just couldn't get any worse.

She treaded water. She was *in water,* again, for the second time today.

"Great, just great," she muttered, as she pulled algae from her cleavage. She glowered at Trevor as he blatantly watched the algae removal. "You're really enjoying this, aren't you?"

"Oh, yeah, I always enjoy a day when I get hijacked, have my truck—which I loved, by the way—shot up, then have to drop it into a lake just to stay alive."

"I think you have a really unhealthy attachment to that truck. I mean, seriously, it's just a truck. No doubt you're divorced."

He was wading down the bank behind the dead tree, looking for a safe place to emerge from the water without being seen from across the lake, and he paused long enough to glare at her, the muscles in his jawline tensed.

"The divorce was the best part of the marriage. And believe me, after today, my attitude about women has gone seriously downhill."

"How anyone would be able to tell the difference is beyond me."

He turned back to the task of finding them a place to emerge.

"You could've kicked me out earlier," she said, surprising him with the subject change. When he didn't answer, she eyed him suspiciously. "So why didn't you?"

"Temporary insanity. Curiosity. That must've been one helluva valuable thing they stole."

"It's really not. At least, not monetarily. But it's important."

They waded through scratchy reeds and big flat water lilies floating on the surface, easing into a little inlet which gave them cover until they could climb the muddy bank into the forest.

"They want something that's not valuable or they'll hurt your brother? Did you stake out full-on crazy, or what?"

"Hey, I have an idea. Let's go back to you muttering and me ignoring you." Then she noticed his empty hands as he directed her toward a safer spot in the woods. "Wait! Where's the gun?"

"Bottom of the lake."

"Are you nuts? We might need that!"

"You really want to be carrying around the gun that was used in the bank robbery?" he asked, arching an eyebrow.

She tried to think of a logical argument, and giving up, said, "Fine. *Be* one of those boring people who always have to make sense."

"Let me guess: you were one of those kids who had a chair dedicated to you in detention in school."

"Was not. They retired my chair after it sort of accidentally caught on fire. There's a plaque there now."

He grinned. "C'mon, Sundance," and they moved deeper into the woods.

C am stood on the hot asphalt road, heat shimmering up in waves as he surveyed the mess from the wreck. He kept an outward appearance of complete professionalism. He was good at that, where Bobbie Faye disasters were concerned. Normally he had Bobbie Faye standing nearby looking all doe-eyed and confused and innocent, even though he was fairly certain she had never been innocent since the day she was born. In fact, in all of the years they'd known each other—been friends, then dated, then became enemies—he had never seen her anywhere near the same zip code as *innocent*. But at least at times like these, she was usually standing within strangling distance, which meant that the disaster was (mostly) over.

Right now, he didn't have a clue where the hell she was and that was very likely a bad thing.

The EMS crew had pulled the unconscious truck driver out of the crumpled cab, amazed that he was relatively unharmed other than being out cold. The patrol officers who'd searched the truck didn't yet see the paperwork which would indicate what his load had been. From the state of the broken bindings, it had been something big and it had cut a swath through a couple of old oaks and saplings at the lake's edge. None of that explained the utter lack of tire marks from the red truck or where the truck could have gone.

The helicopter crew assured him that the truck had not shown up at the other end of the road, heading toward the marina, nor, he knew, had they turned back, and damned if he could figure out what had happened. He was starting to get a very sick feeling in his gut that whatever had plowed down to the lake had taken them with it, and he already had divers on their way to investigate.

When he heard a tonal change in the chatter of the officers behind him, Cam glanced up. Over by the eighteen-wheeler's cab, he saw what he instantly knew was a Fed without the man even bothering to flourish his ID. The man was blond, short (but then, most men were short to Cam, who was six-foot-three), lean, and wore his authority with a sense of entitlement that automatically grated on Cam. The Fed had just stepped out of a government-issue silver Ford Taurus; he was wearing a suit blazer out in this spring heat (already ninety-five in April). The man had the pasty moon glow of an accountant too long behind the adding machine. Cam inwardly chuckled at the man's loafers and the sweat pouring into his white collar. He thanked his last promotion once again (gotten in spite of a Bobbie Faye disaster); wearing jeans and boots and a casual shirt was more of a necessity than a pleasure—as a detective, he needed to blend in, of course—but the casual attire sure as hell made chasing through the swamps after some perp one helluva lot easier than loafers. One of the patrol officers had pointed the Fed toward Cam, who muttered a *fuck* under his breath. Just what he needed.

"Special Agent Zeke Wright," the man said, flashing his FBI badge by way of introduction when he arrived near Cam, and Cam introduced himself back with a brief handshake.

"We've been keeping an eye on this Bobbie Faye Sumrall woman," Zeke began.

"Yeah? You know where she is now?" he asked, suppressing a grin.

Zeke looked around and nope, no clue. "She seems to have disappeared."

"Good job, then," Cam said.

"We believe," Zeke continued, squaring up with Cam and trying to stare him down, "that she's in a lot of danger."

"Bobbie Faye's always in a lot of danger. You'll have to be a little more specific."

"I'm here to assist."

"Well, I hope you have hazard pay." Cam noted the sidestepping of the question and let it go, for now.

"She's just one woman," Zeke said, as if *just* and *one woman* actually applied to Bobbie Faye.

Cam almost felt sorry for Special Agent Zeke Wright in that moment.

"I graduated from the same high school as Bobbie Faye. In one month alone, she caught the school on fire with her home-ec project, then in 4-H, she caused cattle to stampede over the principal's car, and she helped cook the fish for the football state championship pre-game dinner, giving us . . . the entire squad . . . food poisoning. And those were her good days."

"Whatever."

Zeke scanned the opposite bank of the lake, dismissive of any light Cam might be able to shed on what they faced.

Cam simply shrugged. Some people have to learn the hard way.

Chapter Eight

You know, when Bobbie Faye gets ticked off, she makes a bobcat with a toothache look like a day-old kitten.

—*Jessica Cole, the sister of one of Bobbie Faye's former boyfriends*

Hives of dread thrummed up Roy's spine as he waited, still tied to the chair situated in the middle of the blue tarp in Vincent's office. He watched the TVs—as did Vincent, Eddie, and The Mountain. Aerial footage focused on the wreck.

"We still don't know," one older female reporter intoned, "the whereabouts of the alleged red getaway truck rumored to have been driven by an unidentified man who was joined by Bobbie Faye Sumrall, according to witnesses in the bank at the time of the robbery."

A news anchor from the local station cut in. "Dana, is there speculation that the truck may now be at the bottom of the lake?"

"Yes, Robert, that's what we're hearing now, though I haven't been able to get confirmation on that. So far, we haven't seen anyone surface."

Roy stared at the TV. He couldn't hear anything but blood pumping in his ears. It was so loud, it drowned out whatever Eddie was saying (to Vincent? Roy wasn't sure).

Roy couldn't believe Bobbie Faye was gone. It wasn't possible. He'd lived so long with her being indestructible, the prospect that one day she might just not make it hadn't occurred to him. He had to shake his head to force the sound back in, and the glaring audio from the TV startled him. Had it been on that whole time? He oh-so-casually glanced at Vincent, his fingers steepled again, the predatory expression gone, exchanged for one much, much worse. Roy hadn't known there could be a worse, and when he saw it, his stomach did its dead level best to exit his body any way possible.

"Too bad, dear Roy," Vincent said. "We don't really need a hostage, if Bobbie Faye isn't around to bring me the tiara."

Roy gulped. He wouldn't let himself turn to look at Eddie. He'd seen, instead, the light from the windows glint off the knife blade Eddie had withdrawn again, and that light bounced off the wall behind Vincent.

Then The Mountain said, "Huh? Who's that?"

Vincent sat very still and tensed ever-so-slightly as the camera from one of the news helicopters zoomed in to a heavily wooded area adjacent to the lake, focusing on a couple standing there. More accurately, there was a man trying to haul a woman back into the woods, while she gestured wildly toward the crowded bridge that spanned across the lake and led to the marina on Lake Charles.

Roy hung his head and exhaled.

A re you nuts?" Trevor exploded under his breath near her ear as he yanked her back into the cover of the woods. "Of course you're nuts, why am I even asking?" His expression had all of the warmth of barbed wire.

"What's your problem now?"

"They. Saw. You," he seethed, jabbing his finger toward the massive buildup of people on the other side of the lake.

"I saw the Saab. I've got to get to it. What do you care?"

She knew it had been a mistake to let herself be seen; she saw Cam face her across the lake, hands on his hips in his classic "I'm gonna so fucking throttle you" stance. It was dumb and she certainly didn't need Trevor telling her so.

"I care," he said, keeping pace with her, "because we had a shot at a head start. They didn't know where we were, but you might as well have taken out a big neon 'come and get me' sign! I don't get my ass out of this until we get your ass out of this. And you just made it fifty times as impossible."

"I'm sorry! I really didn't freaking *mean* for them to see me, but I saw the Saab and forgot for a minute where I was."

"Typical!" he muttered, and she spun on him.

"Excuse me? What's 'typical' about that?"

"The whole not-thinking-ahead! Women like you—"

"Whoa. Right there." She stepped closer to him, staring hard, her skin flushed. "I have spent this morning becoming homeless, finding out my brother was kidnapped, killing my car, getting robbed, chasing the one thing that might save my brother's life only to get nearly flattened and then drowned, and you're saying that I should have somehow *thought ahead*? It must be nice to live in your universe where people apparently have ESP, but right now, it pretty much sucks in mine and I didn't see any of it coming." Her voice grew more emphatic with every word. "I'm tired, I'm soaking wet, and I'm wearing a 'Shuck me, Suck me, Eat me raw' T-shirt, which, I will guarantee—because this is the way my luck runs—will end up on the freaking five-o'clock national news for the rest of my stupid life, along with my really bad hair, and still I'm managing not to be homicidal. *Yet*. That's about as far ahead as I can handle. Don't. Freaking. Push. It."

She turned and stomped in the general direction of the bridge. Trevor riveted all of his attention on her. She ignored him and kept going until he grabbed her by the back of her shirt and snagged her backwards so hard, she crashed into him.

"What the hell do you think you're doing?"

He studied her a long moment, as if making some decision, and finally said, "Where are you going?"

"Duh," she said, pointing toward the bridge. "To the marina."

"You won't get to the marina, with the police and helicopters knowing where you are now. I'm betting they saw you pointing and now they suspect that's where you're heading. They'll have the road completely covered already."

"Yeah, well, if the geeky boys jump a boat before I can see where they're going on the lake, I'll never be able to track them."

He nodded, agreeing with her. "I know a guy who works at the marina. He'll know what boats have gone out and roughly which direction. We've got to get to another boat and contact him."

"We? So we're a 'we' now?"

"My registration is in that truck. I'm an accessory until we get your brother back safe and can prove your story. I know where there's a boat we could borrow. Maybe we can get to it before the cops figure out we aren't heading to the bridge."

He didn't wait for an answer. Trevor started off at a forty-five-degree angle from their original destination, and Bobbie Faye wanted to protest, just on principle, because she wanted to be the one with the plan, damnit. Nina always had a plan, and it always worked. Ce Ce always had a plan, and it always worked. She could be a planny type. Then she remembered she'd had a plan and look where she'd ended up. So for once, and geez Louise, she hated to do it, she shut up (which was so painful, it made her elbows twitch) and she followed him deeper into the woods, where the trees were so plentiful, the sunlight only filtered through in dappled patches.

They were moving away from the marina. She loathed having to put so much faith in some random pissed-off guy she'd hijacked just an hour ago. But the whir of the helicopters overhead (growing more distant as she and Trevor moved away from the bridge) told her she didn't have a helluva lot of choice at this point. If this Trevor *did* have his name on a registration in that truck (and of course he would, as much as he luuuvved the damned thing), then he might have a point. She knew Cam would take one quick appraisal of this guy and know, without a doubt, her "hostage" could have removed her from his truck any time he'd wanted, so he must be helping her of his own free volition. Which made him an accessory.

Was he telling the truth? Or was he using the accessory bit as cover to try to find out what she was after? He *had* asked about the "valuable" thing the geeky boys took. He clearly knew how to handle a gun. And improvise solutions, something most really good criminals knew how to do. He had that soldier's air about him—part confidence, part street smarts, part "I've killed people, don't annoy me, you could be next." She was going deeper into the woods with a guy who could help her find the tiara, but who could just as easily improvise his way into taking it away from her.

Damn. This was insane. And she had no other choice.

Trevor set a fast pace. Bobbie Faye stayed close behind him, careful to follow as directly in his footsteps as possible, which wasn't easy when she was hyper aware of the gigantic spiderwebs strung between trees and the enormous wood spiders, wider than the palm of her hand, dangling in the center of their webs. All around her were beetles and bugs and animals bigger than a breadbox. She thought it wise to keep as close as she could to this strange, angry man. If nothing else, if they encountered anything hungry, maybe it would eat him first.

Cam didn't recognize the guy with Bobbie Faye, but he could sense from Zeke's satisfied smile that *he* did. Cam had ordered the WFKD news helicopter to stay above the bridge area in case they came out from that direction. He eavesdropped as Zeke pulled out his cell and ordered his own FBI helicopter to pick him up.

"Yes," Zeke said as he walked away from Cam. "Definitely Cormier. Just get here; we can't afford for him to have too much of a head start."

Zeke flipped his phone closed and glanced at Cam, who waited, arms crossed, to see if the Fed was going to pull "need to know" bullshit territorial crap. Instead, Zeke reached for a folded piece of paper his inside breast pocket.

"He used to be an agent."

"Used to be?" Cam asked, opening the paper Zeke handed to him. On it were two photos of a man named "Trevor Cormier"—one from when he was a clean-cut agent, and a more recent surveillance photo where he looked exponentially shabbier, seedier. More dangerous. He was taking what appeared to be a thick envelope of money from men who looked, if possible, even more criminal. Cormier had a steely gaze that would have unnerved most people. The man who'd yanked Bobbie Faye back into the woods had cleaned up some since this photo, but Cam was certain it was the same man. Below the photos, there was a grocery list of crimes, and Cam didn't think this Trevor had left off any of the biggies: there was murder, fraud, grand theft, kidnapping, smuggling . . . Cam looked at Zeke to get the rest of the story.

"It took us a couple of years to realize he was on the take," Zeke explained. "He'd tip off people we were tracking and they'd escape, just one step ahead of us arresting them. Always a lot richer from whatever scam or money laundering scheme or theft they'd planned. Once he knew we were onto him, he went underground. Now he mercs out for a pretty hefty fee. A few weeks ago, we heard rumblings with your Ms. Sumrall's name—"

"She is definitely not *my* Ms. Sumrall," Cam interjected, mostly under his breath.

"—and some sort of moneymaking scam."

"Bobbie Faye? Make money?" Cam shook his head, refraining from the laugh he'd felt at the thought.

"Well, either she's an innocent bystander who somehow got caught up in Cormier's trap, or she's helping him. And he's sharp. He reads people extremely well and knows how to play them."

"You don't know Bobbie Faye. Manipulating her is a little like manipulating a live grenade. In the dark. You don't play Bobbie Faye."

"You don't know Cormier like I know him. He's not only a chameleon, I've seen him con the un-connable. If she's with him, then it's because he wants her there, alive. And before he's done with her, she'll have handed over whatever he wanted, willingly."

Cam stared at Trevor's photo and when he glanced up, Zeke fixed him with an unblinking gaze.

"I will catch Cormier. I have an order to pick him up. If he resists—and I assure you, he will resist—then I am to stop him. Period. If she's anywhere near him . . ." Zeke let the end of his sentence hang in the air between them.

"Knowing Bobbie Faye, she's just a bystander," Cam said, not quite able to add "innocent" to that.

"Well, then, your bystander is about to have a very short life because Cormier will take her out when she ceases to be useful to him."

Chapter Nine

Bobbie Faye would be a force of nature, if she weren't so unnatural.

—Lucy Swimmer, Red Cross disaster director, Southern Region

A s she tromped through the woods, she took mental inventory: she was soaking wet, annoyed, grimy, itchy, pissed off, gritty, irritated and oh, throw in aggravated for good measure. And now she could add feeling inundated and disoriented by the saturation of lush greens in the canopy of the trees above them. The leaves danced and sunlight dappled and mottled them, every undulation teasing and hypnotizing. The shifting vibrant colors plunging into her consciousness so soon after the dark of the lake made her woozy. She kept her eyes down or on Trevor's back to stay focused on every step, trying to avoid stumbling into thorny brambles grown shoulder high. Maybe adrenaline had made her hyper aware of the light in the trees, the periwinkle blue beyond the awning of crisscrossing limbs, the loamy smell of old earth and new growth, the Spanish moss dripping from the tress like gray wax from melted candles. Maybe it was the adrenaline which inspired all her thoughts to swirl and hopscotch subject to subject, so random that nothing made sense.

Had she just been in a truck inside a pipe in a lake?

So she stared at Trevor's back, trying to focus, trying to pull herself back into reality. Instead, all she managed to do was to notice the way his muscles were very nicely toned, the way the triceps were defined when he lifted his arms to move a branch out of the way, the way his confidence in every move he made just oozed sexiness and for crying out freaking loud, she needed to be interested in a man right about now about as much as she needed to grow a third boob, although, think of the money she could make in the freak show.

Geez. Focus.

He was a jerk, she reminded herself, with very questionable motives. Although he was also a jerk whom she'd hijacked and whose truck she'd shot (um, several times) and then destroyed . . . and, okay, maybe he had a teeny tiny bit of a right to be in a bad mood. Didn't matter. She had instituted a no-new-boyfriend rule. Well, a no-dating rule, because she'd hardly call the idiots she'd dated after Cam real honest-to-goodness boyfriends, although that had been the plan.

She was noticing a theme here on the whole "planning" aspect of her life.

No, Cam was a major effing fiasco. The ones that followed were just more or less a parade of losers, and seriously, she'd had her quota of jerks. More than her quota. So no more dating until she had her life a little more together.

At the rate she was going, maybe she'd be capable of dating someone normal once she was in a nursing home.

She decided to avoid staring at Trevor's back and opted to concentrate on his feet while following him, which meant she didn't quite realize when he was about to pause, and when he did, she ran smack into him.

He scowled at her after the third time.

"Did you flunk 'walking in line' in kindergarten or what?"

"Hey, at least I passed 'plays well with others.' "

"Only because you hadn't figured out how to blow them up, yet."

"I haven't blown anything up," she protested. "Lately," she amended.

He muttered something under his breath that she couldn't hear, which was probably a good thing.

She followed Trevor as he hurried through the woods, crossing small muddy creaks and boggy marshes. Bobbie Faye had to hug her bare arms tightly to her body in order to avoid the sharp edges of the thick-fingered palmetto fronds sprouting in clusters which had grown to shoulder height. Trevor used a large stick to knock down the spiderwebs and check the stability of what appeared to be hard soil, but which might turn out to be deep soupy muck with a dried crust. Of course, neither of them thought about doing that *before* Bobbie Faye's boot broke through just one such crusty spot and she had sunk down to her calf in mud.

As she stomped to dislodge the mud, she had let out such a string of expletives, Trevor laughed, shaking his head.

"What?" she asked.

"I saw *three* mother squirrels cover their babies' ears, they were so shocked at your mouth."

"Fuck the squirrels. They get to climb," she said, continuing with the stomping, slinging mud onto his jeans.

"Are you finished being Lord of the Dance?"

"I don't know what scares me more . . . that you made a joke, or that you know about the Lord of the Dance."

He chuckled then, and she felt the energy of his grin surge through her. Wow. It was the first quiet moment she'd had to really look at him, beyond just registering the general hottie factor, and she liked the crinkles around his eyes, the not-perfect face with the lopsided grin, the calm he radiated. That man really should smile a lot more often. She had to mentally shake herself to keep from touching the scar just below his eye.

They stood like that a moment, grinning, and then turned together to head deeper into the woods, keeping up a brisk pace, dodging around thickets of briars, avoiding overgrown blackberry bushes full of thorns, and walking carefully around deadfall to avoid snakes lying in the crevices. She saw deer tracks and then a few minutes later, an area of flattened grass where several doe had bedded down together the night before. Above her, resurrection ferns had leafed out after the recent rain, covering the broad curved limbs of the live oak trees, ruffling in the small breeze like a thick, decorative fringe. The colors and smells soothed her and the calm gave her hope.

Trevor paused near a pine tree, cocking his head to listen to the whir of a helicopter . . . check that, helicopters. There were at least two. So much for *hope.* She watched his face and had the eerie feeling that he not only knew exactly how many there were, but could have told her the model, the payload, and how many people were on board just from the sound. It puzzled her all over again, why he'd let himself get roped into her disaster, because she knew now more than ever that he wasn't a man to *get* roped. It worried her.

Just as she started to ask him, Bobbie Faye saw something move in her peripheral vision. She grabbed his arm.

"Stop," she said, sudden and sharp, and he froze.

She looked around carefully without moving; she wasn't entirely sure what she'd seen at first, but something inexplicable had seized that animal instinct part of her brain, that survival part. To her surprise, Trevor watched her and waited.

And then she saw it.

"Cottonmouth," she whispered to Trevor and he stayed immobile. It was coiled at the base of the nearest pine tree, its jaws wide as it weaved, undulated, preparing to strike. Chills slalomed across her goose bumps, and she tensed, staying perfectly still. The woods around lakes and swamps were full of all types of snakes. This was a deadly water moccasin which they hadn't seen in their speed through the underbrush.

"Striking distance?" he asked, and she nodded. The really bad news about a cottonmouth was that, unlike other snakes which would, if given the option, flee an intruder, the cottonmouth would go after an invader, following it and still striking, even when the invader was trying to leave its territory; simply moving away wasn't so terribly easy. She wasn't sure what to do since the snake was mostly behind Trevor, and at roughly four feet long with an ability to jump nearly its length, the cottonmouth could easily strike Trevor even if he tried to move out of its way. Or strike her, if he moved fast enough.

That's when she saw what she needed out of the corner of her eye—the knife sheathed at Trevor's hip. A Ka-Bar. Ce Ce sold them. The one many military and ex-military favored. The blade alone was seven inches and with the leather-wrapped handle, it was nearly twelve inches long. She eased her right hand to his side and un-snapped the sheath.

"What the hell are you doing?" he muttered.

"Just be still," she whispered, never taking her eyes from the cot-tonmouth. She slowly lifted the knife, thankful that side of Trevor was hidden from the snake, and she balanced its weight in her palm. Trevor started to protest, but something stopped him and she could feel his intake of breath and she knew he was surprised at how she handled the knife. Well screw 'em all, they were always surprised.

She measured the timing of the snake's rhythm against some in-ternal metronome, and she went calm, moving liquid fast, throwing the knife with perfect accuracy, seeing the knife impale the snake's head on the pine tree with a sharp *ssschhhtkkk* sound—

"Oooh, gllrch," she said, slapping her hand over her mouth, shuddering hard, her body wanting to crumple as she turned away from the impaled snake and tried not to throw up.

"You're kidding me," Trevor said, his gaze moving from her to the dead snake. "You throw like . . . a guy, but you—"

"Will totally puke if you don't get that knife and move that thing," she said, shivering again.

She heard him move and grab the knife and she kept her back to him until he came to stand by her again. She knew he was observing her, and she swallowed the bile rising in her throat, willing herself to quit being grossed out, since she had so much more to do in or-der to get to Roy.

"Let's just get going. And watch for those," she said, waving in the general direction of the dead snake. "I can't keep saving your ass over and over."

"You are a real piece of work," he said, muttering more to himself than addressing her.

"Yeah, I get that a lot," she answered.

C am watched Zeke jog over to the FBI helicopter landing on the roadway just clear of the eighteen-wheeler wreck. Another FBI agent stepped out of the cabin, handing Zeke warm-weather fatigues, all nicely folded and pressed. Cam snorted at the army boots, all shiny and new, probably never broken in. The man was going to have blisters.

The FBI agents conferred while Zeke changed right there in the street, and the colleague pulled out maps and drew trajectories. It didn't appear to Cam that they had a clear projection as to where Bobbie Faye and this Cormier guy may have headed. It *was* clear, however, that they either knew or suspected what this Cormier guy wanted and why Bobbie Faye was along for the ride.

Detective Benoit, a dark, wiry Cajun, strode up behind Cam and stood companionably there for a moment, observing the FBI agents as they prepped for God knows what.

"You're not exactly having a stellar day," Benoit noted, and Cam chose to ignore the chuckle in his friend's voice. "They tell you anything?"

"Probably less than half what they ought to have," Cam said, his arms crossed, his fingers drumming against his forearm. He noticed Benoit's glance at his hand and he stilled it. "They're specifically after the guy," Cam said, and then filled Benoit in on what little he knew about Trevor.

"Aw, mon ami," Benoit said, lapsing deeper into his Cajun accent, "you know there's gonna be hell to pay if you let the Contraband Days Queen get killed."

"Fucking tell me about it."

"Hell, you had little church ladies kicking you and altar boys trying to beat you up last time when she was just in the hospital with a concussion."

"Shut up, Benoit."

"And remember that priest trying to make you do Hail Marys?"

"Shut *up,* Benoit."

"And the altar boys threatening to grow up and beat you to a pulp if she didn't pull through?"

Cam scowled at Benoit, who'd amused himself into full-blown laughter. It had been bad enough around town *outside* of the so-called sanctuary of church. Not that he was big on going, though after what he saw all week long, sometimes it helped to go to a place of goodness; Bobbie Faye had managed to invade even that sliver of peace.

"You on the theft thing?" Cam asked.

"Yeah. I'm on it."

"Who's working up background?"

"Crowley and Fordoche."

"Call me when you find the weird thing."

"How do you know there'll be something weird?"

"This is a Bobbie Faye case."

Benoit chuckled. Then, "You going out there?" Cam nodded. "You wearing a vest?" Cam glared at him. "Hey, can I help it that you dated a woman who can shoot better than you can?"

"Get back to the fucking station," Cam snapped, and Benoit laughed again as he headed back to his car.

Cam watched the FBI helicopter lift off, and then turned to one of the officers working the wreck.

"Tell Kelvin it's clear to bring the dogs," he said, and the officer nodded and spoke into his radio to dispatch.

Cam had already ordered his district's helicopter, which would coordinate with the dogs on the ground. He had also ordered a boat to bring the dogs to the opposite bank. It was just a damned shame the FBI had taken off before asking if he had any way to track Bobbie Faye.

The dogs arrived a few minutes later in cages in the back of a truck. The group was a mix of Catahoulas and Redbones and Cam thought them the best trackers in the state. He greeted their handler, Kelvin, a compact, sandy-haired, laid-back man a few years older than Cam's thirty-two.

"You got something for scent?" Kelvin asked, adjusting his baseball cap and chewing on the corner of a toothpick. Cam nodded, walking around to the trunk of his squad car.

He'd meant to throw it away. It was a good thing he hadn't, because he really didn't have time to go to Bobbie Faye's trailer to get something. He opened the trunk and dug into a satchel and Kelvin looked a little surprised when Cam pulled out a nicely folded man's flannel shirt.

"Don't even fucking ask," Cam said. Kelvin laughed and took the shirt.

Cam watched Kelvin get back in his truck and drive over to the boat that would take him and the dogs across the lake. Kelvin would wait until he got to the other side before he'd let the dogs smell the shirt, marking the scent in order to track Bobbie Faye. Meanwhile, Cam had one call to make if he didn't want some sort of voodoo hex on his ass. Not that he believed in that stuff, because he didn't. Not a single whit. He wasn't even sure that Ce Ce believed in it, and instead, wasn't just that shrewd of a businesswoman. No matter. He had to make the call. Having Bobbie Faye in his life was bad enough; he didn't need Ce Ce gunning for him, too.

Chapter Ten

We ask Bobbie Faye to come to the ball games as an ambassador to the visitors. She sits on their side of the field. We have a four-year winning streak.

—*Collins High School Coach Jake Daniels*

Ce Ce had the phone pressed to her ear while she stared up at the TV.

"She robbed what?" Nina said, cracking the whip, and Ce Ce watched her on the small screen, hearing the snap and echo as a couple of would-be pillagers backed away from Bobbie Faye's things.

"A bank, honey. That's what they're sayin' on the news. And she's on the run, and they're sayin' she's with some guy no one can identify."

"Damn. She said something about taking a hostage, but I thought it was just a normal hostage thing."

"Honey, the fact that you think there's a *normal* hostage thing means you've been runnin' that business of yours too damned long." She preferred to stay blissfully naïve of what Nina really did at her S & M Models, Inc. business. "But sweet goodness, she took a hostage?"

"That's what she said. He didn't seem to mind, though."

"Maybe you can make a few phone calls? Some of your . . .

clients . . . might know some gossip about what's going on. I'm not getting specific details from the cops and I can help her better if I know what's up."

"I'll see what I can do," Nina said, cracking her whip again and hanging up.

Ce Ce stood in the little makeshift dining area, a place which typically felt inviting and peaceful, where the early morning sportsmen paused for biscuits and gravy, or deer sausage and boudin balls, a Cajun dirty-rice concoction rolled into a ball and fried. Her Outfitter store was the place where a few early bird customers enjoyed having one last glimpse of the weather forecast and news before disappearing into the Atchafalaya or the woods to the west. Right now, though, every hunter and fisherman who'd come in during the last hour hadn't left and had, instead, stood gaping at her TV at the newest Bobbie Faye disaster. Stood, because the three creaky chipped red Formica dining booths she had constructed ages ago were crammed full of the earlier arrivals and now the store was standing room only. A few customers were just gossiping. She pointedly ignored the cluster of people in the back of the room who were quietly taking wagers on potential damages, or worse, Bobbie Faye's survival. She also ignored the incessantly ringing phone and focused on the TV.

Ce Ce watched the aerial footage of the catastrophe that used to be Bobbie Faye's home. The trailer rested flat on its side; lots of junk aired out on the lawn, a huge crowd gawked, and Nina stood in front of the trailer, wielding her whip. Ce Ce laughed. Thank God for Nina. If it was anyone else out there, Ce Ce would have sent reinforcements. But she suspected that Nina not only didn't need help, but that they would cramp her style.

Then she snapped back to reality.

Bobbie Faye was running for her life.

Ce Ce didn't even know why. That girl was a damned fortress, never letting anyone in, never telling when she needed help. Ce Ce was reduced to being on the sidelines, hoping and praying and trying to conjure up what little magic she knew.

She closed her eyes and rubbed the back of her neck beneath her heavy braids. It was at moments like this she could remember things in fine detail—so fine, it smothered her like a thousand layers of silt. She could still see Bobbie Faye, all of sixteen years old, scrawny, tired, dead broke, half-starved, standing in front of her near closing time, having waited until there were no customers so she could ask Ce Ce a favor in private.

"Her mamma sure was a pretty Contraband Days Queen," Monique said, interrupting Ce Ce's memory. "Before the cancer got her, of course."

Ce Ce opened her eyes to see her friend with her wild red hair spiked at odd angles, a heavy splattering of freckles across her wide face. Monique, a plump fortyish mom of four, had such a benign, benevolent appearance, total strangers would leave their kids with her while she was in line at the grocery store when they had to run back to get "just one" item.

"Too bad she inherited her mamma's nature."

"Nah, honey, that's not from her mamma. Necia's crazy was a lot softer, fuzzy around the edges. She might not remember where she put things."

"Like her kids?"

"You heard about that one?"

"Everybody's heard that one. Left 'em at the grocery store. Completely forgot she'd taken 'em with her, didn't even notice they weren't at home 'til the sheriff called her."

"Yeah, honey, that was Necia. In her own world. Nothing like Bobbie Faye's brand of crazy."

The phone jangled again. It had been ringing incessantly all morning and Ce Ce hadn't answered it since the ruckus started; the media always called her first, trying to get a comment on the record and, standard operating procedure, she wasn't available. If Bobbie Faye called in, she'd use the private line, and anybody else could go to hell, as far as Ce Ce was concerned. And then one of the twins (geez, she really needed to make one of them dye her hair or streak it or something to tell them apart) brought her the phone. When she glanced down, she saw it was the regular line and she started to chastise the girl, who headed her off with, "I think you gonna want it, Ceece. It's Cam. He sounds pretty pissed."

Ce Ce grabbed the phone, snapping it up and said, "You know I'm not about to tell you a damned thing."

"You'd sure as hell better," Cam said, his fury quiet and controlled. "Obstruction of justice, Ce Ce, carries—"

"Oh, hush, Cam, honey. You couldn't get obstruction on me if your mamma gift-wrapped it and mailed it to you directly. I don't know anything, anyway."

"Are you sure? Because I've got the dogs out here, Ce Ce. I'm fixing to have to turn 'em loose and chase her down."

"Don't you be puttin' no dogs on my girl, Cam."

"You want the FBI to get to her first and maybe kill her?" he asked, and Ce Ce felt like she'd just frozen clear to the spot. She listened as he gave her the brief version of the strange man with Bobbie Faye. She knew he wasn't telling her everything, but he was telling her more than he should have because he knew she wouldn't say a word. And, she knew, he was hoping it would soften her up to spilling something he could use.

"Hon," she said, "I don't know a thing. Except . . ." She debated a second. "Except she was pretty scared when she came in this morning. I don't think I've ever seen that girl actually *scared,* you know?"

"Oh, *hell.*"

She knew what he meant. Bobbie Faye was a handful when she was calm and her version of 'rational.' God only knew what chaos she could wreak when she was running scared.

"You keep me updated," she said, and he ended the call without saying anything else.

When she hung up, she gave Monique a nod which sent the other woman to the back room to get more ingredients. One bowlfull of magic was not even gonna begin to cover it.

•   •   •

Roy watched Vincent lower the sound on the TVs and click the stereo on; "Luck Be A Lady" hummed, one of the Rat Pack songs his mom had loved. He remembered her dancing with Bobbie Faye in their living room when he was buried in comic books, too much a *guy* to dance to that weasely music. Eddie glanced up and chuckled.

"Good song, Boss."

Vincent laughed, and headed toward the elaborate liquor bar at the far end of the room, then paused, and danced a few Fred Astaire steps, pulling into a neat slide just as he reached the bar. Roy could never have managed that sort of debonair footwork, though he was a damned fine two-stepper down at Cat Balou's every Thursday night. The ladies loved being swept off their feet and it kept talking to a minimum. He was impressed with Vincent's ability, just a little envious, and he knew he could learn a lot from the man's charm and finesse.

While Vincent fixed himself a Glenlivet, Roy heard him take a call and negotiate the sale of some item, stolen from the sound of it, for which he was asking seven-point-five million. Vincent played hardball while smoothly dancing back to his desk, pausing for a brief moment in front of that antique-looking handwritten book he kept under glass on his desk.

"Ah," he purred into the phone, "Renee, you underestimate me, as always. My asking price will go up in an hour when I call our Iraqi friend. I know he'll pay more, though he's such a hassle to deal with these days, I'd just as soon forgo it for a quick sale, but only at my price. No? Ah, well, too bad, Renee. It would have looked good in your collection."

He hung up, and seemed, to Roy, to be clearly unruffled at having turned down seven-point-two million dollars because it wasn't his asking price of seven-point-five.

Just who the hell are these people?

This might be the worst jam Roy had ever found himself in.

The time with Carmen and the meat cleaver was starting to edge down to number two on the "top-ten" slot, and Bobbie Faye had saved him from that one, too. It had never occurred to Roy that a woman might get angry if the flowery things he'd said weren't exactly true. Of course, he meant them. Each and every time. But people didn't really mean those things permanently, right? He had figured the only people who finally settled down were the ones who didn't know better or the other ones too unlucky (babies, debt) to do anything about it. The idea that a woman really and truly might have wanted to live an entire suffocating life with him boggled his mind. Not as much as Carmen wielding the meat cleaver, mind you, because he never thought women could use weapons. He remembered being genuinely shocked that Bobbie Faye had figured out he was in trouble that day and had shown up in time to throw a blanket over Carmen and confuse the woman long enough to lock her in a closet until the police had gotten there.

"Did you not pay attention," Bobbie Faye had asked him afterwards, "to the fact that her dad is a *butcher*? And no one has seen her ex, what'shisname . . . Joe Thibodeaux, since Carmen caught him dithering that blonde bimbo over at the hair salon?"

He hadn't, in fact, paid attention at all. He had not really thought he needed to. He thought everyone knew he wasn't a forever type of guy.

He was more than worried, though, about what to do now. Eddie and The Mountain looked bored waiting for Bobbie Faye to resurface on TV or call. Eddie had already skimmed through every decorating magazine piled up on the fancy tables in the office. (He kept raving about something called "toile" and something else called "jabots" and Roy prayed to God these weren't some kind of stealth Ninja decorating weapons.) The Mountain had finished his morning nap and was cracking his knuckles, a horrifying noise which echoed in the room with all the subtlety of breaking bones.

Vincent leaned forward, balancing his pointed chin on steepled fingers. "Tell me more about Bobbie Faye, Roy. I am intrigued."

Roy stiffened in the chair. "Why do you want me to tell you about Bobbie Faye?" he asked Vincent.

"Entertainment, my boy. Unless you want Eddie to get bored."

Eddie picked up his knife, pricking the edge of the blade to test its sharpness.

"Oh, no, definitely wouldn't want Eddie to get bored."

"Good. So. Tell me about Bobbie Faye."

Roy thought about all the Bobbie Faye-isms, rejecting the first three stories that popped to mind from when they were kids because they all ended with Bobbie Faye beating the crap out of him for doing something incredibly stupid. The last thing Roy needed was to give Vincent any whiff of suspicion that Bobbie Faye might not be loyal or care what happened to him.

"There was this time," he said, finally remembering a decent story, "when I was in eighth grade and Bobbie Faye was in the tenth. One day after I'd hit on one of the halfback's girlfriends, the guy and his brother jumped me in the parking lot after school with a broken Coke bottle to my throat. The next thing I know, Bobbie Faye was standing there in front of the biggest one—he had to have weighed a good hundred-fifty pounds more than Bobbie Faye—and the only thing she had in her hand to use as a weapon was a pencil. A freakin' pencil! But you'd never know it to see her in action. . . ."

The sound of helicopter blades drumming the air increased. The noise still seemed distant from Bobbie Faye and Trevor's position, though at least one was sweeping toward them in ever wider circles.

"Idiots! It sounds like there's a zillion helicopters up there," Bobbie Faye said. "You'd think we were Bonnie and Clyde. Why the hell do they think they need so many? They're going to run into each other and then they're going to say it's all my fault."

"There are only three, right now," Trevor said, still walking quickly ahead, avoiding clearings or paths which may have opened up the canopy above them. "There's a Bell JetRanger, used by most media outlets. The Bell 47 up there is from your local state police, and it sounds like there's a Huey. Probably FBI."

"Man, you're just oozing the warm fuzzies. Does Hallmark know about you?"

"You're welcome."

"You got all of that . . . from the sound?"

"Sure."

Bobbie Faye stopped, her suspicions confirmed. No normal guy knew that sort of stuff. She knew guys who could tell you exactly what kind of rifle may have been shot just from the sound miles away. She knew guys who could listen to the sound of a truck out on the interstate and tell someone the type of custom muffler it had, down to the year it was made. She'd even dated one guy who could freakishly distinguish the specific factory where a Harley-Davidson motorcycle was built just from the sound of its engine.

Which meant . . . he was a lot more than the good ol' boy he had seemed at first.

"Who the hell *are* you?"

Trevor glanced over his shoulder, saw she'd stopped, and walked back to her.

"Technically, I'm your hostage."

She didn't smile. She no longer trusted the crinkle at the corner of those damned eyes. His expression grew serious.

"I'm the guy trying to help you. I just happen to know a little about helicopters."

"How?"

"*How* isn't important."

"I think it is."

"What difference does it make?"

"My brother's life is at stake. I don't know what would make a difference. I should know these things. I'm running around out here, trusting you to get me to a boat, and it just hit me how much I don't *know* you. I'm putting his life—oh, geez. What if the guy holding him thinks I'm not coming? I haven't called in! I don't have the—the thing! Shit!"

She wanted to run, but she didn't know where they were headed, exactly, and she spun, panic welling from her chest, and she spun again, frantic, desperate for an answer. He caught her by the arm.

"If this guy's as smart as he seems, then he's watching the TV. The media helicopter, remember? He'll know you're alive, and still out here. He'll know you're after it. Whatever the hell it is."

"You're right. Right. Yes. Good."

What if he wasn't?

She was having trouble breathing.

Trevor moved on through the rough, boggy terrain. The minutes ticked away, daggers slicing at her heart.

They'd been silent for a little while when he finally asked, "You said this thing wasn't valuable?"

"Right."

"It's got to have some worth. Somehow. Is there anyone you could call to research it?"

"Why?"

"Leverage, maybe. I don't know. Maybe knowing what it was worth could help you somehow."

"There's no one to call," she said. "It was just an old heirloom kind of thing, a piece of junk, really. My great-great-great-grandfather made it."

"A piece of junk?"

She shrugged.

Obviously, the tiara meant something. The *what* was beyond her comprehension. She'd held it a thousand times at least, feeling every bump and ridge, scratch and indentation. That there was some hidden meaning or value to it clashed so completely with her perception of it as nothing more than a sentimental keepsake, it made her dizzy. The design was basic. Simple as to be almost childlike. There was nothing of any worth inherent in the material used—just plain old iron from a blacksmith's forge. Maybe the blacksmith was famous? Well, then the fame was fairly well hidden, given that the world wasn't exactly putting up blacksmiths' photos on trading cards. She had to get to that tiara. . . .

And then just hand it over? What would make the kidnapper keep Roy alive? Was Trevor right? Could knowing the value give her leverage to save Roy's life? At least the media's attention was very likely buying her that time.

A realization slammed into her: the TV coverage which was, she hoped, keeping Roy's chances afloat, had probably destroyed her shot at remaining Stacey's guardian. She had no money for an attorney and she wondered what kind of jail time she could do if she just took Stacey somewhere safe until Lori Ann was deemed fit enough to parent again. Of course, with Lori Ann, that might not happen. Bobbie Faye didn't know what she would do, because no way was that child going to strangers.

She was caught up enough in the fear that she didn't see a root and tripped, scraping her arm against the bark of the tree; she would have fallen completely, but Trevor caught her just in time. He opened his mouth, probably to say something smartass judging by his expression, then his expression changed, less harsh, and he simply helped her stand and continue. She didn't realize until about forty paces later that she had tears on her cheeks.

They reached a large clearing and circumvented it instead of crossing straight through. She stopped when she heard dogs baying.

"Sonofabitch," she said, her heart sinking. "Goddamnit, Cam." If she'd had any doubts, they were dispelled now. He really did hate her that much, and she wanted to scream in frustration.

"Who's Cam?" Trevor asked, having stopped a few paces ahead.

"You don't want to know." She stood, trying to squelch the panic; breathe in, breathe out. "But those dogs are the best. He's probably getting the biggest freaking kick out of this. God, I swear, I could just kill him."

Trevor cocked his ear toward the sound the dogs were making as if judging the distance from the sound alone.

"You may get your chance."

Chapter Eleven

Wait . . . let me get this straight. You. Want me. To give Bobbie Faye
Sumrall *flaming* batons for the camp talent show? I just don't have that
kind of death wish.

—*Tamar Bihari, Wemawacki's fifth-grade camp counselor*

They ran.

The dogs bayed as branches pummeled Bobbie Faye.
Trevor barged through spiderwebs, drafting long silken
strands behind him like silver kite tails. Where the spiders dove to,
Bobbie Faye did not know and she sincerely hoped she wouldn't
find out. She had to wrap her long hair around one hand and hold it
so it wouldn't fly and snag and trap her in the brambles she passed.

Perspiration slicked her skin as her boots sunk into the soggy
ground and then suctioned back up again. She ached. Her stomach
growled. She wanted to point out to her stomach that this was not
exactly the time to be growling. Her stomach sent a loud memo that
it really didn't give a damn; it hadn't had anything since the biscuit,
and the night before she'd been all diet-conscious and had eaten a
light salad because she had wanted to be able to eat freely at the festival today.

Thwap. Another branch sprang back, smacking her in the face,
snapping her back to the present. No matter how she tried to distract herself, the hounds' baying echoed off the trees. Closer.

And closer.

Being careful wasn't an option anymore. They sprinted flat-out through the woods . . . past snakes, lizards, squirrels, coons, and God knows what else. She knew there were panthers in some parts of south Louisiana, and black bears, and geez, she needed a reverse for her brain to go back to not thinking about the woods' inhabitants.

The barking echoed, moving closer, surrounding her senses.

Bobbie Faye prayed that if Cam was with the dogs, he was somewhere far far behind them. Preferably tripping, falling, and smacking himself unconscious. (Well, a girl could hope.)

She gave herself a mental shaking. She didn't want to think of the baying dogs, or by extension, the man behind them. There were serious things to think about. She was running for her life, trying to get to a boat so she could get to the tiara so she could save Roy's life before she had to kick his ass from here to Texas for being such a screwup as to get them in this mess in the first place. (She was not ranting. She was *listing*. An entirely different thing.)

She was short of breath and hurting all over, but she could do serious. Of course she could. Because she was not going to think random, silly thoughts. Bobbie Faye was not, for instance, going to think about the fact that Victoria's Secret underwire lace bras are so not made for running for your life through the woods. Or anywhere, for that matter. Especially if the breasts were a "C" cup.

It didn't help one whit that her purse strap was slung across her chest, and with the purse itself hanging behind her, bouncing with every step, the straps cut into her shoulders and amplified the pain. In spite of her determination to not think about it, she realized she'd been having the mental background noise of "Boobs hurt, boobs hurt, boobs hurt," with every step (and please, God, let that have been an internal dialog).

At that moment, Bobbie Faye felt an unbridled hatred for every movie heroine who'd ever raced away from the villain in Jimmy Choo shoes, looking all perfectly coiffed and ready for an afternoon tea. That was just wrong. When the pain finally got to her, she tossed pride way the hell away and pressed her free arm across her chest to hold her boobs a little steadier. Unfortunately, that shortened her reach and she was unable to block briars and limbs and vines at face-level. Unwilling to admit defeat, Bobbie Faye held her forearm across her breasts while twisting her wrist so that her hand flapped in front of her, flapping a little to help with deflecting the underbrush, all while holding her hair with the other hand. She hadn't quite perfected the coordination of running to flapping when Trevor glanced over his shoulder. As he turned away, she distinctly heard something that sounded a little too much like "spastic, hobbled penguin."

"Bastard," she muttered. She hoped he came down with a bad case of chiggers in his boxers.

The only way she managed to maintain a (somewhat) positive attitude was to remind herself that all of the running had helped her clothes dry a little, in a rancid sweat-soaked damp sort of way. She hadn't thought she could get any skankier than that morning, but she'd achieved a new personal low. At this point, she figured roadkill had her beaten on the beauty scale. Maybe when she showed up with the tiara, she'd just scare the kidnappers to death and she and Roy could get away safely.

Her relief at finally being dry was cut short when she heard the dogs' deep baritone barking, closer now, frenzied. The goddamned dogs were gaining on her.

Damn freaking Cam and his freaking overachieving ass. It was the thing she had both admired and simultaneously loathed about him. Whether it was winning a Heisman Trophy, tracking a criminal, or flaming out a relationship so angrily that fourteen years of prior friendship were nothing more than crispy ashes in the aftermath, he didn't do anything halfway. Anything. She shuddered and wobbled a moment just thinking about the other things he didn't do halfway, but that was gone. Which was probably just as well, because he was so fucking sure he was always right and their battles had been so epic, she would have had to kill him in his sleep probably a lot sooner than later, and she really didn't look good in jailhouse orange.

Trevor pushed their speed up a notch, and she was panting hard when they stumbled out of the brush and onto a small bayou, about twenty feet across.

More. Freaking. Water.

It was as if she'd kicked God underneath the table and He was smiting her with humiliation. Over and over. Where was that handy pillar-of-salt deal when you needed it? Much, much easier on the smiting scale.

She glanced at Trevor, who was scanning up and down the bayou and realizing, as she'd just grasped, that there was no place where the banks were closer together, making it easy to jump across.

"*No,*" she said. She may have even stamped her boot.

"Big fan of dogs, are you?" he asked, and she could have sworn he had the beginning of a grin beneath those devil blue eyes.

"Remind me to tell you later how much I hate you."

"Sure thing," he said, scanning downstream. "We'll go upstream— that will get us closer to the place where I know a boat is located and if we get really lucky, they'll think we were in such a hurry, we headed downstream because it's more logical if we were heading for the road out."

"But they'll track our footprints."

"Not if we're in the middle of the bayou."

She stared at him a moment, the idea of *more water* in her immediate future. "Really, *really* hating you."

"Got the memo." He pulled out his knife.

Chapter Twelve

Whoa," Bobbie Faye said, backing up a step, her heart rate pinging in the about-to-stroke-out zone. "It was more of a mild dislike, actually. And you're sort of growing on me. In a nonfungus way. And really *really* sorry about that truck."

"We've got to give the dogs something of yours to scent."

"I'm keeping all of my appendages, thanks."

He rolled his eyes, clearly annoyed. "Bobbie Faye, get over here. I'm going to slice a piece from the hem of your shirt."

She cocked her head a bit, assessing him, and then finally stepped forward; he cut a couple of inches from the bottom of her shirt, tearing at the piece until he had made several jagged strips from the original section. Bobbie Faye watched as he found objects along the bank—a small stone, a twig, a larger chunk of bark from a rotting tree. He wrapped the small sections of the shirt around these items, or tucked them into crevices—anything that would give the cloth some weight.

"A good dog handler's probably gonna know this isn't something torn from your shirt in the process of running," he explained as he tossed the lightest one nearby on the bank, and then the next heaviest farther downstream. "But he's gonna have to check it out to be sure and let the dogs scent it and see if there's any trail of us leading from these into the woods somewhere." He continued tossing each piece. "It might buy us ten, fifteen minutes of confusion." The last item was the heavier chunk of wood, which he threw in a beautiful, powerful arc far downstream and across to the other side. It landed with a splud into a tree and the bark disintegrated, and the white cloth from the shirt fell to the foot of that tree.

She gave Trevor a "hang on a minute" gesture and sprinted down the bank in the downstream direction ignoring his sputtering questions behind her. As she stretched her pace into a hard run, she pulled closer to the water, slipping and sliding a little, making fine, detectable footprints and then crossed into the water and waded back upstream to where Trevor waited for her. When she reached him, he had an expression she couldn't quite register; it was almost as if he was marveling at her, but he shuttered the expression as fast as it had appeared.

"We'll get farther, faster, if we swim as long as we can hold out," he suggested as she approached, and Bobbie Faye nodded.

Cam moved through the woods, listening to the dogs twenty yards ahead baying their normal "found the scent" tone, but not feverish enough for Cam to feel as if they had Bobbie Faye in sight. He squatted back on his heels, examining the muddy tracks this Cormier guy and Bobbie Faye had left as they'd hurried, and it was clear from the way Bobbie Faye's overlapped the renegade agent's that she was following the agent and not the other way around. There went the theory that she was taken against her will. Of course, he would have pitied the poor soul who tried to take Bobbie Faye against her will. They'd probably draw back a nub.

Still. She was running *behind* the man. Cormier didn't have a gun on her. It made him shudder to think of someone as accidentally destructive as Bobbie Faye teaming up and helping, however naïvely, someone as purposefully violent as the rogue agent. He wasn't sure the state would survive them both.

His phone vibrated and he snapped it open to hear Jason in dispatch sound a little concerned.

"Cam, the guys in the helo say the Feds are circling closer to your position. They're going to end up on top of you and the dogs in a couple more passes."

"Hang on." Cam stood, surveying the sky. He didn't want the Feds overhead where they might spot Bobbie Faye before Cam could get her in cuffs. After that, they could have their damned agent. "I want a way to contact the WFKD helicopter without patching through to the pilot where the Feds might listen in."

Jason put him on hold, then came back with the cameraman's cell phone. "If it even works up there," he cautioned.

When the cameraman answered his cell and Cam introduced himself, the man asked, "What can we do for you, Detective?" It was the tone of voice that told Cam this was going to cost him something he was going to regret.

"I need you to swerve back toward the bridge and act like you've seen something over there. I need the Feds to get curious and get off my tail over here."

"Hang on," the man said, and Cam could hear him conferring with the pilot. "Sure," he said, "but on one condition."

"Why am I not surprised?"

"You make a statement on the record after all of this is over."

Sonofabitch. *Everyone* knew he didn't comment on the record about Bobbie Faye. People had tried to grab that sound bite for several years now, and the press was especially relentless ever since he and Bobbie Faye had broken up.

"I don't make comments on the record," he said. "But I'll give you an off-the-record comment with details."

"Well, we don't usually try to con Feds, either. Besides," the cameraman said, "I got ways to get most of the details anyway."

Cam listened to the staccato thwapping of the air by the blades of the Fed's helicopter as it flew closer to his position. Goddamn-fuckingBobbieFaye.

Cam suspected the Feds had a sharpshooter buckled at the crew door, watching through a scope, waiting for that perfect shot for Cormier. If Bobbie Faye was still running behind the man, the Feds could accidentally shoot her while trying to get the shot at him. He'd seen enough gung ho hotshot SWAT snipers lose perspective when a hostage situation was relatively calm and stable; this chaos was begging for mistakes. He needed every advantage he could get.

"Fine," he said. "One statement. Only after the whole damned thing is over." He slammed the phone shut. *Assuming I'm still alive.*

He called Jason back, gave him the plan, and instructed him to dispatch their own helicopter over in the same area, mimicking the news helicopter. He doubted it would fool the Feds for long, but if the dogs were as good as they usually were, he only needed a few minutes of distraction.

Cam headed in the same direction as the dogs when his cell phone vibrated again, and he snapped it open without losing stride.

"You said to call when I found the something weird," Benoit said by way of a hello. "This guy, Fred? The thief. He's a professor of antiquities over at LSU. No priors, nothing. Fine, upstanding citizen. I've got Crowe and Fordoche going over his financials."

"He have any history of mental illness?"

"Not before this morning when he was reported associating with Bobbie Faye. Whoa—hang on. *Sacre merde.* His attorney just arrived. It's Dellago."

What in the hell was the sleaziest, highest-paid attorney for organized crime doing defending a joke of a burglar? One who didn't even manage to take anything?

Dellago's appearance could only mean one thing: whatever Bobbie Faye was into was a helluva lot worse than Cam had thought. Arresting her might be the least of his problems. Keeping her alive until time for trial . . . he didn't want to guess how hard that was going to be, if Dellago was involved. He needed to know. He looked around at the sheer manpower (and dog power) chasing after her.

She simply had no chance of escape. She'd be in custody. Safe.

"I'll be there in ten minutes," he told Benoit.

Cam hung up and spun around, heading back to the lake and the accident site. He called Kelvin.

"The dogs are riling up," Kelvin said. "Fresh scent. We're gaining on 'em. Should have 'em in sight in a few minutes."

"You'll have to wrap her up. I've got to go back."

"I'm gonna lose twenty bucks in the pool if you're not the one to cuff her," Kelvin drawled.

"Go to hell."

He hung up on Kelvin's laughter.

As he jogged back to the bank of the lake where his boat was waiting and running, manned by a patrol officer, Cam glanced toward the bridge. Sure enough, the news helicopter had dropped and hovered low over a section of woods a few clicks away from where Bobbie Faye had originally seemed to be heading. His own state police helicopter was circling near it and it looked like the Fibbies had gotten curious and were sniffing around over there.

Kelvin and SWAT could take her. Unless there was a hostage situation, and frankly, he thought he'd have better luck if a cold blooded killer like this Cormier guy was holding Bobbie Faye hostage rather than the other way around. The only good news he could think of was that, if cornered, Bobbie Faye wouldn't shoot the dogs. The men, he hoped, were smart enough not to get in her line of fire.

They swam a half a mile around the bend in the bayou when Trevor motioned for Bobbie Faye to stop. Standing in the middle of the water, they could see a hundred yards upstream where two alligators sunned themselves on fallen logs. Trevor glanced over Bobbie Faye's shoulder. "Going back is asking to get caught. We need to get a little farther upstream before we move out of the water."

"Maybe we can walk past them. I've been told gators are pretty shy."

"You're sure this was someone who actually *liked* you who told you this?"

"Um, not entirely." He caught her unsure expression and shook his head, bemused.

They waded in the dark, brackish water; the strong smell of fish battled the pungent odor of wet earth and rotted leaves in an effort to overtake her senses and render her numb to thought. She needed to think. There was something important tingling somewhere in the deep recesses of her mind.

She felt poised above recognition, like when she was in school, fidgeting in her desk, her pencil hovering over two similar answers on a multiple choice test. Both familiar, and she'd go back and forth, trying to decide if this answer was familiar because it was the right answer or because it was the one she'd said most often, but gotten wrong? This suddenly seemed like the multiple choice test for the decade, where there was something shadowing her answer and she was pretty sure she'd picked the *right* answer, but the nagging feeling of having forgotten something important continued to itch at the base of her skull.

Maybe that nagging feeling was just the stress of the day. Maybe it was because she had thought the most difficult decision she was going to have to make that day was whether to hit the crawfish boil early before they ran out or try to time it for later, when the crawfish were spicier and had absorbed the seasonings better, but when, of course, everyone else would be aiming for them as well. She focused her gaze upstream at the log which protruded almost halfway across the bayou and accepted that maybe that niggling feeling of fear had to do with a ten-foot-long alligator not so far away. Even if they were shy, they were freakishly, primordially scary.

Thinking of alligators, and chomping, reminded her of stub-footed cousin Alfonse, lying in pieces and parts under a tarp. This was not helping. She was not going to think about alligators.

Of course, the very thing you try not to think about is what you think about and maybe she could think about something else, instead, but nope, it wasn't happening. Why couldn't she have decided *not* to think about pretty flowers or chocolate or fluffy bunnies? So her brain complied with the mental image of an alligator chomping and tearing a chocolate brown fluffy bunny and she nearly yelped from the sudden vivid imagery, and she stumbled in the water.

Trevor caught her and, for a brief moment, held her close, presumably 'til her adrenaline subsided enough to take a steadier step. He held her so close she could see the blond and red glints in his stubble, see the stitch marks in the old scar beneath his eye, see the flecks of green in his blue eyes. Then he looked at her, really looked, and his pupils dilated and his whole demeanor changed and holy freaking geez, a man should not have that sort of expression. The kind that said if they weren't standing waist-deep in water in the middle of a bayou, she'd be naked already, and be really really happy about it, too. She felt herself inhale and knew he could feel her heart rev up again.

"You okay?" he asked.

"Mmmmm hmmmm." She didn't trust herself to answer.

"Next date," he whispered, "it's my turn to pick the venue."

She chuckled into his shoulder. Damn. A really good-looking, sexy man who could make her laugh in the middle of a disaster . . . well, that sealed it. He had to be Satan incarnate, or doomed, given her luck with men. At least, she noticed, the helicopters had veered away from them. Maybe all of this was going to work.

C e Ce stared at the TV, watching how the various helicopters (there were three news helicopters now) along with the state police and the FBI had all congregated near the bridge, as if they'd spotted Bobbie Faye. The excitement in the shop was palpable and the nervous energy seemed to radiate off the walls and reflect in the dozens and dozens of crystals displayed everywhere, magnifying the negativity.

She had to do something about that. She needed something to redirect that energy. She nodded to Monique, who nodded back and then ducked behind the counter, heading to one of the back rooms as Ce Ce ripped into cartons of crystals stacked in every available space in the shop.

As Ce Ce surveyed the big crowd, she sighed relief. This much energy, surely, would make a difference. It had to. Now it was just up to her to channel it. She clapped, and Monique carried out a bowl of ashy mixture which Ce Ce had started concocting earlier, only now it smelled oddly of garlic and blood and liver and burnt sage.

"We've got work to do," Ce Ce announced to the crowd, and she started handing out crystals, giving instructions while Monique dribbled some of the ashy mixture around the room.

As Trevor and Bobbie Faye continued walking upstream, Bobbie Faye couldn't pull her gaze from the reptiles; they seemed restless and somehow appeared cocked, as if ready to leap into the water. They should be shying away. And she should be able to think, damnit.

She glanced around at the absolute stillness of the bayou, noting that the baying of the hounds seemed to be moving away from them. There was no breeze, no movement, just stark, green stillness.

Green. Lush, deep, fresh *emeralds* and *olives* and *jades* and *sages* saturating every tree, every grass. Rich, ripe greens.

Oh. Fuck.

"It's the end of April," she whispered, realizing, finally, what it was she'd forgotten.

"Yeah?"

"The only time an alligator is aggressive is when it's a female and someone gets near its eggs. And *now* is usually the time when the eggs are hatching."

"Sonofabitch, stupid fucking moron."

"Hey! I'm sorry, damnit. I didn't mean to forget."

"I was talking about myself," he said, as they turned toward the bank. "I should have thought of that already."

She couldn't help but gape a little at his profile as they climbed out of the water, onto the bank.

Chapter Thirteen

An assessor in our office once suggested that the world needed a "Murphy's Law" for anything Bobbie Faye–related. Then a building immediately fell on him.

—*Kathy Mackel, analyst for the LA Office of Statistical Measurements*

They stood together on the bank. The alligators seemed to have taken no notice of them, and Bobbie Faye wasn't sure what had stunned her more: that there wasn't a catastrophe with the alligators or that Trevor had blamed himself, and not her. She couldn't remember the last time something crazy had happened and the guy nearest her hadn't assumed it was her fault. That was just a world of weirdness, right there. Maybe she could get the address for whatever planet he lived on and manage a visit.

Trevor consulted a compass built into his fancy diver's watch and adjusted their course. They had taken about twenty steps when there was an awful huffing, snuffling sound, and then an outraged, guttural bellow, a battle cry. Bobbie Faye saw the black bear first, not nearly far enough away, and she spun, and sure enough, on the other side of them, bear cubs. Which is precisely when the mama bear charged, closing the gap faster than anyone would have believed.

.   .   .

Cam navigated his way through the gray cinderblock police station, every room painted industrial boring, and not an extra dime spent on passably comfortable. He wove through noisy, teeming, cramped rooms, encountering way more cops than should have been on duty. He knew half of them had volunteered to come in for crowd control and, very likely, to place side bets on just how big a disaster this was going to be. Everyone rubbed up against everyone else; he figured it would be a damned wonder if they didn't need pregnancy tests before it was all over and done.

He flipped through the robber's file on his way to interrogation, glancing at the man's pale, wormy mug shots. Professor Fred looked like the kind of man who slathered on SPF 30 just to walk to his car, not like the kind of guy who woke up one morning and decided to rob a bank.

Cam pushed through the metal door to the observation portion of the dingy interrogation room and nodded to the Captain, a wide, beefy man whose ruddy complexion was heightened by the six-pack of cheap beer he downed every night in front of the TV.

"I knew you'd be headed in when you heard," the Captain said, nodding toward the one-way observation window into the interrogation room. Cam glanced through to the exceptionally massive man sitting next to the Professor, who was now in the jailhouse orange jumpsuit. For a moment, Cam imagined them as a giant mastiff hound spread out next to a quivering, hunched, teacup Chihuahua, only this mastiff had double the jowls and wore a five-thousand-dollar suit and enough diamonds to rival a Tiffany window.

"I love it when they make mistakes," Cam said, as much to himself as to the Captain. The Captain hmphed, which was pretty much his trademark response.

"Good luck with that. You know how clamped Dellago can get," the Captain said. "I think ol' Fred was about to spill everything, but now we'll be lucky if we don't have to mop piss up off the floor in there."

"Did he call Dellago?"

"Nope. Said he didn't have an attorney, then Dellago showed up. Had to have been called by someone besides Fred there as soon as the robbery happened to have gotten here from New Orleans this fast."

Cam entered the interrogation room. Dellago squinted his puffy eyes at Cam, though Cam didn't bother to glance his direction. He knew that barely veiled disgusted expression; Dellago was hoping to draw someone less experienced he could mince and eat for lunch. The attorney subtly moved in his seat, a rare "tell." The man was switching gears.

"Slumming it, Dellago?" Cam asked, still skimming through the Professor's file.

"Hardly, Detective. As you will have undoubtedly discovered, my client is a highly regarded professor with no priors and an impeccable reputation—exactly the kind of client a defense attorney would be proud to represent."

"So, then, all of your previous clients, you know, the ones you pled down in various organized crime cases . . . they weren't the ideal clients, I suppose."

"I fail to see the relevance of this line of questioning, Detective. I was under the impression by your superiors that a deal may be on the table."

"Oh, I'm sure it's of no relevance at all," Cam said, beaming toward the Professor. "I mean, why shouldn't a first-time offender hire the best attorney reputed to represent the top tier of alleged organized crime figures, especially if he can afford him." Cam flipped through the file. "Oh, wait! That's because a professor of antiquities at LSU makes less than forty thousand a year and can't afford something so extravagant. I'm sure Dellago's fee is double that, right Professor?" The Professor gulped, but didn't answer. "Interesting."

Dellago started to respond, his face reddening ever so slightly, but Cam plowed on.

"So, Professor, you had a busy morning." The little man flinched, clamped his lips closed, and stared at his clasped hands.

"My client," Dellago boomed, his deep voice reverberating off the walls, "is prepared to testify against Ms. Sumrall in exchange for reduction to misdemeanor theft."

"Is he now?" Cam leaned back in his chair, an amused grin playing at the corners of his eyes. "Well, that's mighty helpful of him, seeing how he's the one who had the gun, the fake dynamite, and initiated the theft of several thousand dollars."

"Your governor, however, wants Ms. Sumrall behind bars, where she can't keep destroying the state," Dellago said, his tiny slitty eyes boring a stare into Cam. "I can deliver the information you need to put her away. For life."

Chapter Fourteen

Your Honor, *you* try remembering how to manage your anger after you've had Bobbie Faye for a client.

—*former anger management counselor now up on*
destruction of property charges

J ust when in the hell did Louisiana get black bears?" Trevor muttered as they fled through brambles, over logs, with the mama bear steaming toward them, gaining on them fast.

"It's not like *I* invited them!" Bobbie Faye pushed herself to run faster. Everything inside her burned. Her energy . . . chewed and broken. She couldn't keep going. A black bear could run close to thirty miles per hour in quick spurts, and that's all this one was going to need. If she stopped, the bear would be on them. Trevor looked determined to hang back for her; she was going to get them both killed.

Then she saw what she needed.

"Run flat out," she told him through ragged breaths. "Leave me." And when he turned to argue, she said, "Just trust me." She veered from his path and as she expected, the bear paused for a moment, and given the choice between two preys, chose the slower.

She could feel the ground vibrating as the three-hundred-pound bear thundered behind her; its guttural roars pulsed through her skin and ricocheted in her racing heart. Bobbie Faye aimed at what she hoped would save her: a fallen tree which had wedged between two other trees. It slanted at a forty-five degree angle to the ground, and her boots grabbed traction on the rough bark as she raced up the incline, grabbing broken limbs for balance.

The mama bear followed, clawing into the semi rotten wood, shaking the tree in its tenuous lodging in the fork of the other trees, and she knew if they fell, the bear would recover faster. She felt the whoosh of air as the bear swiped behind her just as she launched toward massive clusters of violet flowers and snagged thick wisteria vines dangling from one of the upright trees and she swung away from the furious bear.

See, she had a plan.

Bobbie Faye should have known she wasn't the planny type by now; she intended to grab the nearby limbs of the other tree, and hop down from it, confusing the bear long enough for her own escape. She was far too high up to just drop to the ground and she was afraid she'd lose her grip if she tried to climb down the vine. A simple snag and leap to the next tree was the ticket. She swung on the vine toward the neighboring tree and tried to grab a limb.

She missed.

Which meant she was swinging back toward the tree. Straight toward the bear's massive claws. She was going to make the Darwin list of the stupidest ways idiots managed to take themselves out of the gene pool. The jaws loomed closer: ugly yellow teeth, blasting rotting breath, and there was something she didn't even want to think about snagged on its incisors. The bear roared, jaws wide as her momentum swung her closer. Right for its jagged teeth.

Dellago leaned forward, a smile simpering in his pursed lips. "I've recently had a conversation with our fair governor and he's assured me that you are to cooperate and plead my client out in exchange for that information. Or," Dellago grinned his slimy, little smile, "aren't you important enough to be in on the loop? Perhaps I should speak to your Captain?"

Cam kept a poker face. He knew Dellago probably had as thick a file on him as he had on Dellago. Instead, Cam shrugged. "I don't know of many people who've managed to hold onto Ms. Sumrall and lived to tell about it," he said. "I'm not entirely sure we'd like to be the first to try."

"My client can testify as to how Ms. Sumrall planned this heist and forced him to comply," Dellago continued, his gaze never leaving Cam's face. "You'll have her dead to rights to do with as you want. In exchange, these charges will be reduced and my client will be released immediately."

Cam casually propped his chin in his hand and watched the Professor, who was shaking so blatantly, Cam wondered if he'd vibrate clean out of his loose, pale skin.

"Uh, free?" the Professor asked. "You mean, today? Now?" He looked at Cam. "With—with, uh, with him?" He nodded toward Dellago, who could not have looked more unhappy with his client if he tried.

"Yes. With him. If the D.A. agrees."

"And it would be a wise move, Professor," Dellago intoned in the man's ear, "to heed my advice in this matter. A very wise move."

Cam thought the Professor was turning an actual shade of green.

"But . . . but . . . I'm guilty," he said, leaning toward Cam, a pleading expression overwhelming his trembling features. "I should pay. I'd be happy to pay. Really."

"Nonsense. You have evidence they need," Dellago said, and Cam noted the sinking, grim resignation in the Professor's eyes.

"So," Cam asked, "you're telling me that Bobbie Faye was the grand mastermind behind all of this?"

"Just a minute," Dellago said, putting a beefy hand out in front of the Professor, stopping him from speaking. Professor Fred cringed. "Do we have a deal?"

"Oh, that all depends on just how convincing the Professor's story is."

·　　·　　·

Bear jaws loomed and filled Bobbie Faye's vision until the entire world was reduced to bear teeth the size of the LSU stadium. She suddenly, completely, totally recanted her entire stance on never buying bear rugs on account of some stupid, cockamamie principle. Bear rugs for everyone! For your dog! Canary! Maybe car seats!

She slipped a little on the vine, nearly falling, catching herself as she reached the log just as the mama bear swiped at her. The abrupt swipe shifted the bear's weight, jostling the log, which tilted and suddenly fell away from where it was anchored. Taking the bear with it. The bear and the log hit the ground with a thudding bounce, rolling away from where she hung on the vine until both were very still.

Ohmygod ohmygod ohmygod. She shuddered, nearly falling again, clinging to the vine with the last of her strength. She looked down as she felt Trevor catching the vine, holding it steady as she slowly eased down, arms shaking. She dropped the last few feet to the ground, and the mama bear didn't move.

"She's breathing," he said, "but out cold."

Ohmygod ohmygod ohmygod.

Trevor grabbed her hand and led her away, and she let him, what with her brain set on skipping through a few thousand more *ohmygods*. When they had gone a mile or so, Bobbie Faye knew she had to stop moving. Her body was doing the damnedest thing: it was shaking. Hard. Holy *fuck*, she'd almost been bear breakfast.

Trevor had stopped and was breathing harder than she'd seen him do so far that day, and she knew he wasn't winded from his run; hell, he'd hardly broken a sweat. He was looking at her with a mixture of fury and awe.

"I don't know if you're fucking brave or just plain crazy," he said, fury apparently winning.

"Yeah, that's me. Crazy with a side order of nuts."

"This isn't fucking *funny*. You were almost killed."

"By a *bear*!" She could feel herself rambling headlong into a sort of shocked hysteria and she couldn't stop herself from waving her arms around. "I mean, I know south Louisiana has black bears, it's one of the weird things about this state a lot of people don't know, you know, that bears live here. Even at the salt mines around here, they have bears getting in and the bears are protected by law or something, and they climb the fence and the really fat ones sort of throw themselves over and thump to the ground and then everyone has to stay inside until the bear gets tired of rummaging for garbage and I know all of this and I know that they're here and they're dangerous and *did that help prepare me*? No. *No, it did* not. Because there it was! With the big! And the hairy! And the teeth! And the grrrrrrrrrrrrr!" She rubbed her arms, her voice rising. "And I am allergic to grrrrrrrrrrrrs!"

He looked away a moment, his jaw working in an effort not to laugh; he took a couple of deep breaths, then turned back to her. "That was very fast thinking, though."

She was shaking so visibly now, she was sure he could see it, and the last thing she wanted was to lose it in front of this guy.

"I just," she tried, swallowing to keep her voice from trembling, her voice pitching a little too high. "Well, it's the Bobbie Faye hostage guarantee: we don't let you get eaten by large mammals. Usually."

She ended it with a small chuckle—lame, really—and she felt the shock of the morning rattling her, making her light-headed, and she thought she was in total control when Trevor pulled her into an embrace. She didn't know why. She couldn't understand what he was doing, but all of a sudden, she knew she wouldn't be standing if he wasn't holding her up, and instead of fighting him like she ought to be doing, just this once, she gave in. Just this once, she put her head down on his chest and let someone hold her and she cried. She wouldn't have admitted to crying, and she'd have drop-kicked him into the next state if he said anything remotely mushy or condescending right then, because she, Bobbie Faye Sumrall, did not break down. She just didn't.

He was quiet.

When her nerves settled, she stepped back and faced away from him, taking a moment to wipe the tears from her cheeks. When she turned to him again, he grimaced a little, then stepped forward and used the tail of his shirt to clean the mud from her cheeks. He seemed to take forever as she studied the concentration on his face, mesmerized by the scar just below his eye, well-faded now, noticing the slow rhythm of his breathing. It calmed her, this rhythm.

"You ready?" he asked when he was done. It was as if by silent agreement that the tears hadn't happened.

"I was born ready."

"Yeah, you and General Custer."

They turned back toward the swampy edge of Lake Charles.

Cam watched Dellago aim a hard gaze at the Professor, and the Professor broke out in a sweat.

"Um, well, um," the Professor squeaked, and then stopped and swallowed and fidgeted. "She, uh . . ." He glanced helplessly to Dellago, who simply increased the steeliness of the glare. "Uh, right. Um, she was kinda fed up, she said, with, um, her status in life. I was supposed to get the money and she was, um, going to watch, like an innocent bystander."

"She was just going to watch you rob the bank with you being armed with the fake dynamite?"

"Uh, yes, and she made me bring the gun." Cam noticed him struggle not to keep peering back at Dellago. "I was supposed to kidnap her so everyone would think she was innocent and then we'd split the money later."

"So why didn't you kidnap her?" Cam asked.

"She took over, see. I—I don't know why. Then I slipped and she left me there."

"Right. And you did all of this for her because? . . ."

Dellago intervened, saying, "You know how persuasive Ms. Sumrall can be, once she gets an idea."

Yep, Cam thought, he knew *exactly* how persuasive she could be. But he also knew how smart she was.

"And how long have you known Ms. Sumrall, Professor?"

"Oh, uh. Um. Well. I'm not sure."

"Round it, for me. A few months? Weeks? Days? A year?"

The Professor tried looking toward Dellago, then quickly faced away and proceeded to swallow, cough, and fidget. "Maybe, um, maybe about a year."

"Really? And how did you meet Ms. Sumrall?"

"This isn't important, Detective," Dellago said, scraping back his chair.

"Of course it is. He wants to plead down, he needs to explain how he met her and how long she had this idea."

"I—I—I. I met her at the festival," the Professor said. "Uh, last year."

"Oh, that was the year her sister had to stand in for her as Contraband Queen," Cam said. As an aside to Dellago, "Since Ms. Sumrall had the flu."

"Right! Right, that's it," the Professor said before Dellago had a chance to interject.

"And she came to you to do this because . . ."

"She, she trusted me, I guess. A beautiful woman like that, everyone's always trying to take advantage of her. You know?"

Cam didn't answer.

"So, so, see, she could tell I wasn't the type to do that. I'm not exactly a lady's man. She needed help; she was very determined."

"I think that's enough," Dellago said. "Do we have a deal?"

There was a brief knock on the door and Detective Benoit stuck his head inside. "Cam? You got a call you have to take."

Cam excused himself to Dellago and the Professor and just as he reached for the door, he turned back to them.

"Oh, Professor. You ever heard of a guy named Trevor Cormier?"

The Professor blanched, swallowed repeatedly, and Cam thought he saw the man clamp his legs closed beneath the table. Finally, the Professor shook his head emphatically.

"Uh, no. I can't remember meeting anyone by that name."

Dellago watched Cam as Cam nodded solemnly, giving nothing away as he left the room.

. . .

O ne of the twins handed Ce Ce the private line again, and she was surprised to find Nina on the line.

"Aren't you busy enough?" Ce Ce teased, and instantly regretted it when she heard Nina's tone.

"I'm hearing some bad things."

"What kind of bad? And from who?"

"Just my . . . contacts. In my modeling world."

Ce Ce shuddered.

"I'm hearing there's something B has that someone wants, and he's going to kill her once he gets it."

"What in the hell could that child have that anyone would care that much about? She's perpetually broke!"

"I don't know, and so far, neither do any of my contacts. Maybe if you called Cam? I know B is still furious with him, but—"

"I've already talked to him, honey, and he don't know much more than us. There's some guy with her Cam thinks means her harm."

"The one she kidnapped?"

"That's the same one she kidnapped? This guy that Cam thinks may get her killed?"

"That sounds like Bobbie Faye. Have you learned anything else?"

"Honey, all I know is what I've seen on TV. And that she came and got an advance on her paycheck to pay for her electricity to get turned back on."

"On *this* trailer?"

"That's what she said."

"If she gets out of this alive, I'm going to kick her ass for not asking for help."

"I think you're gonna have to line up behind a few people, honey."

"I've got to go, Ceece. The boys are getting restless over here. I think they're determined to take another stab at the trailer."

Chapter Fifteen

The Bobbie Faye protection charms are our biggest sellers.

—*Eluki B., owner of the New Orleans Voodoo Jamorama*

Once Cam had left the interrogation room, and before he could hear what Benoit had to say, his phone rang. After a moment on the phone with Ce Ce, he knew his suspicions were grounded.

When he hung up, Benoit spoke low, saying, "Got bad news. Kelvin called. The dogs? They lost her."

Cam paused a moment and it took every ounce of willpower not to kick the wall.

Benoit glanced around them, making sure no one was paying undue attention. "They dead-ended downstream and Kelvin turned 'em upstream, but there's a couple of gators sunning themselves and one of our guys spotted a mama bear who's done pissed off and aiming for a fight. Kelvin said he doubted they got by that ol' gal, and even if they did, he ain't sending the dogs that way. He's trying t' go around her now and see if they can pick up the scent."

Cam stared at the cinderblock wall, the industrial gray paint peeling in a few places. He could see why a lot of cops ended up smoking: it gave you something to do with your hands besides punching brick walls.

There were two things of value he'd learned from his quick interrogation with the Professor: one—the Professor was lying about when he'd met Bobbie Faye. She so loved the Contraband Days Festival, she would have dragged herself to the festival even if she'd been shot and was on her deathbed. Her sister had never substituted for her. Cam wasn't entirely sure if Lori Ann had ever even gone to the festival. The second thing was that Bobbie Faye was just as good as dead. Someone high up in organized crime didn't want her around. Dellago would only offer up Bobbie Faye if he was fairly sure she wasn't going to be alive to rebut the Professor's statement and tell whatever it was she knew that could harm them.

"So what was the deal asking him about Cormier?"

"The professor obviously doesn't really know Bobbie Faye. We know Cormier was at that bank. That can't be a coincidence."

Cam pressed his forehead to his fist and leaned against the wall, buying a moment to think.

Bobbie Faye was marked for a kill from two, possibly three, different directions. There was the FBI, who couldn't care less if she got in the way. There was whatever Dellago was up to, probably having something to do with the information Ce Ce had passed along. And that may or may not mean the man traveling with Bobbie Faye was out to kill her, as the FBI suggested.

Apparently one contract out on her life wasn't challenging enough. And she was still running. To what, God only knew.

It occurred to him, just then, how much that summed up Bobbie Faye. She was always running. Running away.

Unbidden, he had a flash of her laughing, her long wild hair flying across her face as she grinned over her shoulder at him. He'd mentioned he might have to go into work that day instead of spending it with her. She'd grabbed his keys in a mock threat to toss them in his backyard, a wooded lot on a lake. He'd been joking, of course, and she'd known that, and was teasing back, and she ran through the house, impish and grinning and eyes sparkling.

She made him laugh. He'd grown up serious, rigid. Straight "A" student, class president, senator at LSU. Everything right and expected. But laughter—deep joy—was new to him. She had a way of looking at him as if he was the greatest gift in the whole world, and she couldn't believe he was for her. She shrieked as he tried to catch her; he'd doubled back through the living room where he hurdled the coffee table and pinned her to the sofa. Only to discover she'd somehow hidden the keys and refused to tell where until he took her to bed.

He hadn't needed a lot of convincing.

He remembered waking hours later to find her kneeling next to him, the light from the bedroom window casting a suffused glow over half of her face, the other half in shadow. She had an odd expression he couldn't quite read, and when he asked her what she was thinking, she had shrugged, saying she was happy.

All gone. Everything. This woman, this person who used to be his best friend, who now hated him.

It shouldn't have been that way.

He paced, ignoring Benoit's amused grin until it grated. "What?"

"You're kicking yourself because she didn't come to you for help."

"Like hell. She's insane, putting everyone in jeopardy, never asking for help. She's pathologically incapable of accepting help. She'll destroy everything before she'll ask anyone, especially me. She's doing this to herself and there's no fucking reason for it."

Damn, he needed to hit something. Soon.

"Yeah, well, if you'd really wanted her to ask you for help, maybe you shouldn't have arrested her sister."

"Fuck off. I was doing my job."

Benoit laughed. "Right. And she took it so well, too. You know, that's the first time I've ever seen armed cops dive for cover and hide from an unarmed person?"

"*I was doing my fucking job.*"

He'd had to arrest her sister, Lori Ann for a variety of crimes, starting with full-on drunk driving and ending with theft, fraud, and check-kiting. He'd known Bobbie Faye was worried about her, he'd known Bobbie Faye was trying to handle the problem, but the arrest fell to his unit and frankly, he thought Bobbie Faye would appreciate that he was kind and gentle with Lori Ann when others wouldn't have been. It had to be done. He knew it, he believed in it. Sure, Bobbie Faye would be upset, but she'd already stated that Lori Ann was a menace to society, so she'd understand. She'd be pissed, but she'd understand.

He hadn't expected the head-spinning, Defcon one, stupendous meltdown that had been Bobbie Faye when she found out he'd been the arresting officer. It was not quite a year later and he still could feel the blisters from her fury.

Hadn't she known what it meant that she was dating a cop? What the hell did she expect? He'd done the right thing. He stood by that. But accusations were hurled and words were said that neither could take back.

"You still writin' checks for that ring every month?"

Cam hated the way Benoit knew him so damned well. The night Bobbie Faye had ended it, Cam had thrown the ring in the lake. She'd never seen it, had never known, and he was never going to tell her.

"Every month. And I'm gonna keep writing them for the next two years just to keep remembering what a stupid idea that was."

"Maybe if it takes writing out a check to remind yourself you don't want to feel the way you do, then—"

"Don't even finish that thought."

Benoit turned and leaned his back flat against the wall, one ankle crossed over the other, arms folded and his brown eyes closed.

"You can't shoot her, you know."

"Don't bet on it."

Bobbie Faye needed to formulate a strategy on how to handle the kidnappers, though she hadn't a clue what it was she could actually *do* until she *had* the damned tiara and knew where she was supposed to take it. She just might, possibly, need help.

She sure as hell couldn't ask Cam for help.

She wondered if it had been her biggest mistake not to call him at the beginning. Of course, even though the kidnappers had said "no police," it wasn't like there were kidnappers out there who had ever said, "Oh, sure, honey, call the cops, we don't mind." So maybe she should have.

Still.

Cam was Cam. Unchanged. Freakishly stubborn. (She resolutely refused to think of any phrases in which "pot" and "kettle" might figure significantly.) He was livid with her, would never see that she'd been right, and if she'd called him, he would have wanted her to go in and do it his way. By-the-freaking-book. They didn't have time for "by the book," and she didn't have time to argue with him.

It would have been one hell of an argument. He'd have turned into obnoxious, bossy cop, the one who knew every freaking thing, who had explained to her that he was a cop, first, a man, second; the one who lived, breathed, and dreamed rules and goddamned ethics. She'd like to tell him where he could plant both, then remembered she already had, rather explicitly, the day he'd arrested Lori Ann. And now . . . well, given the scope of the hunt for her, his hands would be tied—he'd be fired in a heartbeat if he helped her (especially without proof of her story). No, he'd arrest her and Roy's chance would be gone as soon as the media reported she was in custody.

Bobbie Faye raced round and round these worries while she and Trevor trekked through the woods. Another mystifying development: a man who actually seemed to be helping, whoever the hell he was—and could he be trusted? Could he help her when she had to face the kidnappers? Was it even right to ask? Probably not.

She barely tuned into where they were going and frankly, it wouldn't have helped much, anyway. It was just more trees, mud, and water. She kept smacking up against the puzzle of the tiara and no way to solve it when she saw they'd reached a narrow, rutted lane. The fine dust beneath her boots roiled at the injustice of every disturbing step they made, then settled over the encroaching foliage in such fine, light layers that the grass and leaves beside the road looked like they'd been dusted with mocha icing. There was barely enough room for one car to pass, with the swamp lapping at the nonexistent shoulders of the lane. At least there were cypress trees growing thick as weeds to obscure the tiny road from overhead view. Bobbie Faye supposed that the rare times cars met one another, one had to back up to a wider spot to allow the other to pass, which prevented the road from becoming very popular. This was planned, she suspected, by the people who lived this far out of the beaten path; they preferred their privacy.

Bobbie Faye had forgotten about Valcour's Boat Landing until they stumbled upon it, where the road sloped to an end in a small bayou which eventually spilled into Lake Charles. To the side of the landing was a tiny store, a building no more than a shack, really, the wood siding so grayed with age and loose-jointed, it looked like a tired old man, too shrunken for his skin. At one time it had been a meeting spot for fur traders, and it still sported hooks for the pelts to hang from the slatted wood porch. Now, it was the last spot fishermen could buy extra bait, maybe grab a few drinks or snacks for the day before heading out to the lake.

Five dented, rusty pickup trucks with empty boat trailers lined the square of shale where the road sloped down to the water—a poor man's boat landing. The building looked deserted and dark, sandwiched between cypress trees overflowing with gray Spanish moss.

"Maybe there's a phone," Trevor mused, and she watched how he scanned the area.

"You don't think it's too risky? With all of the news helicopters, anyone in there's bound to know what's going on."

"I doubt very seriously they have cable out here, and there's no satellite dish. We'll pretend we're a couple stopping by on our way to our fishing camp."

"Yeah, with no boat, truck, fishing gear, tackle . . ."

"Just act casual." He looked her over. "Okay, never mind. No one's going to look at you and buy 'casual.' Just act like a pissed off wife whose idiot husband knocked you out of the boat and into the lake."

"Do I get to smack you upside the head?"

"Don't push your luck," he warned as they stepped onto the tiny porch.

Chapter Sixteen

Please advise all businesses within the state of Louisiana that they now must include a "Bobbie Faye contingency" in all safety training.

—memo from the National Occupational Safety and Health Administration (OSHA) to the Louisiana OSHA office

Cam needed to get ahead of her. Stop her. Find out what the hell was going on. How in the hell was he supposed to keep her safe with her running amok?

"When are we gonna have background on this guy?" he asked, nodding toward the interrogation room. "Financials?"

"An hour, maybe two. All Crowe would say was she had a lead as to why he may have wanted to rob the bank, but it wasn't too reliable and she was checking it out."

"She say what it was?"

"Nope. You know her. She's not gonna say 'til she knows for sure."

The Captain leaned into the hallway, motioning for both men to step back into the observation portion of the interrogation room. He closed the door behind the detectives.

Through the window, Cam could see Dellago, still seated next to the Professor, swelling with annoyance at their delays. He seemed to be doubling in size while the Professor seemed to be shrinking. If they waited too long, Cam wondered if the Professor would disappear into himself, leaving only the orange jail jumpsuit behind.

"I wanted to wait 'til after your initial questioning to tell you this," the Captain started, "and I didn't want this broadcast over the radio. It's critical we keep this quiet."

Cam knew he'd paled from the frown of concern on the Captain's face. The Captain was going to tell him Bobbie Faye had been killed. He knew it through every cell to the marrow of his bones. He reminded himself that he didn't care, that it no longer mattered, that he wasn't going to have to try to remember how to breathe in and breathe out once the words were out of the Captain's mouth.

He leaned against the door frame (it was not for support, he reasoned, because he leaned all of the damned time), and he looked into the Captain's eyes, but did not see sorrow or sympathy. Instead, he saw frustration and nerves at work, particularly evident in the way the Captain had taken out a quarter and quietly rotated it through his fingers. The joke around the station was that if he got the quarter out, you should probably be worried. If he got it out and bounced it from palm to palm, you were probably fired. If, instead, he got it out and just held it, someone had died. Cam exhaled when he saw the quarter twirling instead.

"I've checked with our resources on Cormier's rap sheet. It's as long as my alimony." The Captain had been paying alimony for twenty-five years. His ex refused to remarry. "All I can tell you," he looked up at Cam pointedly, "is that we are to assist in bringing in this Trevor Cormier alive and unhurt. No matter what."

"What about Bobbie Faye?"

"She's not the top priority here."

Cam's every muscle tensed as he fought to maintain control. It made no sense . . . Zeke said he had orders to shut down Cormier, no matter what. The Captain said to bring him in without harming him, that he was the priority. Two diametrically opposed orders, which means something more covert lay under the surface. Which also meant, of course, that the Captain wasn't at liberty to say.

Cam puzzled over the Captain's oddly blank expression. He was rarely a blank slate, so that, in itself, was a clue that this was far worse than Cam had imagined. Sometimes the government used criminals, made deals, getting them to do the really dirty work no one wanted to have culpability for. Of course, officially, this never happened. Zeke said Cormier had merc'd out, hired out to do the black ops work no one else wanted. It was possible Cormier was blackmailing someone with evidence of their connection to a horrible assignment and that person was trying to take him out and someone else knew of it, and wanted him pulled in. It was also just as possible that Cormier was as bad as Zeke described and Zeke was right to be trying to take him out and Cormier had blackmailed or conned or paid off someone into trying to protect him. There were too many permutations to explain the conflicting orders.

So of course Bobbie Faye was in the middle of this mess. And he was supposed to keep Cormier safe?

"Captain, Cormier's trailing through the swamp with Bobbie Faye. It's a miracle he's alive. It's too much to hope for 'unhurt.'"

"Well hell, Cam, there's your answer," Benoit said, grinning. "Another hour with Bobbie Faye and the man is going to be begging you to arrest him just to get away from her."

The Captain and Benoit chuckled, but Cam kept working the problem backwards and forwards.

"We haven't worked with Zeke Wright before. Did he check out?"

"Nothing off that I could tell," the Captain said.

"Then I'll need Benoit here to continue annoying ol' Dellago in there. I need to get back to the field."

The Captain nodded, leaving the two detectives.

Cam paced a moment, and Benoit waited. "Somebody thinks the Professor's pretty damned important to be sending Dellago."

"Yeah. Are you thinking 'too' important?"

"Last time we had one of those, they mysteriously died in their cell."

"I'll put him in a private lockup and put a guard on him. Vicari's good. Mean as a snake, but good."

They went separate directions, and a few minutes later, Cam was on the district's second helicopter. But not before he'd stopped in to the dispatch office and pulled Jason aside.

Jason was somewhere around twenty-eight, though he barely looked twenty. He was good-looking enough to avoid the "total geek" handle, though he was a communications freak.

"You think you could poke around in the frequencies and listen in on the FBI helicopter?" Cam asked him, and Jason grinned.

"Man, she's got you twisted in a knot, don't she—" and then Jason seemed to notice the look Cam was giving him and not only backed up and put a chair between them, but started apologizing.

"Shut it," Cam said. "I need to listen in to them without them knowing. Can we do that?"

"Officially? Nope. We don't have the same sort of radios."

"Unofficially?"

Jason beamed. "Well, there are a few ways. See, I could—"

"Don't have time for the tech version, Jason. Just see if you can listen without them knowing."

"No prob. Unless it's encrypted. I'd have to be on my home computer to break their codes."

"I'm going to slide right by that one and pretend I didn't hear you say that you can break FBI codes on your home computer, Jason," Cam said. "You might not want to discuss that with anyone else, either."

"Good point."

As Cam was leaving, he glanced back and noted Jason was peering around, making sure no one was watching him. Then he pulled out a different scanner as Cam hurried out of the door.

Chapter Seventeen

No. Just . . . *no.*

—Luke James, local mailman, on learning Bobbie Faye
would now be on his mail route

Bobbie Faye pulled open the ancient, creaking screen door to the landing's store and walked inside into the cooler shade of the room. The place smelled overwhelmingly like fresh peaches and boiled peanuts, a strange mix that seemed to battle in midair. The overhead fan barely pushed the air in and around the impressive stacks of supplies. Items were piled floor to ceiling in every nook and cranny and even right by the door.

From the other side of a stack of saltines taller than her head, an old man's voice chirped, "Help you, miss?" and Bobbie Faye yelped in surprise, spun, forgetting her purse was dangling, and knocked over the entire stack of saltine crackers, which fell into the pyramid of laundry detergent and that toppled into the fishing rods leaning against the wall, which fell dominolike into the cricket bin, knocking it open and setting half of the merchandise free.

Only then did she see the cash register and the two old men sitting in lawn chairs behind the counter.

"Holy freaking geez, warn a girl, will you?" she snapped, trying to pick up the debris.

Trevor hadn't made it past the doorway; he stood there, gaping at the destruction. He checked the sweeping second hand of his expensive diver's watch, and arched his eyebrow at Bobbie Faye.

"Four seconds. I swear, woman, if we could find a way to market that talent, we'd be rich."

Both of the old men behind the counter were laughing when she looked up, and the skinny one nearest the register took off his glasses to wipe the tears from his eyes.

"Leave it," said the other man, a short, round fellow who hadn't risen. "It's slow here in the middle of the day. That'll give us something to do."

"Uh, sorry," Bobbie Faye said. "It's been a kinda stressful morning."

"Do you happen to have a phone we could use?" Trevor asked from immediately behind her, and Bobbie Faye nearly jumped again.

"Don't have a regular line," said cash-register man, "but I have this old cell phone. Reception's pretty crappy and the battery's dying, but you can try it. Seems to work best outside."

"Thanks." Trevor took the phone, and then gave Bobbie Faye an annoyed glare. "Baby, try not to tear the place down, okay?"

"Sure, pumpkin," she said through gritted teeth, barely refraining from giving him the smacking he so clearly needed. "I'll get supplies."

When Trevor stepped over the boxes of saltines and back out the front door, the cash-register man leaned over the counter and motioned to Bobbie Faye to come nearer. He didn't look pervy, and she figured she could take him, so she angled a little closer.

"You okay, Ms. Bobbie Faye?"

She squinted at him for a better look, hoping he wasn't someone she'd run over, folded, or stapled inadvertently. He didn't seem to be giving her a hostile expression and there were no weapons being brandished about, unless he was really slow to lift whatever lethal item he might have.

"How do you know who I am?"

They both motioned her to keep the noise down as they glanced uneasily out the window to where Trevor spoke on the cell phone.

"Everybody knows the Contraband Days Queen," the cash-register man answered, then he motioned to the laptop she could now see propped on the other man's knees. That old man turned it toward her and she could see he had a satellite phone hooked up and was getting the live news feed.

"Playing solitaire gets old," laptop man said by way of explanation. "We saw you coming up the road and we recognized you from your photo here." He tapped the screen. "We wanted to make sure that guy wasn't holding you hostage or doing anything sneaky."

"You sure you're okay?" the cash-register man asked. "We're big fans, you being the Queen and all, and I don't know if we could both take that young man out there, but we could try if you'd like us to. Especially if he's some low-down dirty-dealing dog.

"Whaddya think, Earl?" the cash-register guy continued. "I could distract him, you could hit him over the head with one of those rice cookers." He winked at Bobbie Faye. "They're on sale anyway. Wouldn't be a big loss."

She wasn't quite sure what to respond to first; there was the horror of the live feed (with the news having placed the skank-ugly shot of her at the edge of the forest in the top right corner of the screen) or the way the grainy surveillance video from the bank was apparently on a constant loop.

There it was again: that nervous, wormy guy (she saw a photo of him flash next to hers—ah, his name was Bartholomew Fred) standing in line, moving up to the front of the line. He nicely let a woman ahead of him, then another and another. Then he stepped up, looking jumpy and a few seconds later, here she came into the surveillance frame, walking right into the middle of twitchy guy's robbery.

And handed him the money.

Oh, hell, and talked with him.

Roy was right. It really did look like she was working with the guy and robbing the bank.

Oh, geez, now there was surveillance footage from outside the bank of her jumping into Trevor's truck. The station froze the image of him driving away, with a tag of "unidentified man" underneath and another tag of "considered armed and dangerous."

Great. Just great. Bonnie and Clyde ride again. She was so not going to look good with bullet holes all in her.

Her eyes traveled from the news footage to these two sweet old men offering to fight Trevor for her, both at least eighty, beaming at her like she was a celebrity.

She squeezed the hand of the cash-register man. "I'm okay, really, but thank you. My friend out there's trying to help me. My brother's in trouble and if the police stop me, the people holding him will kill him. I can't explain it to the police—you know how they love to run everything through the paperwork grind first, and I don't have time for that."

"Say no more, Ms. Bobbie Faye," laptop Earl said. "Me and Jean-Luc here have your back. You just let us know what you need."

"A little food, couple of bottles of water? And you never saw me, right?"

"Never," Jean-Luc of the cash-register exclaimed. "But would you sign my cap here? It'd be a real collector's item if you live through this an' all."

"Sure thing," she said, signing his John Deere cap with the Sharpie he handed her, about the time the laptop dinged. She looked at it, puzzled.

"Oh, I'm just IMing Collette at home, letting her know we have a celebrity here."

"Earl!" Jean-Luc shouted. "Turn up your dang-gum hearing aid and pay attention. No one is supposed to know she's here!"

"Aw, Collette ain't gonna tell nobody today. She's gonna save it up for her Po-Ke-No party next Thursday and trump 'em all on the excitement meter. Man," Earl said, switching his attention back to Bobbie Faye, "if you live through this and saw fit to come to that, I wouldn't have to buy Collette an anniversary gift or birthday present for at least a couple of years!"

"I'll see what I can do, Earl. Wait—can I send a text message on that thing?"

"Sure. Hang on." Earl opened up the text message box and

pointed out where to type in the phone number. She plugged in Roy's number just as Trevor returned.

"Young man," Earl addressed him while Bobbie Faye sent Roy a message, "you better damned be careful with our Contraband Days Queen, you hear?"

Trevor frowned at her and she pointed at Jean-Luc and Earl, saying, "Wasn't me! I didn't say a word. They're fans." To prove her right, Jean-Luc proudly displayed his cap with her autograph on it.

"Good job," he said, scowling deeper. "The cops will take one look at this disaster, then see that cap and know we were here."

Jean-Luc immediately shoved the cap into a safe.

Bobbie Faye typed her message, pressing "send" as Earl stood up and waved his cane at Trevor.

"I mean it, young man, you take good care of her. Don't you have any better sense in how to go about helping a lady than to drag her across a bunch of woods and water and wildlife? She gets hurt, me and Jean-Luc here are going to skin you, you got that?"

Trevor looked from man to man to Bobbie Faye. She smiled so sweetly at him and bit back a laugh when she saw him arch an eyebrow, casting her a look of complete incredulity as if he was the one about to get her killed.

"Yes, sir," he said. "I'm going to make sure she's back in one piece."

"One *live* piece, right?"

"The vote is still out on that. Did you get supplies, or are you too busy being Ms. Contraband Days Queen?"

Bobbie Faye grabbed a few prepackaged crackers, energy bars, and bottles of water. Jean-Luc threw a couple of candy bars on top of the heap and refused to allow Bobbie Faye to pay.

"Oh, he was paying," she said, motioning to Trevor, and both old men turned on him with a gleam.

"Well, in that case," Jean-Luc said, "hand it over, sonny."

Trevor cut a look of asperity at Bobbie Faye. She beamed at him as he dug cash from his wallet.

Trevor handed Jean-Luc back the cell phone with a thanks.

"Wait—can I borrow that?" she asked, her voice quivering as she looked down at the live feed on the laptop. "I need to call about my niece, Stacey, and send someone to get—"

"Battery died on me," Trevor said, shaking his head. "C'mon, we've got to go."

Bobbie Faye didn't move, didn't look up at him, and he stepped closer, peering over her shoulder to see what was so riveting. There on the laptop's live feed was an aerial shot of Stacey's elementary school: a crowd of reporters hovered just across the street, along with a growing mob of onlookers.

Sonofabitch. Stacey. *She's not safe.* Whoever had Roy could easily pluck Stacey from that school.

Trevor's hands rested on her shoulders; he squeezed her arms gently, speaking low into her ear. "I found out most of what we need to know before the cell went dead. We need to get moving." He craned his head a little as if listening for the helicopters, then frowned at her. "I think we'd better hurry."

Roy glanced around the room. This was not going well. Eddie flipped the ginormous knife and caught it, causing Roy to nearly seizure on every release, flinching as if it were headed his way.

"You really ought to proceed with another story of your very interesting sister," Vincent purred, "before Eddie gets bored with his play and decides to make you target-practice."

He needed a story that showed she could come through for someone. Something that made her look dependable.

"She saved a man's life, once. He was gonna toss himself off a tall building. Well, as tall as they get in Lake Charles, which is only about four or five stories tall, but still, there he was, all torn up over a broken relationship, and the police got her to come in to help him."

He neglected to mention that the failed relationship had been with Bobbie Faye and that the man had chosen the top of the building from which to jump because Bobbie Faye had suggested, in a fit of annoyance with him, that the bridge wasn't high enough to do him enough damage. Nor had Roy expected his audience to realize that it was the same man who Bobbie Faye had pushed when she'd gotten fed up trying to talk him out of jumping, and as he plummeted toward the large airbag below, he had found religion and was now a superstar radio evangelist who went by the name "Mark in the Morning" and promised listeners he could pray the demons right out of them.

A text message beeped into Roy's phone, and Vincent read it, scowling, and then set the phone down.

"Your sister is working under the mistaken impression that there will be no penalties if she's running late. Perhaps we should start photographing your body parts to persuade her to speed this along."

Roy had trouble swallowing. His mouth had gone dry. He was spared Vincent instructing Eddie to implement this plan when Vincent's cell phone rang. Vincent turned his back to the room, speaking in silken, hushed tones. Roy, frankly, wasn't used to someone speaking so quietly, especially in a tense situation. A shudder rippled through his shoulder blades, and every noise around him turned into senseless buzzing.

"Yes," Vincent said. "Failing that, there's always the sister."

Vincent was speaking quietly because it was about killing Bobbie Faye. That had to be it. Impending death equaled quiet, and Roy found himself rocking against his chair.

Roy had no clue who the call was from. Vincent's voice dropped into a low register, spoken so softly, Roy thought his eardrums would burst from the effort of trying to listen.

"Yes," Vincent said, only slightly louder. "You'll get full payment. No, no, we'll talk about a bonus when you've delivered."

For all his effort, Roy couldn't piece together more of the conversation from Vincent's end of things. He mentally replayed what he'd heard. He needed her to know she was being watched. He needed to give her as much of an edge as possible. He needed to tell her someone was there, planning on killing her.

He had no idea how to do that.

Chapter Eighteen

Do you have any *idea* of just how much damage she could do to a state our size in one day? You've lost your mind. No way are we taking Bobbie Faye.

—*the governor of Rhode Island to the governor of Louisiana*

Bobbie Faye peered through the brush and undergrowth from the hiding spot Trevor had found. He sat on his haunches next to her as they observed a remote fishing camp. It was set back from Lake Charles about a hundred feet or so and looked a bit more like a sprawling compound than one of the more raggedy fishing camps thrown together on so many other lots carved out of the swampy lake's shores. Many camps were barely more than rickety cast-off trailers with porches added on, and there were still a substantial number which were never going to be even that nice. This one, however, looked like a fashionable Craftsman home, something that spoke of architects and designers and planning. Where most other camps simply let the landscape run to the natural vegetation, this place could easily have been the featured spread in *Southern Gardener*. It looked, in other words, like someone refined had chosen this place as a vacation spot and had poured a great deal of care and money and taste into making it a true home away from home.

It was so many kinds of wrong, Bobbie Faye's scalp buzzed. In fact, everything about it triggered warning signals within her, with the shining exception of there being several boats tied up at the end of the pier.

The long pier.

The long pier which seemed to be guarded by a rather disgruntled-looking guy. Meandering back and forth near the fishing camp. At which no one seemed to be fishing, but an awful lot of bustling about seemed to be occurring.

Yes, everything inside Bobbie Faye knew this was a Bad Thing in every way possible.

"Why are we hiding?" she whispered. "I thought you said you knew this guy and we could borrow his boat."

"Technically, the guy I said I knew was the one who worked at the marina. I said I knew *of* a guy with a boat close to where we were."

They watched in silence as the scowling man moved around the main building of the camp, out of their sight. Bobbie Faye checked Trevor's expression, and found him grim, tense.

"Why do I have a really bad feeling about this?"

"Because we're about to do something very very stupid."

Together they headed to one of the outbuildings, something she assumed was a small toolshed. Before Bobbie Faye could ask him what they were doing there instead of getting a boat, Trevor picked the locks of the shed with a little too much ease. He hustled her inside and shut the door, and when her eyes adjusted to the dim light filtering in through the barred windows, she nearly yelped.

It was *gun central*.

A horrible sense of dread spread through her chest and radiated outward, making her arms feel weak as noodles. Trevor busied himself picking out a couple of guns, knives, ropes, and other random supplies Bobbie Faye couldn't identify. He shoved his selections into one of the many satchels hanging there.

"Holy freaking geez," she said, when she could finally speak. "We're robbing *gunrunners*!"

That last word squeaked out in a too-high register and Trevor clamped his hand over her mouth.

"One of their guards is a . . . source, for lack of a better word.

And they prefer to be called 'Inventory Experts for Aggression Control.' Besides, who are you to cast stones, Ms. Bank Robber?"

She tried to exclaim that she *did not rob the fucking bank,* but Trevor had wisely kept his hand clamped over her mouth. He held her there for a moment until, she assumed, he was certain she wasn't going to rouse the suspicions of the guard outside. It was in that moment she caught the gleam in his eye and the way there was a smile tipping at the corners of his very sexy (damn him) mouth. He seemed to be having *fun.*

This was so beyond not a good thing, Bobbie Faye wasn't even sure how to rank it on a scale of *oh shit* to *holy fuck.* What kind of psycho had she kidnapped? What in the hell was his motive?

Trevor turned back to his task, loading a Glock. He started to shove it into her hands, then hesitated a moment with a bit of a grin, and said, "Aim the noisy end at other people this time, okay?"

"Are you nuts? The geeky boys we're going after would be scared of fly swatters."

"The people holding your brother . . . aren't."

He had a point. Dammit. She held the Glock in her hand, balancing the weight of it. If she had to think about it at that moment, she wasn't sure what felt more surreal to her: the fact that she was standing in (no, make that *robbing*) a gunrunner's shed, or the fact that her so-called hostage apparently liked to color so far outside the lines, she doubted he even knew there *were* lines.

She liked that so immensely, she had to sit down. It was a bad thing, she reminded herself. A very bad thing.

Cam had always been all about coloring inside the lines when it came to this sort of thing. She'd like the honor of that, the safety of that. That honor was dead sexy in its own way. But this . . . God help her, was intoxicating. It made her forget everything, including her own rules. It made her want to, oh, holy Mary, *trust* him. (Well, among other things.)

She'd promised herself, never *ever* again. The minute, the *microsecond, you start depending on someone, they leave you with the credit card bill for tips for Mimi down at the Strip & Stare club (and damn, but Mimi makes good tips), or they forget to mention that they're kinda sorta an overachieving criminal wanted by every branch of the government. Or, they seem to be your very best friend in the world, and then they go and arrest your sister and destroy your life. Even with Ce Ce and Nina, she kept her promise to herself: stay self-sufficient. Don't ask for much, try to give back more than you ask, and whatever the hell you do, just don't fucking *need*.

She'd started letting herself make Cam an exception, and look where that got her. No. She watched Trevor as he completed his tasks, clearly way-the-hell more familiar with all of the arms in the shed than any ordinary guy ought to be. A normal guy who'd been taken hostage for something this crazy probably would have let her drown in the truck. Or turned her in at the lake. They definitely would have split along about the time the bear was making out a morning menu. So this guy? Had to have some sort of ulterior motive. And the fact that right now she needed his help? Just pissed her the fuck off. It did not matter that the biceps were a-flexing and the back was well-toned and the ass, well damn, that was a thing of beauty. Did. Not. Matter.

She looked down at the gun again, remembering what the hell she needed Trevor for, and cursed under her breath. She couldn't ditch him just yet and get away from all of those muscles and the abs and the crinkly eyes, holy geez. She had to focus until they safely found the geeky boys and the tiara.

He turned at that moment and saw her sitting on a crate, staring at him. "You okay?" he asked, squatting on his heels, bringing himself blue-crystal-eye level to her, looking sincerely worried.

The *bastard*.

"Yeah, I'm just having a little girl-time here, rethinking my choice in nail color," she snapped, and instead of snapping back, he grinned. He fucking *grinned* at her, that big-cat-stalking-its-prey sort of grin, making her very *very* nervous.

"Cut it out." He only grinned bigger. "I thought we had an agreement going here. You hate all women, I hate you."

"I think I'm making an exception in your case."

"Well *I'm* not."

He looked her up and down, and her skin flamed hot, and his smile grew more wicked.

"Oh, I think you are."

She started to retort as he turned away, but there was an internal war going on, with Lust (which had not been out to play in a long long time) beating the hell out of Common Sense, and she could feel certain body parts placing bets. She opted for ignoring him because she didn't think "nuh uh" was a very convincing comeback.

Trevor opened the doorway a crack and watched a moment until he was satisfied it was clear to leave. They eased down the pier toward the boats tied at the end when the first scowling guard came out of the house. Bobbie Faye knew they were in plain sight, but the guy acted as if he didn't see them, which was just phenomenally odd. As she was contemplating this, a second man walked around the corner of the house and the first guy seemed to be trying to wave away a mosquito or something. Or maybe he was trying to indicate they should get moving.

"Sonofabitch," Trevor muttered. "Head for the white boat at the end."

"You mean the Triton 5220?" she asked, which surprised him enough for him to turn to her with a blank, shocked expression. "What? Girls can know boats."

He didn't get a chance to answer. Bobbie Faye thought she heard a firecracker pop and then *bam*, something hit the pier not far behind them, and they both looked in the direction of the house in time to see the two guards running in their direction, the second one definitely sporting a gun.

Bobbie Faye was pretty sure that if she'd read her horoscope that morning, it would have said something like, "Today the universe hates you. A lot. A whole freaking Grand Canyon lot of hate. Stay in bed. Better yet, dig a hole, hide."

She hauled ass down the pier with Trevor right behind her. They passed a glassed-in Peg-Board set up where all of the keys to the boats were stored, and Bobbie Faye jumped into the boat as Trevor slammed the butt of his SIG Sauer against the glass, shattering it, all while trying to hide his frame behind the skinny wooden stand as the running guards shot at them.

"They're not labeled," he shouted, and then turned to her, shocked again when the engine revved. She'd hot-wired it.

"What is the deal with you being pokey? Get in!"

She ducked down as a couple of the bullets ricocheted a little too close, then aimed at the tie rope binding them to the pier and in one clean shot, severed it.

A bullet splintered the key Peg-Board and Trevor turned and kicked the board into the lake. He leapt into her boat, rocking it hard, and she fell on her ass.

"Geez, you have all the grace of a bull jumping rope," she grumbled. "Cover me."

"What?" he said, firing at the guards, forcing them to stop and take cover. "We don't have time—"

She ignored him, jumping from boat to boat for a few seconds each, yanking the plug wires, disabling the motors.

"Okay, maybe that was smart," he allowed, and she glared at him.

She throttled up their boat and Trevor kept firing on the guards as she backed it out and raced out of the somewhat hidden inlet and into the vast spread of Lake Charles.

"Head over for that canal," Trevor shouted above the roar of the Mercury motor as the boat skipped across the waves of the lake and the wind and water spray slammed the words into oblivion.

"Sure, oh Supreme Commander of the Universe," she grumbled, but turned the boat in the direction he'd pointed.

"I know what I'm doing."

"Riiiiiiggght. Getting us chased by gunrunners on top of everything else. *Genius.* Why the hell didn't I think of that?"

"At least I have a plan."

Trevor started opening all of the various doors and storage areas on the boat.

"Well, Mr. 'I have a plan,' if you were so flipping smart, you'd have figured out that we could use a cell phone right about—"

Trevor straightened up from where he'd been digging and held up a cell phone.

"If I didn't hate you, I'd be real impressed right now."

"These types always keep spares activated for emergencies."

"How the hell do you know that?"

"You could say I'm in the . . . procurement business."

He dialed the phone while she wondered for the millionth time why God hated her.

"Andre?" he asked as his call connected. "What have you got on the pencil necks I told you to watch for?" He listened intently, scanning the lake's opposite shore. Bobbie Faye watched him as his expression grew grim.

"It's not good," he said, finally hanging up. "Andre was on their tail, but he lost them. Last he saw, they went this way. That's where he found their boat. Empty."

Empty. Her brain kept saying the word over and over and wasn't it weird how a perfectly normal word could sound like a jumble of consonants and vowels, marking nothing, making no sense, once it's said repeatedly. Empty. Meaning, they could be anywhere by now, with the one thing she needed to save Roy's life. How in the hell could she find them? He must've still been talking to her, though she couldn't hear him above the roar of the motor. She wasn't sure if the wet she felt on her face was the overspray from the boat or tears, and it didn't much matter.

"Are you listening?" Trevor asked, for probably the second or third time, she surmised. She nodded. "They're probably holed up in a camp somewhere. They'd be crazy to try to head out since there's only a couple of roads on that side of the lake leading out, and I'm sure the cops have them blocked by now. We'll go camp to camp. It doesn't matter how long it takes, we'll find them."

She nodded, and at that moment, she heard the worst thing she could have heard. Motorboats racing toward them. She and Trevor peered back toward the shore of the lake where they'd just been moments before. Three of the boats Bobbie Faye had tried to disable raced out of the inlet where the camp was hidden and headed their direction. Fast.

She'd run out of time.

Chapter Nineteen

I'm sorry, sir, but we don't actually sell insurance to protect the public from Bobbie Faye. No sir, not even if you cry.

—*insurance agent Barbara Vierck, to a customer*

Y a'll keep up the chanting, now," Ce Ce chimed, weaving through the aisles. She'd commandeered several of the customers and placed them at strategic points in the matrix she'd made of crystals to help boost the positive energy flow. "Bobbie Faye, will be safe. Bobbie Faye, will be safe," every customer intoned with her, even macho Maven, who, Ce Ce noted, had positioned himself nearest the gun case so he could shop while he chanted.

"Miss Rabalais? Honey, you want to sit on this box here so you don't have to stand very long?"

The frail eighty-year-old peered through her bottle-thick glasses, slid halfway down her tiny nub nose.

"You think it'll take very long?"

"I don't know, honey. This is a full-out Bobbie Faye event, you know."

"Oh, dear. One of those? Again? She blow up anything yet?"

"Now, now, Miss Rabalais. We're going to think positive, okay?"

"Oh, okay. I am positive she's going to blow up something."

"Seriously, Miss Rabalais, she's going to be safe. Can you hear what everyone's chanting? Now, honey, you chant along."

The old woman motioned for Ce Ce to lean closer, and she whispered, "Is this matrix doohickey we're doing supposed to make you feel . . ." she looked around to make sure no one could hear her, ". . . um, energetic?"

"Energetic?"

The old woman blushed a little. "Yes. You know. *Tingly.*"

Miss Rabalais averted her eyes as Ce Ce scanned the people who were chanting. They did seem to have a bit more color to their cheeks, more smiles. She patted Miss Rabalais on the shoulder.

"It's possible that's a side effect."

"Then," the old woman said, tugging Ce Ce even closer, "can we do this every week?"

"Honey, I'm not sure this town could handle everyone being all . . . *tingly* every week."

"Oh, you never know," Miss Rabalais said. "Could solve world peace."

Ce Ce nodded, a little worried over Miss Rabalais's enthusiasm. They'd just set up the matrix, and if it was this strong, it could definitely help Bobbie Faye, but Ce Ce was starting to worry about what she was going to do with fifty horny customers.

Of course, it was the crystals magnifying the energy. Well, good. Maybe, just maybe, this would help end everything for Bobbie Faye in a safe, quiet, peaceful way.

Just about the time she'd gotten everyone situated, and the chanting going in a nice four/four rhythm, she glanced up at the TV in the corner. The news switched to a view of Nina backed up against Bobbie Faye's trailer, whip ready. The crowd had grown to gawk (and party), but what worried Ce Ce more was the two pickup trucks which appeared to be attached via winch cables to the trailer. There were two clearly overwhelmed deputy sheriffs keeping onlookers from driving into the trailer park and parking all over everyone's lawns. Ce Ce supposed pretty much every other officer was out on the manhunt, chasing Bobbie Faye.

She quickly dialed Nina and watched on TV as Nina answered her cell phone.

"Honey girl, am I seeing what I think I'm seeing?"

"Yep," Nina said, cracking her whip. "The odds on the betting got so high against them, Claude and Jemy decided they could make a bundle if they could prove the betters wrong. I can only do so much with my whip. And with live TV, I can't pull out any bigger arsenal."

"Can't that whip thing puncture a tire with a really good crack at it?"

"I tried. Have you seen those tires? They're off-road, which makes them a lot stronger than your basic wheels. I gotta go, Ceece. I've got pilferers."

Nina hung up and Ce Ce watched the aerial coverage on the TV as Nina cracked her whip again to disperse would-be thieves (one man of a particularly large nature holding up one of Bobbie Faye's pieces of lingerie—a satin teddy—as if trying to judge whether or not it would fit him). Meanwhile, the two four-wheel-drive trucks attempted to use their winch cables to pull the trailer back to an upright position.

It was clearly not working.

"Monique," Ce Ce called, and the redhead waddled toward her, her freckles a calm pale pink. "I need the jar on top of the green cabinet back there."

"The one with the red wormy-looking things?"

"Yep, that's the one. It'll help increase the positive flow, and I think we're gonna need it."

"You ever planning to tell me what those things are?"

"Honey, you don't want to know. Just trust me on this."

Monique nodded and hurried to the back to get the jar.

Bobbie Faye throttled the motor to its maximum speed and kept rubbernecking back at the other boats.

They were gaining.

Trevor was making another call when the motor sputtered and spit and backfired. Apparently, the boat had not read the "escapee contract," obliging it to work perfectly.

They heard gunfire, coming from the gunrunners. The bullets fell short, but at the rate Trevor and Bobbie Faye's boat was slowing down, that was only a temporary reprieve.

Trevor snapped the cell phone closed.

"Hey Mr. 'I have a plan.' In case I don't live to tell you? Your plan sucks."

He ignored her as he jumped to the controls and then to check the fuel line. Bobbie Faye opened the electrical panels.

"Don't touch anything!" he commanded, and Bobbie Faye hmphed.

"Just who the hell does he think he is?" she grumbled while she poked around in the electrical box. "I'm the one who slowed down the other boats by sabotaging them, I'm the one who got this boat started, I'm the one who shot the tie rope"—she jiggled a couple of wires, revving up into her rant—"I'm the one who's going to fix the damned motor so we don't get shot by the stupid gunrunners he stupidly decided to stupidly steal from, the stupid man."

She thought fondly of the moment earlier that morning when she shot his truck and he had gaped at her, furious, and she wished she could go backwards and shoot it a couple more times, just because. Damned man, always thinking he knew what the right thing to do was.

There was a red wire loose from a connection, which was obviously the problem. As she fiddled with it, the boat bounced across the tops of the lake's waves, jostling her. She stumbled a bit and the wire connected to something and *wham,* the boat surged forward, the motor maxed out.

"I fixed it!"

She looked at Trevor, who was trying to steer the boat, and nothing was responding—not the steering, not the throttle—*nada.* He gaped at her.

"I didn't fix it?" she asked, her voice a whole lot smaller.

"What the hell did you touch?"

"The 'fuck up everything' wire, apparently."

Bullets stitched the water just behind them.

Lovely. Just freaking lovely. How could this day get any worse?

Bobbie Faye looked ahead to the shoreline and boggled at what she saw there.

No. No no no no no no no.

There, straight ahead of them in one of the man-made canals dug at the perimeter of the lake was an oil rig on a floating barge. A big oil rig, with a huge crane on board to off-load barrels of product onto waiting barges.

She tapped Trevor, who was still focused on trying to fix the throttle.

"Are those . . . pilings I see?" She pointed to the necklace of huge concrete posts sticking up from the surface of the lake in front of the barge.

They were headed directly at these posts, their boat skimming the surface of the lake at more than sixty miles an hour. Just fast enough to smash into smithereens and not leave anything identifiable behind.

Roy flashed in her mind, then Stacey, and stupidly, the fact that she was going to die in a SHUCK ME, SUCK ME, EAT ME RAW T-shirt for all of the state to see.

So this is what it's like to know you're gonna die, she thought, watching as Trevor jumped forward, grabbing a long rope out of the satchel of goods they'd taken from the gunrunner's shack. He seemed to be frantically tying knots.

"It's not gonna do you much good to tie me up now."

"Don't give me ideas."

Bobbie Faye looked over her shoulder and saw the gunrunners slowing down, gaping at them like they were crazy. Beyond the gunrunners, the WFKD and state police helicopters flew toward them.

"Great. I'll blow up on the news. At least they won't see the shirt."

"Oh, with your luck, I'm sure they'll see the shirt."

"Thank you so freaking much. I'm going to be dead in a moment. Let me have my fantasy, okay?"

Trevor hung one of the satchels over her, then shoved what he could from the second one into her purse.

"Stand here. We've got one shot. Hold onto me, because I won't be able to hold onto you. Got it?"

Well, no, she didn't have it. Not really. Then she saw him start to swing the rope in circles and realized he'd made a lasso and was going to try to nab the crane on the oil rig. But their boat wasn't going to fit through the pilings anyway, and they weren't going to get close enough to the crane to reach it, though she admired him for trying.

She held on tight. Partially because she just couldn't process anything else, and partly because if she had to die, she might as well get to feel his back beneath her arms. She tried to close in tightly to him, to make herself as small as possible and stay out the way of his swinging the lasso, and there were the pilings, right there, a few feet ahead.

Trevor stepped on the side of the boat with a sudden force, tilting it hard, and the motion dipped one side down into the water.

Shoving the other side up.

At that angle, their width scraped past the first row of pilings just as—

Trevor released the lasso.

It arced . . . slicing across the impossibly blue sky, hanging there for a thousand years . . . moving toward the crane . . .

"Hold on!"

The rope snagged the crane and Trevor held the rope as it snapped taut, lifting them out of the boat, the momentum swinging them forward as the boat raced out from under them.

Bobbie Faye strained to hold onto him, her arms burning with the effort. As they glided through the air, she heard his heart jackhammer in his chest, heard him cursing under his breath, smelled the aftershave he must've used that morning.

The boat kept going, racing forward.

Their momentum swung them toward the rig.

The boat rocked back down into the water.

Just as her feet touched the deck of the rig, the boat smashed into the next set of pilings, exploding. The rig's deck jerked and undulated.

Bobbie Faye only had a second to see the horrified shock of the crane operator and the worker on the barge.

"Life rafts!" the barge worker yelled, and pointed. He and the crane operator leapt into one as she and Trevor dove into another. Behind them, flames from the exploding boat licked at the oil rig as Trevor fired up the motor on the life raft and raced up the canal, away from the lake and the rig.

Chapter Twenty

There are five grown men in the waiting room all experiencing shortness of breath, anxiety attacks, dizziness, hives, and one of them has curled into a fetal position, is sucking his thumb, and wants me to call his mommy.

—*Dr. Pam Dumond to RN Jennara B. on the influx of patients during the last Bobbie Faye disaster.*

The state police helicopter rocked hard from the rig explosion; metal shrapnel whizzed outward from the former rig-turned-scrap heap, and a rolling fireball boiled upwards a hundred feet. Cam's pilot regained control, spun around, and faced the lake. There, in front of him, was a forty-foot roiling blaze feeding on the oil from the rig, mirroring the knot in his stomach.

His mind, at first, was a blessed blank.

He stared at the flames, stared at the destruction, and everything was quiet as the color leached out of the world and there was nothing. No feeling, no warmth, no sound, no color. Then, one by one, images of Bobbie Faye ticked into his memory. If he was the kind of man who let his subconscious lead him around, he'd have noticed how he hadn't been able to conjure up one single image of her angry or wild-eyed with fury or giving him a difficult time. Instead, he would have noticed that every image that clicked past was of a moment he had enjoyed, of her smile, or the way she smelled or snuggled into the crook of his arm. But he wasn't that kind of man, and he closed his eyes, pushed the images away. He wouldn't even let himself think about Bobbie Faye. There just wasn't anything to think about; that had been a part of his life that was long over, final, finished.

He had a hard time feeling the radio switch, and he fumbled the mic, his fingers numb, why are they numb? Why is there no sound? And he struggled to remember how to contact Jason, the words robotic as he told Jason what had happened, and to dispatch the emergency crews trained to handle this kind of disaster.

There was nothing to think about. Nothing.

His helicopter hovered a safe distance from the oil rig until the radio crackled with a call from the news helicopter; they'd switched to the same frequency Cam was on in order to coordinate efforts.

"We've got something!" the cameraman shouted over the airwaves. "Seriously, we got something. Y'all have to see this."

Cam radioed back a landing zone suggestion and realized the FBI had been monitoring his frequency when they cut in and announced they'd be joining the party.

Bobbie Faye had felt the force from the blast before she actually heard it. Or, at least, that's what she thought happened, because she never really heard anything. Of course, it was a little difficult to hear with her brain screaming *holy shit holy shit* as if it were trying to gold medal in the freak-out Olympics. The concussion threw Trevor forward, which knocked her down into the bottom of the life raft, and he sprawled on top of her for a long moment before he seemed to shake it off and pull himself up.

He motored them a decent distance away in the canal, a U-shaped affair which worked its way back toward the lake. She sat up and watched him try to tend to a wound in the back of his left thigh where a small, jagged piece of metal protruded. Shrapnel from the oil rig, she supposed. He grimaced and made such a face and, for crying out loud, she'd had worse wounds in her own backyard. She yanked the metal out before he could say anything just to show him how unimportant the wound was.

"Sonofabitch!" he said, gritting his teeth and clamping his hands down, putting pressure on the gash.

"Oh, good grief. It's not even bleeding." She looked closer. "Much." She looked closer still. There was an awful lot of red oozing out. "Ewwww. You really should do something about that," she suggested, and then stepped back in case the "something" which occurred to him would be to toss her out of the life raft.

Trevor throttled the life raft down to barely a crawl as he tried to observe the wound, but he couldn't quite see it, from its position on the back of his upper thigh.

"Oh, fine, give me your knife," she said.

"Like hell."

"To cut your shirt for bandages, idiot."

Trevor pulled up the small trolling motor attached to the life raft, and pulled out his knife and cut his own shirt. They drifted for a few minutes. She crossed her arms, frustrated that he couldn't get to the wound and wouldn't ask for help.

He finally gave in and reluctantly handed her the shirt material as a bandage. She barely resisted the *neener neener neener* comment perched at the tip of her tongue as she expertly folded the material and tied off the bandage.

Trevor examined it thoroughly.

"It worries the hell out of me that the one thing you're good at is tying bandages."

The sound of shotgun shells ratcheting into chambers echoed off the trees around them.

"That ain't all you got to worry 'bout," said a voice behind Bobbie Faye.

"Y'all show your hands," another man's voice instructed, and she and Trevor raised them as the life raft bobbed gently in the water.

"Oh, *hell,*" she muttered just to Trevor, as she had yet to turn and see the men behind her.

"I'll handle this," he whispered. "If it gets bad, swim for the rig. Cops should be there by now."

It wasn't going to help. She'd never make it to the rig; she'd heard enough to know this was a helluva lot worse situation than Trevor thought.

It was everything Cam could do to keep his hands off the controls of the state police helicopter and land faster. He leapt out before the runners hit the ground and sprinted to the news helicopter, meeting Zeke and one of his FBI colleagues halfway there.

"Detective Moreau, this is special agent Wellesly," Zeke explained as they reached the news helicopter together to find the cameraman setting up a playback monitor.

"I'm telling y'all, I think I got them on tape."

The cameraman pushed the tape into the player, fast forwarding until he found where his footage of the boat chase started. He tapped the screen, showing the boat with Trevor and Bobbie Faye.

"I'm pretty sure this is them. I zoomed in here, but as you can see, we're still a little too far away to get a crystal-clear image. This was when we started flying toward them."

Cam watched the speedboat lurch forward. It was Bobbie Faye as he had suspected. He'd recognize her body language anywhere, especially since she was clearly arguing with the man in the boat, presumably Cormier. He held himself spectacularly still as the boat tilted through the first row of pilings and, for a split second, he thought he saw Trevor holding Bobbie Faye just before the boat went down the side of the rig opposite from the helicopter. They disappeared from view and then the boat exploded and a minute later, the rig followed.

"Now see this," the cameraman said, rewinding the tape back to that moment when Cam thought he'd seen Cormier holding Bobbie Faye. The tape froze there. Cormier appeared to be holding something aloft. Maybe a rope? Cam couldn't be sure, but he could see

Bobbie Faye squeezing tightly against the man. As the scene crawled forward, they disappeared from sight, and then the explosion.

The acid in his veins threatened to sear him from the inside out, and he stood, quiet, still.

"We won't be able to get in there for a while," Cam found himself saying. He sounded calm, steady. Strange, how that worked. "The emergency response team is on their way. They'll have to get the fire out and then get the well capped before it'll be safe enough to get any of our CSI in there."

"How long? Hours? What?" Zeke asked.

Cam almost snorted with derision. "We'll be lucky if it isn't days. You don't exactly turn off one of these at a spigot."

They replayed the tape twice more, slowing it down for a frame by frame study, and still couldn't discern any movement of Bobbie Faye and Trevor from the boat.

"Well that's it, then," Wellesly said. "They're dead."

Zeke shook his head. "I'll believe Cormier's dead when I have his body parts in a bag."

Cam ran back to his helicopter. For once, he hoped the FBI agent was right.

I've seen some tick-fevered dogs do some crazy-ass shit, but each-a-you, y'all done take the cake. What the hell were you thinking, stealing my boat?"

"Honestly, there was a mix-up," Trevor said, and Bobbie Faye rolled her eyes at him. That wasn't going to work.

"What?" the man behind her scoffed. "Like you took your brains out and forgot to put 'em back in? That's one hellified mix-up."

"Oh, for crying out loud, Alex," Bobbie Faye said, turning around to face the man leading the gunrunners. "It was just one measly little boat."

"Goddamnit, sonofabitch, I thought that mighta been you," Alex said, and Bobbie Faye and he glared at each other. The gunrunners grinned like a bunch of kids who discovered they were about to have front-row seats to a primo fireworks display as they all studied Bobbie Faye, then Alex, and then back again.

He wasn't much changed from her memory: dark, wiry, muscular, with a hook nose and fierce angles and planes to his face, but the shoulder-length black hair worked for him. He was part Cajun, part Choctaw, and no one would have ever described him as handsome, but he definitely had the kind of charisma that made him a leader and made his men loyal.

The years had been good to him, which pissed her off.

"I saw on the news that you were running loose," Alex continued, and Bobbie Faye noted with a shameful amount of satisfaction that he was seething. "So of course you have to lead the whole damned state to my door. Have you lost your mind? Wait a minute, look who I'm talking about."

"I didn't know it was your crappy old boat, for one thing. If I had, I'd have blown up the whole freaking lot of them."

Trevor turned to her, his expression shot through with incredulity. "Perhaps you haven't noticed who is holding the guns on whom."

"Oh, she knows, all right," said the second man standing near Alex. He was a stump, short and squat, with tobacco stains on his chin from the permanent chew he held between rotting teeth. "They used to date."

"Don't fucking remind me, Marcel," Alex said.

Bobbie Faye watched realization dawn in Trevor's eyes.

"So that's why you knew they were gunrunners. And that's why you're such a good shot."

She couldn't tell what he was annoyed about. "I didn't know it was Alex's camp, though. That one is a lot fancier than the last one. He moves around a lot, since he's a pus-filled, slimy, good-for-nothing waste of human skin."

"Promise me you'll never work as a negotiator."

Alex's face reddened, flushed with fury. "I should have killed you back when I had the chance."

"He got a restraining order on her," Marcel said, "on account of when she blew up his favorite car."

"I was aiming for the camp," she explained to Trevor. "Alex and I never did see eye-to-eye."

"I wanted her dead and she wouldn't oblige."

"I'm beginning to know the feeling," Trevor muttered, and Bobbie Faye cast him an icy frown. "So," he asked Alex, "why didn't you shoot her this time?"

Alex stared at Bobbie Faye. She could see his mixed emotions, but she also knew it was more than that. She had leverage.

The question didn't elicit an answer, though it did make Marcel suddenly regard the men around him. "Y'all show some respect. Y'all can't point your guns at the Contraband Days Queen!"

As a unit, they all swung their guns so that they aimed solely at Trevor.

"Somehow, today," Trevor said, "this makes perfect sense."

"Y'all are all right," Bobbie Faye said to the men. Most of them blushed, though a couple of them looked appreciatively at her belly-baring SHUCK ME, SUCK ME T-shirt and tight jeans. Then they checked to see if Alex had seen them do so, and when they met his glare, they suddenly found their boots fascinating.

"Just what in the hell are you doing out here, Bobbie Faye? And why the hell are you dressed like that?" Alex focused on Trevor. "You let her go outside like this?"

Trevor's expression registered surprise, and then he shrugged.

"You actually expect someone to have some control over her?"

Bobbie Faye wanted to kick them both.

"Hey! What year is it in that universe you live in, Alex? This is none of your business, what I wear."

Alex focused his searing glare back on her. She heard the helicopters whirring somewhere beyond the billowing smoke from the oil rig's fire.

"Fine. So why in the hell are you out here in my backyard, stealing my boat? Bored? Thought you'd light a firecracker up my ass just for kicks and giggles?"

His neck muscles were knotted, tense, and there was a bit of a facial tick, which Bobbie Faye knew was a very bad sign of Alex losing what little grasp he had on his temper. His men looked nervous and sent her pleading looks. And as much as she'd love to mess with him, she didn't have time.

"Actually, I'm in trouble."

"Trouble is your hobby, Bobbie Faye. So what's new?"

"I'm serious."

"Please tell me it's bad."

"It's about Roy. In fact, I need your help."

She'd never actually seen synchronized gaping before. Bobbie Faye wasn't sure who was more shocked at her request: Alex, his men, or Trevor.

"How about I just kill you instead?" Alex finally asked, until he looked around at his men, all of whom were shaking their heads "no."

"Shit," he addressed his men. "Y'all are nuts. I'm not helping her, I don't care if her mamma *was* the Contraband Days Queen for fifteen years."

"But she's the Queen, now that her mamma's gone," Marcel pointed out. "I'm real sorry to have heard about that, Bobbie Faye." Marcel's weaselly features softened. "She was a real good Queen."

"Thank you, Marcel."

"Besides, Alex," Marcel said. "Roy's in trouble."

"You believe her?"

"Bobbie Faye never lies. She's crazier than a raccoon hopped up on Tabasco, but she always tells the truth. And it's Roy. We gotta help."

Bobbie Faye noted the eager expressions on the rest of the men's faces and the rush of the epiphany nearly made her head spin.

"You sonofabitch," she addressed Alex. "You promised me Roy wouldn't work for you ever again."

Trevor stepped in front of Bobbie Faye while Marcel took a step to move in front of Alex.

"Oh, he don't work for Alex no more, Bobbie Faye. Not since the whole car blowing up deal. But he's great at poker."

"Roy always loses!"

"That's what makes him great," Marcel said, and the rest of the men nodded.

Trevor grabbed her around her waist to keep her from lunging at Alex.

If she and Roy lived through this, Bobbie Faye vowed to get even with Alex. Then smack some sense into Roy; he'd been lying to her all these years, still losing all of his money to Alex. She'd like to stomp Alex right now, too, but that was going to have to wait.

"I know you know pretty much everything going on around this lake and these bayous, Alex. You've always had lookouts everywhere."

"What the hell do you want from me?"

"A couple of geeky boys took something of Mamma's," she said, pointedly to the men, "from me, and I have to get it back. The people holding Roy will kill him if I don't."

"So?"

Bobbie Faye watched him. He was normally difficult to read, but she knew him well (too damned well), and she could tell he had more going on here than met the eye. For starters, he didn't seem surprised when she described the boys, and he didn't make jokes about how a nerdy kid was just good gator bait in the swamps. In fact, it was more about what he didn't say than anything else.

"So," she said, giving him a piercing look, "you know where they're going."

"I might have some idea."

"Are you helping them?"

"Nah," Marcel volunteered as Alex glowered at him. "Couple days ago, we heard someone like that was looking for a place to hole up. We didn't know they was gonna be pullin' a job on you, Bobbie Faye. Honest."

"Tell me where they are," Bobbie Faye said to Alex, "and I'll give you your stuff back."

Alex's pupils dilated as his eyes widened, though nothing else denoted just how much she knew he wanted his hands on that stuff again. He glanced around, then back at her, now looking slightly worried that she might say what the stuff actually was. She followed his lead, looking at his men, realizing they still didn't know. She grinned her biggest, most annoying "I have your ass nailed, don't I?" smile at him.

"All of my stuff?" he asked. "Given only to me?"

"Quit worrying about loopholes, Alex. I'll give it back." Eventually, she muttered, though low enough that he didn't hear her. He nodded, very reluctantly, agreeing.

"Hey boss," one of the other gunrunners said. "What do we do with this guy?" he asked, pointing at Trevor.

Bobbie Faye stepped in front of Trevor, surprising everyone. "He's with me."

"Reason enough to put the poor bastard out of his misery," Alex said, and Marcel and the men laughed, but lowered their guns. "Get her out of here, Marcel. Help her find the kids." He pointed at Bobbie Faye, a warning. "But I get all my stuff back. Or else."

Chapter Twenty-one

She got an A+ in demolition. Unfortunately, we weren't *teaching* demolition that week.

—*André Chapoy, high school shop teacher*

Cam's helicopter swooped low over the canals around the rig, staying well clear of the fire, but still close enough to see if any life rafts were nearby. The entire scene at the oil rig was on a loop in his mind, and he wanted it excised.

He pondered what could be driving Bobbie Faye to these lengths. Even if she'd intended to rob that bank, she wouldn't have put this many people's lives in jeopardy on purpose. She was crazy, but she was never intentionally cruel. He could give her that. Reluctantly. Something must be pushing her way beyond the normal level of insanity and the only thing—

He grabbed his phone, and as soon as Benoit answered, said, "Do we know where Bobbie Faye's family is?"

He heard Benoit flipping through a few pages of reports.

"Nope, not yet."

"Find 'em. Just verify their location and put someone on each of them."

"Including the niece?"

"Absolutely."

"Got it. I'll call you back as soon as I've found 'em."

He hung up, pissed that he hadn't thought to find them earlier. One of them was bound to know what the hell was eating Bobbie Faye and, unlike Ce Ce, have no problems blabbing anything anyone wanted to know. He maybe could have stopped this insane chase an hour ago. How in the hell had he forgotten her siblings?

His phone vibrated on his hip and he snatched it open and shouted a little too forcefully, "Moreau here."

"Uh, Cam?" Jason asked, breathless. "You okay?"

"Of course I am," he spat, and he could visualize Jason flinching. "What's up?"

"We've picked up a couple of survivors from the rig. A crane operator and a dock worker."

"And?"

"They said they saw Bobbie Faye, but they don't know if she made it off the rig before it exploded. The workers grabbed the first life raft and raced off toward the lake. The other life raft didn't follow. We haven't found it yet."

"Keep me posted."

"Will do. Oh. On that other thing we were talking about?"

"Yeah?"

"I've had a bit of a breakthrough. Call me from a land line as soon as you can."

They hung up, and Cam debated which was more pressing: hearing what Jason had learned or finding that other life raft before the FBI grabbed it. Bobbie Faye could be injured, bleeding.

Or dying. The imagery of the explosion was on constant repeat. Geez, he needed a new brain.

Cam directed the helicopter to land near the marina and he ran for one of the pay phones out on the pier. When he dialed Jason, he was greeted with, "Hello, Mrs. Lee. I've got that information for you around here somewhere. Is there a number where I can call you back?" Cam read off the pay phone number and within a couple of minutes, it rang.

"What the hell was that?" he asked Jason.

"I wanted to switch to a secure line and I didn't want anyone picking up your cell line and recording this. Besides, the Captain was strolling around.

"I got a snippet. The Fibbies are rotating frequencies, though, not staying on the same channel for very long—probably some sort of automated hack prevention program they have set up to keep anyone from hearing a full conversation. I'm patching it in through the computer to you. Don't worry, it'll be scrambled if anyone else picks up on this line."

Cam made a mental note to sweep his house and office for bugs if he ever pissed Jason off. He could hear computer keys clicking and Jason humming the way he did when he was hyped up on techno-geekism, and then Zeke's voice broke into the silence.

"If I know Cormier, he's after it."

"You think he knows?"

"It's Cormier. Of course he knows."

"You think she'll give it to him?"

"I think she won't know what the hell just happened. I know Cormier. He'll charm it straight out of her hands and make her think it was all her idea."

"If she gets it."

"Oh, he'll make sure she gets it."

"So . . . what happens if he gets it first?"

"Game over."

Jason cut back into the line. "The channel switches there and I lost 'em, but just as they're switching, the first guy asked something. It's too scratchy to understand, and I washed it through the computer a few times. The best I could come up with was something about a 'piece.' I don't know what they're referring to. Maybe the same thing Bobbie Faye's supposed to give to this Cormier guy?"

"Thanks. Do you think you can track down their frequency and listen in again?"

"I can try. I'll call you if I get anything else."

Jason hung up, and Cam tried to imagine Bobbie Faye having something of such great value she'd not only risk going to jail, or dying, trying to get it, but clearly other people were willing to risk as much as well. Aside from one decent car she'd had (used, high mileage), the most expensive thing she'd ever owned was a used laptop computer refurbished by the guys down at the Computer Barn, and even then, it was so far out of date, it barely ran Windows. She had no fancy jewelry (he was not going to think about the ring at the bottom of the lake . . . not going to think about it, not not not not, damnit, and how it would have looked on her), and she had no knickknacks that came from anything except garage sales and flea markets. Anything else of value she'd once owned, she'd hocked, he heard, to pay for Lori Ann's rehab.

He'd offered to pay for that, in spite of Bobbie Faye loathing him, but she'd made it crystal clear she wanted absolutely nothing from him. Ever.

Cam climbed back into the cockpit, directing the pilot to fly south of the rig fire, away from any logical roads out of the area. Anyone wanting to escape would have gone east or west to get to the closest roads out. But clearly, Bobbie Faye didn't just want to escape. She was after something.

Even with the air-conditioning cranked on high, the crowded, humid conditions in the Outfitter store where many people stood or sat, chanting, made the customers look a little too much like dozens of Easter eggs drowned in a pot, coming to a boil. Sweat clustered across their brows as Ce Ce fussed around each one, handing some a crystal, tucking talismans in others' pockets, sprinkling odd spices and ingredients around them all.

"What's that?" Maven asked, his attention dragged from the knife case to the odd blue strings she tucked in his pocket. "Yarn?"

"Sure, honey. Yarn."

Maven squinted at her, suspicious, but she patted him on the arm and continued down the matrix line. No way in hell she was telling him exactly what kind of yarn that was.

The energy seemed to be flowing through the matrix exceptionally well. Quite a few of the customers were looking scads more robust than they had prior to joining in the matrix. They seemed to be feeling, as Miss Rabalais had put so delicately, *tingly,* if Ce Ce could judge by the smiles, the body language, the flirting. She noticed the scores of crystals she had hung around the room seemed to waft toward the door, the same direction she'd focused the positive energy. Sure, some people would say that was probably just the air conditioner jostling the crystals, but Ce Ce knew better.

This was good.

No, this was *very* good.

The phone rang for the billionth time and Allison scrunched her forehead in concern and handed it to Ce Ce.

"Ms. Ce Ce?" It was a youngish woman's voice, tremulous, soft. "This is Mrs. Gareaux, Stacey's kindergarten teacher. We met last open house?"

"I remember, honey. Is Stacey okay?"

"I think so. Well, I mean, yes, she's fine, but I thought I probably should have called you before I let them take her, but it was all official and everything, so I really didn't have a choice."

"Let who take her?"

"The FBI. There was a special agent who came here a few minutes ago. He said he had to take Stacey and put her in protective custody until her aunt Bobbie Faye was found. I know you're the emergency contact to pick Stacey up if something happens to Bobbie Faye—I mean, now, while her mamma's drying out, bless her heart. We just, well, we never talked about what to do if something like this should happen."

"That's okay, honey, I don't expect you'd have that sort of conversation handy."

"True, Ms. Ce Ce, but this *is* Miss Bobbie Faye we're talking about and I just feel terrible that I didn't think to ask this sort of question before."

"Not to worry, honey, I'm sure they were just trying to protect her."

"Yes ma'am. I suppose you're right. It just seemed . . . I don't know. Odd. I just thought you ought to know."

"Thank you, honey. Did you get the agent's name?"

There was a brief pause, a slight intake of air. "Oh, dear, should I have? He had a badge and everything."

"I'm sure it'll be fine," Ce Ce said, and then rang off. Surely, it would be fine, right? She just had to find that child, make sure they were keeping her safe. Get a name. Not a big deal, really. She ignored the gnawing in her stomach. It really couldn't be a big deal. She wasn't sure if she had a spell for that.

Chapter Twenty-two

I'm sorry, Governor, but "her mere existence" isn't grounds enough to register Bobbie Faye as a controlled and dangerous substance to be locked up.

—*Louisiana State Supreme Court Justice Tara Sedalek, to a former Louisiana governor after his run-in with Bobbie Faye put him in a full-body cast for two months*

Bobbie Faye groaned at the incessant busy signal on her cell phone; Stacey's school still wasn't answering. She waited in Marcel's boat while he and Trevor sank the life raft, hiding it from the police.

"What the hell do you mean, you're not coming with us?" Bobbie Faye demanded of Marcel as he and Trevor stepped from the lake shore back into Marcel's boat.

Marcel waved his own cell phone at her while she hit redial.

"I done tracked 'em to a shack, Bobbie Faye. I gotta get outta here. This place is gonna be crawlin' with Feds, and I ain't exactly on their Christmas list. 'Sides, if those kids move from there, we'll know it and I'll call you. I'll take you far as another boat, chere. That's it."

Bobbie Faye smacked the cell phone closed after yet another busy signal, staring at it as she asked, "What could they be doing over there?"

"They're probably getting a lot of calls from parents, which is tying up the lines." Trevor suggested.

That didn't exactly make her feel better.

Marcel guided his boat through small bayous where the trees overhung the stagnant water to the point of obscuring the view from above and the five (at last count) helicopters circling the oil rig fire. She had to give him credit; he was going to great pains to help. He and Trevor seemed to have hit it off well. A little *too* well? This was, after all, a guy who knew exactly where a gunrunner's hideout was. And knew where the guns were stored. And how to use them. And seemed way too familiar with getting into and out of trouble. And . . . wow, her head hurt just thinking about what he could be up to. His procurement business? Was it guns? Or stealing valuable things? Was she leading him straight to the tiara?

Geez. She had enough to worry about.

The bayou they were on curved sharply to the left, but Marcel seemed to be ignoring the curve and was heading straight for a clump of trees and brush.

"Marcel, what the hell are you doing? Intentionally grounding us?"

"Aw, chere, you worry too much. Just 'cuz you dumped me for Alex, don't mean I hold a grudge."

Trevor glanced at her, the mockery clear in his eyes.

"Marcel. *We* did not date."

"We did too. It was a very good date." He turned to Trevor. "We went to a tractor-pull."

"Ha," she snapped. "Y'all tricked me into going, and I ended up covered in beer, cotton candy, and mud!"

"Yeah," Marcel said, smiling, fond of the memory. "It took four men to hold you down so I could hose all the mud off you so you could get in the truck."

"I bet that went over well," Trevor noted.

Bobbie Faye ignored them both, worrying instead over the looming trees, until they suddenly divided in half, swinging open on an electric gate. Marcel held a remote control and grinned, smug.

"Holy crap, no wonder the Feds never find you guys."

"Well, they find the gates sometimes. We've got 'em rigged with alarms and we've got surveillance cameras all over the lake, so we know if one's being staked out or tampered with. Most of 'em, though, are still hidden."

Trevor looked quite appreciative of this creativity. Marcel clicked the remote after they'd passed through, and the gate closed behind them, cutting them off from the bayou and lake. They were floating on an even tinier bayou, one too small for the speedboat and its big Mercury engine to navigate safely.

"This is where y'all switch to the bateau," Marcel announced, and he pointed out a bateau which was tied to a tree a couple of feet away. "There's a trolling motor in good condition, some gas in there, and a couple of paddles. That should get you all the way to the shack."

"Your map is pretty convoluted," Trevor said, reviewing it as Bobbie Faye climbed into the bateau.

"Yeah, well, I could draw you one straight to the shack, but you'd have to cross out in the open in a couple of places or go near a few of the spots where I know the Feds have set up surveillance. This way, you can stay hidden. It'll take you longer, but you're probably a lot safer."

Marcel handed their satchel of stolen guns and supplies over to them. "You're gonna need this more than me," he said. "But Bobbie Faye? Please give Alex his stuff back. I dunno what you've got, but he sure gets real moody when he thinks about it."

"I would imagine a moody gunrunner is a scary thing," Trevor observed, and Marcel nodded.

"You don't know the half of it."

"Marcel," Bobbie Faye said, wrapping her fingers around his forearm, surprising him. "If I get all the way to this shack and those kids aren't there? I'm going to hunt you down."

Trevor eyed Marcel. "I'd suggest you move to Texas, but I don't think it'll do you any good."

Marcel laughed. "It's not too late to save yourself."

"She owes me a truck."

"Oh good freaking grief, it's just—"

Trevor held up his hand, and she shook her head, annoyed.

"Right, right, I forgot. It's never *just* a *truck*."

"I'm sticking to her 'til I get another one, or die trying."

"Emphasis on the 'die trying' part," Bobbie Faye added, and Marcel chuckled as he left them, using a push-pole to guide his boat down the little bayou. He disappeared from their sight as he eased down the left, wider fork.

Trevor sat at the front of the bateau, one hand guiding the trolling motor as he eased them along the narrower passage.

The sunlight barely washed through the tangle of trees laced above them to reflect off the brackish water, which was nearly hidden beneath a layer of duckweed; when she looked farther downstream, the water seemed to disappear under a layer of green to the point where it looked like mossy-covered land instead of the small bayou that it was. From what little she could see of the sun's position, they were heading south, deeper into a vast network of bayous and streams and lands still nearly as virgin as they had been when the country was being explored. Bobbie Faye closed her eyes a moment and listened: birds, bullfrogs, crickets, the rare splash of a mullet jumping in the lake nearby. The boat beneath her glided smoothly through the water, rocking slightly, and a tiny breeze brushed against her face. When she opened her eyes, it was as if she'd moved backwards in time, hundreds of years, to some primordial place where people were insignificant.

How on earth was she supposed to get the tiara to the kidnappers and prevent them from killing Roy or her once they no longer needed either of them? Why on earth did they want her tiara? It was crazy. She wasn't anyone special. She was just a girl whose nicest home had been a trailer; who didn't know, sometimes, how she was going to put the next meal on the table. How in the hell was she supposed to win this?

She shuddered, then hoped Trevor hadn't seen. When she glanced his direction, he seemed to be studying the map. She hit redial on the cell phone. She had to start somewhere, and step one was to get Stacey out of that school and someplace safe.

The Mountain escorted Roy to the bathroom, an area defined more by the stains and mold coating the walls than any actual partitions. There was an awful lot of rusty-colored stuff on the floor and splattered on the walls and Roy decided to pretend that it was some new painting technique gone bad.

"This here's the john," The Mountain said, shoving Roy forward. Roy clamped his jaws against the bile rising in his throat; the stench of something rotting assaulted him and his eyes streamed.

"I figured Vincent woulda had a nice bathroom on account of how his office looks."

"He does. It's on the other side of the building by his office. He don't let the vics use that one. That's what this one is for."

Roy turned to the urinal, trying to ignore the mammoth psychopath behind him.

"This one's the workshop," The Mountain continued.

Roy knew he was going to regret asking, but it was out of his mouth before he could stop himself. "The workshop?"

"Yeah, where we get busy with the breaking and the killing. Vincent don't want none a' that done in his office much 'cuz of the crap that spatters everywhere."

Roy threw up.

With his hands bound in front and ankles loosely tied—the only way they'd agree to let him out of the chair—he rocked out of balance and then leaned against the urinal and hoped he wasn't now wearing his own vomit.

The Mountain, however, didn't seem to notice. He kept on talking as if everything was business as usual. "Hey, you know stuff, don'tcha?" he asked. "'Cuz I was thinking I could get in the *Guinness Book of World Records,* but Eddie says I can't. Eddie says I'd just get into trouble instead, but I think Eddie's kinda jealous."

"Uh, world record?" Roy straightened, zipping his jeans, and then hobbled over to the sink. He prayed for water to wash his face.

"Yeah. For the biggest collection of doorknobs, ever."

"Doorknobs?"

"Yeah! It's cool, man. Every time I crack somebody, I go back to their house later and take a doorknob. So I can keep them with me. I got, like, the biggest collection. You wouldn't believe. Go on. Ask me."

"How—how many do you have?"

The Mountain opened the bathroom door to lead Roy back to Vincent's office.

"One hundred thirteen. I hate odd numbers, though. An' thirteen's really unlucky." They wove past stacked office cubicles, filthy with dust. "I really need to get another one. But don't you think I could get into *Guinness*? I think so."

"Uh, yeah," Roy said, his voice cracking a bit. "I think you have enough right now."

"Really? You think so?"

"Yeah. Maybe you're right, maybe Eddie's just jealous. Does Eddie collect anything?"

"Nah, Eddie ain't smart enough. He's studying on bein' a decorator or somethin'."

"Well, see, there you go. I think you ought to call them, see if they're interested."

"But Eddie said I could get into trouble."

"For collecting doorknobs? C'mon, he's just trying to steal your limelight."

"Yeah. He's just trying to steal my limelight."

"That's right. You deserve to be famous. You put all that hard work into it, and I bet you have 'em all labeled and everything."

"How'd you know?"

"Oh, anybody can see how smart you are at this. It takes real talent. I think *Guinness* would be real interested in hearing your story. They might even do some sort of feature on you."

"Really?"

"Yeah. You should call 'em. Right away, you know, before someone beats you to it. They never print the second person that comes up with something brilliant, you know."

Roy didn't catch The Mountain's answer as he pushed open the door to Vincent's office and ushered Roy inside. Roy shuffled back to his chair on the blue tarp, only just realizing as he passed where Vincent was sitting at his desk that Vincent was on the phone.

His tone, when he finally did speak, was low and lethal and sent shivers up Roy's arms.

"That Professor," Vincent seethed, obviously unconcerned that Roy was listening, "couldn't mastermind his way out of an open cardboard box." Vincent paused for emphasis. "Find out who the double-crossing scum is and bury them."

The thin veneer of sophistication dropped from Vincent for a moment, and the raw, boiling murderous intent evident in his expression made Roy yearn for the warm, fuzzy conversation back in the bathroom.

Chapter Twenty-three

We wanted to do a reality-type show, called *Surviving Bobbie Faye,* but it scared the hell out of the network. They thought we'd be sued for cruel and unusual punishment and we couldn't find contestants brave enough to shoot a pilot.

—*producer Corey Steven New*

Cam's state police helicopter flew low over the southern part of Lake Charles; confused and angry fishermen were being corralled up by state police and rangers from Wildlife and Fisheries, as much for their own safety as it was to interview anyone in the area who may have seen Bobbie Faye.

It bugged him, this "it" thing the FBI were referring to. What the hell was "it?" And was it the same thing as the "piece" they'd also mentioned?

Benoit radioed in, and Cam keyed the helicopter's microphone, asking, "Any word on the family's whereabouts?"

"We've got the sister still in lockdown rehab. The kid was dropped off at school this morning according to witnesses. We can't get through on the phone to confirm. I'm sending a car over there to check on her. And I haven't found the brother yet."

"Check on Brew's Bar. Or Joe's. As a last resort, Podilli's over on

Fifth. Roy's usually in one of them when he gets off a turnaround, hitting on the women 'til he goes home with one."

"Got it."

"And see what exactly Bobbie Faye was doing at the bank this morning."

"Hang on," Benoit said, shuffling papers in a file. "I talked to Mosquito—"

"Melba?"

"Right. She said something about Bobbie Faye cashing a paycheck and looking at her mamma's tiara."

"The tiara? What's it doing at the bank?"

"According to Melba, she hid it there since Lori Ann was selling everything in sight."

"She doesn't usually wear the tiara until the last day of the festival. Did she take it with her?"

"Lemmee see . . . The tape shows she threw the cash in a plastic bag. The Professor grabbed the bag from her and dumped his own money in there. It doesn't really look like there's something else in it. From the angle on her on the tape," Cam could hear Benoit rewinding it and playing it again, "hell, I can't see anything in that bag. It looks empty."

"Let's make sure. And how's the Professor doing?"

"Freaking out. I got nothing else out of him from interrogation. We let him have the jail cell where he can see the TV news on the sergeant's desk. I got tired of him asking what was going on two hundred times. Then he saw something, flipped out, and was about to piss himself in the corner of the cell, but he won't talk. Dellago is still hanging around the station, so I have no clue what's up."

Cam hung up, then stewed. None of it made sense. Of course, Bobbie Faye was involved, so if it had made sense, he would have worried that the end of the world was about to arrive. As it was, he had nothing to go on, except that she was after something that a lot of people wanted. Something people would kill to get.

How that could tie into her looking at that ratty old tiara, he had no clue. *If* it even did tie in.

B obbie Faye muttered, "Damnit," as she listened to yet another round of busy signals on the cell. She itched to throw the damned phone into a tree and it took all her newfound maturity to refrain.

When Trevor raised his eyebrows at her, she explained, "I still can't get through to Stacey's school. Nina's got voice mail on, which means she can't answer, and Ce Ce's private line is also busy."

"I'm just shocked we're down to only one swear word instead of ten. You're losing your touch."

"Yeah, well, I didn't want to get letters from all the mama squirrels."

She stared at the phone a second, then dialed Roy's number. She listened to Vincent's silky answer, braced herself, and said, "I want to know that my brother is all right."

"Not until you have the tiara, Bobbie Faye."

"I'm close to it. I swear."

" 'Close' doesn't interest me, my dear. Get it, or I'll be sending you your brother in a baggie."

"Don't you fucking dare. You hurt him, you'll never see the tiara."

Roy screamed in the background. She ground her teeth at Vincent's smooth chuckle.

"You're disappointing me, Bobbie Faye. Roy had such confidence in you. And by the way—don't threaten me again. Remember, I can pick up your sister whenever I like. It'd be so easy, just waving a vodka martini her general direction. Of course, your lovely little niece, Stacey, is mine to have. You have no idea how easy it is for me to just, *poof*, make her disappear."

"You won't win. Bring me the tiara. You have one hour to get it and contact me again."

He severed the call.

"One hour?" she squeaked, but the phone was definitely dead.

She hugged the phone to her chest, her mind seared blank. This was so far beyond anything she'd faced before. Miles beyond the regular idiots Roy normally crossed. She couldn't feel, couldn't process thoughts, until she realized she'd been staring at Trevor's hands. She caught his expression, something akin to sympathy. Something tender.

"If you even *look* like you're going to give me a hug—"

"Do I look suicidal to you?"

That elicited a small smile from her.

"I've got to find someone to go pick up Stacey. Someone who can protect her in case . . . well. In case the kidnappers decide Roy isn't enough."

She redialed Ce Ce's, only to be met with a busy signal again. Damn it to hell. Hadn't she told Ce Ce for fucking ever that she needed to add call-waiting?

There was only one person she could think of who could handle the heat. God help them all.

When she dialed Cam's phone, she got the voice mail instead.

She wasn't sure when she passed the sign that read, "Hell, Seventh Level, *Home of Bobbie Faye Sumrall,*" but she was going to demand blinky lights and arrows immediately.

She left Cam an inept message, knowing she should probably tell him more, but the battery beeped incessantly in her ear, and she had to save some battery time to try and reach Ce Ce. She held no illusions that he still cared about her, but maybe, just maybe, he still cared about the kid.

Ce Ce knew it was bad news as soon as the woman walked in the door and appraised the energy matrix all the customers had formed. It wasn't just the threadbare navy polyester suit she wore, the too-ruddy complexion, the cast-iron black helmet hair, or the lace-up wedge-soled shoes which set Ce Ce's intuition tingling. No, it was the battleaxe expression, the snide, bureaucratic assurance that she was going to kick someone's ass which warned Ce Ce this was going to be bad. Ce Ce pegged the woman as being roughly ten percent Irish, ninety percent sledgehammer.

"Is there a Ms. Ce Ce Ladeaux here?" the woman asked, spreading her disdain around evenly toward all of the customers still in their matrix.

"I'm Ce Ce Ladeaux," Ce Ce said, stepping forward.

The woman whipped a business card from seemingly thin air and slapped it into Ce Ce's hand.

"I'm Mrs. Banyon, from Social Services. Where's the girl?"

"Excuse me?"

"*Excuse* you? Highly unlikely," Mrs. Banyon snorted, drawing her wide chunky body up, throwing her shoulders back, doing a damned fine imitation of a brick wall. "Not after your stunt today."

Ce Ce looked around, confused. "Honey, why would you care if we did an energy matrix? It's only for positive flow, adjusting the karmic chi—" She stopped when Mrs. Banyon held up her hand.

"I have no idea what you just said," Mrs. Banyon snapped. "I'm talking about Stacey Sumrall. I've been over to the elementary school and she's not there. They gave me some insane story about the FBI picking her up, which is completely bogus. Since you're listed as the emergency person along with a woman of seriously questionable morals, a Ms. . . . ." she referenced a clipboard of notes, "Nina McVey, I can only surmise that you've picked up the child and conspired to keep her from me while your employee, Bobbie Faye Sumrall, is on the run from the police."

"What do you mean, *completely bogus*?" Ce Ce asked, unable to breathe properly. Her heart had stopped beating at those words and it had taken a moment to regroup while the Social Services woman was prattling. "The school called me and said the FBI had picked up Stacey."

"Ms. Ladeaux, I must warn you, keeping a child away from Social Services is illegal."

"Honey, call the FBI, ask them. You'll see that she's—"

"I've already called them. They do not have the child. I insist you produce her at once or I'm calling the police!"

Ce Ce saw the flare in the woman's nostrils and the fury burning in her eyes and knew, without a doubt, that someone had Stacey, and it wasn't the FBI. She thought for a moment that her body was caving in on itself, and then absolute dread took over: Bobbie Faye was certainly going to kill someone when she found this out.

Mrs. Banyon spun slowly. "If you think for one minute, Ms. Ladeaux, that I'm not going to file a report of the utter unsuitability of you as a sitter for this child, you'd better think again. I've heard of your Voodoo reputation, though until I came in here, I thought it was surely exaggerated. None of this is good for that child.

"And yet, as bad as this is, it pales next to the fact that Ms. Sumrall doesn't even have a home anymore, not to mention is wanted by the police. I'm going to take that child into protective custody for her own safety and good, and if you try to stop me, you'll be sitting in jail."

The oppressive heat in the store gained weight and form, as if a heavy wool blanket had covered the room and blocked out the light. Sweat soaked through Ce Ce's shirt and she felt an immense desire to lie on the ground.

Across the room, Monique served the customers water while they waited in their matrix positions, watching the drama unfold. Ce Ce could only think of one thing to do, and she rubbed the back of her neck when she glanced over to Monique, hoping Monique remembered the private signal they'd worked out. Monique nodded and left the room.

"Mrs. Banyon, everyone here can attest to the fact that I haven't left this store all day. Nor have I sent anyone over to the school to pick up Stacey. I am as alarmed as you are, honey. Why don't you sit a moment while I make some phone calls and see if I can sort this out?"

Monique returned with a tray of glasses of ice and a pitcher of tea. Thank goodness. Ce Ce eyed it to make sure it was the correct tea, and not too dark or it would taste bitter.

"Would you like something cold to drink while you wait?" Monique asked, and Mrs. Banyon frowned at Ce Ce.

"It'll take me ten minutes, tops," Ce Ce said, taking one of the glasses and pouring the tea. She handed one to Mrs. Banyon, poured the other two. Monique meandered down one of the aisles while Ce Ce took her own glass over to the counter where Alicia manned the ever-ringing phone.

"I'll only wait ten minutes," Mrs. Banyon said. "Then I'm calling the police."

"That's fine," Ce Ce replied, picking up her phone and dialing the school. "I'll want you to get them involved if I can't find her."

Mrs. Banyon sipped the iced tea, sighed appreciatively, and pressed the cold glass to her forehead.

"This is quite good," she said. "What am I tasting that's different?"

"Oh, just a little mint combination I love. Makes it sweet without having to add sugar."

Mrs. Banyon searched the aisles until she found a low stack of boxes filled with crystals. They were sturdy enough to hold her weight. She settled there, continuing to down the tea. Ce Ce watched her as Monique circled the aisle and eased up behind Mrs. Banyon. The entire crew of customers looked on with morbid fascination, but Ce Ce knew they needn't have worried. Monique was in the exact right place to catch the tea glass when Mrs. Banyon dropped it as she slumped backwards against the shelves.

It was cheating, Ce Ce thought, but no way was she letting that woman file that report.

Chapter Twenty-four

Bobbie Faye? Oh, we just *love* her. You know, from a safe distance, of course.

—Contraband Days fans of Bobbie Faye who wish to remain anonymous

When Ce Ce picked up on the private line, Bobbie Faye bounced for joy and nearly overturned the bateau.

"Oh, honey, thank goodness," Ce Ce exclaimed. "Are you okay?"

"I don't have time, Ceece. This cell's gonna die. Have you talked to Cam? Do you know if he's got Stacey or if she's still at school?"

Bobbie Faye definitely did not like that pause before Ce Ce answered. Because during the pause, she could hear someone in the background saying, "I think she's dead."

"*Who's* dead? Please God, not Stacey!"

"No, no, honey," Ce Ce said. Then Bobbie Faye heard her muffle the phone with her hand and say to whomever had made the "dead" declaration, "She's not dead. She's just out for a little while."

"Who's *out*?" Bobbie Faye asked.

Adrenaline had just hit a line drive up her spine to the base of her brain, smacking her with all its force, as if to say, "You think it was bad earlier? That was just the preliminary round. Watch *this*."

"Um," Ce Ce stalled. "See, honey, this Social Services woman waltzed in here with a really bad attitude, and—"

"*You killed the Social Services woman?*" Bobbie Faye shrieked, leaping up, forcing Trevor to stop the trolling motor and grab her before she fell in the bayou.

She heard Adrenaline's maniacal laugh as Trevor forced her to sit.

"No no no, honey, she's not dead. She's just a little bit unconscious."

"What do you mean, a *little bit* unconscious? How can someone only be a little bit unconscious?"

"Well, it's better than a whole lot dead. Besides, the FBI is supposed to have Stacey in protective custody, only she said they don't and now she thinks we squirreled Stacey away from her and she was about to have us arrested and make sure that you never saw Stacey again, ever. I couldn't let her do that."

"Ceece!" Bobbie Faye said, processing Ce Ce's words a helluva lot slower than she ought. "What do you mean, she thinks you squirreled Stacey away?"

Ce Ce didn't answer. All of the phone's background noises had stopped as well. Bobbie Faye drew the cell away from her ear and realized she didn't have any service.

This was so beyond not funny; she could hear Adrenaline opening the door and welcoming Hysteria and Abject Fear to the party. Her head was spinning, her arms were going to fall off her body, and she was going to shoot into the heavens like some spastic Roman candle with its' trajectory all wonky.

"Breathe," Trevor instructed.

Fat lot of fucking good that was going to do.

C am's phone vibrated that he had a voice mail. How the hell did he have a signal up here? He peered out the window of the police helicopter, scanning until he saw the cellular tower. Ah. He instructed the pilot to hover near it and when he dialed in his password, Bobbie Faye's quietly panicked voice shocked him.

"Cam, I know you're out there, chasing me. I know you're

pissed. I don't have time to explain. I don't have much battery left on this phone. I need you to go get Stacey from school. Just you, nobody else. Get her somewhere safe."

There was a pause, and Cam could picture her closing her eyes, squeezing the phone.

"Please, Cam. I'll explain later. I promise. I wouldn't put you on the spot like this, and I know you're all Rambo about hunting me down and arresting me, but there's nobody else I trust to do this. I— well. Thank you."

The phone went dead.

He was trapped in this hamster cage, not able to get up and pace or hit anything or . . . sonofabitch, it was just like Bobbie Faye to find a new, deeper way to torture him when he didn't think it could be done. Cam forced himself to breathe calmly in and then out again to keep from actively seething and ripping his phone in half.

She didn't have the decency to tell him what kind of trouble she was in, the common sense to let him know where she was so he could pull her out of danger. Sure, he'd have to arrest her, but she had to know there was a veritable army after her now, and the odds in her favor had tanked so long ago, he suspected the bookies had closed the bets.

What in the hell was she thinking? What had crawled up her ass and lit a fire? Idiotic freaking woman.

He checked the caller ID and the number was blocked. Sonofabitch. He listened to the message twice more, trying to pick up on the nuances of the background noises, and got mostly static. Maybe Jason could wash it through the computer and pick up something.

He called Benoit. "Anything else on the family?" he asked, and he heard Benoit swear.

"It ain't tidy, that's for sure," Benoit said. "We've canvassed every bar in the area of those you named. Couple of people remember seeing Roy last night barhopping, but so far, no definitive word on the last place seen or who he might have been with. We're expanding the search grid."

"What about Stacey, the niece?"

"Yeah, that's weird. School teacher says the FBI picked her up a little while ago and put her in protective custody."

Oh, hell. Cam remembered the recorded Fibbie conversation Jason had played for him. They weren't saying Bobbie Faye's "piece." They were saying "niece."

Why in the hell would they have preemptively put her niece under protective custody, but leave the sister in the rehab center?

"Call them, find out where they've taken her, and make sure she's safe."

He was trying not to conjure the image he had of Stacey's fourth birthday, when he'd shown up with a big stuffed green dog and Stacey dove for him, calling him "Uncle Cam." He was not going to think of that hug or the cake in her hair or the big toothy smile. He was not going to get a huge lump in his chest from fear, he was not going to forget how to breathe.

He hung up with Benoit and motioned for the pilot to continue his forward sweep of the area.

He wasn't sure if he was furious with Bobbie Faye for not telling him where she was or what was wrong . . . or relieved she trusted him with something so important.

Or . . .

Had she? Would she stoop so low as to use her own niece to pull him off the chase?

She had to have known that it was the one thing he'd do for her. She had to have known that tremor in her voice would remind him of the times she was really vulnerable, really needed him. Just him. Even though she had a hard time admitting it, he'd drop everything and run to help when she was like that.

Fucking brilliant.

God, he hated that woman.

·   ·   ·

Y ou should eat something," Trevor said, and Bobbie Faye stared at him for a full minute before the freak-out party in her brain subsided enough to register his words.

"I'm sure as hell not carting you out of here if you faint."

She didn't move. Her arms were heavy. How'd they get so heavy? When did she gain two wobbly elephant trunks for arms?

"In your purse. Remember? From the store?" he said, brows knitted together.

She couldn't decide if his scowl was from annoyance or concern.

"You're in shock," he continued when she hadn't moved. "Eat something chocolate—it'll help."

The words slowly connected to meaning, which finally eased into action, and she dug into her purse, pulling out a bottled water and a chocolate bar.

"Can you hand me a soda?" he asked, and she frowned, digging in her purse for a Coke and an energy bar for him.

Soda.

Okay, so he's not from the South. Especially not from Louisiana, where everything was a "Coke" first, and then the next statement would designate the brand. So he was a stranger, not even a native. She might have lessened some of her suspicions of him helping her if he was just a local, one who'd revered the Contraband Days Festival and her mom, the way Marcel and Alex's guys did. Definitely a big fat check mark in the worry column.

She nibbled her chocolate bar.

Her mind swerved from his odd word choice to the image of where they'd purchased the Cokes. Maybe it was the fact that Trevor had mentioned the store, or maybe it was simply that she finally had a moment of quiet to reflect, but the surveillance images of the bank heist that old man Earl had been playing on his laptop looped on a permanent replay behind her closed eyes.

Watching the footage was as close to an out-of-body experience as she hoped to get; seeing it had given her a weightless, disconnected feeling, floating above her own "self" in the lobby.

The images circled again, resetting and starting over, pummeling her senses. Shouldn't she be doing something more productive? She nibbled on the chocolate bar, squeezing her eyes shut, tuning out Trevor, the boat, the world, hoping to find some sort of balance, some blank peace.

And yet, the images moved forward, oblivious to her willpower to stop. There was the nerdy guy, fiddling with his windbreaker, adjusting his collar over and over, rubbing his hands through his hair. It was weird how he was so nervous. She'd thought it had just been her presence, her boisterousness, which had made him so anxious, but when she'd disappeared into the safe-deposit box area, the lobby camera caught him fidgeting and twitching. Then he let a few people up ahead of him, which was just . . . odd. You'd think he'd want to get out of there faster, seeing how he planned to rob the bank. Why let people ahead and prolong it?

This was not helping.

The day's events jumbled together, blending into psychotropic trippy rubble. She was beginning to think she was pathologically incapable of thinking clear thoughts, of being calm in the face of danger. Maybe you only get a certain quota of clearheaded thinking in times of crisis, and she'd used up her allotment. Probably had used it up by age eleven.

It was odd, her thoughts rubberbanded back, just how the nerdy guy had kept looking off toward the safe-deposit room while she was out of the lobby. Why would he keep looking in her direction? Why did he wait until she'd walked out of the safe-deposit room to toss the stick-up note onto the teller's counter?

The beginning of understanding closed in on her, and she focused on that thought. Everything went quiet. The birds and crickets and bullfrogs and wind and trolling motor all ceased as far as she knew. The sun dimmed except for the small pinpoint where she stared into the swamp forests ahead.

He wasn't there to rob the bank.

He was there to rob her of the tiara.

Which meant that someone was trying to double-cross the guy who had Roy.

Chapter Twenty-five

You are insane. We have more than eight hundred miles of pipeline up here,
for crying out loud. Do you know what she could *do* to us? Forget it.

—the governor of Alaska to a plea from the governor of Louisiana

obbie Faye stared down at her candy bar, soft from the heat
and squished to an hourglass shape from her grip.

"Are you okay?"

She looked at Trevor, blank. Unable to register his comment.

"You just turned so pale, I think you went translucent."

"I'm fine."

Someone was double-crossing the bad guys. Someone else
wanted that tiara, and knew where she would be. She had no idea
why they wanted it—that was just as confusing. This nerdy guy had
helpers in the bank. College kids? Right. Could there have been
others in the bank in on the robbery? Or out in the parking lot?

She assessed Trevor, who was consulting the map Marcel had
drawn. Everything about how he reacted to the situation today was
too . . . convenient.

So did that mean that everything about him was wrong?

The frozen surveillance image of him driving his truck as they
sped from the bank flared in her mind, a lit match waiting for a
place to burn.

"What made you help me today?" she asked.

He frowned, giving her the "are you an idiot?" eyeroll.

"Seriously. We both know you could have kicked me out of your truck whenever you wanted. You disarmed me in a split second."

"First," he said, "I *tried* to kick you out of my truck, and then people were shooting at us. I have a real aversion to being shot at, and it was easier to keep going. Once we hit the lake, I figured I was all in, whether I liked it or not."

"Bullshit." She cocked her head, waiting. When he didn't answer, she gave him the stink eye, the evil look she'd mastered when she wanted to convey to Roy that she hadn't believed excuses one through twelve he'd given her for skipping school.

"Look, Bobbie Faye. I'm sure the bank's exterior surveillance cameras caught you getting into my truck and us taking off together. When you said that they thought you'd robbed the bank, I knew they would assume I was an accessory. I figured I'd better help you get whatever was stolen back and catch the real thieves to clear my own name."

"Hmph." She looked away from him, wondering how much of that she really bought, and honestly not knowing the answer. Everything he said made sense, and he said it with just the right amount of annoyance and earnestness to be believable. In fact, it was such a perfect mix, he was so unflapped throughout this whole ordeal, he said everything so matter-of-factly, he couldn't possibly be telling the truth.

"Or," he said, giving her a wolfish grin, "maybe I just liked your shirt."

She looked down at the remaining SHUCK ME, SUCK ME part of her T-shirt and a blush rose from her chest and warmed her face and man, it was a bitch not to have something handy to hurl at his head. She glared at him and he grinned that freakishly sexy grin, and she *really* wanted to bop him, because she'd had more than she could stand of stupid come-on lines and dumb-ass trying-to-get-laid grins in her lifetime, and then she saw by the warmth in his eyes that he meant it. There was something genuine there, something real and sexy as hell, and a connection between them that her body was whooping in delight over, and damn, but a man who could make her feel hot and bothered on a nightmare day like this maybe should get a couple of points in the benefit-of-the-doubt column, in spite of her suspicions.

"I think I liked you better when I hated you," she said, and Trevor laughed.

C am calculated that it had been a little over four hours since he'd seen Bobbie Faye on the bank of the lake, and three hours since the rig had blown. There were a helluva lot of places she could get to in three hours. Especially in south Louisiana. Lake Charles emptied into small bayous, some of which wound toward Lake Prien, and then, south of that, there were more bayous and canals, and then Moss Lake, and ultimately Calcasieu Lake, which had shipping channels and bayous winding to the Gulf.

His radio headset crackled and Benoit popped on the line.

"Any news?" Cam asked.

"If by 'any' you want to include every crank phone call we've had sighting Bobbie Faye, then yeah."

"How many?"

"So far, Collier just counted thirty-six hundred, seventy-three. From all over the state. Either she's cloned herself—"

"For the love of God, don't even suggest that." Cam motioned the pilot to push on in a southerly sweep. "Any word from the roadblocks?"

"Yeah. You're a sonofabitch for ordering it during the festival, according to a few festival-goers. That one's from my mom, in case you're curious."

"Great."

"No word on the brother, yet," Benoit continued, "or the niece. The FBI are stonewalling me. The only good news is we have a fraction of news footage from when the FBI picked the kid up from school. Definitely a guy in a suit, but no one got them getting in a car. There wasn't much press there at that point yet—that's not the major flashpoint, I guess, so it was more second-unit types. They weren't allowed on school property and had set up in front of the school and he must have parked in the back. We're sending this over to the FBI now to make sure they identify him as one of their own."

"But right now, they're not saying whether or not they even have her?"

"Right. As for Roy, a couple of drunks think they saw him leave with a Dora Bernadina, who is married to a roughneck, Jimmy. Jimmy's been out on the rigs for the last month, but came in this morning, and nobody's seen him or Dora and they're not answering their door."

"Get a warrant, get in there, make sure they're not there. Check to see if they've gotten on a plane or bus or whatever."

While they talked, the pilot swooped low and Cam surveyed the canals and woods for any sign of Bobbie Faye. This wasn't a needle in a haystack. This was a molecule in the ocean.

He realized Benoit had said something, and he focused again.

"I said," Benoit repeated, "you should probably know the Professor's acting all weird and shit."

"How weird?"

"Freaking out. Saying he doesn't want his attorney, babbling all sorts of strange conspiracy theories; something about Napoleon figured in one which never did make sense. He's either scared out of his mind or losing it."

"You put him in that private cell?"

"Yeah. Vicari makes a pass in there every fifteen minutes."

"Can you interview him again? Without Dellago?"

"I'll try, if he'll just quit crying. And assuming Dellago isn't still hovering around here."

Ce Ce's positive energy matrix was falling apart.

"People, if you have to go to the bathroom, you'll have to wait until I put someone in your place. Do not . . . I repeat, do not leave your position. You have no idea how much damage you can do."

She looked around the room and knew she was going to have to go for more drastic measures than the energy matrix. They'd been at it for several hours, eating and going to the bathroom in shifts, and still there was no good news. Nothing about Bobbie Faye. Nothing about Stacey. The customers were trying their best, but the cold hard truth was, they were tired of staying in one position for such a long period at a time.

Of course, there was the extra little helping of crazy with a now-unconscious Social Services worker.

"Ce Ce," Monique said, as she took the woman's two legs. "Next time you decide to knock someone out, pick someone smaller."

Ce Ce grunted, having taken the woman's arms. The social worker easily weighed two hundred pounds, and though Ce Ce was fairly well over that mark herself, she hadn't fully appreciated just how much work moving the woman might be. They dragged her to the back supply room where Ce Ce had a cot they could heft her onto, assuming they had any heft left by the time they got back there.

"I think you've been around Bobbie Faye too long," Monique continued. "You think this is normal."

She might have a point with that one.

"What are you going to do with her when she wakes up?"

Ce Ce was wondering if she'd knocked out the wrong person.

"I don't know, honey," she snapped at Monique. "Since she drank almost the whole glass, I'm just hoping she wakes up."

Monique jerked her reddish eyebrows up at Ce Ce.

"Well, honey, you never know how this stuff is going to affect some people. I thought for sure she'd have been out cold by the second swallow. I've never had someone make it through a whole glass before."

"I'm hoping you have a plan."

"Right now, Monique, I've got two hands full of social worker, fifty customers out there doing the pee pee dance because I can't substitute people fast enough, and my girl is running around in the swamps, destroying half of the state. I haven't quite worked out a full plan yet. Give me a minute."

Chapter Twenty-six

Well, ma'am, that $300 warranty does cover all acts of God, but we couldn't possibly afford to cover acts of Bobbie Faye. I'm sorry.

—*salesperson Amanda Eschete to customer*

The helicopter's radio crackled in Cam's headset. He heard Jason's call sign announce and then Jason's excited patter. "Head to Bobbie Faye's birthday, and I can give you some news."

And with that, the radio went silent again. Cam stared at the radio and suddenly guessed that Jason had looked up Bobbie Faye's birthday—June eleven—so Cam flipped to channel eleven.

"I caught something else," Jason said once Cam arrived at the channel and hailed him. "They've ordered an airboat."

"The Fibbies?"

"Yep," Jason said, his voice lowering. "I heard they were putting down at Sabine's Landing."

Sabine's was at the northern tip of Calcasieu Lake, and about three miles southwest of where Cam was currently searching. He closed his eyes, picturing the vast lake that overlapped the Sabine National Forest and the countless rivers and bayous which spilled out into the Gulf. To the east, there were more rivers and then another large lake, appropriately named Grand Lake. He remembered his childhood, sitting in a bateau, fishing back in hidden canals. Never seeing a soul for hours and sometimes days at a time.

If the Fibbies found them first in that vast, nearly uninhabited sprawl of lakes and woods and bayous, they could put a bullet in Bobbie Fay and Cormier and no one would ever know where to find them.

"Where's Ol' Landry?" he asked Jason, and he heard a slight inhalation.

"You're not thinking of sending him after them, are you?"

"You know a better tracker in that area with his own airboat?"

"But Cam. He can't stand the police."

"He hates the Feds more, especially in his backyard."

"Well, he hates Bobbie Faye more than the Feds."

True. Old Man Landry was something of a legend in the swamps. Some people said he had the *eye*. That he could see things that weren't possible to see. Cam believed there was something more logical behind it. (He didn't listen to the rumors of magical insight.) He had seen the old crank work firsthand and concluded his so-called *eye* was born of a well-honed ability to observe little details, to ferret out what others weren't saying by tuning into their body language. Cam had hunted and fished a couple of times with the old man, which hadn't been easy, but Cam had been determined to learn from the best. On his good days, Landry was as welcoming as a porcupine wearing a vest of rusty razor blades.

He never had any good days.

Jason broke into Cam's thoughts, asking, "Did you ever find out why she shot him? Or why he didn't press charges?"

"No. But find him. Tell him what's up and ask him to track the Feds and keep me posted."

"And Bobbie Faye?"

Was this going to be one of the dumbest things he ever did? Or the smartest? No clue. He knew that Landry had trapped and tracked in places around Calcasieu Lake where few people had ever ventured. The man knew that area better than God.

"He owes me. Tell him not hurting Bobbie Faye would even us up."

"Is he big on paying his debts?" Jason asked, and Cam knew it was a question born more from liking Bobbie Faye than it was questioning Cam's authority or judgment.

"I have no idea."

Bobbie Faye found herself amused at the look of surprise on Trevor's face.

"I promise. It's not even worth two whole dollars."

"You called it a tiara when you were on the phone."

"Right," she said. "It's just one of those family jokes, handed down from mother to daughter. I don't even know how far back it went, but one of my great-great-granddads made it for his daughter and it's just been passed down."

"So it has no jewels, no gold, no silver?"

"Nada. It's actually kinda rusty. I need to have it sealed."

She watched him process this information, struggling to hide his incredulity. Was he disappointed? For himself? Or just stunned, as she'd been, at what felt like a completely insane task?

"I know," she said, before he could formulate a question, "it makes no sense."

"Maybe it has some sort of historical value?"

"I don't see how," she said, and they fell silent. The trolling motor hummed as they eased through the shallow bayou.

"Why go to that sort of trouble, then?" she asked him. "I mean, if it's simply historical significance, the kidnapper could have waited until I wore it at the parade and swiped it then. It's not like I'm sporting bodyguards for the thing while I'm moving through the crowds. It would have been much simpler."

"True," he mused, easing them around rotted tree stumps protruding from the still, black water.

"So something made getting it right now a priority. Since the kidnapper wanted me to bring it to him, and there was someone in the bank waiting to rob me of it—"

"Wait," he interrupted. "You didn't say before they were specifically waiting for you."

"I hadn't had a chance to think about it. But I think they were. Which probably means some sort of double-cross."

She turned to look out over the woods they were slowly passing. Her purse was still in her lap, and she'd eased her hand in there as she'd been talking, resting her palm on the Glock he'd given her earlier, one of the ones taken from Alex's storage shed. If he was a part of the double-cross, would he try to dump her now? Or wait until he had the tiara?

"You don't need to shoot me, Bobbie Faye," he said, low, quiet, the words falling softly between them. "I'm not after the tiara."

"Did I just say what I was thinking out loud? Or do you have some sort of microphone in my head? Because, seriously, it's pretty messy in there and I'd like to clean up first if there are going to be visitors."

He shook his head. She wasn't sure if it was from amusement or confusion. Still, she held the gun.

"No, it was a natural thing for you to think. I'm here, I'm helping you, and you know I could have left at any point, especially after the truck went into the lake. So I don't blame you." He watched her a moment. "Of course, that's what any good criminal mind would do right now, try to gain your trust, so you're just going to have to decide if I'm here because I'm trying to help you or because I'm double-crossing you."

She considered his calm demeanor, the way he looked her directly in the eyes, the way he never faltered in the tedious navigation of the bayou in spite of the fact that his life was on the line.

His was the type of calm born from being in too many dangerous situations.

"What made you get a divorce?" she asked him.

His brow furrowed at the non sequitur.

"Why?"

"Curiosity."

"I was an ass," he shrugged. "Then I was never home. Bad combination."

She sank her chin into her hand, studying him.

"Why'd you ask that?"

"To see if you'd tell me the truth," she said.

"And did I?"

"No," she said, giving him a small smile. She put her purse beside her on the bateau's seat. "But for the right reason."

It was the first time during the whole frenzy of the day that she'd seen him look genuinely, utterly confused. She shrugged, refusing to clarify. She could easily be wrong about him. Was it instinct guiding her? Could she even trust instinct? Did a man who still had enough respect for an ex-wife to shoulder the blame have something of honor in him? She met his gaze, seeing the curiosity simmering there. Heat. She'd intrigued him, she knew. What she also knew was that Trevor was holding the map to where the geeky boys were holed up with the tiara. He didn't need her to get to the tiara now, and yet, he hadn't made a move to get rid of her.

Yet, she reminded herself, keeping her purse, and gun, very close.

Roy gaped at the TV screens in Vincent's office. Two of the networks were actively tracking Bobbie Faye "sightings" and a third network was currently interviewing her ninth-grade teacher.

"Oh, she always was a firecracker, that one," the elderly Mrs. Boudreaux drawled, squinting through her bifocals at the camera. "It's not true, though, that she blew up the chemistry lab just by walking past it. She had actually been inside that day, doing her lab experiment just like everyone else. It wasn't her fault those chemicals were mislabeled, bless her heart."

Out of the corner of his eye, Roy caught a too-satisfied smile emanating from Vincent. Roy looked his direction and then followed

Vincent's gaze to the center console. A male anchor, with a badly dyed toupee, yammered, excited.

"And so far, no word on the whereabouts of the niece. In other news, we now have reports that the social worker sent out to investigate Ms. Sumrall's capacity of being a fit guardian for this niece has now also vanished. There have been allegations that Ms. Sumrall may be trying to get out of the country with the niece and there is speculation that the social worker has met with some unfortunate end as a result."

"Holy shit," Roy said, and instantly regretted gaining the attention of Vincent, Eddie, and The Mountain.

"Have no fear, dear Roy," Vincent purred. "Bobbie Faye doesn't have Stacey. I do."

Chapter Twenty-seven

Bobbie Faye tracking charts now available. Red Cross strongly suggests bringing all children and small animals inside for protection. Please stay tuned for frequent coordinate updates.

—*news ticker scrolling across Channel 2 News*

Cam rappelled down a rope from the helicopter onto the airboat waiting below him. The muggy heat from the humid spring day, coupled with the utter stillness of the bayou, smothered him as much as if he'd slid down into an oven. He dropped the last couple of feet, his boots thumping against the airboat's deck, rocking the craft and the milky-eyed man sitting in the driver's seat. The helo moved away, the wind rippling the limbs on the trees and the tall grasses at the bayou's edge.

He took a moment to assess the man. He hadn't seen him in a couple of years, but he looked pretty much the same. The skinny old bastard was barely more than sinew and bone, baked skin taut and suntanned to a deep hickory, leather face lined with so many wrinkles, he was practically an ad for sunscreen manufacturers world 'round. But it was the cataracts that caught everyone's attention. That, and the fact that the man could barely see, but could navigate and find anything he wanted to find.

"You found the FBI?" Cam shouted over the loud thrum of the engine.

Old Man Landry revved the airboat's giant fan, skimming the boat across the top of the swamp. "You ain't looking for the FBI, boy," the old man snarled. "You're looking for that crazy-ass, snake-bit girl."

"And you know where she is?"

The old man gave him a dismissive shrug.

"What makes you think you can find her?"

"I find things, boy. You know that. You cracked your head lately? Or maybe Bobbie Faye cracked it for you?"

"What the hell d'you mean by that?"

"Nothin', you idiot. But when you get ready to find that ring you done thrown in the lake there by your house, you give me a call."

Sonofabitch. Cam reined in his expression, grinding his teeth until his jaw hurt. Benoit was the only person who knew where the ring was, and Benoit wasn't the type to gossip. He liked holding as many cards as he could, so the old man either had a spy or . . . Cam didn't want to contemplate the "or."

"Have you seen her?" Cam asked, pissed that he was forced to do all of the asking. Landry delighted in control. The old man tapped his head by way of an answer and Cam cursed.

He needed to know that he wasn't just going to find her body. He needed to prepare what the hell he was going to tell the Captain. It really wasn't that he needed to have the feeling back in his hands, needed to stop the throbbing behind his eyes, needed to be able to pull in a deep breath and feel like his lungs weren't on fire.

"You never did tell me why she shot you," Cam said.

"None of your damned business, boy," the old man snarled.

"You know it is."

"Know nothing of the sort. You're fishing in a dry hole, there, boy, and you should know better 'n that by now."

"You're a bastard, you know that?" Cam said, finally reaching his limit.

"Yep. Heard that a time or two, but usually from people prettier 'n you." The old man turned his milky-white eyes to Cam. "Ask the question you want to ask or don't bother me."

"Is she alive?"

"Yep. Pissed as hell, as usual."

"How do you know?"

The old bastard just tapped his head again.

"I'm beginning to see why Bobbie Faye shot you."

The old man barked with laughter, wiping away tears.

"Son, you don't know the half of it."

Then he clammed up again, and Cam wondered if he'd ever know the real story between the old man and Bobbie Faye.

They rode awhile in the airboat, going deeper southeast into the swamps, and eventually the old man slowed the boat and the roar of the engine dropped to a tolerable level. He navigated through a small bayou, and every cell in Cam itched to grab the controls and just hurry the hell up.

"When she was a little girl," Old Landry said, startling Cam, "she lost her brother once at the park."

"You knew Bobbie Faye when she was kid?"

"Boy, shut up and listen."

Cam seethed, but did as he was told.

The old man continued. "Like I was saying, she lost her brother. Her mamma was off—drinking, I s'pose, wasted—and it was up to Bobbie Faye to look after Roy. I think she was maybe ten.

"Well, after looking all over the park, she saw a bunch of boys with a tree house fort in the neighboring woods, and they were dressed up as cowboys. They were hootin' and hollerin' and acting like they'd won something. She heard one of 'em braggin' 'bout capturing an Indian and they had him in the fort, so she went over to see what they were up to."

"Roy," Cam said, and the old man nodded.

"Now, all these boys, they were bigger 'n her, and they laughed when she told 'em to let her little brother go. The biggest one, 'bout twice her size, stepped up and shoved her and told her to go away and go cry like a little girl somewhere else."

Cam flinched. He felt sorry for that boy, somehow.

"Yep, she beat the ever lovin' crap outta him. Made him eat dirt. Actual dirt." He laughed. "And the next one that stepped up, too.

The rest of 'em ran off, an' she got Roy outta there."

"So you're saying she's going to be fine."

"No, boy. You really need to learn to shut up. I'm sayin' Bobbie Faye thinks she ain't got nobody but herself to fight what she's up against and she thinks she can win with just sheer force of will."

He turned to look at Cam again. "She can't, this time, boy. Only she don't know it, yet."

Cam would have asked him how he knew, but the man wasn't going to tell him. It was the most Cam had ever heard the old man say in all of the years he'd known him.

"Why the hell do you care? She shot you, remember?"

"Yep. She did. Good shot, too. She coulda killed me if she'd wanted to."

"So why are you helping her? Or are you?"

The old man paused, and Cam saw something of regret pass across his face, then disappear.

"Let's just say, I have a debt to pay, boy, that you know nothing about. And it ain't paid yet. I'd like her to stay alive long enough not to owe her."

The old man slowed the airboat. They were navigating a difficult area where old logs bobbed just below the surface of the water; the green moss covering the trunks blended them in with the dark water.

Cam started to ask the old man if they were close, but the old man put his fingers to his lips to hush him.

While they wound through the bayou, Cam checked the portable GPS he'd taken from the helicopter. Still working, sending off a beacon. He'd punch in a code as soon as he knew he was close and get the SWAT team in there.

He tried not to think about the fact that the old man didn't believe Bobbie Faye could win against the odds this time. If it were anyone else, Cam wouldn't have paid it any attention. He stretched his arms, trying to get the feeling back, trying to breathe.

This wasn't a good day for breathing.

.   .   .

Bobbie Faye had never seen a more beautiful sight in her entire life than the one before her: about a hundred yards away, on a peninsula jutting out where their bayou met a larger canal, was a small shack. It looked out of place in this setting, with its gunmetal gray steel siding, its flaking, rusted tin roof, and industrial windows with security bars. What made it beautiful was that this was the "X" on Marcel's map.

The geeky boys were supposed to be inside.

Finally. Something had to go right, for once that day. Not even *she* had this much bad luck.

Trevor pulled their bateau over to the bank of the small canal.

"What the hell do you think you're doing?" she asked as he climbed out to tie their boat off to a tree.

"Let's just ease up on them, okay? Wouldn't hurt to be safe."

"Out here in the middle of freaking nowhere? What are they going to do? Air guitar me to death?"

She didn't want to have to trudge all the damned way to the shack, through the muddy water along the bank of the bayou. And she knew Trevor well enough at this point to know they weren't going to walk up on the land and leave footprints. No, that would have been *much* too easy.

She might as well have been talking to the fish, for all of the good it did her. Trevor had already slung the gunrunner's satchel-o'-goods over his shoulders, pulled out his gun, and headed toward the shack.

"Next time," she muttered to herself, "kidnap someone a lot less bossy."

Trevor led the way to the shack, crossing onto the peninsula only when grassy undergrowth would prevent them from leaving footprints. There was no way to see into the windows past the heavy black-out curtains so he was being careful. Extra careful with a dollop of pokey on top.

Trevor eased toward the building, sweeping a glance across the ground, pausing to search for other footprints, carefully moving from tree to tree with such stealth he probably could have tiptoed up to a big white-tailed buck and hung bells on the horns.

It was driving her fucking insane.

She (barely) resisted the urge to ram her gun into his ribs to hurry him along.

"Will you quit being all 007 and just go the hell in there?" she whispered, unable to disguise the snarl edging her voice.

"We need to be careful," Trevor whispered back.

"Why? Because they might start chanting algorithms? I think we can take 'em."

They could hear the electronic pinging and whirring and clangy music of some sort of electronic game.

"See?" she said. "They're don't know we're out here. Let's go."

She started to rise from their crouched position behind a tree and he snagged her jeans and pulled her back.

"We need to go slow," he bossed. "You have no clue what's in there. You have to have patience for this sort of thing."

"Buddy, Patience hopped a bus a few hours ago and is slinging back margaritas with a bunch of sailors in some bar on the west coast by now."

She marched over to the shack before Trevor had a chance to pull her back again, then she kicked the door in as Trevor rushed to cover her. He was back to muttering again, something about hog-tying and women, but she ignored him as she went in low, her gun drawn, forcing Trevor to go in high.

As their eyes adjusted to the dim interior, she saw a man sitting in a chair, twirling the tiara. A man whose shape looked a little too familiar, and when her eyes fully adjusted to the dim light in the room, she damned near shot him on the spot.

"Alex! What the hell are you doing here?" she shouted, and he laughed.

"Well, now, chere, I realized something after we left you out there. You have something I want, and you're pretty good at weaseling out of giving it back. I knew where you were heading and I knew you needed something of your mamma's, and I figure this must be it. Now, I think, we're even."

"You bastard," she seethed, pointing the gun directly at him.

His eyes narrowed a bit and he nodded to the opposite corner.

There were two of his gunmen there, guns pointed at Bobbie Faye and Trevor. On the floor next to them were the geeky boys, tied up and gagged, both looking like they'd wet their pants.

"See, now, Bobbie Faye. I've got two men over there who ain't a bit from Louisiana, an' you know what that means?" When she didn't answer, he said, "Dat means, chere, that they don't give two shakes if you're Contraband Days Queen or not."

Bobbie Faye glanced at Trevor, and the second she spun back to Alex, storming over to him, Trevor put himself between her and Alex's gunmen. She stopped just two feet outside of Alex's reach.

"Give me the tiara, Alex."

"Not 'til I get my stuff."

"Goddamnit Alex," she shouted, "I don't fucking have time for this!"

She was breathing hard, itching to pull the trigger just for the satisfaction of wiping the smug-ass smile from his face.

"She's a pretty good shot," Trevor said from behind her. "Even if your guys get me first, she'll still nail you."

"You're the idiot who gave her the gun. Like I'm gonna listen to you. Who the hell you think taught her to shoot?"

"I swear to God, Alex. Not. Today."

"Why don't you just give Alex his stuff back," Trevor suggested, and she hated that quiet reasonable tone with every single cell in her entire being and she very nearly shot him just for being so fucking helpful.

"I don't know where his stuff is."

"Au revoir, chere. You can have this tiara when I get my stuff."

"Alex," she said, flush with fury and heat, "I don't know where your stuff is! My trailer flooded this morning and the water wouldn't quit and I got Stacey out and then the trailer kept flooding and my electricity got turned off which is when Roy called to say he was kidnapped and then the trailer fell off its piers and I don't fucking know where your *love poems* are! So give me Mamma's goddamned tiara *right now* or I'll make sure every single fucking one of them gets *published*."

Alex froze, breathing hard, his face red, and she didn't know if he was blushing or furious, and honestly, she didn't care.

The guards at the opposite corner started creeping toward the door, looking all the world like they were both embarrassed for their boss and aware this was something they really weren't supposed to know. Marcel entered the room from what looked like a closet door and started chuckling until Alex raked him with a heated, furious gaze.

"Sorry, boss," Marcel said, trying hard to stifle the laugh. "I just . . . you know. Luuuuuuuuuuve poems."

"Say another word and you're dead," Alex fumed.

"*Poems?*" Trevor asked, incredulous. He swept a look from Bobbie Faye to Alex and back again. "You're kidding me? This is about *love poems*?"

They were so not kidding. Bobbie Faye and Alex each tried to bore holes into the other with laser-intensity stares.

"They're mine, anyway," she announced, never moving her gaze from Alex. "You wrote them for me. You can't have them back."

Trevor lowered his gun, arching an eyebrow at her, watching her with an intensity she couldn't quite define. "You're still in love with this guy," he said, as if suddenly understanding.

"Hell, no," she and Alex said in unison, and then glared at each other again.

"No," she repeated, evenly this time. "I had sense enough to get off that bus to Hell a long time ago." She glanced at Trevor. "But they're very nice poems. They could be on Hallmark cards."

Alex flinched so hard she thought for a second she'd actually shot him.

"Bobbie Faye," he said, strained. "Do you have any idea how much poetry *pays*? I'm a gunrunner now. I have a reputation to up-hold!"

"Uh, boss?" a guard said, and Alex snapped around to him.

"One word," Alex said, "and you're both dead."

"Uh, no, boss. Not that. This," he said, indicating something outside the window.

Chapter Twenty-eight

Oh, we always check the bobbiefaye.com site for a travel advisory so we know which end of the state is safe for day trips.

—frequent tourists Danette, Joy, and Michael
(last names withheld at their request)

Cam could see the shack right where Old Landry had told him it would be, set on an odd little vee of land where two bayous joined. It was just like the old man to dump him off, claim his debt to Cam was paid, rev the airboat up, and scram out of the bayou, leaving Cam there with not much more than his gun and the GPS unit he'd grabbed earlier. It wasn't cowardice. He'd seen the man handle a bar fight against four men half his age, and they all ended up in the hospital and he didn't have a single scratch. No, Landry just didn't want to be anywhere near Bobbie Faye.

One of these days, Cam was going to have to find out what the hell happened when Bobbie Faye shot the old bastard.

After triggering the GPS, signaling his SWAT team, he crouched and absorbed the sounds and smells of the swamp, noting the distinct absence of birds cawing and the complete lack of humming chirps and croaks from crickets and frogs, a sure sign someone had recently passed through the area. He scanned the ground and tree trunks for any clue. It didn't take but a few minutes to spy a heel print from Bobbie Faye's boot, noting the imprint's worn edges which matched those he'd seen back at the lake earlier this morning. He stayed in his crouched position and noticed grass that had been pressed down as someone passed through; it was rising back into place. They couldn't have been here very long, and were most likely still in that shack.

He rocked back on his heels and thought about the man with Bobbie Faye. A man who was wanted by the FBI, who was supposed to be an ace asshole, a cold-blooded killer. And yet, this man had hung with Bobbie Faye all morning and hadn't yet hurt or killed her, and Cam could barely count three men who'd managed that feat, especially when Bobbie Faye was in full-throttle mode. Which made the guy far more dangerous than a rabid bear, because he obviously wanted something. Anyone going to that much trouble to put up with Bobbie Faye at her ballistic worst wanted something *bad,* and anyone *that* desperate worried the hell out of Cam.

He explored the area and found the tiny bateau Bobbie Faye and Trevor must have used; with a swift kick to the belly of the boat, he cracked the wooden hull. At least they wouldn't be able to slip past him and get away. Now all he had to do was get Bobbie Faye out of that shack.

A rabid bear would have been so much better.

Alex peered around the black-out shades and cursed. *"Je su m'en sacré fou!"*

Bobbie Faye scowled at him and Trevor looked from Alex to Bobbie Faye, a question in his eyes.

"That's Cajun. He just said he's a damned fool," she explained. "No huge surprise there."

Alex glared at her, then back out the window. "I should have known better than to chase after little Miss National Disaster."

Trevor replaced Alex at the window and frowned.

"What's wrong?" Bobbie Faye asked.

"Cops."

"Not just cops," Trevor corrected Alex. "FBI."

Bobbie Faye joined him there and squinted through the window. Three guys in military camo moved through the woods toward the shack; each man kept to some sort of cover as they advanced. Bobbie Faye cocked her head as she studied the shorter, blond guy, and then remembered: he was the guy in the Taurus, the one dressed in a nice sports coat. The one who started shooting at them right after the bank robbery.

"How do you know they're FBI?" she asked Trevor.

"Procurement, remember?" he said, shrugging.

"Beautiful! Man, do I ever know how to pick 'em or what?"

"Hey!" Alex said, his expression dark.

Bobbie Faye ignored Alex and smacked Trevor in the chest with her palm. "You bastard. That guy was shooting at *you* back there at the bank robbery!"

"You robbed a bank, chere?" Alex asked, pride suddenly emanating from him. He dove for cover behind his chair as Bobbie Faye whipped around, gun aimed at his head.

"For the last. Freaking. Time. I did *not* rob the bank."

Trevor pushed her hands down, pointing the gun at the floor. "She's a little touchy about that one. It was her first time."

Bobbie Faye glowered at Trevor, who looked . . . amused. They had the FBI, which were somehow connected to *him,* outside the cabin they were holed up in with a bunch of idiot gunrunners and two geeky boys, who, by the smell of it, were having serious bladder control issues, and he was *amused.* She would show him *amused.* Maybe a bullet in his leg would be amusing.

"Bobbie Faye?" a voice shouted from outside. "I know you're in there. Get your skinny ass out here right this minute."

Everyone in the shack paused a moment as a wave of shock crossed Bobbie Faye's face. *Oh, geez. No.* She stomped across the small shack to the window opposite where the FBI were crouched and peered through the black-out drapes.

Sure enough, there was Cam. Gun drawn and ready. Half-hidden by a giant cypress tree, positioned where he'd get a good shot at anyone coming out of the only door. Sonofabitch. She knew he hated her but sweet chocolate baby Jesus, she hadn't counted on him hating her this much, enough to abandon Stacey. The *bastard.*

Trevor leaned in toward her and peered out the window over her shoulder.

Cam shouted again from his spot near the tree. "I mean it Bobbie Faye. Now!"

"Is there any man in this state you haven't pissed off?" Trevor asked.

"Nope," Alex, Marcel, and the guards all said simultaneously.

Trevor checked his watch, pushing fancy timer buttons, then he showed her the countdown: twenty-seven minutes. She caught his expression and understood: he'd set it when she'd gotten the deadline from the kidnapper. Trevor crossed back to the window to the FBI agents spreading out and he turned to Alex.

"I think it's about time you explained just how you got into this cabin."

W hen he saw the Fibbies sneaking around on the other side of the shack, he knew he had to take control. Quick. God only knew what Bobbie Faye was planning inside, but it was his job to bring her in, damnit, and he wasn't letting the FBI get the jump. He expected his SWAT team to show up in the next five minutes; he could hear their helicopter already, the Huey blades chop-chopping the air. One slight plus to a Bobbie Faye day: the chief practically threw SWAT and any resources he wanted at him with a blessing and a prayer.

Zeke moved to a position where Cam could see him and made a cut-throat motion for Cam to cease calling out to Bobbie Faye. Cam, instead, eased out a bit from behind the tree, his weapon held shoulder high, though still covered from smaller trees and shrubs.

Zeke, livid, motioned him to move back to safety.

Cam ignored the asshole agent.

"Bobbie Faye? I know you're in there. I tracked you. Old Landry helped, so you're not going to get to pretend like you don't hear me. Now get your skinny ass out here or I swear to God, I'm—"

He stopped when the door cracked open an inch. Cam looked back at the FBI's positions and stepped a little to his right to put himself between the FBI and whoever opened that door. The last thing he needed was for the FBI to go trigger-happy.

The door eased open a bit more and Bobbie Faye stood there, her own gun drawn on him.

Holy shit, did she ever look pissed.

"I cannot believe you got that old bastard to help you track me."

Cam grinned. Which just pissed her off a helluva lot more. His gloating was short-lived when he got a glimpse of what was going on behind her. Over her shoulder, several men he couldn't see well and didn't recognize moved behind Cormier. A gang? Didn't fit his profile, but they were, from what little he glimpsed, armed. What little Cam could see of Cormier, the man's appearance was every bit ex-military-turned-mercenary: more dangerous than his photo, and well enhanced by the SIG Sauer the man held.

It looked as if Cormier was aiming at Bobbie Faye's back.

When Cam looked into the man's eyes, he sensed an incredible threat. *You fuck with my plans,* the man's eyes seemed to say, *and she's dead.* Cam looked back at Bobbie Faye and wondered if she knew just how much trouble she was in.

"I said," she seethed, "where the hell is Stacey?"

Cam snapped back to the present dilemma, not wanting to admit to himself that he'd just spent a few extra seconds appraising the fact that she was alive, relatively unhurt except for a few scratches and bruises she got running through the swamps, or the way her green eyes lit up the world, or the fact that he was relieved and could breathe, or how that damned half-a-T-shirt was hugging her and those tight jeans had been his favorites and she looked wild and fierce and sexy as hell and what the *world* was he doing? He needed to get a grip.

"Did you even check?" she asked. He noted the near-hysteria just below her cracking surface. He wanted to put his gun down, he wanted to walk over there, he wanted to hold her, he wanted this all to be over and fixed.

There was no way to fix this.

"Of course I checked," he answered her, moving closer to the door. "The FBI has her."

"No! Ce Ce said they're saying they don't have her. Damnit, Cam, I have never, ever asked you for a fucking thing in my whole life."

He fumed. Of course she hadn't. It was one of things they fought about routinely: she never would lean on him. Or trust him.

"Except not to arrest Lori Ann," she amended, so dead pissed, he thought she might actually shoot him, "and now to find Stacey. Do you hate me so much, you'd let her get hurt?"

She looked at him then with a mix of fury and disgust that burned through every nerve like molten lava.

"Don't you dare," he snapped back, feeling a deep kick to his gut. She had to know he'd never put the kid in harm's way. "They're probably just giving Ce Ce the party line; they're not going to admit anything while all of this is still ongoing, Bobbie Faye. What the hell have you gotten yourself mixed up in?"

"That's enough," Cormier said from behind her, grabbing the back of Bobbie Faye's shirt and pulling her back into the cabin. Cam reached forward to pull her back out, when Bobbie Faye was suddenly gone from view, leaving him and Cormier, gun-to-gun. Cormier closed the door down to a couple of inches.

He had a much better shot than Cam.

"You need to back up," Cormier warned. "You want to live? You back way the hell up."

With that, the door slammed shut and the bolts cracked into place, the metal sound echoing in the utterly silent swamp. Cam saw guns aimed at him from the windows framing the door and he stepped back. There were sounds of arguing from inside the shack (no surprise there) and the guns moved away from the window. He wasn't sure if that was a good sign.

Cam backed about thirty yards away to the cover of the larger cypress and water oaks. His SWAT team had arrived and were waiting at that perimeter.

He turned to the SWAT team leader, wanting a plan to take the cabin without killing everyone inside, and without letting the FBI get their hooks into Bobbie Faye or Cormier.

Then the shack exploded.

Chapter Twenty-nine

Dial 1-B-O-B-B-I-E-F-A-Y-E to report a sighting or a disaster. Please note this line is not for making wagers.

—*memo from Homeland Security.*

Cam saw the ball of fire, the metal splintering into a million pieces of shrapnel that impaled in the trees and limbs and dirt in every direction. Black smoke boiled out of what had been the building where Bobbie Faye had stood, alive, breathing, not five minutes earlier. Blood drummed in his ears. He ran for the burning debris, blinking through the acrid smoke and the fire charring the remnants of the siding when members of the SWAT team grabbed him and carried him backwards to safety.

He didn't want to be safe.

He wanted to dig into that debris and pull the burning wood away with his bare hands and find her, because she was there. She was okay, she was breathing, he knew it. Because it simply couldn't be any other way. He was going to find her, and when he finished yelling at her, which might take a few years, he was going to cuff her and put her in the hardiest cell he could find and goddamnit, she was going to stay put and be safe, if it killed everyone else in the process.

Zeke stormed over to Cam, looking ever-so-slightly unhappy. Losing-the-winning-lottery-ticket unhappy. Cam wasn't sure what

Zeke was going on about, and frankly didn't care. He kept staring at the fire, the black remains of the walls and roof, until Zeke got up in his face.

"You're a fucking idiot," Zeke shouted, "letting that bitch get in the way of—"

Before a single thought had time to form, Cam had Zeke by the throat, slamming him up against a tree. The SWAT team pulled him off Zeke and the agent carefully adjusted his fatigues.

"You're lucky I don't feel like doing the paperwork to get you canned," Zeke said, and Cam laughed.

"Like I give a damn," Cam said, turning back to the burning shack. A cold, numb sensation spread from the center of his body outward; he barely heard the SWAT leader use one of their satellite phones and call for CSI.

Bobbie Faye stumbled down a spiraling staircase, the burning shack now two stories above her. The near absolute darkness was disorienting and heaven knew she was already winging it on the coherent-meter, and even though she was attempting rational thought, she was pretty sure she'd already pinged over into the "losing your mind" red zone. She was a little suspicious that sanity had taken a header off a cliff right about the time Alex shuffled them into the hidden staircase and threw the delay-timer for the explosion.

Trevor descended in front of her and she kept a hand on his shoulder for balance, since Alex was always two turns ahead of them and he was the only one with a flashlight. Her mind raced and dashed and slalomed from emotion to emotion, hitting desperation every other step.

How in the hell could Cam have not gone to find Stacey? He loved that kid. Then again, she'd thought he had loved her, too, but that didn't stop him from destroying her sister and niece's life when he arrested Lori Ann. She couldn't wrap her mind around the reality that he hadn't tried to save her niece; that he hated her so much, he'd rather have her in jail than have Stacey alive. There was something crushing in that realization, and she tried to push it to the back of her mind, but it skipped up front again as they kept descending into utter darkness. Some part of her had thought he still loved her. They'd argued horribly, they'd broken up, they'd moved on, right? Right. But something burned in the center of her chest when she realized he was truly over her. Past whatever they had been together. He'd been *home* to her, once upon a time. There was still some little part of her that had thought he'd eventually come to his senses, see how much he'd betrayed her, and want her back. Really want *her*, not some quiet, proper facsimile.

She could hear Alex's voice echo off the curved stairwell, but she couldn't distinguish exactly what he was saying when Trevor responded, "Salt dome? You're kidding. Here?"

They finally spilled onto a level floor, and she fell. Trevor caught her, and held her for a beat longer than she expected. He rubbed the back of her neck gently, and bent, whispering, "You okay?" She nodded against his cheek as a light snapped on, illuminating a large room. It was probably about thirty by forty feet in size, with a long wall of monitors, and two other exits on opposing walls.

Trevor checked his watch.

"Twenty minutes, Bobbie Faye."

"Where the hell are we?"

Alex clicked on monitor after monitor, creating a three-hundred-sixty-degree coverage of the burning shack, obviously from cameras set up in the swamp. She didn't fully grasp how worried she'd been until she saw Cam alive and conferring with his SWAT team. She exhaled when she saw him, then heard Alex's derisive laugh.

"No, Bobbie Faye, I didn't blow up your boyfriend, though that sure as hell was a missed opportunity," Alex said.

"Ex-boyfriend," she corrected, and when she saw the gleam in his eyes, she held her hand up and said, "Don't even start."

"Aw, chere, I was just going to welcome him to the club. Glad he made it in alive. We should have trophies or something."

"I repeat, Alex, where the hell are we?"

"This is a long-forgotten back entrance to a salt dome. The property changed hands a bunch of times and a better access and offices were built on the other end when it was modernized. And since no one was even aware this entrance was here—"

"Damn," she said. "No wonder the Feds never could figure out how you'd get away." She appraised his satisfied grin, knowing all too well how much he prided himself on strategy. "But, you just blew it up. Are you nuts?"

"He did it to buy us time, Bobbie Faye," Trevor said, and she looked from Trevor to Alex. They clearly had come to some sort of appreciation of each other. Which annoyed the living hell out of her.

"If he bought us time, it was a nice side benefit. Alex thinks about Alex first," she said to Trevor, then turned to Alex. "Like, if you blow it up, they won't find evidence of you having been here, and maybe won't even find this room. You could wait a fair amount of time, build another cabin above this, and be right back in business."

"Now, Bobbie Faye, I'm truly hurt that you don't think I have an altruistic heart."

"Hmph. I'd be impressed, Alex, with proof that you actually had a heart at all, much less an altruistic one."

"Ouch, chere. That hurts."

She looked from him around to the other men, and for the first time since she'd arrived at the shack, really focused on the fact that the geeky boys were there, though they were tied up and held between Alex's guards. She drew her gun on the biggest of the geeky boys and said, "I want to know what the hell was going on in that bank, and I want to know now." She reached over and pulled his gag from his mouth, and he flutter-danced, ducking down and wobbled. If spastic motion was a defense against bullets, the kid was going to be amazingly safe.

"I don't know!" he claimed.

"What's your name?"

"Ben."

"Well, Ben, I suggest you look over there at that man." She nodded toward Alex. "He's a gunrunner, kid. He made sure I knew how to shoot. I shoot better than anyone you're ever going to meet, so unless you really want to sing soprano for the rest of your life, you'd better talk."

The kid looked over to Alex, who nodded and said, "Second stupidest thing I ever did."

Bobbie Faye would have sent him a laser hot glare, but she wanted Ben to break, fast, and intimidation was all she had at this point.

"All I know," he gasped, "is that the Professor said we had to be there as backup. He said he had to get something, and he thought someone might try to stop him. We were supposed to be there in case he got into trouble and we were the drivers."

"What did he have to get?" she asked, and the boy shook his head. She aimed the gun at his crotch and he squirmed.

"Honest, lady, I really don't know! He was really weird about the whole thing, and we're just his teaching assistants, and he said we had to help out on a project. We were supposed to get an extra week's pay if we helped! He said if we got separated, to meet up here, and he gave us a map. That's all I know."

They came *here*.

She whipped around, lunging toward Alex when Trevor scooped her up from behind and held her back. He'd also quickly disarmed her, which was really starting to piss her off.

"The cops will hear the gunshot," he said, by way of explanation, when she threw him an acid glare. "Don't kill your lead time."

When she turned back to Alex, he was still shaking his head. "No, Bobbie Faye, no. I told you, I didn't know that's what was going on. I had a call from a buddy who said he knew a guy that might need to hide a while. The pay was good, so I figured, why not? I had no idea it was something involving you."

"What buddy? What guy?"

"You know. A guy. Someone you don't know. Anonymous."

"Why in the hell should I ever believe you, Alex? You lie for a living."

"Bobbie Faye, do you think that ever, in any universe, I'd want to have to deal with you again? I'm seated firmly in the crazy, but not stupid section, chere."

She was about to retort when Trevor turned her back toward the monitors.

"I think we have a bigger problem," he said, pointing out just what Cam was doing.

Chapter Thirty

I'm sorry, Mr. President, but even though you really like the governor of
Louisiana, you cannot drop a civilian behind enemy lines. No sir, not
even if she *could* take out the whole country.

—an anonymous senior aide to the president

C am stared into the canopy of a tree, trying to ground himself in some semblance of reality. The noises from the
crackling of the fire behind him and the smell of burning
metal and charred grass and the chatter from the SWAT team and
the bitching of the FBI and the thumping of the blades as various
news helicopters flew overhead all blended and swirled, becoming a
cacophony, fueling a consuming rage. He needed to do something to
distract himself from the idea of Bobbie Faye being dead, because he
simply wouldn't let it be true.

He stared into the tree. Ignored everyone yammering at him. Ignored his men trying to get him off the site, into the helo, and back
to the station. He was not leaving.

Not until he found her.

And maybe on some subconscious level he couldn't have explained, he knew there was something odd about the tree.

He needed to find a way into this mess, a way to start wrapping
his mind around what just happened. He needed something on

which to focus, and whatever it was that had caught his eye beckoned him, and he couldn't place why or what it was.

Until he suddenly did.

There was a camera mounted up in the tree. It was inconspicuous at first, disguised as a squirrel's nest. He stepped closer and realized he probably wouldn't have ever seen it if the explosion hadn't blown debris against it, knocking some of the "nest" part away, exposing the waterproof box and a housing for the lens. He turned and scoured the trees around the shack, and found an unusual number of squirrel nests at about the exact same height and size, all positioned in a pattern that nearly ringed the shack.

He circled the cinders and crossed the pier until he found a post topped with what had looked like a birdhouse. With a lens where the bird entrance should be.

Huh.

He scanned the burning shack and hope seeped into the corners of his mind, shushing the rage a little, pulsing with the blood rushing through his ears.

Just one boat tied to the pier. He thought back, remembering seeing at least two or three other people behind Bobbie Faye and Trevor, but he thought he'd glimpsed more. Could that many people have arrived here in that small of a boat? Not impossible. Only, there were no other footprints around the cabin except for Bobbie Faye's and Cormier's.

Odd.

So, how did the other people get into the shack?

Maybe he'd imagined other people. Maybe there really were only two others and that boat was plenty big enough.

Maybe he should quit thinking and do something.

He retraced Bobbie Faye and Trevor's footprints to their bateau.

"What are you looking for?" Zeke demanded. "We already know they were in there."

Cam didn't answer him. He didn't know what he was looking for. Just that there was something else here, and he had to find it. And right then, he really wanted to get rid of Zeke. He must have given away his disdain, lost a grip on his normal poker face.

"I'm not leaving," Zeke said, "until I have Cormier in a body bag. *If* he's dead. Or put him in one, if he's not."

Cam held a tight rein on his expression. This contradicted the Captain's information, but that wouldn't be the first time the FBI had an agenda in one department that the other didn't know about. It did, however, make him even more curious about Cormier.

"You sound like you believe he's alive."

"I never underestimate Cormier," Zeke said. "I can't even begin to count the number of times he was supposed to be dead. I won't believe it until there are body parts on a morgue table."

"So, if the man is so good at what he does, why do you think he needs someone like Bobbie Faye?"

Zeke appeared to be weighing whether or not to disclose more, then he shrugged, as if it didn't much matter now. "We think Bobbie Faye had something valuable he wanted."

This matched up with what Jason had recorded, but Cam needed Zeke to disclose more.

"Bobbie Faye? Valuable?" Cam asked, feigning disbelief. "The same woman who, when her phone rebate check for twelve dollars and eighteen cents blew out of her car window onto a train track, stopped her car and got out to get it, then couldn't start her car and watched as it managed to derail an entire train? *That* Bobbie Faye?"

"All I know is that Cormier doesn't do anything without a plan," Zeke said, looking at the debris, his expression hardening. "Even this."

He paused a moment, and Cam wondered if the agent had seen the cameras.

"He's alive. Somehow," Zeke muttered, more to himself than to Cam.

Cam hoped that plan included needing Bobbie Faye to stay alive.

B obbie Faye knew Cam had seen the cameras; he'd been careful not to be obvious, but his eyes made direct contact with every single lens as he spied where they surrounded the shack. She could see the anger rippling off his shoulders, the tension tying him in knots. Fury. Hatred, with a capital H. It was only a matter of time before he started digging through the rubble to see what was underneath the shack, and that meant they needed to leave.

"Oh, shit," she said, and Trevor followed her gaze: the camera on the pier caught an image of one of the media helicopters hovering not far away from the burning shack. She pulled out the cell phone and saw there was no signal. Bobbie Faye spun, panicked, and Trevor settled his gaze on her.

"I didn't realize the cell wouldn't work in here! The deadline. Oh, shit, I have to make that call. They'll think I'm dead. They'll hurt Roy!"

"I don't think so," Trevor said. "They don't know for sure that you were in the shack, unless the police tell them, and I doubt the police are going to say anything until they know what exactly happened. At best, they'll know you were around here, but they're not going to risk their leverage until it's confirmed one way or the other."

Trevor turned to Alex. "I'm assuming you have a back door, or you wouldn't have brought us here."

"Of course. There are two. One is a long sloping ramp I found that was once used to bring the equipment in for the salt dome below us. I had the door disguised so no one knows it's there."

"Good, then let's go."

"Not so fast." Alex walked over to one of the monitors and pointed to a spot on the ground. "Here's the hidden door to the tunnel. It opens up in the ground right where the FBI are camped out. We aren't going to be able to get out of that door unseen until they leave. That could take more than a day."

They all looked at Bobbie Faye, who shook her head. "I don't have that kind of time."

"I sensed that, chere," Alex said, smiling. "Never the easy way with you, is it?" He raised his hands when she spun toward him. "Sorry, chere. Sorry. The other way out's through the dome."

"You mean . . . down? How?"

"The other end is still being mined. There's an entrance through there." He pointed to the doorway to his right. "You have to take the elevator down to the dome, then cross through an equipment graveyard. The salt rusts it out fast, and it's not worth the time or money bringing the equipment back up to the surface, so they just leave it down there. And there are a couple of large rooms they use as a sort of warehouse. If you ask me, they forgot about a lot of this stuff over the years as they mined the other side."

She looked at the monitors, at the FBI, SWAT, police, and of course, Cam, milling around. There were God-knows-how-many helicopters above it all. No way to get out that exit unseen. But the idea of going down into the dark of a salt dome was like volunteering to walk into your own grave.

She couldn't find Stacey like this. She couldn't save Roy from here. She looked down at the dead cell phone.

"There's an old land-line down there, chere. I think it still works. And the cops wouldn't dream of you going that way so they won't be waiting for you at the other end."

She dropped her face into her hands, feeling an enormous weight pressing against her chest, crushing her heart. She had no choice. She sucked it up, looked up at Alex and Trevor, and nodded.

"Alex? I need the tiara."

He paused, gazing longingly at the tiara. Then reluctantly, he tossed it to her, and then lobbed the flashlight to Trevor.

"Don't say I never did anything for you, chere. You hear?"

"Thanks, Alex," she said, and he nodded.

"I better get my stuff back," he said as he exited the room, heading out toward his own exit as the words echoed off the tunnel walls.

"I'm impressed," Trevor said once Alex was gone and they had turned toward a different exit, the one leading to the dome below.

"Why?"

"You got it from him without shooting him."

"Oh, he knew I'd shoot him. That's why he gave it to me."

"You two must have had an interesting relationship."

"Only if you find pathological liars interesting," she said, then saw his curiosity. "Don't ask. I still don't know how I was so brain dead as to date that man. I definitely didn't know what he did for a living when we met."

"He still cares for you," he said, and she caught an odd note to his tone.

"What do you care?"

"I don't. Just an observation," he answered as they traveled through a hallway toward an old elevator. "The man obviously still loves you."

"He was a poet in school. He loves the idea of love." They stopped in front of the dusty, rusted elevator door. "In the real world, he turned out to be of the 'she's to be seen and not heard' school of relationships."

Trevor's eyebrows arched.

"Yeah, I don't know what the hell he was thinking dating me, either."

She pressed the button to the elevator and nothing happened. She pressed it again, then again. Still nothing. She pounded the freaking button. And yet, there was nothing. No sounds, no movement; no groaning, creaking overtures of an attempt of the elevator car to show up.

Trevor pushed the button and she glared at him.

"Right," she said. "Because if a man does the same thing, it should work."

He chuckled, setting the flashlight down, pulling out his Ka-Bar knife and used it to wedge open the doors. When he aimed the flashlight down into the elevator shaft, it was as if it were a never-ending abyss. He picked up a small rock of salt nearby and dropped it into the shaft, counting seconds until it hit something. Almost ten seconds.

"That's at least eight or nine hundred feet to where the car is stuck. Right now, I'd say you're batting a thousand. I've never seen anyone with such stellar bad luck."

"Go, me. I always was an overachiever."

. . .

C e Ce had no clue how it had come to this. She shook her head, giving up on anything making sense. They had just lugged the Social Services woman to the back room where they'd put her onto a cot when Ce Ce noted the security monitor and saw what she was sure was a plainclothes cop enter her Outfitter store. She flipped on the intercom, making sure the feed was one-way only, to listen to what he wanted.

"I'm Detective Benoit," he announced to Allison and Alicia. The twins smiled and leaned forward onto the counter, showing ample cleavage. He grinned back at their beatific smiles, and Ce Ce reminded herself those girls needed a raise.

"I'm looking for a Mrs. Banyon with the Department of Social Services. She was reported to have arrived here a couple of hours ago. Have you seen her?"

"Well, Officer," Allison said, (or maybe it was Alicia), "there's really been so many people in here. It's kinda a spectator sport at this point. It's hard to keep track of all the people we know, much less the ones we don't."

Crap. Ce Ce stared down at the woman who weighed as much as a lighthouse and was about as solidly built. The first place the cop was going to want to search was the back of the store. She made a mental note: "special" tea plus slow metabolism equals *bad*.

"Where the hell are we gonna put her?" Monique asked, wiping the perspiration from her brow, her red hair standing out in spikes, her pink freckles turning a brighter red with the exertion of heaving the two-hundred-plus-pound woman to the back room. "Hey, I know. We could dress her in one of your costumes, put on a mask, and he'll think she's a wax dummy or something."

"She's snoring, Monique."

"We could tell him it's sound effects!"

The Social Services woman farted.

They both looked down, scrunching up their faces.

"Okay, maybe not," Monique amended.

They heard Detective Benoit give the girls a description of the missing woman. Ce Ce slapped the receiver part of the intercom off in that room and on in each subsequent room as they tugged the heavy, sleeping woman through the cramped hallways. They had to bend her to get her around the junk stacked up in the storeroom, and Ce Ce propped her on a few boxes and an old rug.

"Wanna try the closet?"

"We'll never get her in there. And she could fall over. That door doesn't lock."

Ce Ce looked around the overflowing storage room; there were free-standing shelves jammed against other shelves, all stuffed with every imaginable oddity that she might use in some of her potions and drinks. Spells, some people called them. Alongside that hodge-podge mixture were her books, which tracked some of the more es-oteric facts of south Louisiana's little-known history, particularly anything that recorded old stories of how various salves and drinks worked, anecdotes of those who'd delved into the medicinals before her. In front of all of that, inventory for the store, including more boxes of crystals.

Bobbie Faye may have had a point about the crystals.

The closet was small and crammed with goods. Then, on the in-tercom, she heard Detective Benoit ask the twins, "Then you won't mind if I check the back? See if she's lost back there somewhere?"

"Oh," one of the twins replied. "Well, we gotta go find Ce Ce. We can't give anyone permission to go back there. Just her."

Bless their little peroxided hearts. They really were going to get a raise.

Alicia hustled to the back of the store while Ce Ce could hear the other twin trying to keep the detective distracted. He seemed partic-ularly interested in the crystal matrix and chanting still en force in the store. When Alicia's head popped into the storage room door-way, her eyes bugged and she slid to a stop.

"Don't look at me like that, child. She's not dead. You go distract him some more until we can move her."

"Which way are you going?"

"We'll go on through that back sitting room and then through my office. You go tell him I'm lying down and don't feel well. Tell him I'm real distraught over Bobbie Faye. He'll have to come back later."

Alicia nodded and ran back while Ce Ce and Monique hefted Mrs. Banyon up a little and dragged her into the next room. They got a brief reprieve when Ce Ce heard the detective's cell phone ring, and he asked to step into a back room for that conversation. Ce Ce knew disguising that intercom as a voodoo mask was going to come in handy one day.

Ce Ce and Monique dropped the Social Services lady to the floor with a thud that was a little too loud. They both hovered near the intercom as they tried to glean every word the detective said.

"I still haven't found the kid," the detective said. After a beat, he continued. "Look, Cam, I've squeezed everyone I know at the FBI and they're swearing they don't have the kid. The social worker's missing, now, too. Yeah, I'm following up on that. It's got to be connected. Oh, and Crowe and Fordoche finished the financials on the Professor. He's in debt up to his squirmy eyebrows. Yeah, loan sharks, how'd you guess? Yeah. Looks like he sold something to the sharks to pull his ass out of a fire and word on the street was that the shark sold it for big bucks to a black market art dealer, but nobody knows what or how that ties into Bobbie Faye. When I tried to interview him without Dellago, the sadistic bastard found out and forced me to stop or include him. How's it going there?"

There was a long pause, and Ce Ce wanted to storm into the other room and snatch the phone from him.

"You saw her?"

The detective was silent a moment and Ce Ce and Monique leaned closer to the speaker to get every drop of information they could.

"Holy shit, Cam. Are you serious? How bad was it?" Then, finally, quietly, "Was she inside when it blew?"

Ce Ce grabbed her ample chest and sagged against the wall.

"Well, then, where?" Detective Benoit asked, his voice growing faint over the intercom.

Monique whispered, "I think he's moving our direction. We'd better get her out of here."

Ce Ce helped Monique pick up the woman again, hauling her through another hallway, intending to heave her through the office and onto a private back porch. As they turned from one room to the next, they dropped the poor woman with another loud thud as they encountered Detective Benoit, leaning against the wall.

"Yeah, thanks, Cam," he said into the phone. "Glad to know about the intercom system."

He hung up and looked from Ce Ce to Monique, who had beads of sweat pouring from her from the exertion.

"Well, I'm thirsty," Monique announced. "That was hard work. Anyone else want some tea?"

"No!" Ce Ce shook her head emphatically, her braids bouncing. "There will be no drinking of the tea."

"But the detective might be thirsty. And it's so hot now. It's the least we could do."

Ce Ce pulled her into a conspiratorial stance. "Honey, no. I can't drug a cop."

"But with all of them running around like chickens with their heads cut off, they won't miss him for a few hours."

"No. Tea."

"Especially not your special mix, Ce Ce," Detective Benoit said, obviously having heard everything. He looked down at the Social Services lady. "Please tell me she's not dead."

"Of course not. She fell asleep. We're trying to get her to a cot."

"Asleep. Right. Ce Ce, we need to talk."

Damnit. Nothing good ever came from "we need to talk."

Chapter Thirty-one

We always know when Bobbie Faye is in the woods because there's always a mass exodus of animals in the other direction. We had to make it illegal to hunt using Bobbie Faye.

—*Michele Montgomery, LA game warden*

While the SWAT team waited near a second helicopter which had arrived with Kelvin and his dogs, Cam prowled around the burning shack, contemplating myriad issues. What had the Professor sold to save his ass from gambling debts? What did that have to do with Bobbie Faye? What in hell was driving her? Where the hell was Stacey? Or Roy, for that matter? And why would Cormier tell him to back way the hell up, unless it was because Cormier knew the shack was going to blow? Why in the hell would a mercenary give a rat's ass whether he was blown up? To appeal to Bobbie Faye? She might hate him, but he didn't think she'd want him blown up. Maybe. But then again, why would Cormier know that, or care? Maybe Cormier still needed something from her, and needed her not wigging out to get it. What was it Zeke said? Cormier knew exactly how to manipulate and charm and get what he wanted. Right now, he had Bobbie Faye. Cam had to believe they were alive.

And why warn off someone if you intend on self-destructing? No. They were here. Somewhere. He'd bet a year's salary on it. The trick now? Finding a room, a basement . . . something they'd gone down into; and since they blew their front door, there had to be a back way out.

The FBI agents were scouting closer to the shack, checking in the debris where the fire had died off, looking for clues and bodies. Cam, meanwhile, carefully walked a spiraling perimeter, moving outward from the shack. If it had been his design, and if he'd wanted a back door, he'd want it in the woods, where no one would be paying as much attention.

He moved carefully. Slowly. Wary of destroying any potential evidence, yet needing to examine the terrain. Several times, Cam sank to his haunches, pausing, listening. Smelling the soil, checking for small disturbances.

A broken plant here.

A couple of leaves recently turned over just beyond that.

An odd scrape in the soil just past that.

He waited, instinct telling him he was onto something.

He stood, following what was an almost indecipherable trail, farther down the bayou, where he suddenly found footprints. Men's boots, at least four different sizes. He backtracked farther and found two speedboats, similar to the one he'd seen Bobbie Faye and Cormier in earlier, well hidden in a tiny inlet in the bayou, camouflaged with limbs and fronds piled around them.

Okay, so that's how they got here. Now where did they go?

He moved back to where the footprints ended, picking back up where they must have started being careful. There were the tiniest indentations on the grass, where someone passed by.

Then, nothing. Past that last broken twig, there were no other disturbances, save the footprints made by Bobbie Faye and Cormier, and now his own.

Except . . . there was an odd furrow beneath several of the large ubiquitous wood ferns. A perfectly straight line in the soil, a few feet in length.

· · ·

Bobbie Faye and Trevor stared down the elevator abyss, contemplating options. Trevor gazed back toward the monitor room.

"Is this one of those times when a man won't ask for directions? Because it's pretty much a no-brainer that we're not going down."

He looked at his watch. "Going out Alex's direction is riskier. You realize that?"

"Maybe once we move closer to the surface near the door, the cell will work. I could call Cam, try to convince him I want to give up and that we're somewhere else?"

"He probably won't leave, but it might pull the majority off this detail for a few minutes. It might work."

They turned, and Trevor hung the satchel of guns and odds and ends across his shoulders. They walked in silence back to the monitor room, where all of the view screens had shut off. Timers? Bobbie Faye wondered. They crossed the room and moved up the long, curving slope of the ramp to the other exit.

There was a boom. Echoing down through the tunnel.

Some sort of small explosion?

Then, more small blasts and shouts, dogs barking, people running, boots hitting pavement.

Trevor stopped and she slammed into him. "The cops found Alex's other entrance. Those are smoke grenades. And tear gas."

He spun, yanking her with him.

"You aren't seriously thinking we're going to jump down that elevator shaft?"

"Not jump. Rappel. Have you ever rappelled?"

"Hello? Louisiana? Everything's flat?"

"Right. Sorry."

"What are we going to use?"

He didn't get to answer, for just at that moment, they had entered the monitor room and realized Alex had one last trick up his sleeve: automatic doors on both entrances, which were closing.

Trevor pushed Bobbie Faye through the closing door first, then rolled underneath just as it smashed shut.

"Here," he said, handing the flashlight to Bobbie Faye. "We've only got one chance. They're going to be pulling Alex and his men out of that other end in a few minutes, and it should be pretty confusing until they figure out you're not there. Maybe that'll buy us time enough to rappel."

He handed her the flashlight as he tossed open the satchel and set to work on something about which she had no clue. It gave her a moment to peer down the dark abyss, tossing another salt rock down into the shaft, waiting a million years before it finally bounced and echoed at the bottom.

"Oh, you know, that's just about perfect. I knew when I woke up this morning that this was going to be a special day and you know what I said to myself? I said, 'Gee, Bobbie Faye, you should go find a really sexy guy and plunge eight hundred feet to your death with him. It'll be romantic.'"

"No wonder you have exes littered all over the state."

She squinted at him in the light of the flashlight. "So we're just going to jump into a really deep hole? No definite knowledge as to whether there's a door down there somewhere?"

"Where's your sense of adventure?"

"It died of fright a couple of hours ago."

They heard another round of smoke grenades and tear gas and Trevor sped up his dismantling of various guns. She stared at this man she'd kidnapped, not able to wrap her mind around the kind of man he'd turned out to be. He MacGyvered a makeshift harness and rappelling gear using bits and pieces hacked off from the guns, rope, and other oddball items he'd thrown into the satchel from Alex's storage shed. The muscles in his arms were well defined in the stark light and shadows, and his focus was mesmerizing.

He was, inexplicably, still trying to help.

She had a hard time not just believing that, but accepting it. She'd lived so long by the code of being self-sufficient, it was as alien to her to accept so much help as it would have been to sit in a glassed-in high-rise, dictating to a cadre of accountants. Too strange. Now they were boxed in with a SWAT team and guns and an ex who was pretty thoroughly pissed at her. Maybe if she gave the cops what they wanted, they would help her find Roy. Maybe if she was permanently behind bars, Cam would quit all of the crazy-making chasing and focus on the rest of his job. Maybe they wouldn't be mowed down in the hail of "Hi, Bonnie; Hi, Clyde; nice t'meetcha" bullets she was pretty sure were on their way through the tunnels.

"Can you think of any other options? Have I overlooked something?" When he didn't respond, she quietly asked, "Maybe the police could help me save Roy? They don't know exactly who you are, and you could still leave out through the salt dome."

Without pausing in his work, his fingers flying, tying knots for which she couldn't even begin to guess the names, he asked, "What do you think the guy holding your brother would do the minute he saw you in police custody?"

Barely above a whisper, she answered, "He'd probably assume I couldn't get to the tiara, and that he no longer needed Roy as leverage. He'd kill him."

He nodded, curt and crisp, his hands still working with ropes. They could hear dogs barking, though they didn't echo. They weren't yet in the tunnel. Trevor checked his watch.

"We have about twelve minutes left. We can make it assuming that phone in the salt dome is where Alex said it was."

She studied him as she held the flashlight so he could finish assembling his gear.

"I'm sorry I kidnapped you this morning."

He stopped, his expression odd and frustration swept across his brow. He snagged her, pulling her in, and kissed her.

Hard. There was heat and passion and a tenderness she hadn't expected. He let her go just as abruptly.

"I'm not. Now, let's go."

Trevor tossed all of the extra loose parts not used in the making of the harness back into the satchel and looped it across his shoulders and then stood, facing the abyss of the elevator shaft. With his back to her, she allowed herself a moment to revel in that kiss, and the heat flooding her limbs. She mouthed "wow" to herself.

"Of course," he said, and she saw that he'd glanced over his shoulder.

She wanted to smack him, the smug bastard, but that felt too much like third grade right at the moment. Then she smacked him on the arm anyway, and her inner third-grader cheered.

C am waited, tense. He had his gun drawn and aimed at the open trap door where the SWAT team had entered. Kelvin's hounds were baying not far away, itching to track, still on scent from the shreds of Bobbie Faye's T-shirt that Kelvin had brought back from the bayou. They were putting up such a fuss, Cam was certain the SWAT leader was going to be dragging Bobbie Faye out any moment now.

Instead, the SWAT team leader, Aaron, popped out of the trap-door entrance and motioned Cam to the opening.

"Sir, I've got six males down here. Two of 'em are college kids who are tied up and gagged, and the rest of 'em were armed."

"And Bobbie Faye?"

"Sir, they all claim to not know a Bobbie Faye."

"I know exactly how they feel. Get them up here."

He stepped back and watched as the SWAT team slowly brought up each of the suspects. The first up were two college kids who Cam recognized as the two boys who fled the bank robbery in the Saab. They practically fell upon the SWAT team with embraces and incoherent babbling. It was going to be real interesting to see what light they could shed on this.

He didn't recognize the next three men who came out of the hole, but the last one made him raw with fury, though the most Cam allowed himself as a physical reaction was to cross his arms and watch from behind his sunglasses.

Alex.

Bobbie Faye's ex.

The lowest scum on earth, who'd done more harm to her than

Cam could ever have made up for, who'd lied and cheated and who, rumor had it, was a gunrunner, though no one had an ounce of proof. Alex was a few years older than Cam, and Cam never took the man seriously as a threat for Bobbie Faye's affections when he first started hanging around. He was the kind of guy Bobbie Faye could see through in a heartbeat. Or so Cam had thought. But there she went, getting caught up in his charm and excitement and the pretense of a big family, with all his so-called "friends" hanging around all of the damned time. Before he knew what was happening and had the courage to risk their friendship in order to ask her out, she was dating Alex. Cam had kicked himself a hundred times over for waiting too long, and then he'd had to stand by and be her friend through the whole Alex debacle.

When he did finally ask her out and they started dating, he always wondered if she was secretly bored, secretly longing for that risk, that darkness that exuded from Alex.

Shit. Maybe this thing with Trevor paralleled Alex? Maybe she was attracted to him, in spite of his past? Assuming she knew?

Sonofabitch.

Cam stopped thinking and focused on not pulling his gun when Alex sauntered out of the hole with a demeanor as casual as if he was heading down to the Circle K to pick up a pack of cigarettes. Clearly, he was not the kind of man who would ever give up information, even in the most arduous interrogation. Cam didn't have time for arduous. He would have liked to have made time for an intensive one-on-one, no holds barred, private interview, but that wasn't going to happen. He had made it this far without being one of those cops, though right about now, he was starting to seriously reconsider his code.

It was purely from a professional frustration that he was reacting this way. He was certain of that.

The bastard looked in Cam's direction, and grinned.

She went to that sonofabitch for help, before she came to him?

He'd known she was furious with him. He knew she hated him with a white hot passion. Hell, you could fry eggs on the level of heated hatred she held for him arresting her sister. He knew that. He'd felt the same way, for the things she'd said. He hadn't fully understood that she couldn't trust him. That she'd trust a pathological bastard before she'd trust him. Or, if not trust, at least accept his help.

Cam didn't crack an expression, or let Alex know that he had, in any way, registered on Cam as anything other than another suspect.

"Sir," Aaron said from the trapdoor. "There's tunnels."

"Get the dogs."

The dogs went baying down into the entrance, straining at the leashes Kelvin kept them on. Since they didn't know where the tunnels led, Kelvin would keep them reined in until he knew the tunnels were safe.

Cam watched Alex as the dogs and then Kelvin entered the tunnel. Alex furrowed his brow and seemed to tense. The man actually looked a little concerned.

Good.

That meant Bobbie Faye was still in there, somewhere.

"We're going in," Zeke said in Cam's ear, and he mentally cursed his distraction. He'd forgotten all about the asshole to his left while he was watching the bastard on his right.

"And if we find Cormier," Zeke warned, "you and your men better fucking get out of the way."

Zeke spun away from him, though Cam wouldn't have given him the satisfaction of answering.

He glanced in Alex's direction as he entered the trapdoor and the smug bastard smiled at him. Smiled as if he knew something about Bobbie Faye.

No. He remembered that smile. That was Alex's "I have something of her that you don't have" smile.

Good goddamned thing he had a code and there were witnesses, or Alex would be in the bottom of the bayou.

Cam climbed into the trapdoor entrance after the dogs.

Chapter Thirty-two

The National Hurricane Center came out with its list of hurricane names for the next few months. When it was announced in Louisiana that one of their name choices was "Bobbie Faye," it was the first time in history an entire state flinched.

—*weather anchor Patricia Burroughs on* Dallas Morning News

Trevor tied the tiara to Bobbie Faye's belt loop.

"You're going to need your hands to hold on."

The hounds bayed, the racket echoed through the tunnel and, in spite of the steel door which had closed down between them and the tunnel, filled the room. Trevor hooked his makeshift harness to the elevator cables, turned, and then sat in the harness, hooking the shoulder straps across his chest to hold him in.

"I'm going to have to support your weight. We don't have enough stuff for two harnesses, and since we can't rappel in the traditional sense, you're going to have to hang on tight. It's a quick ride."

He held out his hand to her, ready for her to board the straight-to-hell, do-not-pass-go, do-not-use-any-common-sense express, and all she could do was stare at his long, slim fingers. She was telling her muscles to move. She commanded her legs to walk on over there and step into the little foothold he'd fashioned for her and take his hand. Her legs pretty much said "fuck off bitch, and die."

"Did I ever mention that in high school, I was voted 'Most Likely to Cause Armageddon'?"

He kept his hand outstretched, waiting for her.

Did she trust him with her life?

The sound of the dogs' barking increased and she could hear their grunts and heavy panting, their nails clattering on the concrete floor of the tunnel, the echoing voices of the men who must not be far behind. She turned to Trevor, grasped his hand, and stepped into the foot-harness. She leaned into his body, he wrapped one arm around her, and they adjusted positions a little until he had a strong grip. He handed her the flashlight, its dim beam barely illuminating the murky dark of the shaft, and she squeezed her eyes shut for a second as he reached above her and released the makeshift brake.

They fell.

Plummeted.

Bobbie Faye's nerves screamed at her to clutch onto something solid, anything, to keep from falling, because falling meant dying. They were not exactly helpful nerves. Very possibly, they were a little hysterical. No, no, as a matter of fact, the Nerves had moved just to the other side of Hysterical and were beating the ever-loving shit out of it for being such a blatant underachiever.

She and Trevor plunged down, air rushing past them, and her soul shivered as she inhaled the smell of oil and grease from the old elevator shaft. Dust stung her eyes and nostrils and she buried her face against Trevor's chest.

Still, they fell.

Bobbie Faye half-wondered if she was already dead, if she'd died years ago and was just doomed to live this moment over and over for all of eternity, this falling falling falling forever falling when Trevor applied the makeshift brake to slow them down before they hit the bottom of the shaft, or the top of the elevator car, whichever came first.

The metal brake scraped the elevator cable, slowing them both, and sparks rained down on Bobbie Faye.

Catching her shirt on fire.

She instinctively let go of Trevor to beat out the fire.

"Noooo," he shouted, and that's when she remembered she was supposed to keep holding onto him, not the other way around.

She slipped from his grip, floundering away from him, spinning dizzily, dropping away from him faster as his speed decreased due to his makeshift brake. He released his hold on the brake, accelerating again . . . leaning . . . stretching . . . his fingertips brushing against the tiara, the bottom of the shaft racing up toward them.

The flashlight fell away from her, and for a brief moment, it illuminated his face, furious with concentration, every muscle taut as he reached for her. She stretched toward him, and she felt his hand, all corded sinews and roped muscles, yanking her toward him, applying the brake with his other hand, showering sparks across the top of the elevator car as they smashed into it. The thudding impact thundered up the elevator shaft as the blow killed the flashlight and the sparks in one swift second.

R oy was worried. Frankly, he was about to piss himself and probably should have asked for another bathroom break, but the thought of going back to the bathroom with The Mountain as an escort made certain body parts retract clean up to his neck. He was particularly worried since Eddie had lost all interest in the copious decorating magazines lying around the room and was sharpening his machete-sized knife. Again.

The Mountain kept looking through the discarded magazines, pointing out fancy doorknobs he'd like to collect.

Worst of all was Vincent.

When the phone rang, Roy jerked, reflex, and the ropes bit into his arms. Vincent answered and listened a moment, then seemed to somehow grow more pointy, all violent angles and sharp features.

"You had better," he seethed into the phone, "make sure our little Professor can't tell that version of the story." There was a heavy pause. "No, I don't care what you have to do, or what it costs. Take care of it."

He set the phone down and Roy felt very sorry for whoever the Professor was. Vincent still seemed to be seething, which couldn't be a good sign.

"Twelve minutes left on the clock," Eddie murmured to Vincent, who had returned his focus to the TV images of the burning shack and police activity covered by the news.

"Hey, Vincent," The Mountain squeaked, "ain't that the FBI going in that hole in the ground now?"

"Indeed, my boy, it is." Vincent peered over to Roy. "Which is, sadly, very bad for you. The FBI have a very nasty habit of getting in the way, and your sister certainly won't find the tiara for me if she's locked up in some federal prison somewhere."

"Do we have to wait the full time?" Eddie asked, testing the sharpness of his blade by holding up a magazine page and slicing it diagonally as easily as Roy usually convinced women to go out with him. "There's still no sign of the GPS signal."

Roy would have focused on that latter tidbit except for the fact that Eddie had stopped directly in front of him and had taken a rope and cleanly sliced it lengthways with one swift stroke. Roy tried hard not to picture that blade going through his neck.

"I'll wait until the deadline," Vincent said, and he turned to Roy, a particularly disturbing gleam glittering his dark eyes. Vincent's focus shifted back to the TV, and his momentary bout of smiling, as frightening as it had been, was immediately replaced with a scarier grimace as the news replayed the footage of the police going into the trapdoor. The video zoomed in, capturing close-ups of the SWAT, then FBI, and Roy could feel Vincent's displeasure ripple through the air.

The SWAT team pried the first steel door open and ran across a large room with blank monitors to a second door. A deep, thudding sound of collision reverberated up from the bowels of the earth, and Cam was almost certain he'd heard Bobbie Faye's shriek just a split second before.

SWAT redoubled their efforts to get through that last door.

"How much longer?" he asked the leader, Aaron.

"Not sure, sir. This one's jammed, and it's not a thin sheet of steel, that's for sure. Our pry bars aren't strong enough, and the battering ram won't work. We may have to blow it." Aaron looked around the room. "But I don't know how strong this structure is, or how old. If we blow it wrong, we could collapse the whole room." Then he tapped his foot. "And if we're right, and there's a dome beneath us, we could all drop straight through to the dome. Kill us and anybody underneath us."

E very. Single. Thing. Hurt.

Which was probably the best result, she realized. At least she could feel all of the parts of her which were in agonizing pain and that had to mean she wasn't dead, right? And hopefully, not paralyzed?

She shifted her weight, groping in the inky darkness to get her bearings and figure out where Trevor was. She pressed her elbow into the lumpy terrain beneath her and it grunted.

"Watch it," Trevor growled.

"Uh, sorry." She climbed off him, and onto something equally as lumpy. That flashlight couldn't have gone far, and she groped around in the dark.

"What are you doing?"

"Looking for the flashlight."

"Well, unless you put it down my pants while we were falling, I don't think you're going to find it there."

"Smartass. You find it."

He moved near her, brushing against her several times until there was a lot of clicking as he attempted (she guessed) to get the light on. When it finally illuminated, it flickered grudgingly as if it were not entirely sure it would continue doing them this favor after what they put it through. Trevor aimed the flashlight down and they discovered they'd landed on lumpy sandbags.

"Are we on the floor of the shaft?" she asked, starting to feel a bit panicky. There was no obvious door. Any. Freaking. Where.

"This isn't the floor," Trevor said. "It's sandbags. Or bags of . . . oh, yeah, it's salt."

"So, the elevator car?"

He dug through the sacks and hit something metal. He pounded it with the heel of his boot and they heard a hollow echo.

"Beneath us."

Together they moved the sacks until they found the access door built into the top of the elevator car. He could not pry it open on his own, and Bobbie Faye grabbed a leftover gun part from the satchel, using it as a makeshift pry bar.

Trevor shone the flashlight inside, and the car was empty. They climbed through, landing with a hollow, metallic clank onto the floor of the elevator car. Trevor pried the doors open, and discovered the car hadn't actually been resting on the ground level; there was only a half-a-car's space open as they hovered about five feet above the floor.

Above them, small, concussive explosions rocked the shaft. Dust shook loose of the car and the opening and splattered down onto their heads.

"They're blowing that door," Trevor said.

"How the hell do you know that? Do you have X-ray vision or something?"

"It's what I would do. C'mon, we've got to get out of this car before they get down that shaft."

Trevor squatted and then hopped out of the car, dropping the five feet as smooth as a big cat. He glanced at his watch.

"Hey, four-and-a-half minutes. C'mon."

She turned and scooted backwards on her belly, her feet protruding from the door. Her plan was to shimmy backwards until she could bend at the waist and then she'd just drop down.

Only. There was a great rumbling above her in the shaft. She froze as the elevator car shook.

And started to move.

Upwards.

With her still hanging halfway out.

Trevor shouted something, though she had no clue what, because she was losing her balance and she didn't know how to push off from the position she was in, and then, all of a sudden, something yanked the hell out of the tiara still tied to her belt loop and she slid backwards. Out of the elevator car. Landing on Trevor. Again. In time to see the car whoosh upwards.

She looked beneath her, and it took a heartbeat to register what she was seeing: Trevor, holding the tiara in one hand, which had ripped off with her belt loop when he'd tugged on it.

He had grabbed for the tiara?

He had fucking *grabbed* the *tiara*.

"You bastard! You were waiting to grab this the first chance you got."

"You're insane. I was trying to grab *you*."

"Oh, sure you were. Is that why you've been helping? To get to this thing because you know it's valuable to someone?"

"Another second, the elevator would have sliced you in half. I was trying to keep you alive, you crazy nut job. How many heart attacks do you think a man can take in just one day, anyway?"

He rolled so as to remove her from his chest, and she jumped up, snatching the tiara away from him, waving it at him.

"You try double-crossing me, and I will personally hunt you down for the rest of your very short life."

He checked his fancy diver's watch, pressing a button on the side, which lit up the face a little better for her to see the time. She saw a timer counting backwards, and gulped.

"We've got maybe three minutes, Bobbie Faye. Let's find that land line. You can yell at me later."

Right.

Shit.

Trevor pulled out his gun, faced the electronics box beside the elevator, and without hesitation, shot it out.

"Should slow them down," he said.

"Yeah, well, I hope Alex wasn't lying about a back door."

They hurried away from the elevator, looking for a likely place for a land line.

"It should be near here," Trevor reasoned. "If there was trouble, or if they needed to evacuate for some reason, it would make sense to put a land line by the elevator."

It took two of her very precious three minutes for them to find the phone. The salt fluff from the mine had covered it, blending it in with the wall around it. Bobbie Faye knocked the salt off, and held it to her ear.

Dead.

No dial tone.

Chapter Thirty-three

We made the tragic mistake of asking Bobbie Faye to be the guest of honor at the blessing of the boats. It's the only time in our history someone managed to sink a brand-new shrimp boat with just a bottle of champagne and a good strong arm swing.

—*Father Albert O'Patrick*

Eddie paced in front of Roy, flipping the machete-sized knife with a little too much glee. Roy was trying to remember the Our Father he was supposed to have learned in catechism, except that was probably when he'd been French-kissing Aimee Lynn in the confessional, which probably wasn't the best of priorities, given his present circumstances.

"Two minutes, boss," Eddie reminded Vincent, who seemed to be ignoring them, his rapt attention still glued to the TV screens.

Roy was pretty sure he ought to take it like a man, he ought to watch his killers right up to the fatal blow, except that he was also pretty sure no one was ever going to know that he took it like a man, and so he closed his eyes and replayed some of the high points in his life, which nicely coincided with the women he'd kissed. He'd expected his untimely death to be over a woman, just never over his sister.

He kept his eyes closed and sensed Eddie treading closer and closer with each pass around the room, and he could smell the man's expensive aftershave and hear the rustle of his silk suit. Roy opened one eye and peeked at Eddie as the man rocked on his toes, excitement emanating from him as his lopsided face distorted further with an awful grin.

Roy heard a steady beeping, and knew that the timer was up, and braced himself, closing his eyes.

"Aw, damnit, no," Eddie murmured. "Not fair."

When the machete didn't, in fact, slice him in half, Roy ventured another peek and saw Eddie, The Mountain, and Vincent perusing another TV monitor, which had gone unnoticed by Roy since it had appeared to be off.

"I'm afraid so," Vincent said, though he looked quite happy.

"Uh, what's that?" Roy asked.

"Your lifeline," Eddie grumbled, flopping back into the leather chair, sheathing his machete and looking particularly disgruntled.

"My huh?"

"It's okay, Eddie," Vincent smoothed. "I'll let you redecorate the downstairs apartment."

Eddie seemed to brighten a bit. "Fine. But you cannot veto the toile later like you did last time."

"No, of course not."

"Uh, lifeline?" Roy asked again, and the three men looked over at him.

"GPS signal," The Mountain offered, and then flinched under Vincent's glare. "What? Boss, it ain't like he's gonna live to tell about it, anyway."

Vincent chuckled at that.

"GPS? Whose?"

"You may have been in too much shock earlier when I mentioned I had eyes on Bobbie Faye, dear boy," Vincent said, his fingers steepled as he observed Roy.

"Yeah," The Mountain chimed, a little too enthusiastically. "The guy what was s'posed to grab the tiara and off your sister? He's with her, man. Chasing it down. And this is his way of lettin' us know he's still after it."

"Why wouldn't he just keep it?"

"Easy, m'boy. He doesn't know the value of the tiara, or why I want it. He doesn't get paid until I have it in my hands, and believe me, he charges a very hefty fee. But then, he's the best in the business."

"He'd have to be, to survive your sister," Eddie added, with just enough adoration in his voice to make Roy's eyebrows go up.

Vincent laughed. "Oh, Eddie's got a bit of a crush on our mercenary. Killers often appreciate the finesse of someone who's at the top of the same game."

"I do not have a crush," Eddie griped, though it was clear to Roy that he did. "He's just impressive."

Roy digested this information. So this must be the guy in the truck from the bank surveillance tape. The guy Bobbie Faye must think is helping her, since she hadn't shot him and run to the cops. *She didn't know.*

"Uh, how do you know he's the one who triggered the GPS?" he asked, hoping to find some angle to use.

"Bionics," The Mountain said.

"Biometrics," Eddie corrected, and The Mountain pouted at him and slouched in his own leather chair. "The boss here spared no expense for the gizmos, kid. He doesn't trust a mercenary any more than he'd trust his own mother."

"He really hated his mother," The Mountain offered, and Vincent's glare was so ice cold, The Mountain seemed to shrivel a bit.

Eddie continued. "That particular GPS is programmed to only respond if it's still attached to the mercenary's skin. If he tries to pull a fast one and remove it, it would turn on an alarm here."

Bobbie Faye didn't know she was running with the very guy she ought to be running from. He was going to have to figure out a way to warn her. Something he could shout, fast, when she called in, because he sure as hell knew he wouldn't have time for a full explanation. *If* she called in.

Bobbie Faye stared at the dead phone in the salt dome. This could not be happening. It simply wasn't going to happen this way. She then shone the flashlight all around the phone, as she and Trevor searched for anything to plug in, any wires to reconnect. It was an ancient model, its hard black enamel housing crusted with years of salt fluff, and was attached directly to a wall.

To a wall made of *salt.*

There was no way wires were going through that, and she aimed the light where the phone met the wall and found a small metal conduit pipe running from the phone upwards into the vast darkness that arched above them. The light reflected against the millions of facets of salt crystals making up the walls, and there was no way to see where the pipe eventually led. It looked perfectly fine.

Trevor took the flashlight and tried to find where the wiring went, while Bobbie Faye jiggled the cradle. Then banged it. Harder. Then harder, still holding the receiver in her other hand.

No no no no no, her head chanted, panic in three-quarter time, and before she realized what she was doing, she was using the receiver to beat the living hell out of the telephone, and she may have been shouting. Trevor turned back to her and took the phone from her death-grip, and once the echoes died down from her curses . . .

Lo, there was a dial tone.

"I think you scared it back to life."

"It's a talent."

She dialed Roy's number, white-knuckling the receiver, praying that they'd made it to the phone in time. She looked at Trevor's timer while the phone rang. The countdown was holding steady at zeroes, and no telling exactly how long they'd been lodged there.

The kidnapper's smooth baritone answered.

"I've got the tiara."

"You're late, Bobbie Faye."

"I've been a little busy."

"I don't reward *late,* my dear girl."

She heard Roy scream in the background, and it was all she could do to keep her knees from going out from under her.

"Now, bring me the tiara. You're to go—"

"I want to talk to Roy. Or you don't get the tiara."

"You have too many other family members and friends for me to go after, Bobbie Faye, and you know it. Quit playing games out of your league."

"Oh, sure. You want the tiara? If I don't talk to Roy, and right now, then I'll just wait here. The SWAT team's likely to be here and arrest me in five or so minutes, and I'm sure they'll take the tiara into evidence, and God only knows where it would end up from there. You have no idea how things go missing in Louisiana. Kidnapping anyone in my family wouldn't do you one fucking bit of good then, asshole. Now, *let me talk to Roy*."

There was a soft chuckle from the monster on the other end of the line, and Bobbie Faye shuddered.

"Bobbie Faye, dear girl, I'm going to thoroughly enjoy meeting you."

Before she could respond, Roy came on the line with, "Watch out for—" and just as quickly, was gone again.

"That's it," the kidnapper said. "You've heard him. Now, I want you to meet me at 1601 Scenic Highway in Plaquemine. You have an hour."

"An *hour*? Are you nuts? That's at least two hours from here, if I even knew where the hell here *was*. I'm so far underground, I don't know how long it'll take me to get to the surface, much less Plaquemine."

"Sounds like a personal problem to me."

The line went immediately dead, and Bobbie Faye stared at the phone, unable to form a sentence.

One hour. There was no way, not even if she had the fastest car on the planet and was already in said car, racing across the interstate. One hour.

"Where did he say to meet him?"

She'd almost forgotten Trevor was standing there, waiting.

"Plaquemine. We'll never make it."

"We'll figure something out."

Her brain was humming, her mind reeling, trying to clutch onto some sort of understanding and, instead, it fractured over and over, a kaleidoscope of morbid colors and shock and awe. She couldn't understand this sort of monster; she'd dealt with all sorts of cruel jerks and idiots and people who were just mean or bitter or selfish or greedy (or all of the above), but never, in her entire stellar life of getting slammed by the world, had she ever come up against someone so purely capricious.

"When I get Roy back," she said, "I am so going to stomp this guy's ass."

"If you want to get him, then we need a plan."

"Sure. A plan. Because everything I've planned today has worked out so well."

He chuckled. "Yeah, you're alive and we have the tiara. Which is the key."

"I still don't know why he wants it."

"Then maybe we should find out."

He removed the phone she was still clutching, hung it up, and started to pull her into a hug, but she held back. Then she sighed, exhausted, and rested her head on his chest. He *had* grabbed for her and the tiara to save her. She certainly would have been cut in half if he hadn't acted, right? He was here, he was helping. He was holding her, and not lecturing. That, alone, earned him a little grace in the doubt column.

He rested his chin on her head. "I've never seen anyone go through this for anyone." His low voice hummed through her body.

She shrugged. "It's all I have to give."

And it was. She had no money, she couldn't buy her way out of the problem, and she sure as hell couldn't count on the cops to help her.

"It's a lot more than most people would give."

She looked him in the eye. "They're my family. They're all I have. I'm not going to lose another one of them."

She tried to brace against the fear, for him not to see it, but she knew he had. He folded her in close again, kneading her sore muscles almost as if they'd always fit together like this.

His voice hummed again. "We need to use whatever the tiara is for collateral. If he gets it, and we don't know why he wants it, then he's got all of the cards and there's no reason to let any of us go alive."

"But if we know what it's worth, or what it's for, then we can maybe control that," she continued. "If it's just valuable in and of it-self, then that's a little harder to handle. But if it's really not worth anything . . . if it's a link to something else . . ."

"We get the something else first. Then we hold the cards."

"I don't know how we're going to do that, though, and still get to Plaquemine in time."

"I've got a couple of ideas."

She nodded, and he kneaded the knots in her shoulders.

"But if it's just valuable for itself?" she asked, muffled in his shirt.

He set her back a little. "Then we give it to him. We use it to save your brother's life. No doubt about that."

"Okay."

Behind them, they could hear small explosives echoing down the elevator shaft, and debris raining down the shaft afterwards, spilling out into the open doorway.

"That ex of yours has blown that door to the monitor room." He stood there, looking around as if he was assessing odds at a race-track. "It's not going to take him long to get down that shaft with the SWAT rappelling gear."

He grabbed her hand and they ran into the cavernous, pitch black dome, their flashlight illuminating only a few feet at a time.

Chapter Thirty-four

No, honey, you can't bring in Bobbie Faye as your show-and-tell exhibit for National Disaster Awareness week. I'd like to make it through this week alive.

—*Ms. Pam Arnold, Geautraux Elementary's third grade teacher*

Ce Ce paced. Which wasn't easy, given that she was pacing between the passed-out, drugged Social Services worker on one side, and Monique, whose answer to the day's high level of anxiety was to start early on her own home remedy, a super-strong screwdriver.

She was on her fourth.

Monique was a few Froot Loops short of a bowl to start with, but four screwdrivers later, she had slid so far off the moral center, she had weebled her way to the level of unscrupulous, with a serious leaning toward debauchery.

"We could just drop her off, somewhere."

Ce Ce was ignoring Monique's suggestions. She needed to concentrate on the spell.

"You know, get her all dressed up, like a hooker! That'd ruin her reputation and she couldn't do Bobbie Faye any harm."

"We are not dressing her up like a hooker. Nobody would ever believe she's a hooker, anyway."

"Hunh, 'ave you seen those hookers down on Moreland?"

Monique shuddered. "Honey, she'd pass for high class down there."

Ce Ce glanced down at the currently snoring brick wall with smudged lipstick lying on her storeroom floor. Monique had a point. She shook herself.

Do. Not. Go. There.

"Or, oh! I know! We could call in some exotic male dancers and get some really juicy photos!"

Ce Ce eyed her friend, whose bright red freckles now blended with the deepening ruddy complexion brought on by the vodka.

"I cannot believe they let you into the PTA."

"They had to. I have four kids. They know I'm gonna be around a while so they elected me president."

She whipped out her cell phone and started scrolling through the numbers, and Ce Ce reached over and took away the phone.

"We're not hiring exotic dancers."

"Oh, they do freebies. And they owe me."

"I do not want to know why. Now hush. Let me think."

One of the twins poked her head in the doorway.

"Ce Ce? I think we need to get hazard pay for today."

"What's wrong?"

"You have to do something with this matrix. It's breakin' down out here."

"Honey, it can't be that bad."

"Ce Ce, you ain't seen nothin' 'til you've seen two eighty-year-olds trying to shag each other, almost fully dressed and using one of 'em's walker for support. I think your matrix may have turned up their energy a little too high. We're gonna have to do something, soon. I have had to chase three different couples out of the bathroom already, and twice the woman was Miss Rabalais."

"Oh, Good Lord."

They heard shouting just then, and Allison (oh, hell, Alicia), rushed back out of the room to tend to the problem.

Ce Ce had to come up with a plan. She knew the matrix had been helping. She couldn't explain how she knew, but she was certain the positive energy had kept Bobbie Faye alive so far. That girl had to be exhausted, all this running from the police to God-knows-what.

"Too bad you can't just put a big ol' whaahootzie spell on everyone. Make 'em all forget what egggsactly 'appened, ya know?"

Ce Ce eyed Monique who had, mysteriously, managed to fix herself another screwdriver. She had to have a flask around here somewhere. She shouldn't listen to anything Monique suggested at this stage of the disaster.

Still, there was something to the idea. She'd done a few of the really powerful spells over the years. If she hadn't seen the results with her own two eyes, she wouldn't have believed the spells had worked, but she'd seen and done things that really ought not to be able to be done.

She stepped over the snoring social worker, and started perusing the titles of the dusty, ancient books on her shelves, finally pulling out one weathered, worn tome; she had to hold it close to the lamp to make out the handwritten words.

She knew this spell. It was a powerful protection spell. Scary powerful. The old woman who'd taught her warned her: precise measurements, exact timing. Not a spell to trifle with, and she had had such a difficult ordeal that last time controlling everything to the degree it needed controlling, it had stressed her own immune system completely. She'd had to go to bed for two days afterwards.

But it could work.

She started grabbing supplies.

B obbie Faye and Trevor were in the eleventy-billionth tunnel, which only seemed to lead to more tunnels. They'd moved far enough away from the elevator that they could no longer hear the cutting torch making its way through the metal of the elevator car, but it wasn't going to be long before Cam got through.

Cam would stop her. If he could, he'd put her in jail for years, just for the satisfaction.

If she had to, would she shoot him? Put him in the hospital in order to save Roy? And Stacey? Would she do it for Stacey?

She was a far better shot. He had SWAT with him, of course, but she knew she was a better shot than most of them. The whole idea made her queasy and flush with dread.

They entered a cavernous room, several football fields long, with the dome of the room arching so far above them their flashlight couldn't penetrate the dark far enough to determine the height. Thousands and thousands of salt blocks stacked row after row complicated their perception of the room's size. It was a mammoth crop of salt blocks growing upwards as if trying to reach for the nonexistent sky, all covered with mounds of salt fluff. Each block was a good three feet by three feet square, and most rows were three blocks wide. The light from their flashlight couldn't pierce the well of shadows filling the length of the rows, so there was no telling exactly what was ahead, whether there was an exit and, if so, which direction. They could run through these rows for hours before finding the way out.

"We've got to go up," Trevor said, aiming the flashlight and finding a row where the blocks weren't as neatly stacked, giving him handholds.

"Up?" she said, wishing that tremor in her voice hadn't just been there, hoping he wouldn't notice it.

"Yeah, up. The dogs won't track us up here, and we would be able to see where the exit is and go across the rows if we need to, instead of weaving around."

"Up," she said again, her fear squeaking out a bit. "I'm not real big on *up*. I'd kinda rather go around."

"We don't have time."

He didn't give her a chance to argue. He just started climbing.

"Great. I had to go and kidnap Spider-Man."

She had no choice but to follow, knowing she was going to fall.

When they reached the summit, which was at least forty freaking feet off the floor, she stayed in a squat, hanging onto the top salt block while Trevor stood, calmly surveying the span of the room. Then he turned his attention to where she had a white-knuckled grip on the block, and he squatted down next to her.

"You realize you're gonna have to let that go to get across the room."

"Bastard."

He laughed. "So the tough chick is afraid of something."

"If I admit I am, can we go back down?"

"Not yet." He pointed off to his right. "I think I see the exit over there. We've got to go across these rows to get out." He turned back to her, clearly amused at her immobility.

"Quit enjoying this."

"What? You hunkered down like a monkey? I wish I had a camera."

"I hate you."

"I think we have established that you don't."

"Hmph. I am seriously rethinking that position."

He stood, holding out his hand. "C'mon, Bobbie Faye. We're running out of time."

She grabbed his hand and prayed. Fear hammered in her chest and her adrenaline pulsed so forcefully, it was as if it were turning her inside out, trying to move her against her will. She wouldn't have been surprised to look down and discover that her arms and legs had shed their bones somewhere and she had melted into a noodle-soft pile of goo.

He glanced down and she followed the beam of his flashlight: their footprints were visible in the drifts of salt on the floor below. He scooped salt fluff piled in drifts across the top of the blocks and threw it down onto the tracks. Bobbie Faye stayed very still as he worked around her. When he was done and shone the flashlight down again, the tracks nearest where they had climbed were completely covered.

"Hey, you're pretty good."

"I'm damned good."

"Obnoxious and modest, too."

"Yep. C'mon."

They ran down the row, then leapt onto the next row, just a few feet away, while clanging metal thumps and the muffled hum of men shouting and working echoed in the huge chamber, not nearly far enough behind them.

Sweat rolled down Cam's arms as one of the SWAT guys used a small portable blowtorch to cut through the bottom of the lodged elevator car. He knew they weren't far behind Bobbie Faye and Cormier. Every spark flying off the metal felt like seconds burning.

Aaron, the SWAT leader, tapped him on the shoulder. He was holding a hand up to press his earbud into his ear, and then leaned in to shout above the hiss of the torch.

"You gotta get back to the surface. Benoit's got something urgent for you."

Not. Fucking. Again. He knew he was *thisclose* to cuffing Bobbie Faye. *Thisclose* to keeping her from getting killed in the inevitable cross fire he sensed was coming; he felt it all the way to the cellular level of his bones.

"When you cut through, you lead the team on down. I'll follow as soon as I can."

He climbed the lead ropes with a jury-rigged pulley system to get to the surface and ran through the tunnels. When he got out of the tunnel where he could use the satellite phone, he found one of the SWAT members there, holding it out to him.

"What?" he barked into the phone.

"The Professor's down."

"What!"

"He's not dead," Benoit said, frustration slipping into his cadence, "but he's not good."

"How? I thought you put him in a cell by himself?"

"I did. I also made sure that he wasn't even in a cell next to anyone. We found him on the floor, his lips blue, all sorts of symptoms the paramedic said looked like some kind of poison."

"Who the hell's been back there to see him?"

"Just Dellago, and they were in the general attorney area, not alone, and Vicari watched them, though he couldn't hear what was said. The Professor seemed fine after Dellago left and hadn't ingested anything, and there's nothing yet to prove that Dellago had anything to do with it."

"Oh, you can believe Dellago had something to do with it. I just can't believe he'd be so bold to try to murder his client right under our noses. What have you got on surveillance?"

"Nothing helpful. We're reviewing it. He was brought a lunch, since he hadn't eaten all day, and water. He seemed fine, afterwards, and it was brought to him by Robineaux, and he's damned trustworthy, so I don't know what to think."

"The Prof say anything?"

"He just kept saying *nap, nap, nap* and a bunch of gibberish that didn't make sense."

"Exactly what kind of gibberish?"

"Hell, Cam, I couldn't understand it. Something about boats and naps and one time, I thought he said *gold,* but the paramedic said he was cold, so that's probably what it was. When we moved him out through the lobby area, he raised up and said to me, 'Not corn. Right?' He said it three or four times."

"Not corn? What the hell is that?"

"I don't know. He had corn on the lunch plate, so maybe something was up with that, but he looked so . . . desperate. It was weird."

"Okay, I need you to put a twenty-four-hour guard on his hospital room, and get someone we can trust at the hospital to review all meds going into that room, even if a doctor orders it. He's got to know something pretty freaking big for them to hit him like this."

Cam fumed. Then remembered what he'd originally sent Benoit to do, and his stomach knotted at the lack of news.

"Still no word on Stacey?" he asked.

"Damnit, no. I talked to Ce Ce a while, which was a complete dead end."

"You sound like you think she was telling the truth."

"Let's just say she was highly motivated to cooperate."

"I don't want to know what that is about, do I?"

"Nope. I honestly don't believe she knows anything. Bobbie Faye doesn't confide in anyone, according to Ce Ce, especially when she's got a problem. What about that best friend of hers, Nina?"

"I think Nina already gave us everything she knew. If she knows anything else that she doesn't want to tell, you'll never get it out of her, not even at gunpoint. That is one cold cookie."

Cam heard shouts from the tunnel.

"Do we have a guard on the sister?"

"Yeah. Watts."

"Good. And don't let up on finding that kid."

"Got it."

Cam hustled back to the elevator shaft and shimmied down the ropes faster than was smart to do. As he arrived back in the elevator car the SWAT team were squeezing through the hole cut in the bottom panel of the box and then clipping onto the cables and sliding down to the bottom of the shaft. Cam used borrowed gear to follow them.

As he plummeted to the bottom, he knew Bobbie Faye was running on pure fear. She was afraid of heights, and, something she rarely told anyone, she was afraid of the dark. To have slid down that shaft—in the suffocating pitch black? It had probably scared the living hell out of her.

At the bottom of the shaft, the elevator doors were closed, and it took several minutes for SWAT to pry them open. They clipped on night goggles and swept the area for anything producing heat, and then shook their heads at Cam.

Off came the night goggles and on went their high-beam Mag-Lites. There were footprints in what looked like snow on the floor. He squatted, examining them. Dipped his finger into the fluff and smelled it.

Salt.

The dogs were gonna have a hard time with that.

He looked over the shoe prints. Definitely Bobbie Faye's boots.

He heard a commotion as someone came through the elevator car behind him, and when he spun and shone the flashlight eye-level, he was greeted with a glare from the other man's light.

Oh, hell.

Zeke arrived with his colleagues only a second behind him, and he sported a slitty-eyed, sick predator gleam.

"Where does this dome exit?" the agent asked.

Cam looked to SWAT team leader Aaron.

"Beats the hell out of us. We couldn't find it documented on any map we had. We pulled archival records on our way here when you gave us the location of the shack, just to see what was around here, and that shack wasn't even on the charts. If they mapped it, it never got scanned into the computers."

"We need to secure this room, then," Zeke said. "Cormier will set up somewhere where he can pick us off."

"No, that's not his intent." Cam squatted again near the prints. "Look . . ." He swept the Mag-Lite back and forth, letting the beam rove over the footprints until they stopped and there were several overlapping in one area, like the couple had stood there a moment. Cam ran the flashlight beam up to an antique wall phone, clearly cleaned of salt fluff.

Okay, not what he expected. And weird.

He turned to Aaron. "Put Jason on that line. Get him to run it through the computers and see who was called."

"Doesn't matter," Zeke said. "Cormier's cornered, he's going to set up and take us down, one by one. I know this man."

"Yeah, well, I know that woman. And she's not stopping."

"Then she's going to get in his way, and we'll be finding her body pretty soon."

"Aw, you're starting to sound like you actually care."

"I feel sorry for any citizen who gets in the way of Cormier."

"I think you've been feeling sorry for the wrong person," Cam drawled, and the SWAT team grinned. "You can stay here and set up a perimeter, but I'm going after her."

"You'll be dead in an hour," the agent said then, giving Cam a grim shrug.

Chapter Thirty-five

I'm sorry ma'am, but we can't fill your propane tank if we are within one hundred and fifty feet of any open flame, a barbeque pit, or Bobbie Faye. Especially around Bobbie Faye. I speak from experience.

—Mike M. Wayne, whose eyebrows and hair are growing back. Finally.

As they reached the other side of the cavern, Trevor pointed out the exit. After a moment, he arched his eyebrows at her. "Bobbie Faye? I need my hand back to be able to climb down."

She'd been clutching it with such a death-grip, her own ached.

"Sorry."

They scaled down the salt blocks and when they hit bottom and were on firm ground again, it was everything she could do to keep from dropping and kissing the floor.

"I can't believe I actually made it across that without breaking my neck."

"I can't believe you made it across without breaking *my* neck, either," he muttered as they ran through the exit.

Far, far away, in a tunnel on the other side of the cavern, dogs barked and men's boots thudded, running toward them. She and Trevor kept up an exhausting pace, until something caught Bobbie Faye's eye, and she went back for it.

"What in the hell are you doing?" he hissed.

"Getting directions," she snapped, and she ripped off a placard which had been embedded in the salt wall ages earlier. "Look."

They scanned the faded YOU ARE HERE image and Bobbie Faye was just thankful there wasn't a little icon of Satan and pitchforks. They reversed out of that tunnel, backtracked to one they'd passed up, and turned. A few minutes later, they stood in front of what looked like a much newer elevator.

Bobbie Faye punched the button, and when they heard the elevator car actually moving, she spun and flung her arms around Trevor's neck, impulsively giving him a kiss.

Holy geez, did the man know how to take advantage of it, once the surprise wore off.

He pulled her tight, leaning into her, his hands hot on her skin, his fingertips caressing her exposed back where her shirt had been cut off. She forgot for a full minute where the hell she was and what she was supposed to be doing. Just feeling his stubble scrape her cheek, feeling the muscles corded in his back, feeling his lips on hers, demanding . . . a couple more minutes, she would have forgotten her name.

The elevator dinged behind her, and she broke away, giving him one of her rare, high-wattage smiles, seeing her smile reflected in his own surprised grin. As the elevator doors opened, she spun around, and Trevor looked past her . . .

At an older man dressed in a guard's uniform, his gun still holstered. He seemed just as surprised to see them as they were to see him, and his eyes widened and his hands shook as he tried to pull his gun.

Then he squinted, and recognition drove his bushy brows skyward.

"Oh, no no no! You! You're . . . you're . . . you're that Contraband Days Queen!" and he promptly turned to flee, apparently forgetting he was standing in an elevator car and smacked squarely into the frame of the door, knocking himself out cold. Trevor caught him just before he slammed to the floor.

"Ooookaaaaay," Bobbie Faye said as they peered down at the un-conscious man. "That's a new one."

"You're like some sort of stealth weapon." Trevor dragged the guard backwards into the elevator. "I'm stunned the governor lets you roam free."

"It's not from the lack of trying on his part."

She stepped in the elevator car and the doors closed.

"Let's see that tiara," Trevor said before they pressed the up but-ton. He examined it, running his fingers over the markings and the inscription.

"What does this mean?"

"*Ton trésor est trouvé*? Oh, that just means your treasure is here. You know, found. Like this." She put the tiara on and motioned, voila. She spun and when she turned back, there was a gleam in his eyes that raked her up and down, and she blushed.

"Um, my great-great-great-Paw Paw said this phrase all the time, apparently. You know, like we should treasure ourselves, what we have."

"Not that your, er, Paw Paw wasn't a great guy or anything," he said, "but maybe he meant treasure, like money treasure. As in the real thing. It would explain why this tiara is so important to the kidnapper."

"Couldn't be. My great-grandma said they were really poor. He'd been a blacksmith. She used to joke that there was a sign-up sheet for use of the spoon at supper."

"It doesn't make any sense."

"Welcome to my world."

She took off the tiara and examined it. What the hell had the old great-great-great-lunatic meant by that saying, though? She squinted and turned it to see if she could read the part of the inscription which had worn off over the years, but the letters were too obliter-ated to make them out.

If there had been real treasure, her family would have already grabbed it and blown it on something completely insane and inappropriate—something which would have very likely gotten them into more trouble or destroyed their lives in a spectacularly memorable way. She'd have heard about that by now, if it had happened to one of her great-greats. Nah, her family would have scrabbled after any sort of treasure with all of the finesse of a circus clown.

Then again, just the whiff of the idea of a treasure would make some people crazy. What if someone misunderstood that inscription? What if the guy holding Roy thought this crazy tiara was really worth money?

Trevor punched the up button and she drew her gun, aiming it at the door as the elevator lurched upwards.

Everything was going to have to have precise measurements for the spell to work, and Ce Ce needed to be able to concentrate. Amid the snoring from the Social Services worker and Monique's singing of folk ballads, Ce Ce was a little concerned this might not be the ideal work situation.

She cleared a space on the countertop and sorted out all of the supplies, pulling unlabeled items from her shelves. She had the candles lit, the ingredients ready, her measuring cups and spoons. Boiling water from the kitchenette off her office was nearly ready.

She turned back to her earthenware bowl. It was missing. She knew she'd set it on the counter.

"You know," Monique slurred, "for a place called a Cajun Outfitter and Feng Shui Emporium, Ce Ce, Voodoo ain't really Feng Shui. Didja know that?"

Ce Ce glanced over to Monique. Who was wearing the earthenware bowl as a hat. Ce Ce took it back, explaining, "This isn't Voodoo. It's more positive, affirming. Getting everything to flow the right direction. It's . . . Feng Doo."

"Feng Doo? Doo doo doowhop," Monique sang.

Ce Ce hoped like hell this spell worked.

. . . .

When the elevator doors slid open onto a small, industrial gray room, two guards immediately dropped their weapons and threw their hands up in the air in the face of two guns aimed at them.

Bobbie Faye quickly checked out the room: one large desk, a phone, a TV set (which had a video game hooked up to it), and discarded lunch remnants in the trash.

The older guard, Bobbie Faye guessed him to be about sixty, said, "There ain't a damned thing here but salt, and you're welcome to it."

"But ain't there a safe in the manager's office for payroll?" the young guard asked.

The older guard rolled his eyes and his shoulders sagged.

"Kids," he grumbled.

"I'm not a kid! I'm nineteen."

The older guard turned to Bobbie Faye. "I promise to say he provoked you if you'd just shoot him."

"Why don't you sit down instead?" Trevor asked, indicating their chairs.

He pulled rope from his satchel and cut it into appropriate lengths. As he was tying the older guard, he had the younger one tie up the unconscious guard. The kid kept stealing glances at Bobbie Faye, and then the surprise of an epiphany slacked his jaw.

"Hey! You're the Contraband Days Queen!"

"What the hell is wrong with all you men, recognizing me without makeup? Looking like something roadkill would turn its nose up over. Don't you know the least you can do when you see a woman like this is pretend not to know her?"

"You look the same to me."

"Let me guess. You don't have a girlfriend."

"Or a long life expectancy," Trevor chimed in.

"Hey. Could you autograph my uniform or something?"

Trevor thankfully gagged the boy and Bobbie Faye focused on the markings of the tiara. If someone believed the rumors, if someone had misunderstood the inscription, then they must think the tiara itself was some sort of clue, right? That had to be it, but for it to be a clue, then it would have had to have been made by someone who knew where a treasure was, and there was only one—

Oh, holy fucking shit.

That really couldn't be it.

No. No freaking way.

She rattled around the thought, not quite touching it, and she stared off into space, her breathing slowed, her every movement stilled.

Could it?

She looked at the kid. "Am I going to bring down a bunch of guards if I use this phone?"

He shook his head, and the older guard sighed, clearly annoyed that the kid had no concept of what exactly a guard is for.

"You're onto something?" Trevor asked, moving from tying up the guards to sabotaging the elevator.

She simply turned to the phone, punched nine, got a dial tone, and dialed Ce Ce's private number.

Chapter Thirty-six

We now guarantee all of our ferry rides are 100 percent Bobbie Faye free.

—notice on ferry dock in Plaquemine, LA

Ce Ce had a vial of the crushed leaves of a rare orchid held above her measuring spoon. She needed to put exactly one milligram into the bowl, and as she tapped the vial, her private line rang.

She jumped, snatching the vial away from the bowl and spun, yanking the handset from its cradle.

"Bobbie Faye?"

"How the hell did you know it was me?"

"I kept hoping, hon, that you'd be okay and call. Are you?"

"I'm okay, Ceece. Just running real short on time, so no time to explain. I need to know something important."

"Shoot."

"Was Jean Lafitte a blacksmith?"

"Sure, honey. Everyone knows that. And his brother, too."

"Shit."

"What's wrong?"

"Everything. Look, do you know if he had a special mark or something that he used as a signature?"

"Hang on. Lemme look."

Ce Ce put the vial down safely away from Monique, who was now decorating the snoring Social Services woman with glitter (where in the world that came from, Ce Ce didn't know). It took a couple of minutes to find the right book. She blew the dust off the jacket, the pages cracking and some loosening as she slowly opened it, gently turning to the section she remembered.

While she read the text and scanned the drawings, she heard Monique pick up the phone behind her.

"Heeeeeeeeeeeeeeyyyy, there be Bobbieee Faaaaaye," Monique sang into the handset. "How'ya doin? Yanno, we're gonna have to change your hair, give you some highlights and such if you end up in jail 'cuz I don't think orange is gonna suit you all that great with your coloring."

Ce Ce grabbed the phone away. "Sorry, honey."

"How many screwdrivers has she had?"

"Five, I think. I still haven't figured out where she stashes the flask."

"Did you find the mark in the book?"

"Yeah, honey, it's in here. Old Marie St. Claire had a real thing for Lafitte, apparently. Thought he was handsome. She wrote all about—"

"Ceece. Just the marking. What does it look like?"

"It's a lot of cross-hatching. And if you turn it on its side, it should look like a cursive 'L.' Sort of."

"Sonofoafreakingbitch."

"Honey, you okay?"

"Not yet, Ceece. I've got something to do. Have you found Stacey yet?"

"Not yet, hon, but I'm working on it."

There was silence for a long moment.

"Honey, you've got to tell me—"

"I have to go, Ceece. And thank you. For everything."

The line went dead, and Ce Ce immediately looked at the caller ID: unknown name, unknown number.

Her hand shook as she hung up the phone, and when she turned back to the bowl of ingredients, Monique was playing with the vial of orchid leaves, her screwdriver spilled onto the counter near the bowl. Ce Ce grabbed the vial back before Monique could pour the entire contents onto the Social Services woman.

A re you okay?" Trevor asked, as Bobbie Faye paced back and forth in front of the phone.

"Oh, sure, I'm okay. I'm perfectly okay. Do I not embody the profound okayness of an okay person? I'm so freaking okay, they're going to make posters of me for 'Okay, Central.' Why wouldn't I be okay?"

"Well, the head spinning and fire emanating from your ears might be a sign that all is not well."

She gawked at him as he paused a moment in his efforts to block the stairwell with the guards' desk. "Do you know what this is?" she asked, waving the tiara in his direction as they moved away from the guards, presumably to an exit.

"Well, in *my* universe, it's a tiara."

"Ha! Then you'd be wrong. This, this *thing* my great-great-great-grandfather made is valuable because of *who* he was. Jean Lafitte. *Jean Lafitte*. I'm related to Jean Lafitte. Me. *Related*. To a crazy, black-hearted pirate who ran over everyone to get what he wanted."

"I'd say 'pot' meet 'kettle,' but I like the arrangement of all my limbs."

"I can't believe this."

"What's so hard to believe? He lived around here. Someone's bound to be related to him."

"Oh, no. No, you don't understand. You know what I know? I know that my great-great-great-aunt Cora's corns hurt her whenever she was going to have company, but that conveniently happened every Friday when the local butcher came by to make his deliveries. I know that my brilliant uncle Ansean and his friend decided to rob the liquor store and hung around all night playing pool and drinking and decided when it was getting daylight, that he wanted to take the pool table with him, and he couldn't understand why in the world the police stopped him to question him. I know fifty kazillion *useless* stupid things my idiot family has done and you know why? Because this is the South and we tell every single one of our crazy family stories to anyone who will listen for the sheer entertainment value, so you would think that, at some point, a couple of my relatives could have rubbed a few of their brain cells together and remembered to pass along the little nugget that we're related to a freaking *pirate*. At least I might have known why the kidnapper wanted the stupid tiara."

She stopped venting a moment, having to draw a breath, and heard a rumbling sound she couldn't place, and she looked to Trevor, who frowned.

"I think your ex found the stairwell. And the barricade. It won't hold him for long."

She snatched a leftover piece of rope from what he'd used to tie the guards. "Great. Just freaking lovely." She tied the tiara to a front belt loop. "The way things are going today, Cam will find out I'm related to a pirate and somehow, everything they ever did will be all my fault, and he'll put me in jail so long there'll be another ice age before I'm out."

"What in the hell did you do to him?"

"Why does everyone always assume I'm the one who's done something to the guy, huh? Why can't it be that he did something to me? Is it because there's some sort of testosterone signal that goes out and you instantly agree with each other to blame the woman?"

"Okay. So what did he do to you?"

"He arrested my sister."

"What was she doing? Murder? Aggravated assault? Some other sort of genetically predisposed mayhem."

"Geez. Thanks. It was a simple DUI."

"Ah. You broke up, and he got revenge by arresting your sister."

"No, we were dating. I'd told him she had a problem and I was worried about her and wanted to get her into detox, and he went and arrested her."

Trevor scowled, puzzled. "You were still dating?"

She nodded.

"Seriously? As in, long term?"

"About a year."

"And he arrested your sister?"

"Yep."

"Was he suicidal?"

"What do you mean?"

"Well, assuming he planned on seeing you again and possibly sleeping with you, he'd had to have had a death wish to pull a stunt like that. You don't do that to the woman you're dating, especially if you're serious."

"*Thank you*. He thinks he was doing the 'right thing.'"

Metallic grinding and whirring noises filtered into the hallway and they slowed, listening to the sounds grow as they approached a large manufacturing area. There were giant chopping machines and packaging equipment and shipping conveyor belts all rusted from long-term exposure to drifts of salt. The conveyor angled up up up to what must be an exit several stories above the floor.

Bobbie Faye and Trevor hung back in the shadows. She counted seven workers on the floor and a manager on an elevated glassed-in platform where the glass protected the computer from the salt. On one wall, at a right angle to the manager's platform, there was a plate glass window: a break room. Inside, a TV played the aerial footage of the bank robbery, and the anchors droned on and on. Two workers sat transfixed by the footage. Between the break room and the platform were two secretarial desks facing the promised land: another elevator.

The cutting machine shaved the salt blocks into smaller blocks, which were being wrapped in a plastic label and set on a conveyor. There were dozens of other smaller machines, all banging and whizzing and chirping, doing God-knows-what, motors running loud enough to drown out Bobbie Faye and Trevor's whispered conversation.

She squinted and could see the footage details. She couldn't be seeing what she thought she was seeing.

Her trailer.

Lying on its side.

Broken into halves.

She was going to kill Claude and Jemy, whose trucks and winches were still tied to the trailer as they tried to pull one of the halves upright.

No. Do not think that. She was just going to think positive this time. What was Ce Ce always yammering about? Something about positive thinking creating the reality that you want to live in, and by thinking it, you create it?

So fine. Positive thinking. Positive fucking thinking. She could do positive thinking. Buddhist monks were going to line up to learn how to think as positively as she could think. She'd give seminars.

She heard the sound of dogs baying. Dim, far far away.

Growing louder.

The positive doohickey thing in her brain was apparently in the "off, and fuck you" position.

Chapter Thirty-seven

South Louisiana resident makes first million selling "Bobbie Faye" debris on eBay. Expects to double his sales next quarter.

—lead story in Entrepreneur *magazine*

Cam, the SWAT team, the FBI agents, the dog handler, and the dogs lined up in the crowded stairwell. The disabled elevator forced them up the stairs, which were, of course, blocked. The SWAT had tried kicking the door in, to no avail.

"Blow it," Zeke said.

Cam shook his head, and pressed an ear against the door. He'd heard something. Muffled. Grunting.

"Someone's tied up just on the other side. We can't blow it or we could kill them."

"Well, we don't have the luxury of just waiting around," Zeke barked. "Cormier could be getting away."

"Since when did your mandate include killing innocent civilians?" Cam asked, enjoying the way Zeke had to bite back an answer.

Cam turned to Aaron. "We have any acetylene left?"

"A little."

"Enough to cut off the hinges here? We could pull the door forward to us if we make the cuts right. Then move whatever's blocking the door."

Aaron nodded, and in a few seconds, two of his team flared up the torches, one tackling the top hinge, the other, the bottom.

The key," Trevor whispered in her ear, "is not to sneak over to the elevator because that will draw the employees' attention. Just walk normally, head down like you're reading something."

"Right, so I can walk straight into one of those machines which will probably fold me into some sort of origami figure and mail me somewhere."

"Nah, those machines have large knives. They're cutting the salt blocks. You'd never make it out whole enough to mail. See all of the poles between the workstations? They're pretty evenly spaced. They've got telephones, looks like intercoms to the manager area. If you move toward those, if anyone notices you, they'll probably just mistake you for an employee going to call the floor manager."

Right. Because she looked so much like an *employee* with her SHUCK ME, SUCK ME shirt, now so filthy that the SHUCK ME was barely visible.

Trevor led the way. They walked casually, separated, and then moved around the machinery and the workstations. No one noticed either of them, from what Bobbie Faye could tell. She made her way slowly toward the elevator, backtracking twice to avoid workers she hadn't been able to see until she turned a corner. She bumped into one of the phones on the columns and knocked it off its cradle, and the dial tone was nightmarishly loud. She hung it up fast, pretended to be busy at a machine when she thought someone noticed her.

She waited.

No one was cuffing her. Okay, safe so far. She continued on, leaning past a whirring machine or a stack of boxes to see if the next aisle was clear.

The constant patter of the TV news teams ran in the background, and she tried to ignore it, the constant commentary on her life, her every public appearance since she was three. First, they were finishing up with Susannah—the water company, LSU dean-boinking loon.

"Oh, definitely," the loon was saying. "She's certifiable."

A few seconds later, they switched to another reporter who was interviewing her second-grade teacher. "We all knew Bobbie Faye was a little high strung, but we were very well-practiced on our fire drills!"

She peered around the cabinet again, didn't see anyone, and started to step out when someone snatched her back, hand clamped over her mouth.

Trevor.

Who pointed to another worker she hadn't seen. She would have stepped out in front of him. He pulled her back into a nook out of most of the employees' lines of sight.

"Jeez," she hissed, low, "you could have signaled you were behind me."

"I didn't want the employee to hear."

"I think you just like scaring the crap out of me."

"That, too."

She smacked his arm.

"So, genius, how are we supposed to get out of here?"

"Besides running for the elevator?"

"And then we teleport to Plaquemine? You said you had ideas."

"There are a couple of helicopter outfits not far from here that ferry workers to the rigs. I was planning on stealing a helo."

"Wow, subtle. 'Cause no one's going to miss a whole helicopter."

"I didn't say it was a *perfect* idea."

"Wonderful."

She scowled at him. Then sunk her head into her hands. This wasn't his fault. She had to remember that. She was the one who'd gotten *him* into this. He'd been grouchy, but very helpful. She could deal with grouchy. Especially sexy grouchy.

She stared at the floor, listening to the patter on the TV, then glanced up to see yet more aerial footage of the burning shack.

She grinned at him.

"What?"

"I think," she whispered, "that it's time for someone to get an exclusive on the Bobbie Faye story."

She looked back at the local network station, proudly displaying its contact number at the bottom of the TV screen. She eased around to one of the columns and grabbed the phone. When she was done, it was all she could do not to throw both hands in the air in a mock "touchdown" score.

"We have a breaking news alert," a woman reporter said, interrupting the second-grade teacher's prattling and riveting Bobbie Faye and Trevor to the TV. "Ms. Sumrall's alleged partner in the bank heist this morning has been whisked out of the jail and into an ambulance. We're trying to get word on the scene as to exactly what happened."

She noticed Trevor had been holding his breath and let it out slowly. They both craned around a cabinet to get a view of the TV. The scene switched to Cam's state police station where a mob of reporters were drilling the police representative, Cam's friend Benoit, with questions. He stopped them with universal cop sign, hand up, palm out.

"We don't have any comment at this time."

"Is it true," one reporter persisted, "that he was poisoned?"

"Again, no comment."

"Or," the same reporter continued, "that when you found him, he kept repeating *nap nap nap*? Or *gold*?"

Bobbie Faye watched Benoit adopt a poker face, and she knew him well enough to know he was ticked and that the reporter was correct.

"I'm not sure where you're getting your information," Benoit said, "but you're creating fascinating fiction. The man was cold and he wanted to sleep. I'm sure we'll know more after the doctors can tend to him."

Nap. Man she wanted a nap. Nap nap nap, her brain hummed, as she tried to shut it up.

She peeked out and their path was blocked by two people who'd entered the aisle.

Nap nap nap nap nap cold, her brain sang. Nap nap nap nap nap cold. Nap nap gold. Nap gold. Nap nap gold.

Nap nap nap nap gold, her brain kept singing. Stuck in a groove.

She fingered the tiara for the hundredth time since getting it from Alex, just to make sure she still had it, now re-tied to the front of her jeans.

Nap nap nap gold.

Nap gold.

She looked down at the tiara.

Nap. Gold. *Ton trésor est trouvé.* Nap. Gold. Treasure.

Jean Lafitte had been given Napoleon's gold, just before Napoleon was exiled to Elba. She grew up hearing this story a hundred times in high school and another thousand at the Contraband Days Festival.

Napoleon's gold. Treasure.

Oh, holy hell.

She looked at the odd markings on the backside of the tiara. Marks she'd grown up thinking were nothing more than scratches garnered through years of wear and tear.

"What's wrong?" Trevor whispered as she turned the tiara to catch the light so she could see the markings a little clearer.

"Fuck," she whispered back.

"Sorry, I'm going to need a little more to go on to understand," his voice rumbled in her ear, "because I don't think you're asking for a quickie in the middle of this room."

"I think this is a treasure map."

His eyebrows shot up. "A what?"

"Nap. Gold," she said, pointing to the TV, where they were re-hashing everything which had been said, who'd said it, and what everyone thought about everything that had been said. "I think the bank robber was trying to say *Napoleon's gold.* He was definitely in that bank to get something more than money, and he definitely waited around to get the tiara, and now he's babbling about

Napoleon's gold and it sounds like someone tried to kill him. I think he was saying 'nap' as in Napoleon. And gold."

The anchorwoman broke in again. This time there was a current photo of the Professor in the right-hand corner of the TV screen. He was dressed much nicer in a business suit, posed in front of a well-appointed desk, with expensive bookshelves filled with heavy tomes behind him.

"We've now confirmed the identity of the alleged bank robber, though this seems to have taken his colleagues by complete surprise. The man seen here in this footage—"

There was a new graphic placed under the Professor's photo, which contained the surveillance footage from the bank showing the Professor with his gun and "dynamite."

"—shows the same man now known to us as Professor Bartholomew Fred, Professor of Antiquities at LSU. He has had an esteemed record of discoveries, particularly with old manuscripts and journals, and had been quite excited over the last few days, according to his secretary, who didn't know the Professor's whereabouts today until she saw our footage earlier this afternoon."

The anchor continued with a background of the Professor, all his colleagues either "no commenting" or giving glowing speeches, but Bobbie Faye tuned out and stared at Trevor, who looked oddly back at her.

"Professor of Antiquities," she whispered, and then she looked down at the tiara again.

Holy freaking bouncing Buddhas. She had to be right. Napoleon's gold. She'd been wearing the map to *Napoleon's gold* on her head. For years. When she was too broke to pay her taxes, too broke to pay her electric bill, too broke to buy lunch meat for Stacey for her school lunches and had made do with peanut butter and jelly for the zillionth time.

No wonder the kidnapper wanted the damned thing.

Trevor stiffened, and Bobbie Faye dragged her focus back to their present. And realized: she could hear the dogs baying. A helluva lot louder.

"They got through the stairwell door," he said. "We have to go straight to that elevator. Just pretend you belong here, and we should be able to get there without someone stopping us."

"Right, because two muddy, filthy people who reek of swamp and sweat won't be noticeable."

"Unless you plan on taking everyone in the room hostage, too, I think that's our only choice."

Bobbie Faye looked at the elevator, a good thirty yards away, with secretaries and workers between them and it. Behind her: the banging and clamoring of the dogs slinging through the corridors, and the heavy tromping of boots as the men followed.

Which got the attention of every single person in the room.

And they all turned to see what the commotion was about.

Which meant that there was not going to be any "walking casually to the elevator" plan put into action.

Especially when Bobbie Faye heard Cam as he ran through that corridor, a few steps ahead of the rest of the men (damn him to hell for staying in shape), and she could hear him shouting, "Bobbie Faye! Stay right the hell where you are."

She turned and realized that the nook they were standing in was easily seen from the hallway, and she and Trevor were in Cam's direct line of sight.

Cam was holding his gun, ready to raise it if need be. He was giving her a look, half fury, half . . . what? Fear?

She had her own gun, ready.

She didn't have time to decide.

Trevor shot his gun, aiming it up, into the ceiling, and everyone in the place screamed. Most ran. Several crossed between Cam and where she and Trevor hid, and Trevor yanked her hard toward the elevator.

Chapter Thirty-eight

Our best sales? During a big storm or a Bobbie Faye event. People are trapped and they need to cope.

—*J.P. Paul, beer deliveryman*

C am saw her. Cornered. Trevor standing behind her, one arm around her waist. Cam couldn't tell if she wanted his arm there, or if Cormier was forcing her, controlling her. The fact that she had a gun registered only after the personal space the two escapees seemed to be sharing did. And with that gun in her hand, he knew Cormier couldn't be forcing her; she didn't mind his arm around her. Maybe even wanted it to be there.

Sonofabitch.

The way her eyes darted, measuring the space from where she stood to his location at the hallway opening, told him what was racing through her mind: could she take out the SWAT team before they slowed her down?

He'd never seen such a desperate expression in her eyes, not even the time she'd asked him to let Lori Ann go. There was a wave of absolute primal fear vibrating off her, and he knew she was calculating her shot odds as soon as she'd heard the SWAT running toward her.

Yeah, she might try to take out the SWAT team. Which still left the FBI, who would kill her to get to Cormier.

"Bobbie Faye! Stay right the hell where you are!"

He had his gun ready, but not aimed at her. He saw her think about raising her own, and he gave her a look. *If you do, you'd better kill me.*

He understood, then, he'd let her fire first. He couldn't draw down on her, couldn't put her seriously in the eyesight of the barrel of his gun, not even to wound her.

What in the hell was wrong with him?

He didn't have time to think; Cormier fired upwards, sending everyone screaming and running. Massive chaos put the civvies between Cam and Bobbie Faye as Cormier yanked her toward the elevator, and she stumbled, crashing into a pole, then spun, and as she got her footing, she shot Cam a look that challenged him to shoot her to stop her.

Goddamn her all to hell and back again.

And then she ran.

My God, she thinks she's going to make it to the elevator.

Shooting exploded around him, and Cam knew the time was up. The FBI were in the room, shouting, "Get down, get down," and "Freeze, Cormier," and yelling Bobbie Faye's name. All three of the FBI team had taken up protected positions behind machinery and were firing in the general direction of Trevor and Bobbie Faye.

They weren't even trying to aim. The asswipes. They were peppering the area, not caring what they hit. They had such a hard-on for Cormier, they had forgotten the civilians. And they clearly couldn't care less about Bobbie Faye.

He had to do something. People were going to get killed like this.

There was the elevator, ten feet away.

She zigged through machinery. Ducking. Hearing pings and metallic clanks as bullets whizzed by or embedded in something too close for comfort.

Eight feet.

She lost track of Trevor, and dodged around two desks, rolling down behind one as bullets skipped across the top like rocks on a calm lake, sending paperwork snowing to the floor.

Five feet.

The elevator doors were shut.

She couldn't exactly stand there and wait for them to open. She scanned around the floor, found a stapler which had fallen in the melee, and threw it at the button.

Missed. Sonofabitch.

She crawled to a paperweight, snagged it as another bullet bounced between the desks where she'd just been. Was it Cam who was shooting at her? The other guys?

Her stomach iced over as she thought about how much he must hate her to be shooting at her, to not care if she was dead. She tried not to think about the last time she was lying next to him, listening to him breathing, thinking then that he was, finally, *home*. Her home. Not the house, not a place, but a who.

And now that person was trying to kill her.

She tried to ignore the gnawing, gaping hole she felt in her heart and threw the paperweight.

Bang. Nailed the elevator button.

Watched the numbers trail downwards.

Everyone was going to know she'd thrown that paperweight. All eyes were undoubtedly focused on those doors. She was going to be a sitting duck in that car until those doors closed. She was going to have to shoot back into the room to force them all down. To buy time.

Where the hell was Trevor?

Then she saw him. Several feet away, behind another piece of machinery. Holding something . . . oh, holy freaking geez, he had the tiara. She looked down, and the rope that had held it to her front belt loop had been severed.

She looked back up at him just as the elevator dinged its arrival. She motioned to him, and as soon as she moved toward the elevator, a new carpeting of bullets scattered in her direction. Between them.

He shook his head.

And started to back away, taking the tiara with him.

She had a crisp flash of telling him it was a map. And that look in his eye . . . it had been that look she'd seen in the gunrunner's shed. The one where she knew he was way more than just the "helpful" guy he seemed at the time. The look that said he knew way the hell too much about guns.

Had that look been greed surfacing? Had it always been there? Did he decide somewhere along the way that whatever a kidnapper might go to that much trouble for would be worth a lot, and so he'd play along, pretending to help her to get it?

She knew she shouldn't have trusted anyone. She'd always known; she'd grown up knowing.

The elevator doors slid open, agonizingly slow.

"You go," he shouted. "You've got to get there."

"I've got to have the tiara," she shouted back. "They'll kill him if I don't have the tiara!"

Bullets blanketed the aisles between them.

"I'll meet you."

"Like *hell*. Throw it!"

More bullets slammed around her, then, and she could tell the shooters were getting closer. The antiquated elevator doors were starting to slide closed. She only had seconds.

Then, *pop. Pop pop pop,* the lights shattered above her. Shards of glass exploded and there were more screams and scurrying and running as the place went darker and darker. Men shouted.

Bobbie Faye looked back at Trevor.

He was gone.

The elevator door inched closer to closed.

More lights popped out.

She rolled, then. Somersaulted, actually, and flopped into the elevator car, the doors clipping her and bouncing open a little, then sliding closed again. Bullets embedded in the back of the car, just above her head.

As the doors slid shut, she saw the shooter of the lights, his gun still pointed up.

Cam.

*C*am? Shooting out the lights?

Helping? Motioning her to get down. *Cam.*

And Trevor . . . who'd been helping . . . now gone? With the tiara?

Absolutely nothing made sense.

The elevator crawled its way upwards as the inconsistencies swirled through her overwhelmed mind, her thoughts jumbled, hodgepodge, broken in waves of astonishment.

She had to find purchase somewhere. Some raft of rational thought. Some plan. She was drowning in confusion as the elevator doors opened. Another guard did a double-take from his desk as she stormed out of the car into his lobby. He started to stand, and she drew her gun on him.

"Does it look like I'm having a good day here?"

The guard, mid-forties, took in her rough appearance, with her torn, filthy shirt, stained jeans, scratches, bloodstains. "Can I just lie down on the floor instead of answering?"

"You are a smart man," she said, and read his name tag, "Bertrand. A very smart man."

He flattened himself on the floor and she removed his gun.

"I'm just gonna throw this outside. Wouldn't want you to get into trouble for it completely disappearing."

She turned to go.

"Wait!" he pleaded, and when she looked back at him, "Could you autograph my lunch pail? My wife will never forgive me if I didn't ask."

"On one condition. You tell them I knocked you out and you're not sure where I went when I went out the door. I promise you, it's for a good reason."

"Aw, hell, you're the Contraband Days Queen. I'd be real happy to help."

She didn't have time to marvel at that; she grabbed a Sharpie off his desk and scribbled her name across the closed lunch box set on the corner of his desk, then ran toward the front door when she heard the helicopter blades whirring closer.

With bright yellow call letters emblazoned on the side, WFKD, Channel 2, the media helicopter set down on the outer edge of the large parking lot. She jogged over to it, her gun in the back waistband of her jeans. She beamed the high-wattage Contraband Days Queen smile she'd learned from her mom. The cameraman grinned back.

"Are you for real?"

"As real as it gets."

"We actually get an exclusive?"

"Yep." She pulled out her gun. "While you're giving me a little ride."

"Oh, hell no. You never said anything about a gun, lady."

"Well, duh. Do you usually give people a ride if they call you up and say, 'Hi, have gun, need to take you hostage for a minute?' I promise you, it's going to be a huge story and no one else will have it. As soon as you drop me off, you can tell the police where I am."

She stepped toward him and the cameraman looked at the pilot.

"I heard she's a real good shot," the cameraman said.

The pilot, grizzled, old enough that he probably flew over Vietnam, looked at her and grinned.

"Do people tell you you're really cute when you're carrying a gun?"

"Not if they don't want to be shot."

"Wimps. C'mon. This better be good."

She climbed on board and gave them instructions, and the helicopter lifted off, spun, and headed east.

W hat the hell do you think you're doing?" Zeke yelled, and Cam grinned. God it felt good to annoy that officious jackass.

"Stopping you from killing innocent bystanders."

"Innocent, my ass. That woman had a gun. She aimed the gun at us. She clearly is working with Cormier, and I warned you that if she was, that made her a target. I'm going to make sure you're busted down so many grades, your kindergarten teacher is going to be greeting you next week."

"Be my guest."

"Where the hell did Cormier go?"

Cam shrugged.

One of Zeke's FBI colleagues ran up, short of breath.

"Sir. I tracked him to one of the conveyors. I think he went up it and into the loading dock."

"You run back and bring the helo around here. We'll scour the area. He can't have gotten far. There's nothing but swamp and marshland out there."

One of the FBI agents peeled off back toward the way they came in, while Zeke and his other agent ran back to the conveyor area and started climbing it, much the way Cam suspected Cormier had done earlier.

Cam sent two SWAT team members to tail the agents. "And if you see Cormier, remember, we're to bring him in alive. Unhurt."

He took the rest of the SWAT team up the elevator, where he found the guard lying on the floor, admiring the autograph on his lunch pail.

Cam looked at the autograph.

"You're fucking kidding me. She stopped to autograph this?"

"Uh, yeah. I think maybe she felt bad that she had to knock me out."

"Where'd she hit you?"

The man thought a second too long and Cam knew he was about to lie. Cam put his own gun to the man's head.

"You know what? I'm really tired. Where did she go?"

"I don't know! Out! Out the front door!"

"And then what?"

"Well. There, there might have been a helicopter?"

"Whose?"

The man cut his eyes up and to the right, and Cam suspected he was trying to come up with a lie. He pointed his gun at the man's autographed lunch box, directly on the autograph. The man flinched, aghast.

"What helicopter?"

"WFKD. Channel 2."

Cam rocked back on his heels.

What in the hell was she doing?

She hated heights. Loathed flying. Thought reporters were about ten rungs below maggots after they pestered her so severely during her last debacle. Really detested having her photo taken, and she'd been through a lake, a swamp, and God knows what all.

He and the rest of the SWAT team ran to the front door of the office and out into the parking lot. No WFKD helicopter. He did, however, have a signal on his cell again, and he dialed the other SWAT, only to shut the phone as they ran around the corner of the building to meet him.

"No sign of him," Aaron, said, "but they did determine a truck was missing. The FBI are already calling it in, trying to get an APB out on it."

Cam heard the FBI helicopter overhead and saw it land on the side of the building where Zeke and his men were waiting.

"I've already called ours," Aaron said. "There he is, now."

Once on board, the pilot asked, "Where to, boss?"

Cam had two people to chase, and one bird. His highest priority was Cormier. He had something, the Captain said, that they had to have. Probably some inside lead on evidence the state needed for a big case. He was a mercenary, according to his sheet. He'd probably been promised a big payoff for whatever information he had, which may have had something to do with him not shooting Cam when he had the chance. Kill a cop, the money goes away. In one direction, Bobbie Faye. The other, Cormier.

He made the only choice he could make.

Chapter Thirty-nine

Well . . . I told the boss he had to deal with another Bobbie Faye incident. He started crying and making out a resumé.

—*Shannon Kelsey to Kymm Zuckert, FEMA coworkers*

It took the cameraman almost ten minutes to set up the shot, which wasn't much of a shot, given that the inside of the helicopter was cramped and filled with enough state-of-the-art electronics to send the geekiest of geeks into orgasm. He apologized a little too profusely for his shaking hands and taking so long to set up. He looked at her through the camera, then popped up, a concerned frown scrunching up his chinless face.

"Did you know you were bleeding?"

She looked around and sure enough, there was blood on her hip, and when she pulled at the jeans a little, she saw where a bullet had ripped across the side there, taking material and a hefty gash of her skin with it, which was the cue for her brain to get over the shock and allow Pain to come out to play. She tried not to flinch.

"Great. Look, can we just get this on the record?"

"Uh, yeah, sure," the cameraman said. "You sure you don't need something? Band-Aid? Ointment?"

"Roll the camera."

Best to get on with it. She wasn't going to have another chance to tell her side, and if it turned out the way she thought it was going to turn out, she wanted at least some of the insanity explained. She hated the idea that Stacey would grow up referring to her as "my Crazy Aunt Bobbie Faye," never knowing the truth. Okay, never knowing the other truth, the reason behind the crazy.

The camera's red light popped on, and Bobbie Faye started talking, beginning with that morning and her first phone call to Roy.

B y the time Ce Ce got most of the ingredients poured into the bowl, there was a small crowd gathered in the storage room. Someone had propped the Social Services woman in the corner against a case of broken duck calls Ce Ce kept meaning to return. Ce Ce studiously ignored the fact that Monique had further decorated the woman with pipe cleaners she'd had in her purse. (Although the pipe-cleaner horns wound in the woman's hair were a nice touch.)

"That potion reeks," someone grumbled from the back of the crowd.

"Are you sure it's supposed to smell like that?" one of the twins asked.

"Of course it is."

"Is this Voodoo?"

"It's Stinky Doo!" Monique sang out, and Ce Ce paused a moment to glare at her.

It did emit a bad stench, and she tried to remember if it had smelled quite that awful last time. It reeked something like a sewer crossed with rotting chicken marinated in orange juice: sharp, pungent, rank, eye-watering.

"Hey, we can use these," someone exclaimed, and there was a lot of rushing and bustling about around a set of shelves just beyond her range of vision as she carefully tapped out the ground antler. When she looked up, the entire group had clothespins on their noses and tears streaming down their faces.

"Y'all don't have to stay."

"No, we want to," the other twin said, though quite nasally. "We've got to root for Bobbie Faye."

"Fine. No more complaining."

She had four more ingredients to add, and two of them were going to gross everyone out and, unfortunately, they were the foulest-smelling of all. She decided not to mention that fact or what the origin of the ingredients actually was. She didn't have time for fainters.

B obbie Faye stood in front of the metal recycling yard at 1601 Scenic Highway in Plaquemine, the daylight fading into dusk, a few streetlights blinking on. She yearned to go back into that helicopter cockpit for just a few more minutes. As much as she hated heights and flying and being on camera, all of that combined was suddenly preferable to standing at the entrance to the recycling yard, hoping to be able to face down the psychopath who held her brother. When she'd finished her story and how she planned to face the kidnappers, the cameraman and pilot had become Grim and Grimmer. Not exactly the encouraging rah-rah attitude she'd hoped for, the old music for Rocky on the steps, the feeling that ultimately, this would turn out okay. Now, she was standing near where twelve-foot-tall hurricane fences with razor wire wound at the top flanked the entrance to the yard to keep out thieves who'd steal the metal at night and try to sell it back during the day. Just beyond the gate opening was an empty guard shack, and beyond that, a dusty scale where big trucks weighed their cargo beside an even dustier, decrepit scale house, a tiny box of a building where the computers read the weight of the trucks running in and out all day long.

The entire yard had a veneer of brown, a thick layer of dust kicked up from the unpaved roadways crisscrossing the mammoth yard located on the Mississippi River. She walked through the entrance, her gun in the back of her jeans for quick access but, she hoped, not visible to the kidnappers as she approached. She mulled the idea of picking up something round and tiara-sized from one of the thirty-foot-high metal scrap heaps silhouetted against the fading sun and large pedestal cranes dotting the yard.

The lie couldn't buy her enough time. She might as well face up to that fact.

There was no one on the yard.

No guards, no workers. Quiet velveted the place, eerie and dark.

No Trevor. The bastard. Of *course* he hadn't shown up. He'd been all about the con, right from the beginning.

She wasn't sure where to go, so she continued moving forward until she heard the smooth baritone she'd come to know from their brief phone conversations.

"Stop there, m'dear," the man said. "Where's the tiara?"

"Somewhere safe. Where's Roy?" She tried to fix a location for the voice, but it echoed in the canyons between the mountains of scrap metal.

"First, the tiara."

"Good luck with getting that if I don't hurry up and see Roy."

The largest man Bobbie Faye had ever seen in person stepped from behind a pile of metal, yanking Roy out to stand next to him. Roy's eyes were nearly swollen shut; he was bruised, gashed, lips bloodied, and Bobbie Faye lurched toward him until the mountain of a man held a gun on her.

"Not so fast," the baritone voice said, and the owner of the voice stepped out from behind another large hill of rusted metal. He looked, if possible, genetically mean, all sharp angles and smug smile and with the self-satisfied air of a man who always gets what he wants. "Where's the tiara?"

Bobbie Faye reached behind her to grab the Glock, and instead, someone grabbed her arm and twisted it away, snagging the gun neatly in the process.

"Anh anh ahn," the voice holding her warned. "That would be a bad decision." She craned around to see him, and flinched at the twisted features. He looked like he'd taken a bad beating with the Ugly Stick. Several times.

"The tiara, Bobbie Faye. Now," the baritone said, and he signaled the large man to hold the gun to Roy's head.

"I can duplicate it for you."

"Why would I want that? Where's the real tiara?"

"Stolen. Again."

"Dear, dear Bobbie Faye. That is a shame."

The baritone nodded at the large man, who tugged Roy back a little, as if to avoid splattering the baritone with any brain matter, and Bobbie Faye tried to lunge forward again.

"I know where the gold is. You'll never get it if you hurt Roy."

"Oh, dear girl, I'll get it. If killing your brother doesn't make you talk, and torturing you doesn't encourage you, perhaps I will then move on to your sister or your niece or your best friend. I'm sure, eventually, I'll wear you down."

"Let Roy live, and you'll get the gold a lot faster. I'll go with you. I'll give you whatever you want, without a fight."

"No!" Roy shouted, and the mountain of a man immediately jerked him hard, slamming Roy to his knees on ground filled with sharp metal debris.

"You may be the most fascinating part of this treasure hunt after all, Bobbie Faye," the baritone said, smiling a snake-charming smile. "I have never met anyone so determined in my life. Both you and Roy would have been great students of mine, at any other time, my dear. It really is a shame to have to kill you."

"Would this do instead, Vincent?" Trevor's voice asked, and Bobbie Faye's legs wobbled a little as he ambled out from behind one of the stacks of sheared metal material, twirling the tiara. "It is, after all, worth what? A couple hundred million? At a minimum?"

He was bloody, with at least two grazings from bullets that she could see, and he looked bruised and sore and walked with a slight limp.

God, he was gorgeous.

He actually showed up. He'd shown up for a disaster, fully prepared to help. She'd never actually been in the position of having to apologize for doubting a guy. The absolute elation made her warm and squiggly inside, and she wanted to hug him.

"Ah," Vincent said, facing Trevor, "so I see you figured out what the item was after all. Took you long enough."

Check that. Substitute "kill" for "hug." The freaking bastard had been working with this "Vincent?" All along?

"You fucking bastard. I'll kill you."

"Promises, promises," he answered, and he *winked* at her.

"Yes, he is a bastard, isn't he, dear girl? And an expensive one, at that." Vincent appraised Trevor. "Though worth it, since my hunch was right; if I hadn't hired him, the Professor's double cross would have worked."

"Temporarily," Trevor said, shrugging. "I'm sure you'd have had someone follow the Professor and retrieve it once you knew who had double-crossed you."

"Yes, well, the poor thing's been taken care of."

Suddenly, the universe clicked into focus and Bobbie Faye remembered what Trevor had said he did for a living.

"*Procurement*. I should have guessed."

"One of the best, m' dear. Now, Trevor, I'll have that tiara."

"Not so fast." Trevor backed up a step, and was holding a gun Bobbie Faye would have sworn wasn't there a minute ago. "My price has changed."

Vincent looked exceedingly displeased, and for all that Bobbie Faye currently hated Trevor's ever-loving guts, she appreciated that he was annoying the shit out of Vincent.

"See, dear boy, this is exactly why I didn't tell you what the item was in the first place: I suspected as much from a mercenary. Don't be tedious, Trevor, by turning greedy. It's such a cliché. We agreed on a price and you're going to be fabulously wealthy. I'd rather pay you in a gentlemanly fashion and keep using your services than severing our relationship, and you, right here in this yard."

"Oh, I don't want more money. My fee is fine. I want the girl and her brother."

"Who the hell are you calling *girl*?" she steamed, trying to yank out of the pug-faced freak's grip so she could kick Trevor, but the bastard holding her slammed her to her knees. Shards of metal bit into her skin and she knew they were both bleeding. Then pug-face jerked her back to her feet.

"You prefer *demon*?" Trevor asked.

Vincent chuckled.

"Grown fond of her, have you?"

"No. Quite the contrary. She forced me to plow my truck into a lake, and I'd like to," he looked at Bobbie Faye, "extract payment. I have spent the entire day with her insanity and her deranged bossiness, and I'd like to be able to repay that."

"I? me? bossy?" she snapped, and kicked at the ground, a strong toe-dig which sent rocks and small shards of metal flying at Trevor.

He stepped back to avoid the rocks to his face. . . .

Just as a bullet whizzed over his shoulder, nicking him instead of killing him.

Bobbie Faye scanned back to the spot the bullet may have angled from, and she spied a sniper hunched on the top of one of the metal hills. In the dimming light of the day, recognized the insignia: FBI.

At the same time, Vincent followed her gaze and saw the same figure. He exhaled a brief, low expletive, and in a very quiet voice, said, simply, "Zeke."

Chapter Forty

Ce Ce put the finishing touches on the foul-smelling concoction, looking up to see that most of the gawkers had either edged to the hallway so as to not have to breathe in the stench, or passed out. Only Monique remained happily ensconced next to Ce Ce at the storage room's counter. In fact, Monique stood peering into the bowl, a loopy grin Ping-Ponging amongst her freckles.

"Monique, I need you to stir. Do you think you can do that?" Ce Ce wanted to add, "while you're smashed," but decided not to invite negativity into the room.

"Ohhhhh, surrrrrrrrrrrrre," Monique sang, and she plucked the spoon from Ce Ce's hands and began stirring.

Ce Ce needed to grab the candles and the ingredients to be sprinkled across the top of the bowl as she said the spell. It took longer than she'd hoped to find everything (probably due to the fact that she kept glancing back at Monique to make sure she didn't get distracted and start leading an imaginary band or, God help them, stripping to her own hummed version of burlesque music like she did the last time she'd had that many screwdrivers). Finally, the items were set, the concoction was stirred to the right consistency, the candles were lit.

Ce Ce sure hoped a good, stout protection spell was going to be strong enough for this situation.

God apparently pushed the fast-forward button from what Bobbie Faye could tell in the blur of movement. Shots bounced, snapped, and ricocheted from the FBI as everyone on the ground ran, seeking cover. The yellow glow from the street lamps dotting the recycling yard emphasized the shadows and screwed with her perspective, and she wasn't entirely sure who was shooting at whom.

Vincent hauled Roy with him as his two guards returned fire on the FBI. Bobbie Faye kicked the groin of the ugly pug-faced bastard holding her; when he doubled over, Trevor grabbed her and dragged her away from the line of fire. They were barely around the stacked metal when she kicked his shin, and he flinched.

"What the hell was that for? Are you nuts? Why am I asking that? Of course you're nuts."

"Me? You're calling me nuts? Who the hell *are* you? How'd you get here? And give me that!" She yanked the tiara from his hand.

"I stole a truck and then one of those helicopters that ferry the guys out to the rigs, like I told you, but what's more important is that the guys shooting at us? They're FBI."

"I know that, I can see. Who are *you*? And you were working for that asshole scum all along." She stepped as if to kick him again, but he neatly blocked her and pinned her arms to her sides.

"Look, you can kick me later. I promise. I can explain more when we aren't under fire, okay? I'm here. You have the tiara. We've got to move. Zeke—that's the lead FBI guy—is going to circle around."

"I have to get to Roy."

"I know."

"And I sure as hell don't trust you."

"No, really? C'mon, let's go."

"What makes you think—"

He jerked her out of the way just as a bullet whizzed by, a little too close for her comfort.

"Coming," she said. They moved past a giant shear, its mammoth blade stilled instead of slicing large chunks of metal onto a conveyor. Farther into the yard, they wove around rusted metal stacked stories high, all sorts of recycled objects, from household items to industrial pipes and tools from the local chemical plants.

"Where the hell are we going?"

"To the dock on the Mississippi. Vincent probably has a boat there in case he needs to get away."

"How do you know that?"

"He hates to fly."

"And how do you know *that*?"

"I'll tell you later."

"Why not now?"

"Good grief, you had to have been the most annoying third grader on the planet."

"It is not my fault Mrs. Carmella had to take a leave of absence. She was twitching funny before I even had her for a teacher."

He stopped a second to sweep her with an amused grin.

"Bobbie Faye, you are a helluva lot of fun."

"Most guys don't have that reaction to being shot at with me."

"Yeah, well, I'm not 'most guys.' "

He had a point.

"Give it up, Cormier," the FBI agent's voice echoed off the metal piles. "I know you have the tiara and the girl hostage."

"What is with this *girl* crap? I'll show him *girl*," she muttered, though she followed Trevor around to a slightly better-sheltered area.

To their left, the big shear loomed silently, and to their right, long, high embankments of recycled materials waited to be loaded onto barges. In front of them, there was an enormous gantry crane, several stories tall, its belly high enough above ground, and its tracks set so wide apart, that two train cars could run beneath it, side-by-side. The gantry crane straddled two sets of rail tracks that dead-ended at the waterline of the Mississippi River. Once the shorn metal was dumped into train cars, the crane loaded the rail car filled with sheared metal onto a barge in the canal.

Near a barge which was waiting to be loaded, Bobbie Faye and Trevor spied an expensive looking mini-yacht. They glimpsed Vincent dragging a mostly hog-tied Roy along in that general direction. The mammoth-sized guard and pug-faced guard were planted between them and Vincent and Roy.

"We need to go over those two to get to Roy," Trevor explained, nodding upwards to the conveyor extending out from the shear. She looked up to where the large metal conveyor contraption ran from the shear to a rail car on the other side of both of Vincent's guards and her heart sent out a memo: *no fucking way, or I quit.*

"You want me? To go up there? Near that big knifey thing? With *my* track record?"

He looked up at the shear, then back at her.

"Good point. I'll go up and distract everyone. You run around that end," he pointed to his right, "and then beeline it for the gantry crane. There's a ladder up to that cab up there, and you can lock the cab once you're inside. It's probably the safest place on this yard. I'll get to Roy, but stay there where you're safe."

"Why on earth should I trust you?"

He handed her his gun, then pulled another from his boot.

"If I don't bring your brother back, you can shoot me."

"Promises, promises."

"Look, the ladder's on the other side, so it's relatively protected from the shooting. The train car underneath should keep anyone over here from getting a lucky shot underneath the belly."

"I'm not that girl that has to run off and hide and be safe. I'm a better shot than you."

"True. But are you willing to kill them, Bobbie Faye? Because that's what you're going to have to do if they get close. I doubt maiming them will do the trick. And what about your niece? Who'll take care of her?"

Ugh. She hated it when rat bastards were right.

He kissed her on the forehead and then climbed up the side of the shear, picking his way slowly and carefully up the mountain of metal, keeping large pieces of to-be-recycled debris between himself, the agents, and Vincent's men.

Ce Ce moved the candle over the bowl counterclockwise as the old spell instructed, and chanted the words whose meaning had been lost more than a century ago. As she finished with a flourish of the candle and a last tipping of the candle's wax into the bowl, Monique yelled, "Kick butt!" and shoved her flask forward as if to "toast" with the candle, sloshing a little drop of her screwdriver into the center of the bowl.

Ce Ce froze, watching the gunk bubble and change from the expected bright cherry red to a nasty, malevolent rust color. It gave off an acidic-smelling smoke, which rose and formed a small cloud above the bowl.

"Wow, what a funky color for a whaahozie cloud," Monique said.

"It's supposed to be red," Ce Ce whispered, afraid of what was about to happen.

"I don't t'ink it much likkked, lickered, likedid. Liked"— Monique hiccupped—"my screwdriver. It looks ver' ver' angry."

Ce Ce pulled Monique away from the cloud, which really *did* look angry as it grew and boiled and bubbled in midair, doubling in size every few seconds. It turned, almost as if to look at her, and then it dissipated.

"I don't think it worked."

"Aw, we could try it again. Maybe it needs more screwdriver this time!" Monique poured more from her flask, stirring it into the gunk, which bubbled and roiled, but stayed put in the bowl.

Ce Ce didn't know what to do. She didn't know what she may have unleashed, so she was uncertain if she should do more, or if she did, could it make everything worse for Bobbie Faye?

She slapped her palms over her mouth, worried she'd said that out loud. Cardinal spell rule #1: never suggest anything around a magical spell. You never know what it might do.

Bobbie Faye watched as Trevor climbed debris until he reached the conveyor apparatus, and then he hunkered down, running across the conveyor belt while shooting both down at Vincent's guards and across the piles of debris where the FBI agents had holed up. The flurry of the sounds of the gunshots filled Bobbie Faye's mind with raw fear, and she crawled across the metal, cutting her legs and her hands as she eased around the hill farthest away from her current position and then ran for the gantry crane.

It was a terrible idea, this gantry crane thing. She'd wanted to argue with Trevor, but she had no words left, only fear. Fear of climbing that high, fear of staying down low where the FBI agents or Vincent's gang could wear her down and pick her off. She didn't have enough ammunition for a prolonged fight with them, and maybe Trevor understood that, too. Mostly, she didn't want Stacey to have to go to her funeral. Which meant she had to trust someone to help her.

It was a hard thing to let go and trust him.

Once she got to the ladder, she shoved the gun into her waistband again and anchored the tiara on her head so that her hands were free. The blood running down her arms from the metal cuts should have freaked her out; her adrenaline was such that she couldn't feel. Finally, adrenaline was useful for something.

She thought, briefly, how that was such an apt analogy for so much of her life, bleeding and not feeling, too busy surviving to stop and assess, and as this idea pierced the fog of her thoughts, something grabbed her foot.

Vincent.

"I'm sorry, m' dear, but I'll be taking that tiara now."

The bastard had climbed up behind her, and she'd been so lost in musings, she hadn't heard him or felt him jar the ladder. He held her foot with one hand, and the other arm, looped as it was through the ladder, pointed his gun in her direction.

"Where's Roy?"

"Oh, safe for now."

It was the self-satisfied grin that finally snapped her instincts to life. The smug expression of an asshole used to getting his way just because of his penchant for hiring very expensive thugs ticked her off. She kicked the ever-loving crap out of his face, slamming the heel of her cowboy boot down into his pointy chin.

"Bite me."

He fell backwards, snagging a rung of the ladder on his way down, but it bought her enough time to beat him to the cab and lock the door. As she slammed it shut, she had one last glimpse of the dock area and saw Trevor pulling Roy out of the yacht.

Whaddaya know. He could be trusted. This might be some sort of anomaly. At least she was finally safe.

Then she heard Vincent climbing again, threatening, "Bobbie Faye, dear girl, I want that tiara. I will get it, my dear, if I have to invite everyone in your family, and every friend you've ever had, to a private little get-together in your honor."

Chapter Forty-one

Zis . . . Louisiana governor . . . the one they say is crazy . . . he says he
offers us a new weapon, a woman. Claims she can destroy any country we
wanted. He'll trade her for money to repair his state. Zis is good, no?

—*(possibly) the Russian prime minister to his secretary [translated from Russian]*

Cam had chosen to track the WFKD helicopter with Bobbie
Faye inside, knowing she hadn't thought about the fact that
the craft had a transponder signal and would be easy to
find. He arrived just as Jason called in the WFKD pilot's report of
what had transpired and where they'd dropped Bobbie Faye. Cam
saw the FBI helo on his way in, already on the ground, which meant
Trevor had to be here as well.

Gunfire erupted and he could hear shouting, but was too far
away to distinguish who was speaking. It sounded like Zeke.

The return fire was sporadic. He and the SWAT team had to
spread out and circle around, being careful to not only not get
caught in a cross fire, but not be in a position where they had to fire
without seeing who they were shooting.

It conjured his worst nightmare: going on a "Bobbie Faye" disaster call, firing at someone to protect her, only to find her body, his
bullets the cause of death.

He shook it off. He couldn't be thinking about that now.

More gunfire. He was closer.

For a brief moment, he thought he saw Bobbie Faye climbing up the gantry crane, but then he blinked and maybe it had been the light playing tricks on him. No way in hell would she ever willingly climb something that tall.

B obbie Faye ducked underneath a control panel inside the cab as she heard Vincent climb onto a precariously small foot ledge where the ladder terminated. He shot into the crane's side window and she scrunched down as small as she could, trying to hide as the bullets bounced around the steel walls of the cab.

She heard him laugh.

Then he was quiet.

Too quiet.

Moving around that foot ledge had to be difficult, especially dressed in a suit, but he made no noise, and she itched, antsy and anxious. She whipped around to see where he'd gone, forgetting she still wore the tiara. It caught in the wires that hung beneath the control panel, and her hair was knotted in the tiara's curves.

She tried to disentangle herself from the tiara, and it from the wiring, being careful of the electrical connections . . . when she realized the cab had grown perceptibly darker. Someone was blocking the streetlights from shining in the cab's window.

Vincent.

He'd moved around to the front of the cab where a crane operator would view the boom and control the loading, and from the look of satisfaction, she knew the sick bastard saw her. He shot the front window, raking out the glass with the butt of his gun. She tried to twist to pull her gun from her waistband while still trying to navigate the wires.

The tiara tangled even more in the wires.

Vincent stepped carefully over broken glass, one foot on the control panel, one foot still outside the cab, and she knew she had to move, had to do something. She yanked, hard, on the tiara, and it pulled wires, short-circuiting the controls. She broke free of it while it dangled there, and sparks flew, electricity arcing across to the metal portion of the cab, electrifying it. Bobbie Faye flattened herself onto the rubber floor mats while Vincent held onto the metal ceiling of the cab for stability, and the jolt surged through him.

He spasmed, letting go, falling out of the window and as the shorting wires caught fire, a nasty, rust-colored, violent-looking smoke filled the cab. It smelled moldy and nasty and, somehow, like rotten oranges, as the rubber from the wires melted and flames arced across the control panel. She expected to hear Vincent shout as he fell, expected to hear a horrible thud as he landed, and instead, there was silence except for the crackling of the arcing wires.

The gantry crane lurched and she held onto the operator's seat in front of the control panel, which finally seemed to have stopped arcing. Though the crane's engine was now somehow *on*.

Vincent wasn't at the window.

The crane swung, slowly to the left. She didn't have a clue what it was doing, but it seemed to have a mind of its own as it swung hard to the right and then back to the left. The crane's boom extended out with a hard pitch, and then slammed out to its maximum length, nearly thirty feet out, jerking the crane in the process.

The tiara swung hard in the knotted wiring and she was afraid to let go of the seat to grab for it with the crane careening to the left and back to the right, faster and faster, a broken metronome speeding up out of time. She eased up on her knees, hung onto the armrest, and peeked out the window

There was Vincent, out on the end of the boom.

Clinging. Slipping. About to fall.

He dropped his gun.

She didn't know how to stop the crane. There was an Alaskan-sized part of her which wanted to be evil and twirl her moustache and let him fall, but she didn't want to kill him. She wanted him punished. For a very long time in really awful ways, but she didn't want to kill.

Bobbie Faye pushed at controls, trying to understand which

knob did what, but nothing seemed to work as the boom lurched from side to side.

The crane shimmied so violently on the last swing, it catapulted Vincent off the boom . . .

. . . and slung the tiara so hard, it broke loose of the wires, bounced against one cab wall, flipped midair just past Bobbie Faye's outstretched hands, and fell . . .

. . . out the shattered window.

Tumbling down, bouncing off the gantry crane with a thudding clunk in one direction while Vincent flew through the air.

She didn't know which horror to watch.

The tiara took one last bounce, sailing out over the dock, heading for the deep Mississippi. She glanced back at Vincent flying through the air and then averted her eyes as he landed, impaled on a metal spike protruding off the conveyor.

She was going to be sick.

She bit down, gritting her teeth against the bile rising in her throat, and then looked out over the churning Mississippi waters, no sign of the tiara to be had.

It was gone.

The Mississippi, with its ever-shifting muddy bottom and churning waters, rarely gave back anything it had sucked into its black heart.

Leave it to her to lose an heirloom passed down for a couple hundred years. Perfect. Just perfect.

She could picture her mom on the last parade float, wearing the tiara, waving, waving, waving to the crowd. Handing it down to Bobbie Faye, telling her how important it was to keep for the family. For tradition.

Bobbie Faye buried her face in her hands.

The shooting had stopped.

She was so tired, so worn, she wanted to lie down and go to sleep, but she needed to find her family. She climbed down into the darkening night and the stillness was oppressive, the heat and dust seemed to hang and form a wall to push through.

As soon as she stepped off the ladder, Trevor moved out of the shadows, followed by the FBI agent now holding him at gunpoint.

"I ran out of bullets," Trevor said, keeping a light, amused expression for her.

"I can't take you anywhere," she quipped back.

"Stop right there, for your own safety," the FBI agent said. "I'm Special Agent Zeke Wright, Ms. Sumrall. If you'll please turn over the tiara, I can take this scum in and get him out of your hair."

Bobbie Faye had her gun drawn on him before he could move, but he didn't seem terribly concerned; another FBI agent stepped out of the shadows to her right, his own gun trained on her.

Cam found one of the FBI shot; he was alive, but unconscious. In his SWAT ear-com, he heard Aaron, saying, "Cam. We've got a wounded guy in a suit over here. Face is all kinds of ugly. And another big-ass guy sitting on the ground next to him, holding more than twenty brass doorknobs, and he's crying."

"Did he say anything?"

"Just that they're beautiful and perfect, and now he's not going to get to have his Guinness entry. Whatever the hell that means."

"Okay, get them out of here. I see something happening underneath the gantry crane. I'm coming up from the south end."

"Meet you there."

When he got there, his blood drained to his feet: there was a face-off between the agents, Cormier, and Bobbie Faye, with Zeke apparently holding a gun on Cormier. There was blood on Bobbie Faye's hands, her legs, her hip. It was everything Cam could do not to just shoot everyone around her right then and there and get her to a hospital.

What he didn't understand was why Zeke wasn't just arresting Cormier. Or why Bobbie Faye had her gun drawn on a federal agent. He studied his ex's expression, and knew she wasn't buying the cajoling spiel Zeke was giving her. Why, he wondered, was she suspicious?

And then it hit him. The cell where Benoit had put the Professor . . . it was the one with a view of the desk sergeant's TV. Not a good view, but a view. The Professor had flipped out over the name "Cormier" in the interrogation room. Then drugged, poisoned, the Professor had babbled: "Not corn. Right." Cam would bet his next paycheck the Professor was trying to say, "Not Cormier. *Wright.*" Agent Zeke Wright. Could the Professor have seen the agent on the news coverage and learned Zeke's name and so had been trying to tell them? Zeke had claimed to be hunting down Cormier as if he had the authority to do anything to get his man, but the Captain had told Cam to bring Cormier in unhurt.

Cormier must be undercover. Zeke was the rogue agent. And Zeke clearly wanted something from Bobbie Faye.

Sonofabitch.

He'd led the man to Bobbie Faye all damned day long.

Cam moved slightly and put himself in her line of sight so she'd know he was there and he could back her up. She did the damnedest thing. She gave him the little ear tug sign they'd had for years. It meant, "Wait. Something's going on and I can handle it."

She had clearly lost her mind.

"You were at the bank," she said to Zeke, who twitched a little, and looked oddly antsy. "When I ran out of the bank, I saw you there, waiting in your car. And now you're here. Wanting the tiara. Why don't I think that's a coincidence?"

"Look, Ms. Sumrall," Zeke said, his voice smooth as if talking to a child while he scratched at his upper arm and chest with his free hand.

That wasn't going to go over really well.

"This man," Zeke continued, "has been trying to double-cross you. He's a mercenary, and he's been after the tiara all along. Now I'm arresting him, and I need the tiara for evidence."

"Evidence? So it can conveniently disappear later on?"

"Quit being ridiculous, Ms. Sumrall. Hand it over."

Cam watched her lower her eyelids and give Zeke the expression he'd come to know as the "slitty glare." Cam caught himself grinning, even though Bobbie Faye could still see him.

Bobbie Faye looked down at the ground, glancing around her as if something had fallen.

"What are you doing?" Zeke asked.

"Well, you must think my brains have fallen out of my head if you think I'm going buy a crap story like that. Trevor could have taken the tiara from me at pretty much any point today. If he was double-crossing me, he'd be long gone. Which leaves us you. I'm sort of amused that of all the people who are interested in the tiara, you happened to be in the parking lot at the time of the robbery. Was that your idea? Steal it from Roy's kidnapper? Did you know what was going on and decide to take it for yourself?"

Cam caught Bobbie Faye's eye and nodded.

The muscles in the back of Zeke's neck tensed and knotted and he scratched more emphatically at his neck and arms. Zeke's colleague seemed washed in a sudden sheen of sweat, and Cam could smell the fear from where he stood.

Then Cam pinged on the fact that she'd said, "kidnapper." And "Roy." No wonder she'd pushed like the Terminator hopped up on steroids.

"Look, bitch," Zeke snapped, "you're just a stupid girl who's about to get herself and her whole family killed. This isn't funny."

"Oh, really? You know what *is* funny? When you lose the 'whose dick is bigger' contest to a 'girl' like me. You're never going to get that tiara."

"You should concede now, Zeke," Trevor said. "This could get embarrassing."

"No ignorant set of tits is going to beat me." Zeke's voice curled with satisfaction in spite of him rubbing an ever-reddening blotchy cheek against his shoulder. "Especially when I have her niece."

Bobbie Faye froze, and Cam couldn't catch her eye. He could tell she was calculating, when Zeke laughed.

"Exactly. Let's just say she's in *protective custody*. So you give me the tiara, I shoot Cormier here, who is the bad guy as far as the cops are concerned, and then you get your niece back."

"You bastard," Bobbie Faye seethed. "Where is she?"

"With an agent of mine."

"Would that be Baker?" Trevor asked, sounding even more satisfied than Zeke had. "Because he isn't an agent of *yours*, Zeke."

Cam could see Bobbie Faye assessing Cormier, and when she looked back at Zeke, it was clear she believed Cormier.

"You're not that stupid," Zeke snapped. "You're not going to risk her life on what this mercenary says. He's played you all along, and you're too fucking naïve to realize it. Hand over the tiara."

"How about, instead—" she said, lifting up her shirt, and Cam flinched, wanting to cover her, feeling protective, until he saw what she'd done: there was a microphone wire attached to the center of her bra and a little sending unit under her arm.

"—you wave to the pretty camera over there in that pedestal crane," she finished, pointing toward a crane nearer to the entrance of the scrap yard. She smiled, big, and said, "You got it, boys?"

And sonofabitch if the helicopter cameraman and pilot didn't wave to them from the pedestal crane, and the streetlight glinted off their TV camera.

"Yaaaaaaaaaahoooooooo, we got it Bobbie Faye," the cameraman shouted back. "All of it! Live!"

Bobbie Faye looked directly at Cam then, acknowledging his presence there, signaling that's all she had, and he stepped out, aiming at Zeke while she aimed at the other FBI agent.

"We've got it, too," he said, and Zeke spun.

In a flash, Zeke turned back as if to shoot Bobbie Faye. Before Cam could plant a slug in him, Cormier disarmed the agent and had him on the ground, aiming Zeke's own gun back at the prone agent.

Without looking away from Zeke, Cormier said, "You're Cameron Moreau, right?"

"And?"

"Call your Captain. I'm FBI, undercover. He's already had the information confirmed; we couldn't tell you until we'd flushed out this asshole once and for all."

Bobbie Faye squeaked a little when she asked, "You're—you're FBI?"

Cam glanced at her and she looked a little woozy.

"Ohmygod. I kidnapped an FBI agent. I am so going to jail."

Cam placed a call to the Captain while his SWAT surrounded Cormier, Zeke, and the other agent, and disarmed them all.

Zeke's neck had started breaking out in horrible hives.

"Please, for the love of God, let me move so I can scratch. Are there oranges around here? I'm allergic. I swear, I'm going to have seizures. I need a doctor!"

Roy stumbled out from behind one of the mountains of metal, his face nearly swollen shut. Bobbie Faye ran to him.

She hugged Roy first. Then yelled at him. Then hugged him again, tears running down her face.

They had all been through hell and back, and Cam was convinced *it hadn't needed to be that way.*

She wouldn't have had to go through any of it, if she'd called him first. It made him livid. She put herself and everyone else in danger because she was too damned pig-headed to ask for help. To admit she might need something.

From him. Especially from him.

His veins grew cold and the iciness seeped into every pore, every heartbeat. He was furious with her for having put her life on the line. Every scrape she had, every cut, every bruise assailed him and taunted him with the clear indication that she didn't need him. Never did. Never would.

He made sure the ambulance was dispatched and he turned his back on her and walked away, knowing Aaron could handle the rest of the details.

Ce Ce and everyone who could cram themselves into her Outfitter store stood in front of her little TV, completely slack-jawed and gobsmacked as the live coverage spun across the screen from the scrap yard in Plaquemine. There were ambulances there, a body being carried out by the Medical Examiner, and more cops than anyone could count, including SWAT and FBI.

And there was Bobbie Faye, in living color, looking like she'd almost been beaten and pureed, but alive.

"Where am I?" a muffled voice asked from the storage room, and Ce Ce nearly jumped out of her skin at the realization: the Social Services woman. They'd forgotten all about her in the excitement of seeing the live footage.

Ce Ce quickly conferred with the crowd and they all knew their parts to play. Maybe, just maybe, they could stay out of jail.

Chapter Forty-two

She's alive. It's over. Now we can all get back to our own normal lives.

*—first comment on the record after any Bobbie Faye event by Detective
Cameron Moreau, Ms. Sumrall's ex-boyfriend, as told to WFKD*

Bobbie Faye watched Cam walk off, and everything in her
ached with fury. Tears welled up and she flat refused to let
them slide. For a brief moment there when he was watching her handle Zeke, when he saw what she'd been up against and
what she'd deduced, she thought she'd seen something akin to
pride aimed in her direction. But no, he'd walked off, without a
backwards glance, anger radiating off him in a too-familiar way. So
as she stood there watching the paramedics do a preliminary
check on Roy and get the wounds bandaged, and as another set
worked on her, it surprised the hell out of her to feel Trevor's palm
soothe the back of her neck, kneading the knots of tension from
her shoulders as if he'd been the one she'd known all her life and
had dated.

"I've called the agent protecting Stacey," he said, "and she's fine.
She might be a little hopped up on sugar. I think she conned him
into buying her every snack this side of the Mississippi, but she's in
great spirits. I'm having him meet you at your home; I know it's destroyed, but I suspect you'll want to go back there first?"

She nodded, not trusting herself to speak.

"Good. I've got a thousand reports to fill out."

And with that, he, too, walked away.

L et me get this straight," the groggy Social Services woman said to Ce Ce's crowd while they all stared at her, wide-eyed and a little too innocent. "First, I fell asleep on the box over there?"

They all nodded in unison.

"Then I walked in my sleep and offered to dance the tango with, let me understand this, that gentleman over there?"

She pointed to tall, quiet Ralph, and everyone nodded in unison.

"And after that, I suggested we all go to a stripper bar? Where I was going to 'bust a move'?"

They all nodded in unison, Monique a little more enthusiastically than the rest.

"And I'm supposed to believe this?"

"Well, honey, I don't know what on earth makes people do strange things when they sleepwalk," Ce Ce offered. "But maybe you should see a doctor about that."

The woman glared at her and Ce Ce smiled as innocently as possible.

And everyone nodded in unison.

T he view of her trailer from the aerial footage had not prepared Bobbie Faye for the carnage that had been her home, and she would have lain flat on the ground from the weight of the depression, had a big black Ford not driven up at just that moment and out hopped Stacey, blond pigtails askew, Popsicle stains (several colors in fact) all over her face and hands, and something that looked remarkably like ice cream sprinkles all over her cheek. She was dragging a stuffed elephant that was slightly bigger than she was, and Bobbie Faye scooped her up and held her so long, so tight, she was pretty sure the sprinkles were permanently implanted in her own cheek, and she didn't care a bit.

"Aunt Bobbie Faye! It was so much fun! Me an Uncle Baker—"

The new agent nodded a greeting.

"—we went to the zoo and the pony rides and the merry-go-round and the planannniiinium—"

"Planetarium?"

"Uh huh, and then we went to McDonald's and—whoa."

Stacey's attention focused on the trailer lying on its side in several pieces.

"It's okay, Stace. We'll figure something out. Okay?"

"Uh huh. Can Uncle Baker come back again tomorrow?"

She turned her little pig-tailed head his direction, beaming at him, and Bobbie Faye tried to hide her laugh as he blanched and nearly ran back to his car.

"Stace, honey, I think Uncle Baker might need a little while to recover."

Twenty-four hours later, Bobbie Faye was still pulling the little rug rat off the counters and the back of the sofa. She was beginning to wonder if the kid had mainlined the sugar instead of just ingesting it.

She looked at that kid, and her heart squeezed in her chest, and she couldn't let herself think of how close she'd come to losing Stacey. Or Roy. As much as she wanted to knock him in the head herself, it had all been too damned close. She didn't know if she was ever going to recover from it all. They'd just returned from seeing Roy at the hospital, where the doctor had said he was going to be fine. And Roy was already hitting up on the nurses, so clearly he was feeling better.

Now Bobbie Faye sat outside her small trailer lot, watching the mobile home company move in her new (used) trailer. They had agreed to give her a good deal on it, with payments she almost could afford, in exchange for her occasionally appearing in a TV ad touting that their brand of trailers were tough enough to withstand a "Bobbie Faye" day.

Nina moved away from overseeing the trailer installation and sat next to Bobbie Faye in a lawn chair someone had loaned them.

"Any word on whether or not the reward from the stolen crap in the kidnapper's office will pay for all the damages?"

"Not yet. Benoit told me they're putting a detective, Fordoche, on it. She's supposed to be very good, honest, and anal up the wazoo, so hopefully, half of it won't disappear."

They sat in companionable silence a few minutes, watching the chaos of the trailer being moved in with three different men all trying to be the boss and giving five different sets of directions to the driver.

"Oh, by the way," Nina laughed. "I heard where Dora went."

Roy had filled Bobbie Faye in on just where he'd been when the day had started.

"She went to her mom's, all freaked out because she didn't want to deal with Jimmy coming home after the kidnappers had taken Roy. So Jimmy comes home, sees she's run home to her mom, thinks it's because she found out about him and Susannah the loon, so he goes over there to apologize and try to win Dora back. It's a good thing Roy's protected in the hospital right now, because Dora told Jimmy about Roy and the two of them turned Dora's mom's into a regular *Jerry Springer* show, especially when Susannah showed up."

Bobbie Faye whiplashed, as she turned to catch Nina's wicked gleam.

"Yup. And Susannah thought he was divorced already."

Bobbie Faye tried not to feel too evil about smiling right then.

"Oh, brace yourself, here comes 'Just Call Me Sunshine.' "

Bobbie Faye looked over to the driveway where a car had pulled in. Cam. Looking distinctively peeved. She met him halfway between her chair and his car. From the way he slammed his car door, she thought he was about to lecture her.

Instead, he was cold. Stone fucking cold.

"I've spoken with the Department of Social Services," Cam said, barely looking at her. No 'how are you?' or 'glad you're okay' or 'fuck you for not coming to me,' which she suspected was the thing eating him. "They've agreed to accept that you're providing Stacey with a good home, and they're going to drop the new charges of putting Stacey in danger during this fiasco. You can keep the kid."

"Seriously?" She was shocked. Ce Ce's description of the completely furious Social Services worker after she'd awakened from being drugged was not pretty, and Bobbie Faye expected them to try to take Stacey from her permanently.

"Your Cormier guy put in a call for you. Said he'd been trying to catch this agent for more than a year, and if you hadn't done what you did, not only would Roy have been killed, but he would have lost both Vincent and Agent Zeke Wright, both of whom were responsible for your cousin's death and quite a long list of other crimes."

"Really?"

"Yes."

This had to have impressed him, that she'd made the right choices. He kept his stony expression.

"And?"

"And, nothing, Bobbie Faye. I told them I agreed you had no choice and they've dropped the charges. I thought you'd like to know you'll be able to keep Stacey."

She didn't know what to say. At that moment, everything seemed possible, and it hit her like a tidal wave just how much she loved her niece. She looked at Cam, his arms crossed, his glare stoic.

"Thank you."

"I didn't do it for you. I did it for the kid. She's been through enough."

"Wait. Let me get this straight. You just said I had no choice, you vouched for me, and you're still furious with me?"

"Damned straight."

"*You're* the one who *chased* me, who nearly got me killed, more than once. And you're pissed off at *me*? You're nuts!"

"*I'm* nuts? You put everyone in danger, including yourself. You nearly get yourself killed and in the chaos, did more than a couple of million dollars worth of damage, all because you wouldn't fucking call me and ask for help."

"Yeah, because the last time I did that, it worked out so well for me."

They both seethed, breathing hard, heat radiating between them. He had come through for her, she reminded herself. He had shot out the lights when he couldn't have known the FBI agents were the bad guys; he'd broken his own rules to help her.

He spun to leave and she reached out for him and he pulled his arm away.

"Don't, Bobbie Faye. Just. Don't."

And just like that, he walked away.

Her throat burned with fury and words logjammed there. Then she turned and rejoined Nina at the lawn chairs.

"What the hell is with the two of you?" Nina asked. "You know you still love him. And he still loves you. I swear, if any more electricity passed between the two of you over there, we'd be putting out brush fires. Why can't y'all get over yourselves and have a life together?"

Bobbie Faye watched Cam slam into his car and back out of the drive, never looking in her direction, not even once.

"He doesn't want to be in love with me." She faced her friend. "And that makes all the difference in the world."

Later that night at the Contraband Days Festival fairgrounds, Bobbie Faye sat in a lawn chair positioned in a makeshift throne made from a bateau. Twinkling lights dressed every tree and shrub and lamppost, crowds mingled and swirled to music from a terrific local band, and a *fais do do* was in full swing. Just about everyone had on pirate gear with eye patches, fake swords, and brightly colored shirts. There was barbequing, and the beer and soft drinks flowed freely. Bobbie Faye was amused to watch Old Mr. Zachary get drunk enough to get up the courage to ask Old (widowed) Mrs. Ethel to dance, while Stacey and four or five other kids about her age were running amok, shrieking with joy and Popsicles, all of their tongues a disgusting blue from cotton candy known as the "Bluebeard." There was also a suspiciously signifi-cant exchange of money as bets were paid off, and Bobbie Faye was treated to enthusiastic waves from the crowds.

She shrugged her shoulders, trying to let go of the sadness and tension. Several riverboat captains in attendance at the festival had conferred over her tiara dilemma and informed her that finding the tiara was virtually impossible, though a few offshore divers hovering around volunteered to try. When Bobbie Faye had learned about Lafitte's journal, which Vincent had bought after the Professor had been forced to sell it, she'd had hopes of reconstructing the tiara and using the journal information to decipher the map. Unfortunately, the FBI held Lafitte's journal for evidence, and no telling what was going to happen to it or if it would ever be given back to her family.

At least everyone was safe. That was the important thing. She slowly felt a sense of peace being there, in the hometown that she loved, watching the crazy people live full out. Even Ce Ce and her gang had shown up and they were all jabbering about the exciting day (getting ever more exciting in the retelling, with each and every one of them in the starring role).

Bobbie Faye breathed in the scent of the grilled chicken and pork ribs and exhaled slowly, her eyes closed, when she realized she smelled . . . *him*. She looked up and around, and there was Trevor, sitting in another lawn chair, lounging back, his ankles crossed like he'd been sitting there for a while, watching her.

"Okay, that's creepy," she said, and he smiled.

She smiled back.

He moved his chair to sit beside her.

"How's the Professor?"

"Pretty good," he said. "They figured out what the poison was and he's recovering. We still don't know how it got in his food, though. Probably his attorney paid off someone. Your state police are doing a pretty thorough investigation. By the way, how's your brother?"

"Oh, he's fine, I guess. Or, rather, he's back to normal. While he was in the hospital he made dates with three nurses, and two hus-bands have shown up already to beat the crap out of him."

Trevor laughed and then picked up her hand from the chair's armrest, playing with it.

They were silent a moment, until she said, "I still don't quite get something."

"Just one thing?" He grinned and she smacked his forearm.

"Seriously. This agent—Zeke—was on the take from Vincent, and Zeke decided to double-cross Vincent and get the tiara for him-self." She looked to Trevor for confirmation before she continued, trying not to get distracted with him holding her hand, his thumb purposefully tickling her palm. "So Zeke forced the Professor to rob the bank? He was going to wait outside and "catch" the bank rob-ber, taking him and the money—and tiara—into evidence?"

"Right, where it would conveniently disappear as you guessed. He was going to claim the Professor acted on his own, so Vincent wouldn't know Zeke had double-crossed him."

"Leaving the Professor to hang as far as Vincent was concerned."

"Exactly."

"So, the Professor decides to double-cross Zeke? And he brings two kids to help him get away from Zeke—"

"Who wasn't expecting any resistance because he had too much leverage on the Professor, who had major gambling debts and needed some money if he wanted to keep his legs and his family."

"So, a triple cross. And you knew this all along?"

"Not the Professor stuff. I knew that Zeke was planning some-thing. Zeke believed I was corrupt and working for Vincent as well. He knew you would have to go to the bank to get the tiara, and I thought he was going to try to take it from you there himself. I hoped to catch him in the act. The whole robbery part was com-pletely left field."

"So you would have stopped Zeke, then taken me and the tiara to Vincent and done whatever super FBI thing you do to save Roy."

"That was the plan."

"But then you tried to kick me out of your truck!"

"When I knew the boys had stolen the tiara, I thought I could get to them faster, and I was trying to protect you."

"You changed your mind when you saw Zeke behind us?"

"Yep. No way was I letting him get his hands on you."

She eyed him. He looked more relaxed, and sexier, if that was possible, but also a little more . . . dangerous . . . now that he was focusing directly on her and not running for his life.

"Are you really FBI?"

"Pretty much."

"I'm never going to make bail, am I?"

"You think we want you in a jail cell where you can incite riots? We are not Stupid, Inc., thank you very much."

"I'm not going to be arrested? For all that stuff we did?"

He leaned her direction and her heart rate doubled, and she was definitely trying to shush all of her other parts.

"I've been trying to nail Zeke for a year. You made that happen. I owe you."

"Am I going to hear about that damned truck forever?"

"Nah. It's just a truck."

"What!"

He laughed. "I knew the truck was bugged, which is why I didn't clue you in when you first leapt up in there. I had to stay in character. I was pretty sure the watch was bugged; it was a GPS thing given to me by Vincent. If, at any point, I had broken character, he would have figured out I was a Fed and he'd have killed your brother."

"I can't believe you tormented me about that truck."

"You're rather fun to torment."

"Bastard."

"Yep."

But he grinned at her, a blindingly sexy grin. Good damned thing she was sitting down.

"So," he said, still smiling at her, and holy geez, did it just go up twenty degrees? "Tomorrow? You busy? I thought we could do something a little less high profile."

"What? Like outrun nuclear warheads?"

He laughed again, and the crinkles around his blue eyes and the tan and oh, holy shit, he was going to be trouble. Big trouble.

"After that day, you want to go out with me," she stated, a little bit lost. Most guys would be running. Or giving her a list of things she had to change about herself in order for them to stick around. "Are you sure?"

"Yes," he growled, and his confidence was intoxicating.

He stood and pulled her up, into his arms and against that amazing chest and said, "Let's dance."

Yep, he was going to be trouble. She could see it. He was freaking FBI. She regularly destroyed things that were Federal. This had disaster written all over it in huge neon print.

She let him lead her onto the dance floor and into his arms, swaying and spinning to the music.

Acknowledgments

There's just no way to amply thank everyone who's partici-
pated in this journey and helped me achieve this dream; I
am, frankly, gobsmacked when I think about how many
people encouraged me and sustained me in some way. I am immensely grateful for everything you all have done. In my shabby attempt to name a few, I have not mentioned others who had a
dramatic and profound impact—particularly my friends. If I tried to
name all of my friends and all that they have done, it would fill a
book and then some. Yes, I am freakishly lucky, and I hope my
friends know how much I love them.

So, to name a few key players without whom this book would
not exist:

To Julie Burton, one of the finest friends and first readers anyone
could hope for, who handed it to Rosemary Edghill, who became
the mentor of my dreams and whose own brilliant advice and en-
couragement helped me find my way. And to her sister, India
Edghill, one of the best cheerleaders in the world. This book would
not have happened if it were not for the three of them. (You people
should read Rosemary's and India's books; seriously, you are missing
out on some fine storytelling if you don't.)

To Lucienne Diver, agent extraordinaire, who is a most amazing,
wonderful, trusted friend and astute business partner. Quite simply,
you hung the moon *and* the stars. I could go on for pages, so I'll
leave it at this: I am beyond the luckiest writer *ever*.

To Nichole Argyres, my brilliant editor at St. Martin's Press, who is a world of fun and another trusted friend. Your insights and style and enthusiasm made the whole editing process a blast while simultaneously making me a better writer and this a much better book. You totally rock.

To the terrific, supportive, and encouraging Matthew Shear (publisher) and Matthew Baldacci (marketing director) and the fantastic people in marketing, PR, and art. I am extremely fortunate to work with such a stellar team whose own wonderful enthusiasm and support for this book was beyond my dreams. I hope you all know how much I greatly appreciate all your efforts. And to Ed Chapman, the phenomenal copy editor without whom you all would know just how much my grammar sucks . . . thank you.

To Rae Monet (for FBI advice) and Lieutenant Cathy Flinchum of the Louisiana State Police (Public Relations): thank you both for being so generous with your time and answering tons of questions. Any mistakes in procedure left in the book are entirely my own.

To the city of Lake Charles, LA, for being the extremely cool place full of people I am proud to call family and friends. I may have made up a few locations and, okay, moved a few places around a bit, but I promise that when I was done, I put it all back to the way it was originally. I think. I mean, if you run into a salt dome where it isn't supposed to be, let me know and I'll try to put it back where it belongs; that was one slippery little sucker to get situated and it may have escaped a time or two and moved somewhere else when I wasn't looking.

Just so you know, the Contraband Days Festival is the real deal and I highly recommend it for a fantastic time; there are events scheduled for families as well as just for the adults. If you want to learn more, visit: www.contrabanddays.com.

To my family who believed, supported, encouraged, cheered, commiserated, and helped many times over. I could never have done this without you. This is true of my whole family (I am extremely lucky), including Amanda Eschete (whose assistance kept my sanity intact—well, more intact than expected); my brother and his wife (Mike and Allison McGee); and my in-laws (Marion and

Patsy Causey); but especially to my dad and mom, Al and Jerry McGee, whose shining example of hard work and tenacity taught me to never give up, in spite of the odds. (And their love and hours and hours of baby-sitting made it possible!)

To my kids, Luke and Jake, who discovered the hard way that it was probably best not to get Mom to cook when I was writing lest there be fire alarms and billowing smoke (a regular occurrence), who survived (and sometimes took advantage of) my dazed expressions when they stood at my elbow asking questions, waiting for me to shift out of the imaginary world and back into the real one, and who would say with pride when someone asked, "My mom's a writer." (Yes, insanity runs in the family.) I love you beyond measure, and you have been the joy and laughter and fun and chaos (also good) in my life. I cannot imagine a world without you both, and no success would matter if you aren't here to share in it.

And finally, to Carl, the love of my life and my best friend. You supported me in bad times and good, cheered me on, believed in me, and worked many many extra jobs and hours to give me the chance to pursue my dream, maybe never realizing you already had just by being there. None of this would have meant a thing without you.

More trouble on the way for BOBBIE FAYE!
Coming from St. Martin's Griffin Spring 2008

B obbie Faye Sumrall was full up on crazy, thank you very much, and had a side order of cranky to spare. It had been that bad of a week, and she hoped to have just one night, one measly little night, to sleep well. That wasn't too much to ask, right?

Apparently, the Universe thought it was.

She and the Universe wee like warring spouses locked in an eternal battle, trying to blow up one another while pretending all was okay when they were at couple's therapy. She was beginning to think no one was buying the act anymore. Still she tried. She went through her nightly routine: she squeezed into the tiny bathroom of her small, almost-not-ratty trailer, fantasizing about actual hot water while she grabbed a tepid shower, and then to wind down, poured herself some juice and nibbled a cracker. Luckily, her five-year-old niece, Stacey, had been invited to spend the night at a friend's house. No matter how much she loved the little rug rat, at least there wouldn't be fourteen billion attempts to hog-tie the kid into bed for a whole five minutes of sleep before she bounced up again, determined to drive Bobbie Fay out of what little was left of her mind.

When Bobbie Faye did finally stretch out on her lumpy mattress, it was only to sink into disturbing, hallucinogenic dreams, all disjointed, a half-step two-step out of rhythm, bits and pieces swirling in a kaleidoscope of confusing colors. At one point, she saw herself and damn, she looked odd. She could have sworn her boobs were off kilter, like one was higher than the other, but maybe it was just that striped butt-ugly shirt she was wearing, the one she'd won back in high school for that dumb "spirit week" contest. She was twenty-freaking-eight-years-old; why couldn't her subconscious mind be a team player and clothe her in something über cool and sexy? And why did her normally long brunette hair look so . . . strange? It seemed all wrong: shorter . . . stiff, like she'd emptied a can of hair spray and shellacked it into a helmet.

Great. Bad dream *and* bad hair. But at least she wasn't bald, like that little schlumpy guy she was talking to.

Oh. Wait. Make that the schlumpy little guy she was *shooting*.

Why in the hell was she shooting this guy? Five times. Damn, but it was a beautiful pattern. At least her dream got that part right. Still, he didn't remind her of anyone she knew. He was way too schlubby to be IRS. Stupid subconscious. Why couldn't it at least let her pretend to take out some of the jerks driving her insane? Mr. No-Extension-For-You IRS Guy would have topped her list. Then her dreams swirled again, and she felt the rush of wind tangling her hair, her arms wide as if she were flying under the streetlights in the small commercial district of her tough, no-nonsense industrial hometown of Lake Charles, Louisiana.

When she woke up, she had a raging headache, her mouth was painfully dry and then she peeled her eyes open, and *holy fucking shit*.

There was something definitely . . . bloodlike in her hair. Just beyond the foot of the bed, her closet was open. She instantly glanced down, dreading what she'd find, but no, she still had on the sameT-shirt she'd worn to bed. So it'd been a bad dream. A way too realistic bad dream. Note to self: ease up on the chocolate suicide cake after dinner.

When she turned her head, she froze, her body running cold and clammy because her Glock was right there, on her bed, *in her right hand*. It was supposed to be locked up. It was always locked up, especially with Stacey living there now. Bobbie Faye gingerly sat up and checked the clip.

Five bullets were missing.

Clearly the Universe thought it was payback time.